Megan's arms slipped around his waist.

"I don't expect you to take on my problems. You're my boss, not my fairy godmother."

Daniel chuckled. "Yeah, I'd look pretty silly in a dress carrying a wand, and I'm not such a great boss at that."

"Why do you say that?" She looked up at him through watery green eyes. "You're great."

"Because a good boss doesn't go around kissing his employees." He stared down at her damp cheeks, his belly flipping. "Right now, I want to be a very bad boss."

Her eyes flared with desire. "How so?"

"I want to kiss you. Again."

She sucked in a breath and bit down on her lip before saying, "I told you, I quit. That means you're not my boss."

He leaned his forehead against hers and sighed. God, he wanted to kiss her. "I'm not accepting your resignation."

"You don't have a choice," she said, her lips so close.

PROTECTING THE COLTON BRIDE & COLTON'S COWBOY CODE

NEW YORK TIMES BESTSELLING AUTHOR
ELLE JAMES
MELISSA CUTLER

♦ HARLEQUIN® ROMANTIC SUSPENSE

ISBN-13: 978-1-335-08159-9

Protecting the Colton Bride & Colton's Cowboy Code

Copyright © 2019 by Harlequin Books S.A.

The publisher acknowledges the copyright holders of the individual works as follows:

Protecting the Colton Bride
Copyright © 2015 by Harlequin Books S.A.

Colton's Cowboy Code
Copyright © 2015 by Harlequin Books, S.A.

Special thanks and acknowledgment are given to Elle James and Melissa Cutler for their contributions to the Coltons of Oklahoma miniseries.

Recycling programs for this product may not exist in your area.

Printed in U.S.A.

www.Harlequin.com

CONTENTS

Elle James, a *New York Times* bestselling author, started writing when her sister challenged her to write a romance novel. She has managed a full-time job and raised three wonderful children, and she and her husband even tried ranching exotic birds (ostriches, emus and rheas). Ask her, and she'll tell you what it's like to go toe-to-toe with an angry 350-pound bird! Elle loves to hear from fans at ellejames@earthlink.net or ellejames.com.

Visit the Author Profile page at Harlequin.com.

PROTECTING
THE COLTON BRIDE

Elle James

This book is dedicated to my father, who left his home in Arkansas to join the US Air Force and gave twenty years of his life to his country. He ultimately followed his heart all the way back home, where he lives today and is happy to stay there. Home was where his heart was, and his heart was in Arkansas. I love you, Dad!

CHAPTER ONE

DANIEL COLTON SWEPT the brush over Rider's black coat, comforted by the scent of animal hide, manure and fresh-cut Bermuda. With every swish of the horse's full black tail, hay dust sparkled in the air, reflecting the afternoon sunlight streaming through the open door of the Lucky C breeding barn.

This was home and there was nowhere else Daniel would rather be.

"Are you about done brushing Rider? Halo's practically champing at the bit to get outside for her afternoon run."

Daniel lifted his head and stared over the black quarter horse stud's back at the woman on the other side. She was brushing the beautiful palomino mare, one of Daniel's many successes in his quarter-horse-breeding program at the Lucky C Ranch.

His chest tightened and his breath caught. It wasn't the horse he couldn't take his gaze off. It was the halo effect the sun gave Megan Talbot's strawberry blond hair. The palomino's registered name was Angel's Golden Halo, but the woman deserved the moniker more than the animal. For the first time in the four months since Megan had come to work for him, she'd worn her hair loose. Normally those long, curly locks were twisted into a braid, pulled back from a face sprinkled lightly with freckles. Some would call them flaws in her pale complexion, but Daniel found each freckle adorable and hard to resist.

A light breeze blew through the door, lifting Megan's hair, making it dance in the sunshine. The horse shifted nervously and Megan patted her backside. "Shh. We'll leave soon." She turned and smiled at Daniel with her bright green eyes. "Ready to saddle up? I don't know if Halo can wait any longer. She's more hyper than usual."

Daniel jerked his attention back to his horse, reminding himself that he was the boss, Megan worked for him and he had no business staring at her hair or any other part of her perfectly shaped face or lithe, athletic body.

"Let's saddle these two." He was ready to get out of the barn and gallop across the pastures of his father's ranch. Working around the animals, training, feeding and riding, he was more at home than at the big house with the rest of the Coltons.

Big J Colton was the patriarch of the Oklahoma Coltons and the owner of the Lucky C Ranch. As his bastard child, Daniel had grown up with his half brothers and half sister, accepted by everyone except his stepmother, Abra Colton. Because of her antagonism toward him and the fact that Big J had taken in a child who wasn't hers, Daniel had never felt he quite fit in with the others.

Megan was first to the tack room. When she emerged, she carried a blanket. "Is Greta back from Oklahoma City?" she asked.

"Not that I've heard. Why do you ask?"

With a shrug, Megan threw the blanket over the mare's back and followed Colton into the tack room. "I thought I saw her earlier. I might have been seeing things. With a wedding to plan, I doubt she has time to go back and forth between Tulsa and Oklahoma City often."

Daniel snorted. He grabbed his saddle and a blanket and squeezed by Megan in the confines of the barn. The scent of strawberries wafted in his direction from Megan's hair hanging down around her shoulders. Why did she have to be so darned beautiful? If she wasn't also so efficient and helpful, he might reconsider her employment at the ranch. She was a distraction and growing more distracting every day. "Don't know what takes so long in planning a wedding. All you need is a bride, a groom, a preacher and a ring."

Megan laughed as she lifted her own saddle. "I'm with you. If you know you love someone, why all the fuss, anyway? Married is married whether you have a big wedding or stand in front of a justice of the peace, say I do, sign the papers and call it done."

Daniel chuckled. "And I thought all women were romantics."

Megan's pretty coral lips twisted. "I think it's just me. My parents tried to convince me to earn an M-R-S degree, but I was too busy studying genetics and cell biology to be interested in the boys on the UCLA campus."

"M-R-S?"

Her brows rose. "You know. Mrs. someone." She shook her head. "They wanted me to marry well, be a social butterfly on the arm of my husband and stop playing in yucky stuff like parasites, tissues, and horse and cattle semen." Megan tossed her saddle up onto the mare's back with little effort.

Strong and beautiful, and she knew what she wanted out of life. In Daniel's mind, that was a killer combination. Why waste brains and talent by making her some man's arm candy?

He threw the blanket on Rider's back, followed by the saddle. "Didn't you grow up on a ranch? You know your way around horses like you've been doing this all your life."

Megan reached beneath the horse to grab Halo's girth, threaded the strap through the ring and tightened it. "My parents own a nice spread in California," she answered, pulling hard. "But they didn't let me work with the animals. I was barely allowed to ride. They were afraid those big ol' horses would hurt little ol' me." She laughed, the sound brightening Daniel's day.

Daniel frowned at how he'd grown used to the sound and looked forward to it. As he cinched Rider's girth and looped the leather strap, he concentrated on sticking to facts, not emotions. "You're an excellent rider."

"I didn't get that way *because* of my parents, but more *in spite* of them. What they didn't know was that I'd go to my room, saying I wanted to read for a while. Once there, I'd slip out the window, climb down a tree and race off to the pasture. Because I didn't want to get caught, I rode bareback and without a bridle."

An image of a gangly young woman with long strawberry blond hair riding bareback across the hills of California flashed in Daniel's mind. "No bridle? How did you get the horses to go the way you wanted?"

Megan lowered the stirrup and patted Halo's neck. "They could feel the pressure of my legs and responded accordingly. I also bribed them with apples and sugar cubes."

"I'm impressed." Daniel adjusted his stirrup and slipped the bridle over Rider's head. "Your parents didn't know what they were missing. You're very good with the horses."

"They didn't need the help with their horse-breeding program. We had a staff that managed the animals on the ranch." Megan sighed. "I'd love dearly to bring my horses out here someday."

"Why don't you?"

"My parents haven't forgiven me for moving to Oklahoma. Every time I speak with them on the phone, they ask me when I'm moving back. Remember last month, when I went home because my father was sick?"

Daniel nodded. She'd been gone an entire week, and he'd missed her more than he cared to admit. "You could have brought your horses back with you then. We have room here on the Lucky C for them."

Megan gave an unladylike snort. "Don't you think I would have if I could have?" She shook her head. "My father is using them as leverage, threatening to sell them if I don't move back to California."

Daniel shot a glance her way. "And are you?"

Megan blinked. "Am I what?"

"Moving back to California?"

She laughed. "Oh, heavens, no. I love it out here. I love my parents, but they stifle me. I've been calling my father's bluff about selling the horses. I hope he has a change of heart and lets me have them. Besides, I have no desire to live their lifestyle. It's not me."

Grabbing his stallion's reins, Daniel asked, "And what lifestyle is that?"

Megan's mouth twisted. "Servants to do everything for you, smiling at people you don't know at social events you don't really care about. Wearing skirts, heels and makeup all the time. Never getting your hands dirty or breaking a nail."

Daniel studied her fresh, makeup-free, freckled face. With her light red eyebrows and blond-tipped eyelashes, she was beautiful just the way she was. He wouldn't change a thing.

Tearing his gaze away from her, he led Rider out of the barn. He walked away from the woman who was far too often in his thoughts both at work and at night when he lay in bed, trying to sleep through a growing hunger that had nothing to do with food.

Behind him, he heard the sound of hooves pawing the ground and then thumping against the hard-packed dirt.

"Whoa, Halo," Megan said, her voice tight.

Daniel glanced over his shoulder.

Halo, normally calm and gentle, reared, her front hooves pawing at the air.

Daniel took a step back into the barn, his hand still holding Rider's reins.

Megan held on to Halo's bridle, talking softly, soothingly. When the horse came back down on all four hooves, Megan chuckled shakily. "You really are raring to go, aren't you?"

"Need a hand?" Daniel asked.

Her mouth firming, Megan frowned. "I don't need your help. I'm perfectly capable of handling Halo."

A smile tugging his lips, Daniel led Rider out of the barn. "Touchy, are we?"

"I'm not fragile like my father and mother seem to think. Haven't I proven that?" she demanded.

"Absolutely," he said, unable to fight the grin spreading across his face. "If you didn't look so good in your jeans, I'd mistake you for one of the guys."

Megan's frown deepened for a moment, then cleared. Her lips quirked upward along with her brows. "You like the way I look in jeans?"

Daniel was saved from responding by Halo rearing again, jerking Megan up off her feet for a second.

"We'd better get going before Halo takes off without you." Daniel jammed his boot in the stirrup and mounted Rider. He had to remind himself Megan was his employee. He couldn't flirt with the staff. It wasn't right. He leaned down and opened the gate to the pasture, rode through and waited for Megan.

She stuck her boot in the stirrup, but before she could sling her leg over the top of the saddle, Halo spun.

Megan held on, managing to get her leg over the top. "I don't know what's got her riled, but she's not acting right."

"You want to take another horse?"

"No," Megan grunted, fighting to control the horse and aim her toward the open gate. "She needs to get out and run."

Daniel waited for Megan and Halo to pass through before he closed the gate.

Megan released one hand from the reins to pull her hair behind her and tuck it into the back of her shirt. "I should have braided this—"

Before she finished her sentence, Halo reared, tossed her head and yanked the reins from Megan's hands. Before Megan could reach out to retrieve them, Halo leaped forward and bolted across the pasture.

Daniel dug his heels into Rider's flanks and raced after her, his pulse pounding as fast as the horse's hooves. At the speed Halo was going, all it would take was a quick change of direction or halt and Megan would be thrown.

Rider's hooves thundered across the ground. Daniel leaned forward to decrease wind resistance, slapping the reins behind him against the horse's hindquarters, urging him faster.

The stallion's eagerness to be first in the race would have made him move faster even without Daniel's bidding.

Halo had a good head start, but Rider slowly closed the gap.

Megan held on, bending over the horse's neck in an attempt to grab her bridle, without success.

As Daniel rode up beside her, pressing Rider against Halo's side, he yelled, "Grab on!" Reaching out, he looped his arm around Megan's waist.

She grabbed around his neck and held on as he lifted her out of the saddle and slammed her hard against his chest.

His legs clamping tight around the horse, Daniel adjusted his balance for Megan's weight and pulled on the reins. "Whoa, Rider."

The horse strained against the command, determined to catch up and overtake Halo.

His grip loosening around Megan's waist, Daniel's breath caught and held. If he didn't get Rider under control soon, he'd drop her and she could be crushed beneath the horse's powerful hooves.

MEGAN CLUNG TO Daniel.

Rider had been just as spooked by Halo's behavior as she had been. In his mad dash to catch up to the other horse, he was ignoring Daniel's one-handed attempt to bring him under control.

She was deadweight on Daniel. If she could get her leg around to the back… Swinging her leg behind her, she couldn't quite reach the back without Daniel losing his grip on her. The front was closer and had a better angle.

"Whoa!" Daniel yelled at the crazed horse.

Megan made the decision to go for the front. She looped her leg over the saddle horn and straddled Daniel's lap, facing him.

Daniel immediately released her and reached around her to take the reins in both hands.

Trying to make herself as small as possible, Megan pressed her face into his chest so that he could see over her. Daniel's thighs tensed beneath her as he dug his heels into the stirrups and pulled back hard on the reins. Rider slowed, whinnying his protest, as he settled into an agitated trot.

Daniel let off on the reins just a little.

Rider took that as an invitation to leap forward. He was instantly brought back by a sharp tug on the reins.

The horse reared.

Daniel leaned forward, his chest pressing into Megan's, his breath stirring the loose hair at her temples.

Her pulse hammered in her veins, but she kept her cool and held on until Rider stamped to a complete stop, pawing at the dirt.

When she was certain Daniel had the horse settled, she lifted her head, her face inches from Daniel's. Adrenaline spiking through her system, her breaths coming in ragged gasps, she was hyperaware of every point of contact between her body and his, from her legs resting on his muscular thighs to her chest pressed against the hardened planes of his. She could barely breathe.

His arms still around her, holding on to the reins, Daniel breathed out a long sigh. "You had me scared."

Megan let go of a nervous laugh. "You? I could do nothing to stop her. That was stupid of me to let go of the reins." The wind lifted her hair and blew it across her face. Before she could shove it behind her ear, Daniel reached out and did it for her.

"You couldn't have known Halo was going to take off like she did." Daniel's fingers curled the hair behind her ear, and he dragged the backs of his knuckles across her face, tracing a line from her ear to her jaw. "Watching her fly off like that with you on her back the reins dangling…"

Mesmerized by his gentle touch, Megan couldn't move away, nor did she want to. Daniel had never made a pass at her, nor had he indicated any attraction toward her in the four months she'd worked for him. Oh, but she'd been attracted to him from the day they met, when she'd interviewed for the job of his assistant.

Now, with her heart racing for an entirely different reason, her breath lodged in her throat and held as she waited for him to make the next move.

Daniel's gaze shifted to her mouth. He cupped her cheek, and his thumb brushed across her lips. "You don't need makeup."

"My mother would disagree. She hates my freckles," Megan whispered, her breath mingling with his.

"I think they are one of your best features." He leaned forward and touched her freckled nose with his lips.

Megan's eyes widened. Had he just kissed her? Was she dreaming? Her lips tingled in hopeful anticipation of a kiss that met her mouth, not her nose. She swept her tongue across her suddenly dry lips, and she stared up into his eyes.

Daniel's thumb brushed her lips again. "Don't do that."

"Do what?"

"This." He leaned forward and touched his mouth to hers, his tongue sweeping across the seam of her lips.

She opened to him as naturally as a morning glory opened to the sun. Her hands curled into his shirt, dragging him closer.

Daniel crushed her to him, his arms tightening around her. His tongue slipped past her teeth, claiming her in a long, sensual kiss that made her blood burn a path all the way to her core.

When at last he raised his head, he stared down at her as if seeing her for the first time.

Suddenly she felt shy. Her cheeks heated and she stammered, "Thanks for coming to my rescue."

Her words seemed to shake him out of his trance, his body stiffening. "Right. You're welcome." He glanced away, looking anywhere but at her. "I'd have done it for anyone."

He could have stuck a pin in her ego, as deflated as she felt after that incredible kiss and then his complete brush-off. A rush of adrenaline-induced anger made her back straighten. She was sitting in his lap, for heaven's sake, and there was no mistaking his obvious attraction to her pressing against her.

"Here, let me help you down." He gripped her arms and started to lift her off him.

Megan's arms slipped around his neck, refusing to let him dislodge her from his lap. Damn it. She didn't want down. Where she sat was exactly where she'd ached to be for so long. She wanted to scream with frustration that he now seemed determined to put her back in her place.

Megan tilted her chin in challenge. "I know you would have rescued anyone. That's the kind of person you are. But would you have *kissed* anyone like you just kissed me?"

CHAPTER TWO

DANIEL HELPED MEGAN slide around him to ride double behind him. Then he turned back for the barn.

"Aren't we going after Halo?" she asked.

"We're closer to the barn. I'll come back to get her when she's had time to calm down."

All he got from Megan was a soft snort. He could feel her anger and was torn between regret and relief. She was his employee. He had no right to kiss her like he had. Instead of holding around his waist, she gripped the rim of the saddle's seat and didn't say a word.

Her silence made Daniel's gut knot. This was the reason he didn't mix business with pleasure. And holy hell, it had been all pleasure, the feel of Megan's lips on his, her body pressed tightly to his. But when you crossed the line, you couldn't go back. The easy camaraderie they'd had before the kiss might be gone for good.

Jack, the oldest of Daniel's half siblings, and his younger brother Brett stood by the barn, sunlight glinting off their dark brown hair. They draped their arms over the wooden fence rail, their brows rising when Rider turned, revealing Megan behind Daniel.

Jack frowned. "Run into trouble?"

A grin split Brett's face. "Or creating some of your own?"

Daniel glared at Brett.

As soon as they reached the barn, Megan slid off the horse's rump, her cheeks bright pink. "I'll go look for Halo," she said, turning toward the barn to find another horse.

"Don't worry about her. Jack and Brett can saddle up and help me go after her."

"Fine." Megan, her face averted, ran for the barn.

Brett's smile disappeared. "What happened?"

"Something spooked Halo."

His younger brother's gaze followed Megan. "Not the horse. Megan. What happened with Megan?" He faced Daniel.

Heat suffused Daniel's cheeks and spread all the way out to his ears. "When the horse bolted with Megan, I pulled her off. She rode back with me. That's all." He narrowed his eyes, willing his brothers to stop with the inquisition about Megan. "What did you think happened?"

Brett's mouth twisted. "I don't know, but Megan just ran off like a scalded cat."

Daniel blew out a breath. "The point is, Halo spooked and nearly hurt Megan."

Jack's brows drew together. "That's not like her. Halo's one of our gentlest mares."

"I know. All the more reason to bring her back and find out what's wrong with her." Daniel looked from Jack to Brett. "Are you coming or not?"

Brett spun and trotted toward the barn. "It'll just take us a minute to saddle up."

Daniel dismounted and led Rider to the watering trough, watching through his peripheral vision for Megan to emerge from the barn.

By the time his brothers had captured and saddled

their horses, Megan still hadn't come out of the barn. Daniel knew it had been a mistake to kiss her. Now she was too embarrassed to come out while he was still around. She was the best assistant he'd had. Okay, so she was the only assistant he'd had. Now that his breeding program was doing well, he needed all the help he could get.

Megan was smart, computer savvy and great with the horses. He hoped she didn't quit because of one little kiss. One completely soul-defining, world-shattering kiss.

Daniel groaned.

"Got a bellyache?" Brett asked, leading his bay gelding out of the barn, followed by Jack.

"No, just thinking."

Jack swung up on his horse, carrying a lasso in his right hand and reining with the left. "Thinking these designer horses aren't the way to go after all?"

"No, not at all." Daniel had put a lot of thought, planning, research and sweat into the horse-breeding program, and it was just beginning to pay off. He wasn't giving up now.

"I told you, Jack," Brett said. "With Daniel's eye for excellent breeding stock and Megan's record-keeping capabilities, we're finally starting to take off. It won't be long before the Lucky C becomes a household name in progressive horse-breeding programs."

Daniel's chest swelled. "I'm determined to continue that progressive trend. Has Big J considered my proposal to purchase semen from the Kennedy Farms?"

"He's thinking about it. You already know how I feel," Jack said. "The Lucky C is a cattle ranch. We've always run cattle. The horses should be secondary, for running the cattle, not breeding."

Daniel respected his older brother's ability to manage a ranch the size of the Lucky C and his love and determination to protect his family. But the man was pragmatic and often slow to change. In order to let loose of the funding to purchase the semen needed to move their program forward, Daniel would have to convince both his father and his older brother it would be worth the investment.

"Come on, Jack," Brett said, nudging his horse to catch up with Jack's. "Daniel's already got other breeders looking at the Lucky C lines. He knows what he's doing, and it doesn't hurt to diversify our holdings."

"Yeah, well, we don't even know if the Kennedys will sell to us." Jack shot a glance at Daniel. "What's the latest?"

"They are all about the pedigree," Daniel said. "They hand-select the programs they want to contribute to."

"You have some of the best horses in the country," Brett noted. "Why wouldn't they want to add to your lines?"

Daniel snorted. "Their pedigree requirement extends to family and heritage."

"So? The Coltons are full of family and heritage. You think they might not sell to us because of family?" Jack's brows dipped. "I'll bet the Lucky C Ranch has been in the Colton family as long if not longer than the Kennedys have owned their ranch."

"Yeah, but I'm the one running the horse-breeding program here. I'm the main contact," Daniel reminded him.

"And?"

"Well, I'm not exactly a blue blood or a purebred."

Jack reined his horse to a stop. "What the hell are you talking about?"

"Yeah, what are you saying?" Brett reiterated. "You're just as much a Colton as the rest of us."

"I'm the bastard," Daniel said, his tone flat.

"That's not how we see it," Brett said.

Jack, Brett, Ryan and Greta had always treated him as one of the family, even though Daniel's stepmother had resented the fact that Big J brought him to live with them when his own mother had died.

Abra hated Daniel. She hated that Big J had an affair with the nanny when Abra had been halfway around the world on another one of her trips. The woman couldn't stand to be around her own kids. They made her nervous.

Daniel's mother, full-blood Cherokee, had left the Lucky C when she discovered she was pregnant with Big J's child. She'd returned to the reservation, where she'd instilled in Daniel pride in his Cherokee heritage and the love of horses.

"You're as much a Colton as the rest of us," Jack said.

Brett snarled. "If anyone says differently, they can take it up with all of us."

"Not everyone sees things the way you, Ryan and Greta do," Daniel assured them. But his heart warmed at the conviction in his brothers' tones.

When he'd come to live with them at only ten years old, he'd thought he'd be miserable, losing the mother he loved and moving in with a father he barely knew. He figured on staying until he was old enough to leave home.

And here he was twenty years later. He no longer lived at the big house, having moved out when he finished college. Now he lived in the cozy two-bedroom cabin close to the breeding barn. It was small but enough for a bachelor and away from his stepmother.

"There she is," Jack called out, pulling Daniel back to the task at hand.

Halo stood in the middle of the pasture, pawing at the ground.

As they neared, she reared and whinnied.

Rider answered, sidestepping nervously.

"She's all wound up," Brett muttered. "Did she get hold of some bad feed?"

"No telling. But whatever is bothering her isn't normal." Daniel nudged Rider forward.

"Let's go get her." Jack lifted his lasso and urged his mount forward.

Daniel rode up to the mare. With only twenty yards between them, the mare bolted and ran. Rider quickly caught up to her on one side. Jack's horse swung to the opposite side as he tossed the lasso, his aim true. The rope circled the mare's neck.

Jack tied off on the saddle horn and slowed his horse by pulling on the reins.

Halo pulled against the rope around her neck, tossing her head, dancing sideways to avoid Jack. Daniel was on the other side. He reached over and grabbed her reins.

Between Jack and Daniel, they slowed the mare to a halt. Her chest heaved, her sleek cream-colored coat was slick with sweat and her eyes rolled, showing the crazed whites.

"Need a hand there?" Brett called out, riding nearby in case the horse broke free.

"We have her."

The two Coltons led the horse back toward the barn, Daniel speaking to her softly, trying to soothe her.

Brett was first off his horse. He took over for the other two and held the horse's reins.

When Jack loosened his hold on the lasso, Halo tried to rear, but Brett held tight, pulling her head down.

"You're right," Brett said, straining to hold on to the horse. "Something isn't right with her."

"Let's get her into the squeeze chute. I want to take a blood sample." Daniel dismounted and led Rider into the barn, tying him off to a post before helping Brett get Halo into the chute.

Jack backed away. "If you two can handle this, I'll take care of the other horses."

"We have it," Daniel assured him. "All I need is a syringe—"

Megan appeared, carrying a syringe and a couple of cotton balls soaked in rubbing alcohol.

Daniel breathed a sigh, happy that she hadn't decided to quit because of his indiscretion.

"Daniel keeps telling us how efficient you are," Brett teased. "Now you're a mind reader?"

Megan shook her head. "It's logic. Halo wasn't acting herself. There has to be a reason."

Brett and Daniel held Halo's head while Megan swabbed the horse's neck, felt for the jugular and slid in the needle.

Halo jerked, but the men held her steady while Megan pulled the plunger, filling the syringe. She removed the needle, swabbed the injection site and massaged it for a moment. "I'll put this in a tube and drop it off at the vet pathology lab in Tulsa on my way home."

"Better leave now if you want to catch them before they close for the day."

"Will do." Megan hurried back into the barn with the syringe without making eye contact with Daniel. She'd always been open and smiling around him.

Daniel could have kicked himself for ruining everything. He wouldn't have been surprised in the least if she came in the next day with her resignation. "Can you take over with Halo?"

"Sure." Brett gripped the mare's bridle and backed her out of the chute.

Daniel ran into the barn, where Jack had tied off his and Brett's mounts beside Rider. He was in the process of removing the last saddle.

Megan was nowhere in sight.

Jack shook his head. "She's in the office."

Without a word, Daniel entered the office.

Megan was at the desk they shared in the cramped space, transferring the blood from the syringe into a tube. "Is there anything else you need dropped at the lab?" Megan reached for a padded envelope and dropped the tube inside.

"No. Just that." Daniel rubbed his sweaty palms down the front of his jeans. "Megan, I want to apologize."

Megan's cheeks reddened. "Don't."

"I'm afraid my actions might have given you the wrong idea."

Her head jerked up and she stared straight into his eyes. "Are you going to tell me that you kissed me by accident? Or that it was a huge mistake?"

"No. I mean, yes." He bit down on his tongue to keep from saying something stupid.

"Save your breath, Daniel." She crossed the room with

the package in her hand. Her jaw was set, lips pressed into a thin line. "I agree. The kiss was a big mistake."

He let go of the breath he'd been holding, but the tightness in his chest didn't loosen. Though he thought the kiss was a mistake, he hadn't known how he'd feel to hear her echo his thoughts. Had the kiss meant nothing to her?

"Good, then." Daniel straightened, determined not to let any of his chaotic thoughts show in his expression. "I just didn't want things to change between us. You're the best assistant I've ever had."

Megan rolled her eyes. "Daniel, I'm the only assistant you've ever had. But if you want to pretend nothing happened and everything between is just like it was this morning, I can play that game, too." She stopped in front of him and poked a finger into his chest. "But it would be a lie. You might wish you could, but you can't take back that kiss or the way it made you feel. Because I sure can't. It wasn't entirely one-sided, in case you hadn't noticed."

MEGAN LEFT THE office and ran out of the barn. She hopped into her Jeep Wrangler and sped down the road leading to the gate to the Lucky C Ranch. Soon she was on the highway into Tulsa, where she had a depressingly small apartment in an inexpensive but not too sketchy neighborhood.

Determined to make it on her own without her parents' vast wealth, she'd managed to put down a deposit on the apartment and pay rent and her utilities with the money she made working for the Lucky C Ranch.

The drive into Tulsa didn't take long, and soon she was on the bypass circling the city to get to the veterinary laboratory before it closed. She hadn't factored in the evening rush-hour congestion. Swerving in and out of traffic, she finally pulled into the parking lot with two minutes to spare.

She ran the blood sample inside, wrote out her request and left the package with the receptionist.

Then she drove to her apartment complex and parked, her hands shaking as she sat behind the steering wheel, letting the events of the afternoon wash over her in a tidal wave of emotions. One thought stood out over all others.

Daniel Colton had kissed her.

The incessant buzzing of her cell phone pierced her hazy cloud of schoolgirl giddiness, and she dug in her purse.

Perhaps it was Daniel calling to tell her that the kiss hadn't been a mistake and he was deeply, madly, completely in love with her. Megan found the phone, stared at the caller ID and groaned before punching the talk button.

"Hi, Mother. What do you want?" she asked, the irritation in her voice more pronounced than usual.

"Ferrence Small is back home from New York City."

"That's nice."

"I understand he's a lawyer now, working with a large pipeline company out in Wyoming. If you can tell me the next time you'll be home, I'm sure I can set up a chance for you two to meet."

"Mother, I'm not interested."

"Sweetheart, your father's health isn't what it used to be. He's a very sick man."

"I know. I was out there last month. We had a lovely visit."

"Honey, you can't keep slaving away in the tornado-infested center of the country. I can't stop worrying. And you can imagine all the stress your father is under."

"I'm sorry, Mother. But you and Daddy can manage your ranch in California. You don't really need me there. However, the Lucky C needs me here. I have important work to do, and I don't need care packages, cards and letters begging me to come home. I'll be home for visits. That will have to be enough."

Her mother clucked. "Oh, darling, I didn't want to have to tell you..."

A sense of dread slipped over her. Her mother only used that I-hate-to-stick-it-to-you-but-I-will-if-I-have-to voice when she was about to drop a bomb on some poor unsuspecting sales clerk who displeased her while shopping. Only this time, the bomb would fall on Megan.

"Your father is on the line, and he has something to say to you."

Her hand tightening on the cell phone until her knuckles turned white, Megan sucked in a deep breath and said, "Hi, Dad. What is it you wanted to say?"

"I have an auctioneer coming out tomorrow to look at your horses."

Megan's heart plummeted to her knees. "Daddy," she said. "I've only just started putting money away for the horses. It will take me years to have what I need to pay you for them."

"I'm sorry, sweetheart, but if I can't go out to Oklahoma to talk some sense into my daughter's head, I can damn sure get her to come to me. The Triple Diamond Ranch is your legacy."

"Daddy, it's *your* legacy. You and Mother never wanted me to help with it. Now I want to make it on my own." She'd left the rich debutante lifestyle behind after she'd lost her fiancé and nearly lost her life. Megan had no intention of going back.

Her father snorted. "You do not have to work for others when you have servants who can do all that for you."

"But, Daddy, you don't understand. I love working with the horses. And I'm good at it."

"You're a woman. You shouldn't be working around animals big enough to crush you."

"Those horses are big enough to crush the men I work with as well as me. The thing is, Daddy, I know when to get out of the way."

"Damn it, Megan, you are our only child. I want to know when I die…" He coughed. "I want to know you will be here to take over the reins. You need to come home, settle down, get married and have children to shoulder your obligation to your heritage."

"I'm sorry, Daddy, but I have to live my life the way I want to, not the way you dictate."

Her mother's gasp echoed over the line.

"Very well," her father said in a steely voice. "If you're not home in one week and actively looking for a suitable spouse, I will sell all of your beloved horses to a glue factory."

Blood drained from Megan's head, and her stomach flipped. "You can't do that. Those horses are beautiful animals, and they should be with us. The horse-breeding program at Triple Diamond Ranch is one of the best. You can't condemn them to a glue factory or even sell them just because you want me to come home."

"I can and I will. If you care about the horses, show you care about your legacy and the future of Triple Diamond Ranch. One week, Megan."

CHAPTER THREE

DANIEL TOSSED ALL night. When he actually fell asleep he dreamed of Megan, her hair flying out behind her on a runaway horse. He chased her. For a long time she was just out of reach. When he finally caught up with her, he snatched her off her horse and into his arms. Then they kissed. The kiss turned into more and suddenly they were in his bed, making love.

Daniel jerked awake, hot, sweaty and more aroused than he'd ever been in his life. All stemming from a kiss that shouldn't have happened.

Before dawn, he rose from his solitary bed in the cabin close to the breeding barn and pulled on a pair of jeans, a shirt and his boots. He couldn't go back to sleep knowing Megan would be in his dreams, lying naked in his sheets. Everything about that image was wrong.

He'd be lucky if she even showed up for work today. And if she did, she'd probably come only to turn in her resignation.

By the time the sun came up over the horizon, Daniel had fed the horses, checked on his studs and prize mares and stacked twenty bags of feed in a corner of the barn. With his pulse still pounding and blood burning through his veins, he snapped a lunging rope on Rider's halter and walked him out to the arena.

Daniel twirled the end of the rope and clucked his

tongue. Rider started at a walk, more interested in an easy pace than actual exercise.

"Come on, boy. You need this as much as I do." Daniel continued twirling the loose end of the rope. He clucked his tongue again and tapped the horse's hindquarters with the rope.

Rider stepped up the pace and trotted around the circle, tossing his black mane in protest.

The monotonous circling calmed Daniel and the horse, and they settled into a rhythm of walking and trotting. Fifteen minutes passed before a voice called out.

"Daniel!"

Daniel's hand tightened on the rope. Rider immediately came to a halt.

Heat rose up his neck and into his face as Daniel turned toward the voice.

Megan leaned over the arena's metal fence, her arms folded over the top rail, lines etched across her smooth forehead.

Though he was happy Megan had returned, Daniel couldn't erase his concern over the content of his dreams, and he worried his thoughts would be easily discernible in his eyes. Without meeting her gaze, Daniel nodded. "Good morning, Megan," he acknowledged, gathering the rope until he held the horse on a short lead.

The normally reserved and always confident young woman chewed on her lower lip, and her brows puckered. "We need to talk," she blurted.

His stomach knotting, Daniel braced himself. "Yes, we do. Let me take care of Rider first. Then we can talk uninterrupted."

"Okay," she said, biting on her lower lip again, driving Daniel nuts with the nervous movement that only drew his attention to the mouth he'd kissed so hard the day before.

He opened the gate to the arena and led Rider through.

Megan closed the gate and trailed behind Daniel and Rider, following them into the barn.

Not certain what he was going to say, Daniel chose to concentrate on the horse, putting off the talk as long as he could, hoping he could say something that would make sense and put things back on an even keel. He liked Megan. A lot. And he didn't want to lose her over something as stupid, and inconsiderate, and completely unforgettable as a kiss.

Holy hell, he couldn't even come up with an apology when he wasn't at all sorry he'd kissed her. He'd be sorry only if she left because of it.

After grabbing a brush, Daniel stalled by running the brush over Rider's back.

Megan fetched another brush and took the other side, working quickly, her strong hands smoothing over the horse's sides, meeting Daniel over the horse's hindquarters. She stared across the animal's rump and said, "Daniel, I have to quit." Then she spun and paced away from him.

"Won't you at least give me the chance to apologize properly?"

Her head down, her boot heels pounding the dirt, she marched to the end of the barn and back. "Normally I'd give two weeks' notice. But that's impossible."

His chest tightening with each of her words, Daniel stood with a brush in his hands. How could he salvage this situation and keep her on the Lucky C? "Under the circumstances, I don't blame you, but I wish you'd reconsider."

She paced, shaking her head, her long French braid whipping side to side. "If there was any other way, I wouldn't go, but I don't see another option."

"Again, I don't blame you. I blame myself." He set the brush on a workbench and gathered Megan's hands in his. "I wish there was something I could say or do to make it better. Please don't go. I need you here."

She stared up into his eyes. "I don't have a choice. If I don't leave, he'll sell them all." Her eyes swam with tears.

Daniel stared down at her. "What are you talking about?"

"My horses." She frowned. "What did you think I was talking about?"

A wave of relief nearly made Daniel weak. "I thought you were mad about yesterday."

Her frown deepening, she stared into his eyes. "Yesterday?" Then her eyes widened and her mouth formed a kissable O. "Yesterday." Twin flags of color flew high on her cheekbones. "The kiss."

"The kiss." His hands slid up her arms and stopped before he pulled her close and kissed her again. "I thought you were going to leave because I crossed the line."

"You think I'd leave because of a kiss? I thought you knew me better than that."

"You had every right to quit. As your boss, I shouldn't have kissed you."

"For your information, there were two people involved in that kiss. It was not one-sided. And that's not the reason I'm leaving."

"Then what is?"

"My father." She pulled in a long breath and let it out.

"He gave me an ultimatum. He's going to sell my horses if I don't come home to live."

Daniel's fingers tightened on her arms. "I thought the horses at the Triple Diamond were quality stock. They are ranked right up there in standing with the Kennedys' breeding program."

"Yeah, well my father doesn't really give a damn about the horses. It was just a project he took on at my suggestion until I left."

"Can't you buy them from him?" Daniel couldn't wrap his mind around throwing away some of the best horseflesh in the nation.

"If I had the money my grandmother left to me." She shook her head. "But I won't get that until I'm married. It's a stipulation of her will. Even then, I'd have to purchase them through a third party. My father would never sell them to me. He wants me home, and this is his leverage."

"Didn't you say he was sick?"

"Yes, but I can never tell how sick he is. He always tries to manipulate me and make me live according to his standards. I don't want to go back, but I don't have another choice. I have to go home. I can't let him sell those horses. They're top breeders…and…my friends."

Daniel gathered her in his arms and stroked her head. "It's okay. We'll think of something."

She rested her cheek against his chest, her fingers curling into his shirt. "There's nothing to think about. I have to go. The sooner the better."

He tipped her face up. "When is he selling?"

"He gave me one week to get home or the horses go on the auction block." Her eyes filled with tears.

"Well, that gives us a week."

"One week isn't enough." She shook her head. "I don't see any other way. If he sells them as breeding stock, they'll go high. I won't be able to buy them. I barely have enough money to pay next month's rent. So you see, I have to go home." She took a step back and stood in front of him, her shoulders slumped, the first tears sliding from the corners of her eyes. "I thought he was bluffing. But I can't bet those horses on a bluff."

The anger he could handle. But as the tears slid down Megan's cheeks, it felt like a large fist had clenched around his heart and squeezed. He pulled her against him again and held her close, resting his cheek against the top of her head. "I have a little money saved."

She laid her face against his chest. "I can't take your money. This isn't your problem. It's mine."

"Well, don't do anything today. Give us some time to come up with some solutions."

"I'm out of solutions," she said, pressing her face into his shirt.

"Just promise me you won't leave right away. Can you do that?"

"It'll take time for me to organize my apartment, shut off my utilities and inform my landlord. But once I have all that done, I have to drive to California."

"Just hold on for a day or two. We'll think of something."

Her arms slipped around his waist. "I don't expect you to take on my problems. You're my boss, not my fairy godmother."

He chuckled. "Yeah, I'd look pretty silly in a dress, carrying a fairy wand, and I'm not such a great boss at that."

"Why do you say that?" She looked up at him through watery green eyes. "You're great."

"Because a good boss doesn't go around kissing his employees." He stared down at her damp cheeks, his belly flipping. "Right now, I want to be a very bad boss."

Her eyes flared with desire. "How so?"

"I want to kiss you. Again."

She sucked in a breath and bit down on that lip before saying, "I told you, I quit. That means you're not my boss."

He leaned his forehead against hers and sighed. How he wanted to kiss her. "I'm not accepting your resignation."

"You don't have a choice," she said, her lips so close.

Daniel could almost feel how soft they were. He wanted to kiss her so badly his lips tingled. The warmth of her breath feathered across his mouth. His hands shook with the effort it took to resist.

Then he pushed her to arm's length. "I can't screw this up. If we find a way to save your horses without you moving back to California, you'll still be my employee. I don't want to risk losing you as an assistant."

Megan sighed and dropped her arms. "Okay, boss, I'll be here for another day, but I'll only be able to work half a day tomorrow. I have a lot to do to get my stuff packed for the move."

"Don't start packing yet. We'll come up with a solution. In the meantime, I need you to call the vet lab and see if they came up with anything from the sample you took in yesterday."

"They won't have had time to process it," Megan argued.

"Then research other breeding programs. The Kennedy deal might not happen."

"Why? You have a fine program here. You're a rising star in quarter horse breeding."

Daniel snorted. "As far as the Kennedys are concerned, that isn't enough."

"Why?"

"I don't want to go into it. Just do that research for me, will you?"

She popped a salute and gave him a crooked smile. "Yes, boss." Then she turned and marched into the barn office.

Daniel let go of the breath he'd been holding since the urge to kiss Megan again had nearly pushed him past reason. He had to come up with a plan to help Megan get those horses or he'd lose her. After working with her for only four months, he knew she'd be impossible to replace. In more ways than he'd ever imagined.

MEGAN ENTERED THE office, closed the door behind her and leaned against it. Her face burned and her heart hurt so much she could barely think straight. She'd wanted to kiss Daniel. She'd almost thrown herself at him. After yesterday's kiss, she'd thought there might be something between them. But today he'd pushed her away. Apparently he wasn't as infatuated with her as she was with him.

Since the first day she'd come to work with Daniel, she'd known he was special. The man was quiet and dedicated. He loved horses as much as she did. His Cherokee ancestry didn't hurt, either. He was tall and handsome. That dark, dark hair and even darker brown eyes made her crazy with longing. Maybe she should leave. Staying at the Lucky C and falling in love with Daniel would only set her up for a whole lot of pain.

The irony of it all was that all problems would have been solved if he'd professed a secret love for her and asked her to marry him. She'd have the man of her most sensual dreams and meet the stipulation of her grandmother's will. She'd inherit her grandmother's sizable financial holdings upon her marriage. That money would be enough to purchase the horses from her father and she'd never be subject to his threats again. Her life would be her own to live the way she saw fit.

Megan drew in a long, steadying breath and let it out on a sigh. If wishes were horses, beggars would ride. She held out no hope for another solution to her situation. But two more days with Daniel were better than nothing.

She sat behind the desk and thumbed through her contacts to find the number for the vet lab in Tulsa and called. When she reached one of the lab techs, she explained she was calling for the Lucky C Ranch.

"Oh, we're so glad you called. We had a lull in samples, so we were able to get right on the one you left last night. I'm surprised that horse is still standing. The sample you left us indicated she was poisoned." The tech gave her the scientific name of the poison, which Megan wrote on a pad.

"It affects the animal's nervous system, making her jumpy and overstimulated."

"How would a horse get hold of something like that?"

"It's not like it grows around here. Either it was present in the food she was fed, something brought it into her environment or someone gave it to her."

Megan's gut clenched at the final option. They fed

all the breeding horses the same feed, and Halo was the only one to show any symptoms.

"Okay, I'll let the boss know. Thank you for the information." Megan hung up and stared at the phone for exactly two seconds. Then she pushed to her feet and ran out to the stalls.

"What's wrong?" Daniel had just finished mucking Rider's stall and stood the rake against the wall.

"The vet lab said Halo was poisoned."

"What?" He hurried to Halo's stall with Megan.

The mare stood with her head sagging, her breathing labored.

"She seemed fine early this morning when I checked on her." Daniel entered the stall and ran his hands over her neck, checked her eyes and looked down her throat. "Call the vet."

Megan ran back to the office and dialed the veterinarian who serviced the animals on the Lucky C. He was there within twenty minutes, and they spent the rest of the afternoon working to save Halo.

Megan and Daniel cleaned her stall thoroughly, took samples from her trough and searched the barn for anything contaminated that she could have come in contact with. Nothing stood out.

After the vet left with strict instructions on how to take care of the very sick horse, Megan stood by Daniel. "What now?"

"We wait and see how she does by morning. We've done all we can do."

Megan stared at Daniel's worried face. Neither one of them had eaten lunch, and the work they'd done all afternoon had depleted Megan's personal store of energy.

It had to have taken a toll on Daniel's. "It's nearly supper time. Why don't we grab a bite to eat?"

Daniel shook his head. "I have deli meat and bread at the cabin. Help yourself. I'm staying with Halo."

Knowing Daniel needed to fuel his system for what appeared to be an all-nighter, Megan left him in the barn and hiked over to his cabin. It wasn't the first time she'd gone to the cabin to make sandwiches. The man didn't take care of himself. As his assistant, she'd helped him set up a robust database to track horses, feed, lineage, exercise and all the other nuances of running a breeding facility. She'd also learned what kind of sandwiches he preferred and made sure he ate.

She entered the cabin through the front door and headed for the small kitchen. Having little in the way of decorations, the cabin reflected the male occupant through the dark leather furniture and large television screen for the occasional football game he liked to watch. The furnishings were spare and serviceable.

In the kitchen, his refrigerator held five bottles of beer, a couple bottles of water, one moldy orange, a few bottles of condiments, a jug of soured milk and a package of deli meat. Megan gave the meat a smell test. Thankfully it passed.

After throwing together two sandwiches, she grabbed the bottled water and hurried back to the barn, not wanting to be away from Daniel and Halo any longer than necessary.

Daniel was where she'd left him and Halo lay on the ground beside him.

Her heart went out to the horse. "She doesn't look good."

"The vet said tonight would be the big test."

Megan held out the sandwich she'd wrapped in a paper towel. "Eat. You're no good to anyone if you pass out from hunger."

"I don't pass out," he mumbled, refusing to take the sandwich. "I'm going to wash my hands first."

"I'll be here." Megan sank to the ground beside Halo, unfolded the napkin around her sandwich and took a bite. She had no real interest in eating when such a beautiful creature was lying sick because of some toxin with a source they had yet to locate.

Over her shoulder, she heard the jingle of the phone ringing in the office. She struggled to stand but settled back on her bottom when Daniel's deep tone said, "Hello. Yes, this is Daniel Colton. Mr. Kennedy, I'm glad you called."

Megan stiffened. From the sound of it, Daniel was talking to the owner of Kennedy Farms. Excitement had her leaning toward the office, straining to hear the conversation. This was the call Daniel had been hoping for. Marshall Kennedy didn't bother to talk to breeders unless he already had a good opinion of their programs.

Rider whinnied from his stall. Angel, Halo's mother, answered, the noise drowning out whatever Daniel was saying.

The office door swung closed, shutting out the sound of the horses and cutting off any eavesdropping Megan hoped to accomplish.

Not that it mattered. She'd soon be on her way back to California to live the life her father and mother deemed appropriate for a debutante. All interest in the sandwich she'd prepared disappeared and she laid it on the napkin beside her.

Sleek, the black barn cat, trotted over to her side and sniffed at the discarded food.

"Go ahead. You can have it. You'll need your strength here more than I will." It appeared the cat would outlast Megan's stay at the Lucky C.

CHAPTER FOUR

"I'VE HEARD A lot about the Lucky C Ranch lately," Marshall Kennedy's voice boomed in his ear.

Daniel held the phone in a tight grip. This call might mean the difference between a good program and an excellent breeding program that could gain international attention. "Thank you, sir," Daniel said. "I've selected from only the best lineage."

"I assume that's why you're looking at purchasing semen from Striker's Royal Advantage."

"Yes, sir. I've done my research, and I believe a foal from Striker and Big J's Lucky Coin will be the most sought-after registered quarter horse in the country."

"I'm impressed with Big J's Lucky line, but I don't sell to just any farm that comes along with enough money to pay for stud service."

"I understand, Mr. Kennedy."

"I want to know my horses are being bred and cared for by a fine, upstanding family. Good family is just as important, if not more so, than money. From what I've learned about the Coltons, there are a few skeletons in the closets. You being one of them."

Daniel bit down on his tongue to keep from telling Kennedy that people couldn't always choose their lineage like people could choose a horse's bloodline. "I'm as much a part of the Colton family as any of my siblings, and I'm just as proud of my Cherokee blood." Realizing he was coming across too strong, Daniel drew in a calming breath and continued. "If my heritage will be a sticking point in this deal, perhaps this conversation is over."

"Whoa, young man. I didn't say your bloodline was at fault."

"Then what is it you need from me to convince you the horses produced from your lines will be well cared for?"

"I want you to convince me the Coltons are the right family to invest in. I'm speaking at the annual Symposium on Equine Reproduction a week from now in Reno, Nevada. I want you to attend that symposium. I'll be there with members of my family. If at that time I feel that the Coltons are worth the risk, we can discuss the details of the sale. Are you still interested?"

"Yes, sir," Daniel said, not really understanding how meeting Kennedy at a symposium would change the man's mind if he'd already made his decision. "I'll be there."

"Good." Marshall Kennedy ended the call, leaving Daniel no closer to knowing whether he'd get the semen he wanted to take his breeding program to the next level. With one of his mares down and no guarantee she'd pull through, and his assistant likely quitting, he wondered if it was too soon to take this step. He'd be gambling a great deal of Colton money on a dream. Not all of the Colton brothers were in agreement on taking this project forward. Big J liked a family consensus before funding was released.

The bright spot in the mess of the past few days was

that Kennedy hadn't said no. He hadn't said yes. But there still was hope.

He stepped out of the office and returned to the stall, where Megan sat in the dying light beside Halo, stroking the animal's neck. The horse didn't look any better, and Daniel wasn't sure she'd live to see the sunrise.

Too many strange things had happened on the ranch in the past few months. The main house had been robbed and his father's wife, Abra, had been attacked and left in a coma. Now someone had tried to kill one of his prize mares.

Daniel wasn't ready to give up on Halo, yet. And he still had to come up with a solution to Megan's problem or he'd lose her, too.

Megan smiled over her shoulder at him. "I kept Sleek from eating your sandwich."

The barn cat sat beside Megan, licking its paws. The stray had been an asset to the ranch and kept the mouse population down.

The sun had dipped below the horizon while Daniel talked on the phone with Kennedy. With his world tilted on its axis, Daniel wasn't sure what the next day would bring or how to keep everything he'd worked for from falling apart.

"You can go home. I'll stay with Halo," he said to Megan.

She shook her head. "If it's all the same to you, I'd rather stay. I know it doesn't make sense, but I feel like it's my fault Halo's in the shape she's in."

"Unless you purposely poisoned her, I don't see how it could be your fault."

"I should have realized something was terribly wrong with her and dealt with her immediately." She scratched behind the horse's ear. "Then you wouldn't be as sick as you are now, would you, baby?" Her tone was soothing, and Halo's ears twitched.

"We wouldn't have known anything sooner," Daniel said. "The lab had to make that determination. It wasn't until this morning that she went downhill."

"Still, I was the last one to ride her."

"Stop." Daniel held up a hand. "We'll both stay with her."

She gave him a crooked smile. "Thanks. I'd like that."

He left her in the stall and went about the task of feeding the other animals. When he returned to the stall, he carried several clean horse blankets and a section of hay. He spread out the hay on the ground.

Megan took one of the blankets from him, laid it over the hay and sat on one side of it, patting the spot next to her. "Sit and eat your supper."

Daniel sat and took the sandwich from Megan. When their hands touched, a spark of electricity shot up his arm, reminding him of that kiss and the subsequent dreams that had plagued his sleep the night before. At least if he stayed awake all night with Halo, he wouldn't be dreaming of lying naked with Megan.

"Was that Marshall Kennedy on the phone?" Megan gave him a half smile. "Sorry, I overheard a little."

Daniel chewed on a bite of deli meat, mentally going over his conversation with Kennedy. Megan had been with him when he'd researched the studs and breeders. She knew as well as he did what they needed at the Lucky C to make it a world-class operation, and she deserved to know the outcome of that conversation, even if she did quit in two days' time. "Yes."

"Well?" She leaned forward on her knees, her green

eyes bright in the soft glow from the overhead lighting. "Is he going to deal with us or not?"

Daniel shook his head. "Jury's still out."

"Then why bother calling you?" She sat back, her excitement replaced by a frown. "Either he's going to sell to you or he's not."

"It's like I told Brett and Jack. The man has a thing about family. He looks at the lineage of the horses, but he's concerned about the family raising those horses."

"Then it should be a slam dunk. The Coltons are well respected as ranchers not only in Oklahoma but also across the United States."

"Ranching cattle. But we're new at horse breeding and not as well proven. That's not what he's concerned about, though. He wants to know his horses are going to a good family."

"Again, the Coltons are well respected. What could he be concerned about?"

"He's specifically worried about me. He called me a skeleton in the Colton closet. From what I've learned, the Kennedys are socially elite and proud of their status."

"Sounds like my parents. They would hate to have me mess up their standing by marrying beneath me." Megan shivered. "I've met too many of their social picks." She snorted. "No thanks. Do you think that's what's holding the Kennedys back?"

Daniel nodded. "I'm the stick in the man's craw. The bastard son of a Colton, and a Cherokee to boot."

Megan's face reddened and her eyes flashed. "Is he refusing to sell to you because you're half-Cherokee?"

"He didn't say that, but I'm betting he's not comfortable selling to the bastard son. I don't have the social status of a Kennedy."

"Daniel, you're just as much a Colton as any of your siblings."

"Not according to my stepmother."

"Abra is a bitter old woman who doesn't even like her own children. She's more interested in social status than love and family." Megan clapped a hand over her mouth and then sat back. "Sorry. I couldn't stop myself. I've seen how she treats you and your brothers and wanted to tell her what I thought about that. How can a woman dislike her own children?"

"It doesn't matter, and it doesn't bother me anymore." Not since he'd moved out of the main house. He didn't come into contact with Abra Colton as often and it suited him just fine.

"The point is, Kennedy can't hold an accident of birth against you. You're a good man. You're good with horses and have a great eye for quality. If he could only see that, he'd sell to you with no further questions asked."

"Well, that's just it. He'll get the chance. I meet with him face-to-face in exactly one and a half weeks."

"What?" Once again Megan sat forward. "When? Where? I'd love to be a fly on the wall at that meeting."

He wished Megan could be at his side. She'd be a great asset because of her knowledge of horse breeding from the Triple Diamond and her pedigree from an impressive family tree with a long line of Talbots raising only the best Talbots and horses. Kennedy would fall in love with Megan's charm and capabilities just like he had.

She assured him, "Kennedy will see what a great program we have started here at the Lucky C." Her lips twisted. "I mean, the program you've started."

"I couldn't have even tempted the man without your

help putting the data together to send to him. Why don't you come with me?" Then he remembered Megan was leaving the Lucky C to go home to California.

Megan sighed. "Unless I'm willing to let my horses be sold, I can't. I'm headed to California in the next week."

"Damn. I wish you didn't have to go." Daniel leaned forward and checked on Halo, racking his brain for a solution to both their problems. The horse lifted her head and stared at him with her big brown eyes as if to say she wished he could fix her problem, as well.

"You'll do fine," Megan said, leaning back against the wall. "The most important thing right now is to get Halo back on her feet."

"You're right." Daniel settled back against the wall beside Megan.

She closed her eyes, stifling a yawn behind her hand. "I don't know about you, but I didn't sleep worth a darn last night. My dad's threat and my ride on a sick horse weren't conducive to pleasant dreams." She yawned again and laughed. "Sorry. I'm supposed to stay awake all night with Halo. I won't be of much use if I fall asleep."

"Come here." Daniel slipped an arm around her shoulders and pulled her close. "Lean on me. I'll stay awake and let you know if there's any sign of change."

Megan snuggled up against him. "I thought you didn't mix business with pleasure?"

"You said it yourself. You quit." What could it hurt to hold her? It might give him a chance to come up with a plan to rescue her horses from being sold off, or find a way to impress Marshall Kennedy with his family when he wasn't even part of the official Colton line.

Megan closed her eyes again. "Mmm. This is much

nicer. I should have quit sooner." Her breathing became deeper and her body relaxed against Daniel's.

If only she knew how hard it was for him to hold her and not kiss the tip of her nose or press his lips to her temple, she might not be so willing to fall asleep against him. All thoughts of being a good boss and not touching his employee flew out the barn door while he held Megan in his arms.

Halo stirred, lifting her head a little, her hooves kicking out just once before she settled back in the straw.

Daniel prayed that she'd make it through the night and he'd come up with a way to keep Megan. She'd been instrumental in his research and planning for his breeding program. She was good at what she did, and her parents would squander her assets, forcing her to go to social events she couldn't stand.

Sometime in the night, Halo shook out of the effects of the poison and got to her feet.

Daniel was so relieved, he almost woke Megan to tell her, but she was sleeping soundly and he hated to wake her. Instead, he lay down on the bed of straw and blankets and pulled her up against him. As he drifted into a deep sleep, he found himself wishing he could go to sleep every night with this amazing woman in his arms.

MEGAN WOKE TO the soft thuds of hooves pawing at the dirt. She cracked an eyelid to see Halo standing in her stall, impatient for her feed and getting more impatient by the minute.

Joy filled her heart at the sight of the mare standing straight and proud, the effects of the poison worn off. Megan turned to tell Daniel, but he was asleep, his manly face softened in the gray light of dawn that snuck through the open door of the barn.

He must have been awake all night, worrying about Halo and wondering what to do about the meeting with the Kennedys.

Megan was loath to move away from the warmth of his body. It felt so firm and strong beside her.

One big obstacle had been cleared for Daniel. Halo would live. She was one of his best broodmares. Her loss would have been a big hit to his breeding program. Now all he had to do was impress the Kennedys. The irony of the situation wasn't lost on her.

Her family was among the socially elite of California. The Talbots' horse-breeding program at the Triple Diamond Ranch was nationally acknowledged. Daniel needed a boost on the social front in order for the Kennedys to consider him eligible for inclusion in their equine breeding efforts. What he needed was to marry into a family like the Talbots to give him social clout.

And if she and Daniel married, she'd satisfy the conditions of her grandmother's will and inherit a trust fund sufficient to purchase her horses from her father.

Megan could see herself married to a man like Daniel. He respected her mind and her ability to work with the horses, and he wasn't stiflingly overprotective. He'd worked hard to get where he was, earning his keep on the Lucky C, giving back to the family that provided him a home when his mother died. Yes, he was the kind of man she could easily fall in love with and probably already had.

If the ache that had settled in her chest when she thought of leaving the Lucky C and Daniel was any indication, she could see herself falling for this amazing man.

All her problems would be solved if only Daniel was interested in her as more than just his assistant.

"Do I have dirt on my nose?" Daniel stared up at her, a sleepy smile curling his lips.

"No," she answered. "Why?"

"You were staring at me and frowning." He swiped his hand across his face and sat up. "What were you thinking?"

How much she cared about him and wished he returned the feeling. Heat filled her cheeks, and she bit hard on her tongue to keep from blurting out her thoughts. To avoid answering, she turned to Halo. "When did she get up?"

"Around two in the morning. One minute she was lying as still as death, and the next she rolled to her feet as if she was done being sick."

Megan smiled. "I'm glad. I'll leave feeling much better knowing she is okay."

Daniel's brows dipped. "About that…" He stood and reached down for her hand. "I've been thinking."

Megan laid her fingers across his big palm, bracing herself for the rush of heated awareness to shoot from the point of contact throughout her body. And it did, leaving her feeling slightly breathless and off balance. Oh, yes, she was well on her way to loving this man, and he didn't have a clue.

If she were smart, she'd keep it to herself. He obviously wasn't of the same mind or he would have kissed her again. He'd had an opportunity while holding her through the night, and hadn't made a move.

Daniel pulled her to her feet. "You're frowning again, and I haven't even told you my idea."

"Oh, sorry." She slipped her hand free and stepped away from him to keep from making a fool of herself. "I guess I was thinking, too."

"Well, it's like this—and tell me I'm crazy if this sounds too insane to pursue—"

Megan watched as the man blushed and stumbled over his words. It wasn't like Daniel to be embarrassed. Nor was it like him to beat around the bush. Megan leaned back against the wall, enjoying this side of Daniel she hadn't seen. "It can't be all that bad. Your ideas are usually spot-on." She smiled, encouraging him to continue.

"You need the money to buy your horses."

Before he finished his sentence, she shook her head. "I told you, I won't take your money."

"That's good, because I don't have enough to buy the Triple Diamond breeding stock. But I might have a solution for both your problem and mine."

Megan's heart skipped several beats as Daniel's cheeks turned a ruddy red.

"You need a husband. I need an injection of social elitism that will impress Marshall Kennedy."

Her heart stopped. Her breath caught and held, refusing to move past the knot in her throat as she waited for what she'd only dreamed would come next.

Daniel shoved a hand through his dark hair and frowned. "I can't think of any other way to accomplish both, or I'd do it, but I'm fresh out of ideas."

"Daniel!" Megan said, her voice breathy. "Get to the point."

"Why don't we get married?"

Even though she'd known it was coming, it still hit her square in the chest. The air rushed from her lungs, and a tsunami of feelings washed over her. A surge of joy made her heart beat so fast she felt faint. She crested that wave and slid into the undertow of reality. "A marriage of convenience?"

"Exactly." He reached for her hands.

When she hid them behind her back, he dropped his arms. "It wouldn't have to be forever. Just long enough to satisfy the stipulations of your grandmother's will and keep your horses. That would help me get past the Kennedy gauntlet. We could leave today, find a chapel in Vegas and spend the night. It would be over in less than five minutes."

With her heart smarting, Megan forced a shaky smile. "Way to sweep a girl off her feet."

He waved his hand, and Halo tossed her head. "If you want, I can make an official announcement in front of my family."

Megan shook her head. "No."

"No, you won't marry me?"

"No." She pushed past him to pace down the center of the barn. "Your plan is insane."

"Do you have a better one?" he asked. "I'm all ears."

The plan was the same as the one she'd been thinking of before Daniel had woken up. Only when she'd dreamed it up, it didn't sound as cold and impersonal as Daniel's proposal. Somewhere in the back of her mind she'd hoped that a marriage to Daniel would be something more than one of convenience.

After yesterday's kiss, she wasn't sure she could be around Daniel for long periods without wanting another. And another.

"The problem is, my only other choice is to move home and live under my father's thumb."

"And you don't want to do that, do you?" he asked.

Megan faced Daniel, her back straight, her chin tilted up. "I'd rather die than live like my parents want me to. If it were just me, I'd stay and tell my father no thank you." Then her shoulders sagged. "But I can't abandon my horses."

"Is there anyone else who'd come to their rescue?"

"No." Megan glanced around, looking for the answer. Her gaze returned to Daniel. "If you're serious about your offer—" she paused, then went on "—I'm in."

As soon as she said the words, she wanted to take them back. This was not how a proposal was supposed to be. She should have been ecstatic, giddy with excitement for the man professing his love to her. Instead they'd hop a plane to Vegas and wham, bam, thank you, ma'am, they'd be married by some pathetic imitation of Elvis in a drive-through chapel on the Strip.

Daniel's lips quirked. "Why do I get the feeling you're not happy about this?"

"I don't know." She flung her hands in the air and fought back tears. "I guess I expected...well...not this."

"It's not as if it will be a real marriage. Once we're both in the clear, we can get a quickie divorce, and you will be free to marry whomever you prefer."

Megan stared at the man. He really didn't have a clue that she was falling in love with him. "Yeah. But the man of my dreams would have to do a better job of proposing."

"You deserve the best, Megan. If he doesn't care enough to do it right, don't marry him."

She raised her brows. "And your proposal was the standard to measure by?"

"Oh, hell no." Daniel grasped her hands and pulled her closer. "If this were a real proposal, I'd have taken you out to dinner at a nice restaurant or, better yet, on a picnic to your favorite spot on the ranch, because I'd know you didn't give a damn about all that fancy stuff. You love being out in the fresh air, close to the animals you love."

Megan could picture this scenario. He'd take her out to the hill with the ancient oak tree near sunset and wait to ask until the bright orange globe settled at the edge of the horizon, brushing a glorious palette of colors across the clouds. She sniffed. "A picnic would have been nice."

"And I'd have brought along a bottle of wine."

She cocked her brows. "To get me liquored up?"

"Can't have my girl turning me down, now can I?" He grinned and pulled her closer. "Then at sunset, I'd have gone down on one knee."

Megan's breath caught in her throat just as it would have had he been performing according to his script. Her chest tight, she forced a chuckle, hoping to ease the tension rising inside.

Daniel's brows dipped. "What are you laughing about?"

"On a cattle ranch, you would have put your knee in a cow patty."

"Anything for the woman I was about to ask to marry me." Daniel held her hands, his gaze intense, the smile sliding away. "I'd have asked you properly, saying something flowery and sincere, like this. 'Megan, you outshine the stars in the sky and make my heart beat faster whenever you're around.'"

Megan laughed, the sound catching in her throat. "That would be a good start."

"'Would you marry me and make me the happiest man alive?'" He nodded to her. "And you would fall into my arms, crying happy tears, shouting yes at the top of your lungs."

A real tear slipped from the corner of her eye and trailed down her cheek.

Daniel caught it on the tip of his finger. "You've got the idea."

"A proposal like that would make it hard for a girl to refuse."

"That's where the liquor comes in to seal the deal." He curled his fingers around hers. "So, Megan Talbot, will you marry me for however long it takes to sort out our troubles?"

Her heart breaking just a little, Megan wanted to say no. Daniel still had a long way to go before he fell in love with her, if he ever did. Then again, if she wanted to save her horses, this option seemed to be her only recourse on her father's short deadline. If she married, she'd have the money she needed, and her father couldn't expect her to come home to California to live.

He let go of her hands and stepped back. "Want time to think about it? I know it sounds crazy. You might feel better if we put the agreement in writing. I don't want your inheritance, if that's what you're afraid of."

"No, I trust you, and no, I don't want time to think about it. My answer is yes." If she thought about it too long, she'd talk herself out of it, and she couldn't afford to pass up the offer. "For the horses."

"Right. For the horses."

CHAPTER FIVE

DANIEL CIRCLED THE single-engine Mooney as he went through his preflight checklist of the airplane. Flaps. Check. Horizontal stabilizer. Check. Ring?

Panic struck. He stopped in the middle of his inspection and dug into his pocket for his grandmother's wedding ring. He wished he'd had time to take it to a jeweler to have it sized properly and fitted into a pretty box for safekeeping. But after they'd made their decision, they'd agreed they had little time to dawdle.

In the past hour, he'd taken care of the animals and informed Jack he'd be leaving. Then he'd arranged for someone to take care of the breeder barn in his absence and check on Halo through her recovery.

He'd barely had time to pack a bag and file a flight plan with the Tulsa airport. In less than thirty minutes, he and Megan would be on their way to Vegas to get married.

Holy smokes! He was getting married.

Granted, it was a marriage of convenience, but it was no less nerve-racking. Megan came from a family far above Daniel's social class. Hell, for the first ten years of his life, he'd lived on the reservation in a trailer. Megan grew up in the lap of luxury, surrounded by people who took care of her every need. How could he compete with that?

He'd never truly been one of the elite Coltons, either. He'd never felt like he quite fit in.

Now he was marrying into a family known nationwide for their wealth and prestige. Megan's parents were often in the news attending various events.

Then he reminded himself that she'd given up that lifestyle to come to work for him. She was willing to muck stalls and get her hands into the dirty and not so pleasant tasks of raising horses. Her fancy upbringing hadn't slowed her down one bit. She was tough and fearless when it came to working with the large animals.

Megan had driven back to her apartment in Tulsa to throw some clothes into a suitcase and get back to the ranch. She'd be here any minute, ready to climb aboard the small plane the Coltons owned.

Damn. Where was that ring? When he couldn't find the pretty emerald-and-diamond ring, he nearly had a heart attack.

"Daniel!" Ryan Colton, Daniel's half brother, emerged from the darkness of the hangar into the bright Oklahoma sunlight. "Heard you were heading to Vegas."

"I am," he said, digging deeper into both front pockets.

Ryan's eyes narrowed. "Forget your key to the plane?" His lips twitched.

Daniel's fingers connected with metal, and the tension in his shoulders released. The ring was safe in his pocket. "No, thank goodness, I have it."

"Dude, the plane doesn't take a key."

His mind on the trip ahead, Daniel ignored Ryan's comment. "What brings you out to the hangar?"

"Jack informed me Halo was poisoned. What's going on?"

The tension returning for an entirely different reason, Daniel's chest tightened. "The lab reported they found poison in Halo's blood. We have no idea how it happened."

"Maybe she got hold of something in the barn or in the field."

"Megan and I went over the entire barn, thoroughly cleaned Halo's stall and couldn't find anything that would have poisoned her. We don't use rat poison in the barn."

Ryan smiled. "That's why we have Sleek."

"Right, and we have too much invested in the horses we keep in the breeder barn to risk storing anything poisonous there."

"Do you think someone might have given it to her?"

Daniel had considered that option. "Who would want to hurt Halo? She's one of the best mares in my breeding program, and she's got the best temperament."

"I don't know." Ryan scratched his chin. "Do you know of any competing breeders who'd go to the trouble of sabotaging your horses?"

Daniel shook his head. "It's not like she's a race horse with the potential to win a derby." He shrugged. "It makes no sense."

"I'll nose around and see if I can learn anything that'll shed some light."

"Thanks."

"Hey, on another topic, is Greta back from Oklahoma City?" Ryan asked.

His half sister, Greta, had been in Oklahoma City busily planning her wedding to Mark Stanton, the son of one of the wealthiest families in the state. He missed her expertise with the horses. She was one of the best trainers he'd known.

"Not that I know of." Daniel checked beneath the plane for any leaks. "Why do you ask?"

"I could swear I saw her at the hardware store yesterday." Ryan shrugged. "Must have been seeing things."

"I'll be glad when she's done with this wedding planning business." Daniel straightened.

"You and me both. It's not like her to get all girlie."

Megan emerged from the shadows of the hangar and out into the open, rolling a suitcase behind her. She wore jeans, boots and a green blouse that exactly matched her eyes. Her hair was damp but pulled back in her normal French braid. Other than the nice shirt, she looked like she was ready to go to work, not to her wedding in Vegas.

Daniel's heart skipped several beats. Megan could wear a feed sack and make it look great. With those long legs, the subtle sway of her hips and the way she smiled…his groin tightened, and he wanted to hold her close all over again. Keeping her at arm's length would be a challenge.

"Hey, Dan." Ryan waved a hand in front of Daniel's face.

Daniel barely saw the hand, his gaze on the woman walking toward them.

Ryan turned. "Ah, Megan. Are you going, too?"

Megan rolled her case to a stop, nodding. "Yes, I am." Her gaze shot from Daniel to Ryan and back.

Daniel took Megan's bag and loaded it into the plane. "I have a couple more checks. Then we'll be ready to go."

"So, what's in Vegas besides the usual—gambling, wedding chapels and shows? I haven't heard of any of those involving horses." Ryan stared at Daniel, then Megan.

A flush of pink rose in Megan's cheeks. She glanced at Daniel and gave him a slight shake of her head.

Taking Megan's cue, Daniel replied, "We're going to see a man about a horse. If the Kennedy Farms deal doesn't work out, we want to have a backup plan." Daniel didn't like lying to his brother, but Megan wasn't ready to announce their plans, and that was okay with him. He wasn't certain how he felt about what they were about to do.

"Well, then, I won't keep you." Ryan held out his hand. "Be careful. I understand there are some storms heading this way."

"I've already checked the weather. We're flying north of the system." Daniel took his brother's hand.

"Good. We kind of like having you two around." Ryan shook Daniel's hand and then pulled him into a hug. "See you in a day or two?"

"It might be closer to a week."

"A week?" Ryan stepped back, his eyes wide. "What kind of horses take a week to look at?"

Daniel's lips firmed. "After we stop in Vegas, we're going to California to check out more horses. I have a meeting scheduled with Marshall Kennedy in Reno in a week. We'll be back at the Lucky C long enough to regroup and head out again."

"Sounds like a nice vacation. Wish I could go along with you." Ryan nodded. "Again, you two take care and come back in one piece."

"We will."

Ryan stood back as Daniel helped Megan into the plane and climbed in after her. She settled in the copilot's seat and Daniel sat beside her, going over the remainder of his preflight check. When they were finally ready, he showed her how to wear the copilot's headset and slipped his headset over his ears.

"Ready?" he said into microphone.

"Ready." Her voice came to him over the sound system.

As they taxied down the grass runway and lifted off into a westerly breeze, Daniel gripped the yoke, his pulse racing as he thought about what lay ahead. In a few short hours, they'd be in Vegas getting married.

MEGAN'S FINGERS CURLED around the armrests as the plane left the grass strip and climbed into the sky. When they were far enough away from the ground that she didn't have to worry about crashing, she settled back and relaxed.

"I knew the Coltons had a plane, but I didn't realize you all knew how to fly it."

"Not all of my brothers have learned."

"Just how long have you been flying?"

"Since I was about fifteen and Big J bought the plane. He paid for my flight lessons while he learned to fly, as well. It's always a good thing to have a copilot in case something happens to the pilot."

Megan's stomach fluttered as she stared at the yoke in front of her. "Just so you know, I don't have a clue how to fly this thing, but I'm willing to learn."

He smiled over at her. "It's not a requirement, but I'm glad to hear you're willing. Not many people are interested."

She liked it when he smiled at her. He had the faith in her to think she could learn to fly an airplane. She'd always been interested in flying, but her parents wouldn't have allowed her to take flying lessons any more than they wanted her working with large animals. To say they were overprotective would be a gross understatement. Hell, she'd learn to fly if it was something Daniel wanted.

"My parents are likely to flip when I come home with a husband. Just so you know. We're likely to incur resistance."

"I can handle it," Daniel assured her.

"I placed a call to the attorney who handled my grandmother's will and arranged an appointment with him in two days. I also arranged to meet with a horse broker."

"Good thinking. By this time a week from now, we should be sitting pretty. You with your horses, me with my breeder stock semen."

Megan nodded. "Sounds easy enough. However, I've never known anything to be that simple."

Daniel shot a glance her way. "True." He held out a hand. "We'll get through this together. We make a good team."

She took his hand, that same sharp crackle of electricity shooting through her. She had no doubt they'd make it, and she refused to think about what would happen afterward, when their marriage of convenience was no longer needed.

"Hey." Daniel squeezed her fingers. "It's going to work out."

She nodded, comforted by the gentle pressure on her hand.

"You didn't get much sleep last night. Why don't you relax and take a nap? I might need you later to spot me through the mountains."

Her heart leaped into her lungs. "Mountains?"

"Unless you want to take the long way around, we'll be flying just south of the Sangre de Cristo Mountains in New Mexico."

She bit on her bottom lip.

Daniel let go of her hand and brushed his thumb across her lip. "Don't worry. I've flown this route several times."

"I have, too. In a 747, not a crop duster." She stared out the window at the ground several thousand feet below them. "Something tells me it will be a lot different than flying over at thirty thousand feet."

"It is, but I think you'll like it."

Megan settled into her seat, letting the hum of the engine lull her into a trance while they were still over the flat terrain of Oklahoma and the Texas Panhandle. At least the danger of the flight took her mind off her coming nuptials.

She must have fallen asleep somewhere between thinking about crashing into the mountains and a cheesy wedding in Vegas, because the next thing she knew, they'd hit a speed bump on the Vegas Strip.

Megan's eyes popped open, and she stared around the interior of the airplane. It hadn't been a speed bump they'd hit. The little plane hit another pocket of air and jerked.

She sat up straight and stared out at a darkening sky. Thunderclouds rose high to her left, lightning flashing. "Is everything okay?"

"Should be," Daniel said through gritted teeth. His fingers gripped the yoke, his knuckles white. "Remember that storm my brother was talking about coming out of the southwest?"

"I thought we were going around it?"

"That's the idea. Only it's getting bigger as we speak. We won't be going through it, but we're getting some of the bumpy air around it."

Mountains rose ahead of them, their snow-covered peaks appearing beautifully dangerous. Megan's heart lodged in her throat. "I thought we wouldn't be going through the mountains on this trip."

"In order to go around the storm, I'm having to fly farther north. We're nearing the Sangre de Cristo mountain range."

Megan's pulse raced, her breathing becoming shallower. "Just how much experience do you have flying through mountains?"

He laughed, though it sounded strained through the headset. "Too late to ask now, isn't it? But for what it's worth, I have over two thousand hours flying this plane."

"That sounds like a lot. How many of those hours were in this kind of weather?"

"There are never enough hours flying in this kind of weather. The idea is to avoid these conditions."

"Should we put down?"

"Can't. Not here. The best we can hope for is to swing wide."

They hit more turbulence, and the plane dropped like someone had pulled the rug out from under them.

Megan swallowed a scream and held on.

Daniel moved his feet and scanned the instrument panel, his hands steady on the yoke. "Just a little farther and we should clear the side of this storm."

She caught and held her breath as they neared the snowy crags a lot lower than she liked.

Lightning flashed nearby. A rumble of thunder

sounded over the roar of the engine and through the muffling of her headset.

Megan had never been so frightened in her life. But seeing Daniel in the pilot's seat, his jaw set, all his concentration on flying the airplane, made her feel a little safer.

Until the next big dip brought her even closer to the jagged peaks. Her stomach clenched, and she bit down hard on her tongue to keep from screaming again. Daniel didn't need a crying woman in the cockpit with him. She had to be strong, even though she shook from head to toe.

The clouds billowed higher, blocking the sun, making the sky ominous.

Megan found herself leaning away from the turbulence, willing the little plane to fly safely around the storm and up over the mountains.

They seemed to be heading straight into the mountains instead of flying over the top, and the storm appeared to be engulfing them in its fury.

Tearing her gaze away from the mountains, she risked a glance in Daniel's direction. His face was tense, a muscle flicked in his jaw and his knuckles were white on the yoke.

"It's going to be okay," she said softly, as if speaking the words out loud would make it so. She sent a silent prayer to the heavens to deliver them safely through the storm and over the mountains they were racing toward.

"Hold on," Daniel said in her ears.

Her fingers dug into the leather of the armrest. She closed her eyes, trusting Daniel to deliver her safely over to the other side of the storm and the mountain.

Another drastic drop forced her eyes open in time to see the ragged peaks directly in front of them.

Daniel struggled with the small plane, pulling back on the yoke at the last minute, narrowly missing the edges of a giant outcropping.

Once over the top of the mountain, the clouds parted, and they blew through as if spit out by the storm. Slowly the turbulence subsided, and they flew out of the black clouds, into an entirely different world of sunshine and blue skies.

"Wow." Megan pressed her hand to her heart and drew in a long, steadying breath, then let it out. "You were amazing."

Daniel scrubbed a hand down his face. Beneath his Cherokee complexion, his face had paled.

Megan reached out and placed her hand over his on the controls.

Eventually he unwound his grip, transferring it to her hand. "I'm sorry. I shouldn't have tried to outrun the storm. We could have been killed."

"But we weren't, thanks to your superb flying skills."

"I feel like we should find a place to land and rent a car for the rest of the journey."

"No way. I've never flown into the sunset in a single-engine airplane. And it appears as if we're going to have an outstanding display."

"As long as you're okay."

"I'll admit, I was shaking in my boots about the time we hit that last really bad dip."

"You and me both." He squeezed her hand. "But from here to Vegas it should be smooth."

"As long as you're flying, I'm okay." She smiled

across at him and settled back, refusing to release his hand unless they hit another intense storm.

Megan figured if they could survive something as insanely intense and dangerous as braving that storm and nearly crashing into the mountain, things could only get easier. They'd land, check into a hotel, find a twenty-four-hour wedding chapel and tie the temporary knot.

What could be hard about that compared with the flight over?

CHAPTER SIX

"WE'RE SORRY, BUT the hotel is booked for the weekend," said the clerk behind the counter of the newest of the big casino hotels.

"Every room?" Megan asked.

"There's a huge techie convention going on. I've had to call several hotels to find rooms for walk-in guests. There just aren't any available. I'm sorry, ma'am, but I can't help you."

Megan couldn't believe their luck. The one weekend they decided to fly to Vegas to get married and every hotel they'd been to thus far had been completely sold out.

"Come on. We'll walk next door." She hooked Daniel's arm and dragged him to the exit. "I have a feeling there will be a vacancy there."

"We've been walking the Strip for over an hour with no luck." Daniel covered her hand on his arm and glanced down at her with a crooked smile. "We might have to sleep in the plane at this rate."

"It'll be okay. There has to be a room in one of these hotels. I'm determined to have a shower. I still smell like the barn, and that's no way to go to a wedding." She winked up at him.

"Which reminds me." Daniel's lips firmed. "We still have to find a chapel."

"Excuse me, sir," someone said behind them.

The clerk they'd been speaking with ran to catch them at the door. "I just got off the phone with a cancellation. Our special honeymoon suite is available."

Megan was already shaking her head. "A suite? Isn't that expensive?"

Daniel stepped toward the clerk. "We'll take it."

"But, Daniel, we don't know how much they're asking."

"I don't care. It might be the only room available in all of Las Vegas, and we have a wedding to go to. It only seems fitting."

Daniel followed the clerk back to the desk and slapped his credit card on the counter. A bellboy appeared and collected their bags.

Soon they were shown to a large penthouse suite with floor-to-ceiling windows overlooking the brightly lit Las Vegas Strip.

Megan walked to the window and stared out at the glitzy lights of the city, worried that Daniel was spending too much of his own money to make this farce of a wedding happen. "I would have been fine sleeping in the plane."

Daniel stepped up behind her and rested his hands on her shoulders. "This is better. And we need to take a few pictures of us in this suite when we return after the wedding to show your parents."

Megan leaned back against him, the solid strength of Daniel easing her misgivings and stirring in her a deep longing to be held in his arms for longer than a temporary arrangement. "You're right. I just hate spending your money for my troubles."

"You're helping me, too, so we're even."

Megan turned back to the spacious living room with a table and chairs for intimate dining and a sofa for two in the middle of the sitting area. A door opened into a bedroom with a king-size bed made up in crisp white sheets and a classic white comforter. One bed. Two people.

"We can worry about sleeping arrangements when we get back from the chapel," Daniel said. "I'd like to take a quick shower. How long do you need to get ready?"

"About twenty minutes. I want to shower, too, but you can go first."

Alone with Daniel in the hotel suite, Megan tried to keep it all businesslike, but one look at the bed and her pulse kicked up. A second look and her core heated. If this were a real wedding between two people in love, the room would be perfect for consummating the marriage.

For the hundredth time since Daniel had made the suggestion of getting hitched, she reminded herself it was temporary. Daniel had shown little interest in a relationship between the two of them over the past few months she'd been working for him. And he'd been pretty adamant about their marriage being a business arrangement, nothing else.

Daniel set Megan's bag on the luggage stand. "You know, maybe we should revisit the idea of a prenuptial agreement."

His statement hit her square in the chest. "What?" She faced him, frowning.

He paced away from her and back, raking a hand through his thick, dark hair. "You're a potentially wealthy woman. You need to protect your assets."

"Isn't it a bit late to get an attorney to draw up a prenuptial agreement? We're getting married as soon as we can get showered and dressed."

"At the very least, we could write it out on a piece of paper and each sign it in front of a witness."

"My grandmother's trust fund isn't a huge amount."

"Megan, you don't have any siblings you haven't told me about, do you?"

She shook her head.

"You're an only child. You stand to inherit everything your parents own."

"I don't want what they have," she insisted. "I would rather they spent it all before they die." She'd left California to get away from that life and had no need of their money or land holdings. "I couldn't give a damn about my inheritance as long as we save those horses. If my parents should pass away before we end our relationship, I'd give all their money and property to charity. You could have it."

Daniel's lips thinned. "I don't want your parents' money. I prefer to make my own way in life."

Her back stiff, her chin held high, Megan said, "Same here."

"But you'll have a fiduciary responsibility to their wealth should they leave it all to you. I'm sure they have people who depend on them for their livelihoods. You want to protect them."

Megan's mind flew to their housekeeper, Mrs. Gibson, who'd been with the Talbot family since Megan could remember. She'd practically raised Megan when her parents were off to all corners of the world. Then there were the groundskeeper and the ranch foreman, both of whom had worked for the Talbots for decades.

"Okay, so I can't just walk away from it. But we don't have time for a formal agreement and all the attorneys who should be involved."

Daniel rested his hands on her arms. "Let me get my shower, and while you're getting yours, I'll write up something. We can both sign it and have a bellboy witness it."

"I think it's a lot of trouble. I know you are a good man and you wouldn't do anything to jeopardize my horses. Otherwise, I wouldn't consider marrying you, even if it is temporary." She cupped his cheek, rose up on her toes and dared to kiss him. "But thank you for thinking of it."

Daniel stepped around her, unzipped his suitcase and dragged out a garment bag and his toiletries. "I'll only be a few minutes." He entered the bathroom and shut the door behind him.

Megan opened her suitcase, removed the dress she'd packed and stared at it with a critical eye. She hadn't kept many items from the vast wardrobe her mother had insisted on buying for her on Rodeo Drive in California. But she'd brought a couple of her favorite dresses to Tulsa when she'd packed up and left home.

When she'd stood in the little bedroom in her apartment going through her closet, she'd almost wished she'd brought more. Then she'd found the simple white cocktail dress she'd purchased with her own money on sale in a shop in downtown Tulsa. It had been marked down significantly and looked good on her. The best part about the dress was that she'd bought it with her own money. She hadn't paid a ridiculous amount, and it fit and looked as good as anything she'd left behind.

She shook out the wrinkles and hung the dress in the closet, trying to ignore the sound of water running in the bathroom. A door separated her from a very naked, very wet Daniel. She didn't have to use much of her imagination to envision him nude.

On many occasions through the heat of summer at the Lucky C, he'd gone shirtless while he worked on the ranch. His chiseled chest and taut abs glistened with sweat in the sunshine.

For a moment, she leaned her cheek against the bathroom door and closed her eyes. Water would be streaming over his broad shoulders, down his thickly muscled chest and lower. What would it feel like to touch his naked skin, to run her hands over the hard planes of his body?

Her blood burning through her veins, she reached for the doorknob before she realized what she was doing. The cold, hard metal woke her. Her breath hitched and she jerked upright, her eyes wide. Why torture herself? The man wasn't interested.

Megan left the bedroom and wandered around the suite, counting the minutes until the faucet shut off and Daniel emerged from the shower.

She was standing at the floor-to-ceiling window in the sitting room when a sound behind her alerted her to his presence.

"The shower's all yours."

When Megan turned to face him, her stomach fluttered and blood rushed south to her core.

Daniel wore dark trousers and a white shirt open at the neck. He worked the buttons on his sleeves. "Damned buttons weren't made for big hands."

Her throat dry, Megan stepped forward. "Let me." She nudged his hands away, her skin tingling where it brushed against his. She made quick work of the buttons, finding it hard to breathe. With him standing so close, she was surrounded by the potent scent of his aftershave.

"You smell good," she said and quickly stepped away.

He dug in his pocket and pulled out a bow tie. "You don't happen to know how to tie one of these, do you?"

She smiled, her heart thudding hard in her chest. She should have told him no and walked away. Instead, she took the tie from his hand and wrapped it around his neck. She was so close to him, their breaths mingled. "I used to tie my father's neckties." Her fingers fumbled with the cloth, but managed to knot the tie perfectly.

Almost faint from not daring to breathe while she stood so close, Megan started to back away. Now she really wanted to kiss Daniel.

His hands captured the back of her head. "This is going to be harder than I thought." Then he bent, his lips crashing down on hers in a bone-melting kiss.

With his tongue he traced the seam of her lips, and she opened to let him in. He swept past her defenses and conquered her, caressing the length of her tongue in smooth, dangerously sensual strokes. One of his hands slid down her back and cupped her bottom, pressing her closer.

Megan leaned into Daniel, the hard ridge beneath the fly of his trousers pressing into her belly. The urge shot through her to rip the bow tie from around his neck and loosen all the buttons of his shirt. Her entire body burned with the need to feel his body against hers.

At last he pushed her to arm's length and stared down at her with enigmatic brown-black eyes. "You should get your shower."

Her knees shook as she stepped away from him. Her arms slipped down his chest to fall to her sides. Then she turned and stumbled through the bedroom. She didn't stop until she was in the bathroom with the door closed between her and Daniel.

Her heart racing, Megan leaned her back against the door and pressed her fist against her pulsing lips. How could this arrangement remain all business when there was nothing businesslike about the way they'd just kissed?

If Megan hadn't run when he'd told her to get her shower, Daniel might not have been able to let her go. That kiss had shaken him more than he cared to admit. Dragging in several deep breaths, he forced himself to focus on what needed to be done.

While the shower ran, Daniel found a sheet of hotel stationery and wrote out a statement that, once married to Megan Talbot, he would not retain any rights to her inheritance. He'd have someone witness him signing the paper later. He folded the paper, slipped it into his pocket, grabbed the room key card and left.

He took the elevator down to the lobby and went in search of the concierge. The man at the counter helped him call around to the marriage registration office and nearby wedding chapels to find one that could fit them in for a quickie wedding.

The first one didn't answer. The second chapel was booked until the following day at two in the afternoon.

The third was booked through the next week, and the fourth had one opening if they could make it there in five minutes. Otherwise they would have to wait until the following morning at nine. Daniel thanked the woman and called the next number the concierge offered.

The receptionist on the other end of the call answered,

"This is the Graceland Wedding Chapel. You bring the bride and groom, we provide everything else."

"Do you have any openings for wedding ceremonies tonight?" Daniel asked.

"Yes, sir. We're open 24-7."

"I'd like to make a reservation for an hour from now."

"I'm afraid we can't do that," the receptionist said.

Daniel's hopes slid into his boots. What the hell? This was the town of gambling, partying and the wedding destination of people wanting to tie a quick knot. So far, things hadn't gone as smoothly as he would have liked. The near-death experience in the Sangre de Cristo Mountains, then the almost failed attempt to secure a hotel room and four calls with no wedding chapel were wearing on him. If he were as superstitious as his ancestors, he would have read it as a sign the wedding wasn't meant to be.

"We've only had one cancellation, sir. The time will be thirty minutes from now, and there might be a wait."

His heart lightening, Daniel gripped the phone, his optimism returning. "Will it be a long wait?"

"Depends on when our Elvis shows up."

Daniel ground his teeth at the vagueness of her answer. "How many couples are waiting on him?"

"There are two couples waiting right now."

Wanting to reach through the phone, throttle and then hug the young woman, Daniel asked for the address, committed it to memory and ended the call.

He made arrangements to have champagne and roses delivered to the room while they were out. By that time, he'd been gone long enough that Megan should have been showered and ready to go.

Daniel entered the elevator. Before the doors could

close, two women entered wearing skimpy black dresses and impossible leopard-print stilettos. They giggled and leaned on each other, and they reeked of perfume and alcohol.

"Oh, baby, aren't you the handsome devil?" the brunette cooed, letting go of her friend to drape herself on Daniel's arm. "Please tell me you're in Vegas to have fun."

He smiled and peeled the woman off his arm. "I'm in Vegas to get married."

"Oh, well, now. Isn't that sweet?" the brunette said. No sooner had he untangled himself from her than she wrapped her hands around his arm again. "So you aren't married yet?"

"Headed in that direction now." Daniel prayed they'd hurry and stop on the woman's floor.

"The important item to note is that you aren't married, yet." She leaned across and pecked his cheek. "You still have time to back out."

"I'm not backing out," he assured her.

The blonde with too much hairspray poofing her hair out at strange distances, took her friend's arm. "Denise, sweetie, you need to leave this poor man alone. He's not going out with you when he's got his own honey waiting for him at the altar."

"You look good enough to eat. Don't get married. It only destroys your waistline and makes you bitter." Denise poked a thumb toward her chest. "Ask me. I know all about crappy marriages. Celebrating my freedom tonight. Ditch the bride and come with us for the night. No regrets. No divorce attorneys."

Her friend nodded. "Trust her on that one. It can get ugly."

The elevator bell dinged and the door slid open. "I believe this is your floor." Daniel held the door open.

"If you change your mind, join us." Denise gave him her room number and stumbled out of the car.

Daniel was glad when the door closed and continued up to the penthouse. He had no reservations about Megan. In the few short months he'd known her, he'd learned she was trustworthy and had a big heart. Possibly too big a heart, as evidenced with her agreement to marry him only to save a few horses from being sold.

He'd marry her even if he didn't need the social clout, just to foil her family's attempt at extortion. What kind of father would threaten to sell the horses his daughter loved just to get her to come home and live by his rules?

The elevator arrived at his floor and he got out, more convinced they were doing the right thing. He swiped his key in the lock and entered.

The sitting room was empty, and he didn't hear the sound of a shower or blow-dryer. Silence greeted him and made his heart skip several beats before racing to catch up.

"Megan?"

No answer.

Daniel stepped toward the bedroom and came to an abrupt halt.

Megan appeared in the doorway, wearing a white dress that plunged low between her breasts, hugged her waist and hips and then floated out around her thighs to the tops of her pretty knees. She'd pulled her hair up and away from her face, the long strawberry blond tresses cascading down her back in soft, loose curls he wanted to bury his hands in. Her eyes widened, her cheeks flushed and her full, lush lips curved upward in a smile.

"Wow. You look amazing." Daniel swallowed hard and clenched his fists to keep from reaching out and taking her into his arms. Remaining platonic would be the biggest challenge he'd ever faced when she looked so damned gorgeous and kissable.

Her brows furrowed and her smile slipped as she glanced down at her dress. "Too much?"

He shook his head. "No, you're perfect." God, he wanted to pull her close and hold her until his pulse slowed and he could get a grip on the rising passion threatening to overwhelm him. But he knew that if he succumbed to his desire, his pulse wouldn't slow until he'd stripped her naked and made love to her all night long. Only when he fell into an exhausted sleep would his heartbeat return to anywhere near normal.

Megan touched his arm. "If you've had second thoughts, we don't have to go through with this. My problems aren't yours. I can figure out something that doesn't involve you giving up your freedom to save a few horses."

Daniel nearly groaned. Standing before her, he inhaled the fresh scent of Megan. She had to be nearly naked beneath that dress. All he had to do was pull her into his arms, wrap those legs around his waist and…

He dragged in a deep, fortifying breath and let it out. "Unless you've changed your mind, we're going through with the plan."

"You just seem so tense."

A short, hard laugh erupted from his throat. "I promised to keep this arrangement purely business." He leaned back and raked her with his gaze. "But I'm finding it difficult. Now, if you're ready, I have the address of the wedding registration office and a chapel. But we have to rush."

He offered her his arm, bracing himself for that electric jolt he received each time she touched him.

Her hand curled around his elbow, sending that spark of sensations shooting through him, straight to his groin. Yup, keeping this marriage platonic would either prove he was a saint or kill him. Daniel suspected it would kill him. "Let's go get married."

CHAPTER SEVEN

MEGAN SAT IN the backseat of the taxi beside Daniel, her heart pounding, her mouth dry and more nervous than she'd been when she'd left home to strike out on her own. Though this was a marriage of convenience, she couldn't help but feel as though it was a particularly momentous occasion.

After taking them to get their marriage license, the taxi stopped in front of a little white wedding chapel, the blue sign lit up with white neon lights. A smaller sign below had an image of a dancing Elvis Presley painted on it.

Daniel leaned forward. "Are you sure this is the address?"

"Yes, sir. This is the place."

Megan fought back a giggle at the scowl that settled on Daniel's face as he paid the taxi driver and he helped her out onto the sidewalk.

"I don't know," he said, staring at the dancing Elvis. "This isn't quite what I had in mind."

Megan squeezed his hand. "It's exactly what I had in mind."

"Are you sure?" He didn't look convinced.

"Absolutely. It's Vegas, baby." She winked. "Lighten up. If the certificate is valid, that's all that matters."

Still frowning, Daniel led her into the lobby of the

little chapel. Against either wall was a couple seated on a bench. One pair wore black jeans and leather jackets. The young man's hair was shaved in a Mohawk, and he sported a one-inch gauge in each ear. The woman had piercings in her lip, nose and eyebrow, and her ears were rimmed in studs. Her hair was shaved on one side and long and black on the other.

Megan gulped and shifted her attention to the other couple. They appeared to be in their late forties or early fifties. She wore a short sequined dress and spike heels. The man with her wore a suit and tie.

"We can look elsewhere," Daniel whispered close to her ear, causing tingles to spread throughout her body.

"No," she said, her voice breathy. "This will be fine."

They were met at the front desk by a woman wearing a '60s miniskirt and go-go boots. Her lips were painted a pale pink and she chewed gum, smacking it loud enough to echo in the room. "Welcome to the Graceland Wedding Chapel. How can I help you?"

Daniel stepped forward. "We want to get married."

The woman pointed to what appeared to be a menu. "Which package would you like? The Las Vegas Elvis Wedding Package or one of our traditional wedding packages?"

Though afraid to ask, Daniel did. "What's in the packages?"

"All of the packages include use of the chapel, photography, music and wedding services. The officiant fee and marriage certificate are separate. If you select the Las Vegas Elvis Wedding, the bride may choose to have Elvis walk her down the aisle."

Daniel stared at the different options and turned to Megan. "Really, we can go somewhere else."

Her heart warmed at his concern, and she squeezed his arm. "I love this chapel. It's quaint and we don't need much. We could do the basic traditional package."

At that moment, the Elvis impersonator entered the building, wearing a dark, bedazzled shirt, open down the front. He displayed a significant amount of chest hair. He wore sunglasses and tight black pants. His dark hair was slicked back with the signature lock falling across his forehead.

"Anyone here for a wedding?" he called out and pulled Megan into a bear hug. "How about you two?" He pointed to Daniel. "Is this your hunka-hunka burnin' love?"

Megan's cheeks flamed, and she was happy to see Daniel's turn ruddy. "Yes, he's my fiancé. But these people were here first." She glanced at the older couple and the pierced pair.

"Let's get these weddings rollin'."

An hour later, Elvis had performed the ceremonies for the older couple and the pierced one.

"If you'll give me a few minutes, I'll get out of the Elvis gear and we can perform your ceremony."

Megan glanced at Daniel. "If it's all the same to you, I'd rather just get started. No need for the minister to change. Are you okay with that, Daniel?"

Daniel's brows twisted and he stared hard at her, then sighed. "If you're okay, I'm okay."

The receptionist handed a modest bouquet of red and white roses to Daniel and a boutonniere to Megan.

Megan attached the flower to Daniel's lapel and patted his chest. "It's going to be okay."

His brow cocked as he handed her the bouquet. "If you say so."

"I do."

"Sweetheart, save the *I do*'s for the ceremony." Elvis nodded toward the front of the chapel. "Now if the groom will take his place at the altar, I'll escort the bride down the aisle."

Megan's hand shook as she laid it on Elvis's arm and waited for Daniel to take his position at the front of the chapel. When he turned to face her, the music started and Megan's heart squeezed hard in her chest.

The receptionist handed Elvis a microphone and he sang "Can't Help Falling in Love."

Slowly, Megan and Elvis walked down the aisle in time to the music, the words bringing a lump into Megan's throat and making her eyes sting. The closer she came to Daniel, the more she realized just how the words to the song fit the way she felt.

This half-Cherokee man who loved horses as much as she did and who didn't quite fit in, just like her, was the only man she could imagine spending the rest of her life with. If this wasn't love, she was even more on her way to falling in love with him.

As Elvis ended the song, he handed her off to Daniel and took his position in front of them.

"Megan, do you promise to love Daniel tender and love him true for all of your days?"

Megan gulped hard to clear the knot from her vocal chords and answered, "I do."

"And, Daniel, do you promise to love Megan tender and love her true for all of your days?"

He held Megan's hands in his and answered in his deep, resonant tone, "I do."

"Do you have a ring?" Elvis asked.

Megan gasped. "I didn't even think about rings."

Daniel smiled and dug in his pocket, pulling out a beautiful ring with an emerald center stone surrounded by white diamonds. "I did. This was my grandmother's wedding ring. It's not much, but it meant a lot to her."

He slid the ring onto her finger, echoing the words Elvis prompted him with. Megan wished she'd had something to give to him, but then, this wasn't a real wedding and this wasn't going to be a real marriage. But still…

"I'm sorry I didn't have time to get it fitted," he whispered. "We can do it when we get back to Tulsa."

The ring fit a little loose, but Megan didn't care. The ring had belonged to his grandmother and was something he obviously cared about.

"By the power vested in me by the state of Nevada and the Graceland Wedding Chapel, I pronounce you husband and wife. You may kiss the bride." Elvis sang "Love Me Tender."

For a moment, Daniel hesitated. Megan held her breath. Then he bent, gathered her in his arms and kissed her.

The photographer's flash blinked close by, but nothing penetrated their embrace until Elvis's song ended and he cleared his throat.

"All you two need is the certificate and you can commence with the wedding night." Elvis escorted them back to the receptionist's desk, where they signed the marriage certificate and the photographer snapped more pictures. Then they were on their way with a marriage certificate and a DVD documenting their nuptials.

A white limousine stood at the curb, the driver holding the door for them.

Daniel handed Megan in, gave the address to the driver and slid in beside her with a huge sigh.

She shifted the bouquet to her other hand and touched Daniel's shoulder. "Tired?"

"I don't know what I feel. That was the most bizarre wedding ceremony I've ever seen."

"I don't know. I thought the Elvis impersonator did an excellent job with the accent and the songs." She held up the DVD. "If I thought my parents would come unhinged by my marrying, wait until they see these wedding photos."

Daniel took her hand in his. "I'm sorry. Your wedding should have been more…"

Megan raised her eyebrows. "Boring?"

"I don't know." He shook his head. "Classier."

"Personally, I liked the Elvis touch. I promised myself I'd never marry a man who lacked a sense of humor."

DANIEL COULDN'T RESIST Megan's smile and grinned himself. "I almost laughed out loud when he first walked in the door."

"And how perfect were the song choices for a wedding?" Megan giggled and hummed "Love Me Tender."

The sparkle in her green eyes captured and held him as they drove between the brightly lit casinos.

"Do you want to go dancing?"

"You dance?"

Daniel frowned. "I've been known to two-step on occasion."

"I'd love to dance. But not tonight. I'm pretty tired from all that's happened in the past forty-eight hours." She leaned against his arm. "You sure know how to show a girl a little excitement."

When he helped her out of the limousine, she didn't

release his hand until he had to get the key card out of his pocket to open the door to their room.

When she started to walk through the doorway, he tugged her back. "We have to do things right, even if they are only temporary." He swept her off her feet, crushing her against his chest. "Now, Mrs. Colton, welcome to the honeymoon suite."

She draped an arm around his neck and stared around the room. "It looks different." Then her eyes brightened and her smile grew wider. "Flowers and champagne? You shouldn't have." Her arm tightened and she kissed his cheek. "But I'm glad you did."

"You deserve so much more. I hope that one day when you marry for real, your husband does it right."

Her smile slipped and she sighed. "You've set the bar high, Daniel. I don't know how any man can come close. Thank you for giving me an unforgettable wedding day."

Daniel couldn't think of a reason to hold her in his arms longer, so he lowered her feet to the ground and stepped away. Then he crossed to the table, where an ice bucket held a bottle of champagne. Two champagne flutes stood beside it.

He popped the cork and sparkling liquid spilled onto the table. Quickly filling the two flutes, he held one out to her. "To us."

She shook her head and winked. "No. To wedded bliss, however long it might last."

Daniel's chest tightened as he stared across his glass at Megan. She made a beautiful bride with her cheeks flushed and her hair tumbling over her shoulders in long, loose curls. The dress hugged her figure like it was a part of her, swirling around her legs when she moved.

Daniel drank the liquid all in one gulp, wishing it

were whiskey, something with a bit more of a kick to take the edge off his desire. But it might have had the opposite effect, lowering his inhibitions, making him forget his promise to keep this marriage a strictly business relationship.

At that moment, as Megan stood in her white dress with her back to the dark sky and bright lights of Vegas, there was nothing businesslike about the way Daniel felt.

"You can have the bedroom. I'll take the sofa," he said, his voice gruff.

Megan glanced at the sofa and shook her head. "That's not even a real sofa. It's more like a love seat." She turned to him, settling her hands on her hips. "I'm smaller. You can have the bed. I'll sleep out here."

When he opened his mouth to protest, she raised her hand. "You're doing me a great favor by marrying me. The least I can do is let you have a decent night's sleep. You'll need that to get through the interrogation my parents will put you through in a couple days."

"I won't make you sleep on the sofa."

"Then are we both sleeping in the bed? Because you are not sleeping on that." She pointed to the sofa. "Don't even bother to argue."

He shrugged. "Then I guess you can have the bathroom first."

"Damn right I will." Her lips quirked and her eyes flashed as she marched past him into the bedroom with its adjoining bathroom.

Scrubbing a hand over his face, he realized just how tired he was. But when Megan was in the room, his body seemed to go into hyperdrive, the adrenaline powering his blood, keeping him alert to her every move.

The woman was playful, resilient and amazing. Most

women would never consider an Elvis wedding appropriate. Megan showed her ability to adapt and her sense of humor, smiling and humming to the music the impersonator sang.

Her parents had no idea what a treasure she was. They should have just let her live her own life. The more Daniel was around her, the more he suspected he was falling in love with her. But he couldn't.

Megan came from money.

Daniel came from the res and a single-wide mobile home that had seen its better days two decades before he and his mother lived there.

He wasn't really a part of the Colton family even though Big J had taken him in. He didn't have the family tree his other siblings could claim, coming from both Big J and Abra Colton's lineage.

Megan deserved a better man with a better family. A man who knew how to act in public and wouldn't embarrass her or her parents.

His stomach knotted at the thought of meeting her parents for the first time and announcing they'd been married. He was without a single doubt that they'd be disappointed in Megan's choice of a husband.

Daniel poured more champagne and drank it, the bubbly fizz not his drink of choice. He stood in the door frame of the bedroom, staring toward the bathroom.

"Daniel?" Megan chose that moment to crack the bathroom door and peek out, her hair falling forward over a very naked shoulder. "Could you hand me my bag?"

His heart stood still as he stared at her.

"Please?" she prompted, pushing him out of his stupor.

Daniel grabbed her bag from the floor and handed

it to her. When her fingers touched his, jolts of fire rippled through his veins, sending heat throughout his body and south.

"I'm headed out for a few minutes," Daniel muttered, backing away from her. "Don't wait up for me."

Her eyes widened. "Where are you going?"

"It's Vegas. I thought I'd get in some gambling."

"Oh." The disappointment on her face almost made him change his mind. He couldn't. If he stayed in the suite with Megan, he'd forgo his promise, pull her into his arms and make love to her the rest of the night and well into the next day.

"I'll have my cell phone if you need me." Daniel left the room and hurried down the hallway to the elevator. If he had to stay up all night gambling, so be it. He couldn't go back to the room when he wanted to kiss his new wife and make mad, passionate love to her.

CHAPTER EIGHT

MEGAN LEFT THE bathroom wearing a pale blue baby-doll nightgown. A lot of good it would do her. Daniel had run out of the room so fast, he left skid marks on the carpet.

He definitely wasn't interested in her or in making their marriage real.

Megan wandered around the bedroom, her hand skimming across the comforter, wondering what it would be like to lie naked beside Daniel in the king-size bed. She ached so badly inside that she wouldn't be able to keep her hands off him for long. Maybe that's why he'd agreed to sleep in the bedroom, where he could close and lock the door to keep her out.

Megan found a blanket in the closet and took one of the pillows off the bed. At least she could get a good night's sleep, even if Daniel didn't. She spread the blanket, plumped the already fluffed pillow and lay down, bending her legs to get all of her on the sofa. The settee was much too small for either her or Daniel.

She lay for a long time staring up at the high ceilings and out at the Las Vegas night sky.

Where was Daniel? Megan checked her cell phone just in case she'd accidently turned it off or set it on silent. No calls, texts or voice mails. An hour passed and she couldn't sleep, not knowing when he'd come back.

Pushing to her feet, Megan returned to the bedroom

and entered the bathroom, closing the door behind her. All the effort she'd put into looking good in her nightgown had been wasted. She pulled her hair back into a high ponytail to get it out of her face.

A noise in the other room made her catch her breath. Had he come back? Would he want to kiss her? *Please let him want to take me in his arms and make love to me.* "Daniel? Are you back?" She flung open the door and scanned the bedroom and the room beyond.

Megan stood perfectly still in the doorway, her heart beating hard against her ribs. "Daniel?"

Again, no answer.

Her pulse picked up, thrumming through her veins— not in anticipatory excitement but because of the creepy feeling she had someone other than Daniel was in the living room.

Megan stepped backward, closed the bathroom door and quietly turned the lock. If Daniel spoke up and let her know he was in the room, she'd unlock it quickly. But Daniel hadn't responded, and there was definitely someone out there.

The plush carpeted floor muffled even the heaviest footfalls.

She'd carried her cell phone through the suite and into the bathroom earlier, hoping Daniel would call. If she had to, she could call 9-1-1. With someone already in her room, would anyone arrive in time to save her?

When the doorknob turned, Megan nearly fainted. Whoever was out there wanted in. Megan curled her hand around the knob and held it, keeping it from turning, just in case the lock didn't keep the intruder out.

The knob stilled.

Megan backed away from the door, dove for the cell

phone on the counter and hit Daniel's number. It rang four times while Megan held her breath, praying he would pick up before whoever had come into their suite got creative and jimmied the lock.

At last Daniel answered, "Megan. Are you okay?"

She pressed the phone to her ear and whispered into the receiver. "There's someone in our room."

"What do you mean?"

"I'm locked in the bathroom and there is someone in the room."

"I'm on my way. Stay on the phone with me."

"I will." She clutched the phone like a lifeline, listening to Daniel's reassuring voice, while her other ear strained to hear movement beyond the door. "You didn't order room service, did you?"

"No."

She bit down on her lip to keep it from trembling. "Me, either."

She stood in the middle of the bathroom, staring in horror at the door, her thoughts running the gamut of self-defense classes she'd taken as the child of a wealthy family. All her life she'd been taught not to trust anyone and beware of strangers who could commit random acts of violence or people who might want to kidnap her. Now all those lessons flew out the window with her nerves.

The knob twisted again.

This time Megan wasn't near. It wiggled as if someone was jimmying the lock. She stared at the door, willing it to hold back whoever was on the other side. "He's turning the knob," Megan said, her voice shaking.

"Yell out loud that you're calling 9-1-1," Daniel said. "I'm in the elevator now."

Megan held the phone away from her mouth and yelled, "I'm calling 9-1-1!"

The knob stilled.

"Help, someone is breaking into my room," Megan said loudly and clearly enough that whoever was on the other side of the door would hear and leave. She recited the details of her hotel and room number to make it sound official.

"Good," Daniel reassured her. "Is there anything in the bathroom you could use as a weapon?"

Her heart hammering, Megan glanced around at the towels, tiny plastic bottles of shampoo and a small bar of soap. All of her toiletries were in the other room. "Not really." She grabbed a towel from the rail and held it in front of her, ready to throw it in the intruder's face if he should break through the door.

"I'm almost to our floor."

"Good," she said. Something hit the door hard. Megan yelped.

"What happened?"

"He's trying to break down the door." She yelled more loudly, "Hotel security is on its way up, and the police are less than two minutes away!"

Another loud thump and the door rattled on its hinges, but held.

Megan's instinct was to get as far away from the door as possible, but she figured if he burst through, his momentum would throw him into the bathroom. She could toss the towel over his head and duck past him while he untangled himself from the terry cloth.

Sure. And pigs could fly.

Into the phone she whispered, "I'm putting you on

speaker and setting the phone on the counter in case I have to run."

"Okay," Daniel said. "I'm just one floor short. Hang in there. I'm almost there."

She held her breath and braced herself for the next blow to the door.

A moment or two passed and nothing. She strained to hear any movement on the other side of the panel. Her heart stood still as she waited, holding the huge luxury towel in front of her, spread like a fisherman's net.

Something slammed against the bathroom door so hard, the door frame splintered. Another slam and the door crashed open. A man in dark clothes and a ski mask fell into the room.

Megan tossed the towel in the man's face and ducked past him.

She had almost cleared the door when a hand reached out and snagged her arm, jerking her back. Megan twisted, employing one of the escape techniques she'd learned long ago. She freed her arm and ran through the bedroom, into the sitting area and straight for the exit, footsteps pounding behind her.

A sob rising up in her throat, she reached for the door and yanked it open. Before she could run through, a hand hit her hard in the back, slamming her onto the floor. She landed on her hands and knees and rolled to the side, away from her attacker. At that exact moment, the elevator dinged, indicating the arrival of the car.

"Daniel!" Megan screamed.

The man in the ski mask leaped over her sprawled form and ran for the stairwell at the opposite end of the hall.

The elevator door opened and Daniel leaped out.

"Megan?" He ran to her and dropped to his haunches. "Oh, baby, are you okay?" His hands skimmed her body, her arms and legs, his assessing gaze sweeping across her.

Tears pooled in her eyes as she pushed to a sitting position. "I'm okay. He went that way." She pointed to the stairwell.

Daniel paused. "Did he hurt you?"

"No. I'm fine."

Daniel held out his hand and helped her to her feet. "Go into the room and lock the door, chains and all. Call hotel security and wait for me to return. Don't let anyone in but me or security."

Her heart racing all over again, she touched his arm. "Where are you going?"

"After your attacker." He ushered her to the door and bent to brush a quick kiss across her lips. "Lock it." Then he was gone, racing down the hall to the stairwell. As he ran, he shot a glance over his shoulder. "By the way, I love the outfit." With a wink he pushed through the door.

Warmed by his comment, Megan watched until he disappeared. Once he was out of sight, a chill shivered across her skin. She ducked back into her room and closed and locked the door as promised. She hurried over to the phone on an end table and dialed the operator. "Hotel security."

"One moment while I connect you," the operator said. "Security."

Megan sighed. "Someone just broke into my room." She gave the details, assured them the intruder was gone and then hung up to wait for their arrival.

All through the call, her mind was on Daniel, praying he was okay. Part of her wanted him to catch the intruder while the other part of her didn't want him to get hurt in the process. She paced to the door and looked through the peephole into the empty hallway, wishing Daniel would come back. She turned and leaned against the door, her gaze panning the room. Why had someone broken in? They didn't have anything worth stealing.

She walked through the sitting area, through the bedroom and into the bathroom. Nothing appeared disturbed. In the bedroom, again, nothing seemed out of place. No drawers were opened. Her purse sat on the dresser in the same position she'd left it. In the bathroom, she slipped into the fluffy white hotel bathrobe. She grabbed her phone and held it, willing Daniel to call and let her know what was happening in the stairwell.

A knock at the door made her jump and yelp.

"Hotel security."

Megan hurried to the door and peered through the peephole. Two men wearing the uniforms she'd seen in the casino stood outside her door.

She slid the chain off and unlocked the dead bolt. Her hand shook as she opened the door.

"Ma'am, we understand you've had a break-in. We notified the police, and they are on their way. We're here to protect you until they arrive."

"Thanks." Megan stood in the robe, wishing she'd taken the time to get dressed, feeling uncomfortable in a bathrobe with nothing more than a sexy nightgown beneath it. Where was Daniel?

DANIEL RAN DOWN the stairs, leaped over the railing and dropped to the next level. He stopped and listened. Below he heard footsteps pounding on the stairs. He leaned over the railing and caught a glimpse of someone in black three or four floors below. Fueled by the sound and the sight of his prey, Daniel continued downward.

The metal clink sounded of a stairwell door opening and closing. Daniel leaned over the railing again but didn't see anything. He was still several floors from ground level.

His heart beating rapidly, he continued downward from the penthouse level until he reached the ground and burst through the door.

Multicolored lights flashed, and the constant ringing of bells and the musical cacophony of the casino assailed his senses. He scanned the immediate vicinity for a man in black. There were a couple of older men wearing black shirts, standing at the slot machines, but no one appeared to have been running down multiple flights of stairs.

Daniel hurried past row after row of slot and video poker machines. At one point he thought he saw a man in black duck around a group of people at a roulette table. Upon closer investigation, he discovered a woman with dark hair and a black blouse drinking a martini and laughing up at her date.

As large and confusing as the casino was, Daniel knew it was a lost cause to continue his search. The longer he was away from Megan, the more he wanted to return to her and make certain she was okay.

He took the elevator back to the penthouse level and hurried toward their room. The door was open, and a couple of security guards stood inside.

When he entered through the open doorway, the guards blocked his path.

Daniel held up his hands and nodded toward Megan.

"That's my wife." The words rolled off his lips, feeling so natural and right.

Megan's cheeks reddened. "You can let him in. He's with me."

Daniel slipped around the security guards and pulled her into his arms. "Are you okay?"

"Yeah. More importantly, are you?" She pushed to arm's length and stared up into his eyes. "Did you catch him?"

He frowned and shook his head. "He must have gotten off on one of the higher floors. I went all the way down to the bottom and never saw him." Glancing over her shoulder, he asked, "Anything missing or disturbed?"

"Nothing. He was in the room long enough to grab my purse, but he didn't even touch it."

A minute later, the police, the hotel manager and the assistant manager arrived, filling the room. The police took Megan's statement, dusted for prints and looked around, leaving shortly afterward.

The hotel manager and assistant manager stood in the hallway with Megan and Daniel until the police left. When they were gone, hotel maintenance staff entered and wiped away all traces of fingerprint dust and splintered wood from the door frame. "We'll have someone fix the frame tomorrow," said the manager. "Please accept our apologies. Your room will be comped and our security staff will be working closely with the police, going over the video footage to help them identify your intruder. We'll have guards on the floor for the remainder of the night."

"Thank you." Daniel held the door for the hotel manager and his assistant. When they'd passed through, he closed it and turned to Megan.

Her face was pale and her eyes were rounded, with dark circles beneath.

Daniel opened his arms. "Come here."

Megan fell against him, burying her face against his chest.

He held her close, resting his cheek against her soft hair, breathing in the scent of her. After the insane race to get to her before the intruder did and then the race down the stairwell to catch the bastard, Daniel didn't think his heart would ever slow. Who the hell would attack an innocent woman? Was it a random event or had he targeted Megan?

"I've never been more scared in my life," she muttered against his shirt, her fingers curling into the fabric.

Daniel's jaw hardened, his arms tightening around Megan. "I'm here now. I won't let anyone hurt you."

She slipped her arms around his waist, her body shaking against his. "I didn't think you'd get here in time."

Daniel hadn't, either. He'd prayed all the way up in the elevator, watching the numbers tick at the pace of molasses dripping. "Did he hurt you?"

"He pushed me down. Other than a little rug burn on my hands and knees, I'm fine. I'm just glad *you're* okay."

He shook his head. She'd been the one attacked, and yet she was concerned about him. His chest swelled. Megan was an amazing woman. "Come on. You must be exhausted." Tucking her in the curve of his arm, he walked her toward the bedroom. "You can have the bed. I'll take the sofa."

Her arm clamped around his waist. "The sofa is too small."

"I'll make do."

"You'll be uncomfortable and won't sleep."

"It won't hurt me for one night." He stopped beside the bed and let his arm fall from around her.

Megan didn't let go of his waist, nor did she move from where she stood beside him. "Stay with me," she whispered.

The softly spoken words went straight to Daniel's heart. He wanted to wrap his arms around her and hold her until all the bad in the world turned good, but if he lay down beside her, he wasn't sure he could stop at a hug. "I can't."

"At least until I go to sleep." Her head dipped. "I'll understand if you don't want to."

Daniel closed his eyes, his fists clenching. "It's not that I don't want to."

Megan turned her face up to his, her brow creased. "What do you mean?"

He shook his head and gripped her arms. "I want to. Hell, I want *you* and that's the problem."

Her chuckle made his groin tighten, the sound soft and sexy, stirring his blood. "Daniel, we're married."

"Only in name." He let go of her and shoved a hand through his hair to keep from dragging her into his arms and kissing her like there might not be a tomorrow.

She touched his chest, sending warning signals throughout his body. "It doesn't have to be in name only."

"This is supposed to be temporary. You have your life. I have mine." He forced himself to take a step backward. "I don't belong in yours."

Her frown deepened. "My life is at the Lucky C Ranch and so is yours. How different are our lives?"

He shook his head. "You are the daughter of a very wealthy man. I'm a bastard son of a Colton. We're worlds apart."

Megan planted her fists on her hips. The image of her in her fluffy terry-cloth bathrobe, her trim legs peeking out from the hem, and her pretty little feet bare against the carpeted floor almost undid Daniel. She tossed her ponytail back over her shoulder. "You make it sound like I'm stuck up, when in actuality, you're the one who's stuck up."

"I'm not stuck up."

"Look, Daniel, I don't judge you based on your family or where you came from. I take you for the man you are now. The least you could do is give me the same benefit of the doubt."

"It's different."

"The hell it is." Megan pointed to the door. "Go. Sleep on the sofa. I'll be just fine on my own." She reached for the sash around her waist and untied it, letting the robe drop to the ground around her ankles. Then she tipped up her chin and pushed her shoulders back, making her breasts rise in the sexiest sheer nightgown Daniel had ever seen in his life. The garment revealed more than it covered and sent his pulse rampaging through his veins. "Too bad you won't be along on this honeymoon."

When she started to turn away, Daniel grasped her elbow and yanked her back and into his arms. "What are you trying to do, damn it?"

"Nothing," she said. "Absolutely nothing."

He swept his hand along the side of her face and up to pull out the elastic band around her hair, letting it fall down around her shoulders. "Well, you're doing a whole lotta something to me, and I can only take so much."

She stared up into his face, the anger melting from her eyes, her tongue coming out to wet her lips. "That's your problem," she said, her voice soft and breathy.

"No, it's our problem." He cupped the back of her head with one hand and bent until his lips were a hair-breadth from hers. "This is so damned wrong." He fought to keep from taking it a step further, knowing he was losing this battle and fast.

"Then why do it?" she asked, her words warm against his lips.

"Because it feels so right." He lowered his mouth to hers, intending only a light brush, telling himself he'd just get a little taste of her and go away. Control flew out the window when their lips touched. He could no sooner back away than stop breathing.

Daniel crushed her body against his, the soft curve of her breasts pressing against his hard chest, her thighs straddling one of his, her arms circling his neck to bring him closer. This was where he wanted to be. Not in the other room, lying cramped on the impossibly small sofa.

She opened her mouth on a sigh, and he swept in to claim her tongue in a long, hot, wet caress.

He slid his hand down her back to cup her bottom, pulling her closer until his straining member rubbed against her belly. The kiss went on, the heat building between them, the need to feel her skin against his becoming a physical ache.

Megan broke the kiss and stepped away.

Daniel groaned, reaching out to bring her back within his embrace.

She shook her head and reached for the buttons of his shirt, flicking them free one at a time all the way down to where they disappeared into the waistband of his trousers. Gripping the fabric, she pulled it loose and freed the remaining buttons with quick, deft strokes of her dexterous fingers.

Impatience sent Daniel over the edge. He shoved her hands aside, unbuckled his belt and jerked it out of the loops, slinging it across the floor. Then he grabbed the hem of her gown and yanked it over her head, tossing it aside. He swept her with his gaze, lingering on her perky breasts, the nipples puckered and beaded into tight little buds.

A slow flush rose up her neck and into her cheeks. With exaggerated care, Megan loosened the top button of his trousers and slid the zipper down, unleashing his straining member into the palm of her hand. Her lips curled upward and her brows cocked. "Commando?"

"Always." He toed off his cowboy boots and his trousers slid down his legs.

Once he stood naked in front of her, he sucked in a deep breath and let it out in an attempt to rein in his galloping pulse. "If you want, you can back out now."

"You're wrong," she said, gently squeezing his hard staff. "I couldn't back out even if I wanted to. I need you. Now. Inside me." Tugging gently, she backed toward the bed. "Don't fight it."

"I'm past fighting. I concede this round to you and your gorgeous body."

CHAPTER NINE

A THRILL SHIVERED across Megan's body. "Victory at last," she murmured, aroused beyond reason, barely able to form a coherent thought.

Daniel scooped her legs up and laid her on the bed. He hooked his finger in the elastic band of her panties and dragged them down her legs.

Now we're getting somewhere. She ran her hand up her torso and plumped one of her breasts, hoping to entice him into moving this along a little faster. Her core on fire, she needed him to quench the blaze.

He crawled onto the bed, leaning over her, his arms bulging, his member nestling in the mound of curls over her sex. "I didn't go into this deal with sex in mind."

"Consider it a bonus." Megan wrapped her legs around his waist and urged him closer.

"Uh-uh. Not yet." With one hand he reached back and disengaged her legs. "I want this to be as good for you as it will be for me."

Was he kidding? Any more excited and she'd burst into flames. "Oh, I have no doubt it'll be good," she said, her voice low and husky.

"Shh. Anyone ever tell you that you talk too much?"

"Sometimes—" He cut off her words with a kiss, darting his tongue into her mouth. He tasted of mint and coffee and smelled of the outdoors and aftershave. She opened to him, offering him everything in exchange for one night of passion.

After ravaging her lips and mouth, he trailed hot kisses along her jaw and down her neck.

Megan tilted her head back to allow him better access to all those sensitive places in his path. When he reached her breast, her back arched automatically, her body taking over, reacting to his every touch.

Daniel tongued her nipple, flicking the tip and rolling it around between his teeth.

She cupped the back of his head, running her hands through his thick, dark hair, urging him to take more. When he switched to the other nipple, the cool air across the first one only made her more aware of her nakedness.

Though she wasn't a virgin, she had never been so very aroused and aware of a man's body as she was with Daniel. His huge frame, thick muscles and hard staff made her want to get even closer. She wanted him inside her.

Daniel abandoned her breasts and seared a path with his tongue and lips down her torso, dipping briefly into her belly button but not stopping for long. He finally reached the apex of her thighs and parted her folds with his thumbs.

Megan stiffened, waiting for his next move, her breath hitched in her throat, her fingers knotting the sheets at her sides.

His head lowered, and he tapped his tongue to that strip of flesh alive with nerves. The touch sent sparks of electricity shooting through her body. A tingling sensation built at her center, radiating outward. "Do you know what you're doing to me?"

His chuckle blew warm over her wet entrance. "I hope I do."

"Don't stop," she cried.

"Yes, ma'am." He tapped her center again.

Megan moaned and reached for his head, digging her fingers into his hair, pulling him to her.

His wet tongue stroked her again and again, then moved down to her damp entrance, swirling around in her juices before returning to her aching, needy flesh. While he tongued her, he slipped a finger into her channel, her wetness coating him, making it easy for him to slide another inside, and another.

She writhed, her body moving to the rhythm of his tongue and fingers, the heat building, her insides tensing, rising to that peak she reached for with all her might.

One final flick sent her rocketing for the heavens like Fourth of July fireworks in sudden, glorious bursts, shooting out in all directions.

Megan rode the rocket to the moon and back, her hips moving to the pulsing beat of blood hammering in her veins.

As she returned to the earth and her senses, another ache filled her, and she urged Daniel up her body, dragging at his hair.

"Hey, that's attached." He laughed and complied, sliding his body over her torso and breasts until his lips hovered over hers. "Are you ready?"

"Oh, you have no idea."

"I think I have a little bit of an idea. But first…" He leaned over the side of the bed, reaching for his trousers and the wallet in the back pocket.

Thankful he'd had the wherewithal to remember protection, Megan grabbed the foil packet from his hands and ripped it open, then slid the contents over his rock-hard member. She tossed the empty packet to the side. "We aren't done yet."

"Are you always this insatiable?" He smiled, his eyes darker than dark, his lips wet from pleasuring her.

"Baby, it's you." She gripped his bottom and brought his staff to her entrance. "I can't seem to get enough."

"It goes both ways, sweetheart."

"Then don't let anything stop you now."

He nudged her opening.

"Oh, please, don't take it slow," she begged.

Hot and wet from the most incredible foreplay she'd ever experienced, she was ready.

Daniel drove into her, burying himself hard and deep.

Megan raised her hips to take him even deeper.

He withdrew and entered her again. His length and girth filled her, stretching her channel in the most glori-ous, sensual way. Megan bucked beneath him, digging her heels into the mattress to meet him thrust for thrust.

He rode her hard and fast, his long, steady strokes building speed, the friction inside heating her, sending her back up to the top of the peak.

One last time he powered into her, all the way until he could go no more. There he held her, his body rigid, his member so thick and solid, yet throbbing and warm, pulsing inside her to the rhythm of her own heartbeat.

When at last his muscles relaxed, he collapsed on top of her and rolled over, taking her with him, retain-ing their intimate connection.

Megan lay with her cheek against his naked chest, her body limp and replete after the most mind-blowing sex she'd ever experienced.

Daniel pulled her into his arms and rested his chin against her temple. "That was amazing."

"I have no words, except...wow."

He stroked a hand down her arm and along the swell of her hip. "We should get some sleep."

"I haven't even thought about tomorrow."

"We have an entire day of honeymooning and another night here. You don't have to think beyond that. Not yet." He kissed the top of her hair, then pressed his lips to the tip of her nose and finally her lips.

Megan wove her fingers into his hair and deepened the kiss, holding on for as long as she could before breathing became a necessity.

Her body stirred against him, and his flaccid member grew hard all over again.

"I assume sleep is not on your mind," she teased him, her finger trailing down his chest and belly to the tip of his shaft which pressed against her stomach.

"Not now. And not for the rest of the night if you keep doing that."

"Is that all it takes?" She circled him with her finger. This time she rose up over him, straddling his hips, her knees sinking into the mattress, her warm wetness easing down over him.

"Who needs sleep, anyway?" Daniel thrust up into her. Holding her hips in his big, calloused hands, he guided her up and down in a hot, rapid ascent until they climaxed together, calling out each other's names.

Megan lay over his bare chest, her racing heartbeat matching his. Exhaustion melted her into him, and she could barely move enough to slip onto the bed next to the big Oklahoman. "Sorry, that's all I had in me. Give me a couple hours of sleep and I could do it all over again."

"Is that so?"

"You bet." She looked into his eyes. "Promise me one thing."

"What's that?"

"Tomorrow." She yawned and closed eyelids so heavy she could barely keep them open. "No regrets."

DANIEL LAY AWAKE for a long time after Megan fell to sleep, staring into her fresh, beautiful face. Her strawberry blond hair fanned out over his arm in burnished-gold, silken strands. Her full, soft lips were swollen from his kisses, and her fingers rested against his chest, curling ever so slightly as if to hold on to him.

No regrets.

As soon as she'd said it, a dozen thoughts had powered through his head, every one of them a strong reason for him to step away from her as fast as he could. He was a good man, but he wasn't the kind of man who strove for wealth and power. He liked living on the ranch and taking care of horses.

His goal was to establish a viable horse-breeding program, not to conquer the world one corporation at a time. He had no desire to be a big shot in an office. Horses were his passion, and no matter how little he made at what he was doing, he wouldn't want to do anything else. He loved the animals, felt most comfortable around them. More so than around humans.

Except Megan. She'd fit right into his life without so much as a bump in the road. Her passion for horses equaled his, and her desire to live simply paralleled his own. Then why did he think she was a debutante to be coddled and protected until the day her parents handed her off to some rich playboy? He'd provide for her, protect her and see to it she never lacked for the most beautiful things money could buy. But would he let her do the things she loved? Would he love her like she deserved to be loved?

No regrets?

Daniel's only regret was Megan's accident of birth. If she had not been born of insanely wealthy parents, he could have seen being with her for the long haul. But he didn't have enough to offer her.

He must have drifted off in the wee hours of the morning. When he opened his eyes, sun streamed through the curtains of the honeymoon suite.

Megan stirred beside him, rolling onto her back.

Daniel slipped his arm out from beneath her and propped himself up on his elbow to stare down at the beautiful woman. Tall, slender and curvy in all the right places, she was absolutely gorgeous. Never in all the time she'd worked for Daniel had she expressed an interest in him, nor had he encouraged it. He respected her as his employee. Though he'd considered her hands-off, he couldn't change the way his body reacted to hers when they worked in tight quarters.

Even now, as she lay sleeping in the bed, his breath quickened and his member hardened.

If he didn't move immediately, he'd be touching her again like some sex-starved teen.

Daniel eased off the mattress and stood. They needed at least one day in Vegas to make it look like a proper honeymoon before heading on to California to meet with her grandmother's attorney. The sooner they got the ball rolling on her inheritance, the sooner she'd be able to purchase her horses.

While in California, they'd meet with her parents,

an encounter he didn't look forward to. They'd be upset she'd married beneath her. Daniel hoped they didn't make a big deal out of it.

Megan was old enough to make her own decisions and live life the way she planned, not the way her parents felt she should. The least he could do was show her a proper honeymoon for an unusual wedding. He stepped into the bathroom, past the jagged edges of the busted door frame.

His heart stilled for a moment. If the attacker had been successful, what would have happened to Megan? Had he been there to hurt, kidnap or kill her?

And why? What did Megan have that an intruder would want? Kidnapping made more sense. Her parents were rich. If they loved her, they'd pay anything to get her back alive. Killing her made no sense whatsoever, unless it had been a random break-in and the burglar was on an insane mission to murder.

Daniel glanced at the sleeping Megan through the doorway and decided to leave the door open enough that he could hear if anyone were to break in and attack again. He'd keep her close until they returned to Oklahoma. For that matter, had her horse been poisoned in order to cause injury to Megan? Perhaps he was putting two and two together and coming up with five.

He switched on the shower and stepped beneath the cool spray, hoping the water would wash away the fog of uncertainty and make his thoughts clearer. The danger they'd encountered had to stop before Megan got hurt.

Whatever he did that day, he needed to keep his hands off his bride. This was supposed to be a marriage of convenience, not the real deal. As soon as she acquired her grandmother's inheritance, she wouldn't need him anymore. Daniel had to remind himself of that fact. Megan would be his ex-wife and, if she chose to stay at the Lucky C, she'd be his employee again. He had to keep their relationship on a business level. No more making love into the dark hours of the morning.

The cool spray of the shower did nothing to tone down his rising desire. Just the thought of a naked Megan lying in the bed made his insides heat. The water warmed as he lathered a bar of soap, spread it over his face and body and then stepped beneath the showerhead to rinse off.

Cool air fanned across his backside. Slender fingers circled his waist, and a warm body pressed against him.

Daniel's body reacted immediately and with profound lust. He leaned his hands against the cool tiles and let the water wash over his head and shoulders as he gathered his wits and held tight to his slipping control. "You are making it extremely difficult to remain hands-off in this marriage," he grumbled.

"You were the one who wanted this marriage to be hands-off." Megan pressed her cheek and other, more interesting parts against his back. "How's that working for you?" Her hands slid lower to fondle his hard staff.

"I'm failing miserably." He sighed and turned to face her, gathering her in his arms. "Especially when you look so damned beautiful in nothing but water and soap."

Her brows rose. "I don't have any soap on me."

"Guess we'll have to fix that." He lathered his hands with the bar and set it aside. Starting at her neck, Daniel spread the suds across her shoulders and over the swell of her breasts. He stopped to tweak each of her puckered nipples, swirling the slippery bubbles around and around until Megan captured one of his wrists and guided his hand lower to the tuft of hair over the apex of her thighs.

"There's no soap here," she said, her voice gravelly and sexy.

Daniel cupped her sex and slid a finger between her folds.

Megan's breasts rose on a long, indrawn breath. "Yesss." She gripped his upper arms and closed her eyes, holding on while he touched her again.

Daniel studied her face as he toyed with the special place that made her crazy when he stroked her. He liked watching her eyelids flicker, her tongue dart out to wet her lips and her hips gyrate with every movement of his finger. Her response made him ready to take her there against the cool tiled wall.

He slipped his soapy hands around to her back and down over the rounded swells of her bottom. Then he lifted her, and she wrapped her legs around his waist. Poised at her opening, he was sorely tempted to thrust up inside her.

With her hands braced on his shoulders, she tried to lower herself, but his hands on her hips stayed her descent.

"No. We can't do this."

She drew in a deep breath, her breasts within reach of his lips. "Protection?"

"It's in the other room."

"Then let's go into the other room." She cupped his chin and smiled down into his face, the shower pelting her chest, the water dripping off the tips of her breasts.

Daniel groaned. "It's more than just protection. We can't keep doing this. When the charade is over, we have to go back to being us."

"And this isn't us?" Her fingers raked through his hair, and she tipped his head toward hers. "It could be."

"It shouldn't be," Daniel said. "I promised I wouldn't take advantage of you."

"What if I want you to?"

His lips quirked on the corners. "It doesn't make it right."

Her mouth pressed into a thin line. "I swear, Daniel Colton, you have the hardest head of any of the Coltons. What does it take to get you to look past the nose at the end of your face?"

"What do you mean?"

"Nothing." She loosened her legs around him. "Let me down."

Now that she'd asked him to put her down, he was certain he didn't want to. But he complied.

Megan stepped out of the shower onto the mat and slid the curtain shut in his face, fire flashing in her green eyes.

Daniel didn't like that she was mad, but perhaps it would be better if she stayed that way. The less she liked him, the easier it would be to go back to their former way of getting along.

Staring down at his erection, he doubted they'd ever go back to the way it was before they were married. Who was he trying to kid?

He rinsed under the lukewarm water and switched it off. When he pulled the shower curtain back, Megan had left the bathroom and closed the door behind her.

His pulse leaped at the thought of her in the bedroom alone with a possible intruder. Daniel dove for the door, his wet foot slipping on the tile floor. Instead of opening the door silently to check on her, he crashed into it headfirst and slid to the floor.

His head throbbing, he pushed to his feet and regrouped. He flung open the door, throwing a towel around his naked waist.

Megan was halfway across the room, headed in his direction, a frown denting her brow. She wore a black lacy bra and matching panties, the darkness of the scraps of material enhancing the paleness of her skin. "I thought I heard something fall in there."

"You did." He straightened, his pulse settling into an uneven rhythm with her almost naked in front of him, the undergarments almost as enticing as her nude body. "I just—" he cleared his throat "—wanted to make sure you were alone."

Her brows lifted, and she glanced around the room. "I believe we are the only two people in the suite at this time."

"Good." He marched into the room, grabbed his clothes and kept going into the sitting area, thus avoiding temptation.

"Hey, cowboy." Megan leaned in the doorway, her arms crossed, her lips quirked. "You can run, but you can't hide from the way you feel."

"It's not right. We're only in this for a short while."

Megan dipped her head. "So why not enjoy each other's company in the meantime?"

"It's not right. My mother and father did that, and what did it buy them?" He jammed his legs into his blue jeans. "A bastard child."

Megan's arms dropped to her sides, and she crossed the floor to where he stood pulling his shirt over his shoulders. She laid her hand on his arm, all amusement wiped from her face. "Daniel, a child of ours wouldn't be a bastard." She nodded toward the papers on the end table. "We're legally married."

"For show."

"It's legal."

He shook off her hand. "You deserve a better match."

Her frown returned, and she spun away from him. "For the love of God. You sound like my parents." Megan disappeared into the bedroom. Drawers slamming and the rasp of a suitcase zipper were the only sounds coming through the open door. Then she appeared, pulling a dress down over her head. "That marriage license has to be legal for me to collect my inheritance."

"I realize that."

"Fine," she said, straightening the hem of her dress. She turned and gave him her back. "Zip me."

A chuckle rose up his chest, and he crossed to where she stood in her stiff, fiery anger.

He dragged the zipper up the back of the dress. Before she could get away, he turned her to face him. "Look, let's make this day a good one, no matter what happens in the coming days. We have all of Vegas to explore and no one to please but ourselves." He held out his hand. "Deal?"

She stared at it, her eyes narrowed. Then she relaxed and slid her hand into his, her frown easing. "Deal. We'll make it a day." Letting go of his hand, she glanced up at him, her eyes narrowing again for just a moment. "But I still think you're discriminating against me because of my family." She poked him in the chest with a finger. "I. Am. Not. My. Family." She reentered the bedroom, calling out, "The sooner you get that, the better." Slinging her purse over her shoulder, she emerged in the doorway. "Ready to paint this town red?"

He grinned. "Let's do it." Daniel pushed aside all his misgivings about this marriage of convenience for the day and concentrated on showing Megan a good time, while keeping a close eye on her in case the man who'd broken into their room showed up again.

CHAPTER TEN

MEGAN SMILED AND laughed through the day, walking along the broad sidewalks of the Vegas Strip. She and Daniel toured several of the more notable casinos from the pyramid of the Luxor to the MGM Grand. They ate a sumptuous lunch at the Eiffel Tower Restaurant in the Paris Las Vegas Hotel and Casino and walked beneath the sky-painted ceilings of Caesars Palace.

The day passed in a whirl of activity and fun. Megan hadn't realized how entertaining Daniel could be and how special he made her feel, always opening doors for her and holding her hand everywhere they went.

At The Venetian, Daniel hired a gondola to take them through the beautiful canal winding its way through the spacious hotel and casino. The oarsman paused long enough to use Daniel's smartphone to snap a picture of them in each other's arms, drifting beneath an arched bridge.

Despite the nature of their agreement, Daniel went above and beyond what was necessary to make the day special. If she hadn't known better, Megan could almost have believed they were truly on their honeymoon.

At the end of the day, they stopped in front of the Bellagio in time for the spectacular musical light show. Daniel slipped his arm around her and she leaned in to him, tired but happy. Their fake honeymoon had been everything she could hope for in a real one. And she'd spent it with the man she was falling madly in love with. Her heart swelled with the last strains of music.

"Ready to get dinner?" Daniel asked. "Or would you rather go back to the hotel and order room service?"

Megan didn't have to think twice. "Room service." Back in their hotel room, she wouldn't have to share Daniel with a thousand other people. Even if he didn't want to be intimate, he would be with her. She would be happy with any scraps he threw her way. But she'd be beyond ecstatic if he carried her back to the bed and made sweet love to her through the night.

On the walk back to the hotel, the lights of the city shone all around them, neon illuminating the night sky, masking the stars she knew were just beyond the halo of garish brightness. "Though Vegas is fun, I'll be glad to go home to Oklahoma. I like my nights filled with stars."

Daniel reached out and grasped her hand, pulling it through the crook of his arm. "You and me both. Nothing makes me happier than to lie on the ground and stare up at a clear night sky and count the stars until I fall asleep."

"My father's ranch is over fifty miles north of San Francisco, but the lights from the city fade the stars." She leaned against his shoulder. "I much prefer the nights on the Lucky C."

Cars moved past them on the street, and a steady stream of humanity passed them on the still-warm concrete sidewalks.

Daniel pulled her to a halt at a crosswalk and pressed the button for the pedestrian light. "We can cross here."

Their hotel was on the other side of the busy thoroughfare. Just a few more feet before she had Daniel all to herself.

The light changed and the traffic pulled to a halt, the little walking man figure lighting on the crosswalk sign.

Megan stepped out on Daniel's arm, ready to be back in their room, with all the possibilities of how the rest of the evening might go racing through her mind.

Screeching tires made her turn to glance at one of the cars waiting at the intersection. It jerked forward, the scent of rubber burning against the pavement as whoever was driving floored the accelerator.

The car careened toward Megan and Daniel.

People scattered, screaming.

Daniel shoved her hard, sending her flying out of the way of the oncoming vehicle. She hit the ground and rolled to the side, the tires barely missing her as it raced by.

A loud thump made her blood run cold. Megan stumbled to her feet, her heart lodged in her throat. "Daniel!" she cried out.

The vehicle sped on, disappearing into a red sea of taillights. On the ground before her, Daniel lay on his back.

"Daniel!" Megan rushed forward and fell on her knees on the pavement.

"I'm okay." He lifted a hand as if to prove it, though he didn't get up immediately. "Just bruised my backside. Give me a minute to feel if anything is broken." Slowly he moved his legs and arms. Finally he sat up.

People gathered around them even as the light changed to green for the waiting cars.

"Hey, mister, are you all right?" A woman stepped up to them. "I'm a nurse. You should stay down until an ambulance arrives." She held a phone to her ear. "I'm calling 9-1-1 now."

Daniel was already shaking his head. "No. Don't. I'm okay. Just a little shaken up."

"We saw that car hit you, dude," a teen said. "I swear he did it on purpose."

"Yeah," another teen said. "If you hadn't rolled over the hood, you'd be a dead man."

Daniel pushed to his feet and gave the teens a wry smile. "Thanks. I think I get the picture." He hooked Megan's arm and led her out of the street to the relative safety of the sidewalk.

"At least go to the hospital and let the ER doctor check you out for a concussion," Megan urged him.

The nurse had followed them and stood beside Megan, nodding. "He really should. Sometimes you think you're okay, but you could have head trauma and intracranial bleeding."

Megan's stomach lurched. "You're going to the hospital." She turned to wave down a cab. When one pulled up to the curb, she opened the door and pointed. "Get in."

"Really, I'm fine," Daniel insisted. "I jumped up on the hood. The vehicle didn't hit me."

"You landed on your back and probably hit your head in the fall. Which would explain why you can't seem to focus enough to get into the cab." Megan tapped her toe. "Are you going to get in, or are two women going to have to manhandle you into the car?"

Daniel glanced from Megan to the nurse and back before he raised his hands in surrender. "Okay, okay. I'm getting in."

The nurse sighed. "Good. Just let a doctor check you out. I'm sure you're fine, but it doesn't hurt to have the doctor confirm."

Megan turned to the nurse and held out her hand. "Thank you."

The nurse smiled and shook her hand with a wink. "Your husband is too cute to lose to a freak accident. Take care."

Megan climbed in beside Daniel and told the cab driver to take them to the hospital.

Daniel sat beside her, rubbing a hand over the back of his head. "We could be ordering room service," he grumbled.

"We can still order room service when we get back. They serve 24/7." Megan scanned his face and body for injuries. Other than a scuffed elbow, he looked fine. "Let me feel the back of your head."

He leaned forward. "I've got a knot from the fall."

"Where?" She leaned close. He captured her hand and guided it to the spot, where she felt a chicken-egg-sized bump. "You did get a bump, poor baby."

He removed her hand from his head and used it to pull her close to him. "Mmm, you smell good."

"After a day tromping around Vegas, I shouldn't."

"Damn, Megan." He set her away from him and stared down at her hands. "Your hands are raw." He leaned back and studied the rest of her, including her skinned knees. "How did you get those?"

She smiled. "A certain cowboy shoved me out of the way of a speeding car."

"Oh, baby, sorry I pushed you too hard."

She shook her head. "I'm okay. If you hadn't pushed me as hard as you did, we would both have been hit. I'm just sorry you took the brunt of that maniac's bad driving skills."

"Good thing we're going to the hospital. The doctor should be able to help you."

"I've only got skinned knees and hands. My head didn't connect to the ground. How did you keep from getting crushed by that car?"

"I was pretty good on the vault in high school. I planted my hands on the hood of the car and swung my legs to the side. A great vault, but a terrible landing."

"You're alive. That's what matters." She wrapped her arms around him, the sound of his body thumping against the metal of the vehicle replaying in her mind. "Wow, you could have been so messed up."

He chuckled and winced. "Ouch. Careful how hard you squeeze. I suspect a bruised rib."

"Sorry." She sat up straight and carefully moved away. "What's happening here? First the attack in our room, now a hit-and-run."

Daniel's lips thinned. "It can't be a coincidence."

Megan shook her head, her hands trembling. "It's as if one or both of us are being targeted."

The cab drove up to the ER entrance. Megan got out and extended her hand to help Daniel.

He ignored her hand and climbed out on his own. "Thanks, but I really am okay."

"If it's all the same to you, I'd rather hear the doctor say that." Megan led him into the hospital and up to the registration desk.

An hour later, after Daniel had his head scanned and Megan had her knees cleaned and bandaged, they left in another cab. When they arrived back at the hotel, they looked pretty banged up and hurried to their room.

"You can have the shower first," Megan offered. "I'll order room service."

"If they come before I'm out of the shower, don't answer the door," Daniel warned her.

Megan's heart warmed at his concern. "Not everyone is out to get me."

"Maybe not, but that's three near misses in as many days. If you're not getting a persecution complex by now, I'll get one for you." He pointed at her. "Don't open that door for anyone. I'll answer it when I get out."

"Yes, sir." Megan popped a smart salute and smiled. "You can answer the door. In the meantime, I'll call in a dinner order."

Daniel entered the bathroom and left the door propped open.

Megan couldn't help peeking as he dropped his jeans and shed his shirt.

He turned, caught her staring and winked. Then he stepped into the shower, closing the curtain between them.

Megan's cheeks heated. "Tease!" she called out.

"Peeping Tom!" he shouted back.

Still smiling, she lifted the phone and called room service, ordering a couple of steaks and a bottle of wine.

When she hung up, she entered the bedroom and scrounged through her suitcase for something to wear. She settled on an oversize T-shirt and a pair of shorts. Not exactly a sex goddess outfit, but she wasn't planning on seducing Daniel after he'd been knocked around.

Her cell phone rang in the other room. By the time she reached it, it had stopped. Checking the caller ID, she noted it was her parents. Rather than spoil the rest of her evening, she decided not to return the call.

The choice was taken out of her hands when her phone

rang again and startled her enough that she pressed the receive button.

"Megan?" her mother's voice sounded in her ear.

"Hi, Mother."

"Why didn't you answer the first time I rang? Is everything okay?"

Megan sighed. Her mother worried far too much about her, to the point of obsessing. "I'm fine, Mother." If *fine* meant almost being thrown from a horse, having her room broken into and nearly being run over by a crazed driver, she was just dandy.

"You don't sound fine. When are you coming home?"

Her heart thumping against her ribs, Megan took a deep breath and dove in. "As a matter of fact, I'll be home tomorrow."

Her mother gasped. "Tomorrow? Why didn't you tell us sooner?"

"I only knew myself today," she fibbed just a little. She'd known since the day before, but one day's difference didn't matter that much.

"What if I'd had an appointment or a meeting to go to? Fortunately, my calendar is free tomorrow, so I can pick you up from the airport in San Francisco."

"I won't be flying into San Francisco, Mother." Megan bit her bottom lip and forged on. "I'll be flying into the airport at Santa Rosa."

"In a regional jet?" Her mother had a fear of small aircraft, almost as strong as her fear of her daughter riding horses. "I wish you'd come in something much larger."

"I'm flying into Santa Rosa in a four-seater. We want to rent a car from there, so no need to meet us."

"A four-seater? Oh, baby, that's worse than I thought."

"I'll be fine. My pilot is exceptional."

"But it's such a long way from Oklahoma to California in something that small."

"I'm not flying directly from Oklahoma, Mother."

"You'll be stopping along the way?"

"Stopped. We flew into Las Vegas yesterday. We're flying out tomorrow. I'm not sure what time we'll be leaving, so don't wait at the airport for me. I'll call when we're on our way out to the Triple Diamond."

"Your father won't be happy to know you're flying in a death trap."

"It's not a death trap, Mother. I'll be safer than if I drove out to California."

"Oh, dear." Megan could picture the normally unflappable Josephine Talbot wringing her hands and clutching the phone in a white-knuckle grip.

She hated worrying her mother, but she hated worse being smothered by her mother's fears for her. "Mother, my phone battery is about to die."

"Charge it. I'm sure your father will want to talk you out of flying tomorrow."

"It's not his decision. I have to go now. The battery light is blinking. Bye, Mother." She ended the call and turned off her telephone.

"Your parents?" Daniel asked from the doorway. He had a towel slung over his bare shoulders, and he wore a pair of clean blue jeans and nothing else.

Megan's breath caught in her throat, and her belly tightened. The man had no right to look that deliciously sexy. "Yes, that was my mother. She thinks flying in anything less than a 777 is a—how'd she put it?" Megan tapped a finger to her chin. "Ah, yes—death trap." She smiled up at him. "What do you say to that?"

"Sounds like she worries about her daughter." He

raised the towel and rubbed it through his dark hair, standing it on end. Then he turned and strode back into the bathroom to deposit the towel. "The shower's all yours."

"Thanks." She gathered her shirt, shorts and panties. "The steak's on the way. I'd like to meet with the lawyer in Santa Rosa before we go to my parents' home. They live farther out." Megan turned her back to him. "Unzip, please."

"Are you always this demanding?"

"Don't worry. I won't demand you do anything you don't want to." She glanced over her shoulder, forcing an innocent look. "You do want to unzip my dress, don't you?" Megan fluttered her lashes for effect.

Daniel groaned. "Now who's being the tease?" He unzipped the dress and then slapped her bottom. "Go on. I'm not waiting for you if the food comes before you're out."

"I wouldn't expect you to." She marched into the bathroom and purposely left the door open as she pushed the dress off her shoulders, letting it float to the floor around her ankles. When she stepped out of her panties and straightened, naked, she cast a glance toward Daniel.

"Tease," he said.

"Peeping Tom." Megan winked and stepped into the shower, proud of herself for daring to flaunt her naked body. The cowboy had a huge complex about the difference between his background and hers, and she meant to pick that complex apart and get down to their similarities. She loved horses. Daniel loved horses. She loved seeing him naked. Apparently, Daniel wasn't immune to seeing her naked. Score one for the debutante.

Unfortunately, this battle had yet to be won. Tomorrow would be a huge skirmish with her parents. One she hoped they'd come out of unscathed and with her precious horses intact.

DANIEL CONTINUED TO stare at the closed shower curtain even after Megan disappeared behind it. He could imagine the water running over her pale skin, dripping off the tips of her breasts and down to that tuft of hair between her legs. He groaned.

Megan poked her head around the curtain, exposing a wet breast. "Did you say something?"

"No." Daniel choked on his response and turned away from the enticing view, his member hardening beneath the denim of his jeans. How was he supposed to keep his promise to himself and to her when she was so damned beautiful and sexy and, well, hell—Megan was everything a man could want in a woman. Soft skin. Silky, long, strawberry blond hair. A body a model would envy. And she was good with horses, wasn't afraid to get dirty and loved staring up at the stars at night.

He glanced out the window of the sitting room at the bright lights of the big city and wished he was back at the Lucky C Ranch in Oklahoma. Life was simpler there, and he didn't have to worry about cars running over him or his wife.

Wife.

He wasn't used to that word where Megan was concerned. But the more he said it, the better it sounded. And his grandmother's ring looked beautiful on her hand.

"It's gorgeous, isn't it?" Megan came to stand beside him, wearing a softly worn T-shirt and a pair of jersey knit shorts that hugged her buttocks and thighs like a second skin. Her hair hung halfway down her back in long, straight, damp tresses, a few strands curling as they dried.

Without makeup and dressed like a college student with bare feet and her bare breasts pressing against the cotton T-shirt, she was even more desirable than in the sheer teddy she'd worn the night before.

Who was he kidding? She could wear a paper sack and he'd be turned on.

A knock on the door forced him to focus on something other than the way her distended nipples formed tiny tents in the cotton shirt.

Daniel grabbed a five from his wallet and hurried to the door.

A man in a hotel uniform wheeled a cart in with two covered dishes, wineglasses and a shining bucket with a bottle of wine chilling in ice. Daniel tipped the man and held the door as he exited. He closed and locked the door, turning the dead bolt and sliding the chain in place.

Megan arranged the plate on the bistro table in the corner and smiled across at him. "Ready?"

He was ready for so much more than food, but he forced himself to take a seat across from her.

"Did you tell your parents why you were in Vegas?"

"My mother was more concerned about what I was flying in than why I was in Vegas. I guess it didn't occur to her I might be eloping. Now, if my father had been the one on the phone, that would have been his first question."

"Tell me about your father."

"My father is a taciturn man used to getting his way on the ranch and in the boardroom. He doesn't suffer fools well, and he can tell when someone is blowing smoke. So our stories have to match perfectly, or he'll figure it out."

"No pressure, right?" Daniel cut a slice of steak and popped it into his mouth, chewing on the food and the information Megan was feeding him. He swallowed. "Your father likes it best when you march to his beat, I take it."

"He does. I believe he thinks I'm an adolescent still in need of his protection. I'm surprised he didn't try to stop me when I moved to Oklahoma. He probably would have if I hadn't told him I was going out to visit an old college friend. I guess he couldn't conceive of the idea that I wouldn't come home." Megan glanced down at her plate, the food untouched. "I couldn't stay in California."

"Because of your father?"

"Mostly."

Daniel figured there was more to her story than her father's overbearing ways. When she was ready to tell him, he'd be there to listen.

They finished their meal in silence, sharing the bottle of wine. The alcohol took the edge off Daniel's desire and eased the tension between them. When they were done, they brushed their teeth at the double sink in the bathroom. For a moment, Daniel felt as though they were an old married couple, sharing the simple moments of married life. Megan finished before him and left the room.

When he was ready to call it a night, he walked into the bedroom, fully expecting to see Megan in the bed. It was empty.

He frowned and went to find her in the sitting room, curled up on the sofa, a pillow beneath her head and the comforter from the bed wrapped around her. She'd closed her eyes, but Daniel could tell she wasn't asleep.

"You can have the bed."

"I'm fine," she said and stuck one of her legs out from under the comforter, laying it on top. "Just a little hot."

Daniel stared at the long, slender leg as if willing her to cover it. Finally he stepped back and turned for the bedroom door, his rib hurting and a few other aches making themselves known from his tussle with the speeding car. "Good night."

"I hope you sleep well," she called out.

He could swear he heard a muffled chuckle, but when he turned back, she was lying still, her eyes closed. He must have been imagining the chuckle.

As he stretched out on the king-size bed, his arm fell over the empty space beside him, and he wished she was filling it. Daniel had to remind himself they were from two completely different worlds, and though she had assimilated well into his, he didn't belong in hers. The next day would prove that more than he cared to admit. Meeting her parents would help to keep him on track and focused on getting through this ordeal and back to his life at the Lucky C. There he and Megan would go back to being boss and employee, if she even wanted to return with him.

Daniel couldn't fall asleep knowing Megan was in the other room. Fear kept him awake—fear that he wouldn't hear if the door to the suite opened and the attackers returned. After fifteen minutes of straining his ears to hear every movement, he got up, marched into the sitting room and scooped Megan off the sofa.

"Hey," she cried. "What are you doing?"

"Getting a good-night's sleep." With her pressed against his body, he doubted that would happen, but he'd rest easier knowing he could protect her if she was in the same room as he was.

"What if I don't want to sleep with you?" She crossed her arms over her chest. "Put me down. I can walk."

He shook his head. "We're already halfway there," he said as he entered the bedroom and tossed her on the bed.

Megan landed with a grunt. "You don't have to be such a caveman," she groused, sliding over the mattress to the far side, away from Daniel. "I was perfectly fine in the other room." She pulled the sheet and blanket up over her arms and chest.

"Yeah, you might have been all right, but I wasn't." He lay down beside her and turned his back to her. "Just go to sleep, will you?"

"Sure." The bed moved, the blanket shifted and then her bottom bumped against his. "If that's what you want."

"It is." He swallowed hard to keep the groan rising in his throat from escaping. Sleep was the last thing on his mind. Making love to Megan was foremost in his thoughts and every nerve in his body.

A soft snort sounded from the other side of the bed. She knew.

Daniel gritted his teeth and forced his eyes closed. He'd keep his hands to himself if it killed him. And it likely would.

For a long time he lay there trying not to feel every move Megan made. Making love to her in the first place had been a big mistake. Now that he knew what it was like to hold her in his arms and thrust deep inside her…

His member thickened, and he started all over trying to turn off that part of his body. It was a battle he was destined to lose. One he would stay awake into the small hours of the morning fighting.

The best he could do was think about his bruises and the pain they gave him, along with the terror of seeing that vehicle coming straight at Megan. For the entire day he'd been out with her, he'd sensed something wasn't right, as if someone was watching them. Every time he'd turned around, no one stood out.

As he finally drifted off to sleep, Daniel was assailed by a sense of impending doom. The same feeling he'd had the moment before the car's engine revved and the driver barreled toward him and Megan.

CHAPTER ELEVEN

MEGAN WOKE BEFORE Daniel and slipped into a designer dress she knew was one of her mother's favorites, hoping to soften the shock of her daughter's elopement.

Her mother would protest, but deep down, she cared about Megan. To a fault.

Frank Talbot was another matter altogether. He'd be furious and ready to call in the lawyers to annul their union. The man was a complete control freak. If the deed wasn't his idea, it wasn't worth the legal documents it was written on.

Megan had to convince him that her marriage was what she wanted and that she loved Daniel with all her heart. Hopefully her father would buy it and leave it at that.

Megan buckled the strap of her stilettos and stood, teetering. God, she hated heels. She preferred wearing her boots every day instead of the trappings of a debutante. When she'd left California, she'd vowed never to wear high heels again. And here she was, ready to break an ankle climbing in and out of an airplane in them.

She had to remind herself she was doing all of this for the horses. A thrill of excitement rippled through her at the thought of seeing her beautiful horses again.

"Do you want to eat breakfast before we go?" Daniel emerged from the bedroom, wearing blue jeans, a crisp white button-down shirt and a brown leather jacket. His dark hair hung longish, nearly to his shoulders, and one errant strand dipped down over his forehead, giving him a roguish flare.

Megan's heart fluttered over Daniel Colton. He was a beautiful man with his high cheekbones, rich complexion and eyes so dark a woman could fall into them and never want to come out.

His sooty brows sank. "Are you okay?"

Megan shook herself out of her lust-fest over the half-Cherokee man. It was *his* fault she couldn't concentrate. She was almost certain that if he'd given in and made love to her last night, she wouldn't have been so off-kilter now. Focusing on his words, she answered, "I'm fine. Why do you ask?"

"I also asked if you wanted to have breakfast before we left, or would you prefer to wait until we get to Santa Rosa?"

"I prefer to wait. My stomach is knotted."

Daniel held out his hand. "Everything is going to work according to plan."

She laid hers in his. "I hope so."

He squeezed gently and then released it. "Let's go. I can file our flight plan once I get to the airport."

"How long is the flight?" Megan asked.

"An hour and a half."

That would put them in around lunchtime. "I'll call the attorney's office and see if we can get in right away."

"Good." He reentered the bedroom and came back out carrying his bag and hers. "Did you sleep all right?"

She smiled brightly and lied, "I did, thank you. How about you? Did you sleep okay?"

"Yes." The dark shadows under his eyes and the firmness of his jaw told a different story. Megan had felt his every move through the night and had chosen to let him suffer as much as she did. She'd been sure to bump up against him on purpose so that he'd be reminded of what he was missing. She'd thought maybe, just maybe, he'd turn over, pull her into his arms and make love to her.

That hadn't happened, shaking Megan's belief that he was as aroused as she had been. But seeing how tired he was gave her a thrill she wouldn't admit to Daniel.

He'd have to get over his prejudice against her for her lineage. To her, its only advantage was to provide a little leverage in Daniel's negotiation with Kennedy Farms.

It had been a wake-up call to her, reminding her of why she didn't belong in the fast-moving, big-spending limelight of her family's wealth and notoriety. Had Chase lived and they had gone through with the wedding, their marriage wouldn't have lasted an entire year.

Chase Buchannan was charming and sexy. He lived life in the fast lane. Having grown up the son of a high-powered movie producer, he'd been everywhere and done everything, including drugs and racing. He loved his cars fast and his women faster. Why he'd asked Megan to marry him was a mystery to her.

She had accepted his proposal to shock her parents. Unfortunately, her desire to shock had backfired. Chase's connections met with her father's approval, if not her mother's. Megan had hoped Chase loved her for herself. Only later did she realize she'd desperately wanted to be loved to the point she would have married a man completely wrong for her. Chase was more in love with living on the edge than he ever was in love with her.

Megan gathered her purse and followed Daniel out

of the hotel room, studying the man who'd offered to marry her to help her save the horses she loved so much.

If Daniel was as passionate about a woman as he was about his horses, he'd be a man who would love her completely and sacrifice everything to protect her and make her happy.

He worried that his heritage made him a bad match. In Megan's view, it made him even more appealing because he had to work hard to prove himself. The boys Megan grew up with tended to be lazy and took everything for granted, including their friends.

Daniel was as loyal to his friends as he was to his family. If only he could see that he was not inferior stock. His Cherokee blood made him even more appealing to Megan along with his lack of pedigree. He wouldn't always be targeted by the paparazzi, his life on display for everyone to see and criticize. Married to Daniel, Megan could live her life the way she wanted. The way she'd done for the past four months.

She loved it and had learned so much from Daniel about breeding horses and caring for the animals and people he loved.

Daniel hailed a cab that took them to the airport where the Colton plane was parked.

After a thorough preflight check, he filed his flight plan, loaded their luggage and helped her up into the plane.

A short taxi on the runway and they were in the air, flying west to face her parents and the attorney with the real marriage certificate for their fake marriage.

Feeling a little let down by the entire affair, Megan sat silently for the majority of the ride, speaking only when she had a question about the plane's instruments.

She enjoyed the scenery from the small windows, marveling at how close the plane flew to the mountaintops.

Daniel piloted the craft with skill and confidence. By the time they cleared the Sierra Nevada Mountains and descended into the Santa Rosa Airport, Megan had gone over every possible scenario that could happen when she introduced Daniel to her parents. Her nerves were stretched taut as the landing gear kissed the runway.

Daniel brought the plane to a halt at one of the general aviation hangars and shut down the engine. He turned to her and smiled. "You look like you're about to face the firing squad."

"I feel like I am."

He sighed and held out his hand. "It'll be all right. The marriage certificate is legal. We've consummated the marriage. Your parents can't undo what's been done."

Megan shook her head. "You don't know my father. He has the most expensive attorneys with the most clout on retainer. The man can do anything he wants to do."

"Except order you around. That's what I'm for." He winked at her and reached across to unbuckle her safety harness, his knuckles brushing against her belly, sending flickers of electricity shooting across her body. "Come on. We have an appointment with your grandmother's attorney. One step at a time will get you through this."

Megan held on to his hand when he would have pulled it free. "In case I haven't told you, thank you for doing this for me. You didn't have to marry me."

"Remember, I'm getting something out of this marriage, too. I should be thanking you."

"Don't thank me until you get Kennedy to agree to sell you the semen for your breeding program." She let him help her out of the plane and onto the ground, liking the feel of his hand on the small of her back as they caught a shuttle to the rental car companies.

A half hour later, they were driving away from the airport in a sleek black SUV.

Megan used her cell phone's GPS to get them to the office of her grandmother's attorney, Lloyd Young. A receptionist showed them into a conference room and offered them bottled water or coffee. When they declined, she left.

An older gentleman with graying temples strode into the room. Megan recognized him. He'd read her grandmother's will four years ago. He greeted her with a warm handshake. "Megan, it's good to see you." He held out his hand to Daniel.

"Mr. Young, this is Daniel Colton. My husband." Megan stumbled on the word. It was so new to her.

Daniel held out his hand and shook the lawyer's.

Mr. Young's brows rose. "This is a surprise." He grinned and glanced back at Megan. "Congratulations. When was the happy occasion?"

"Two days ago," Megan answered. She hooked her arm through Daniel's.

The attorney nodded. "I take it you didn't come to pay a social call."

"Not really," Megan admitted. "I've come to claim the trust fund my grandmother left me."

The attorney nodded. "Let me check the wording in the will. Seems to me the trust wasn't released until your thirtieth birthday or until you married, whichever came first."

Megan dug in her purse for the marriage certificate and handed it over to the lawyer. "Seems I met the marriage clause first."

Mr. Young took the certificate. "I'll have a copy made and return it to you. Please, make yourselves comfortable while I go over the will. My secretary will see to your needs."

"Thank you." As soon as the attorney left the conference room, Megan's shoulders sagged. "I hope this doesn't take too long. I'm sure it's been four years since Mr. Young looked at that will. I can't remember the exact wording. I know I had to be married. But I'm not sure there wasn't another stipulation associated with the trust."

"We'll know soon enough," Daniel said.

"Either way, we won't get the money today. It's probably tied up in a bank, and I'll have to sign for it."

"Once you have it, you'll be closer to purchasing your horses from your father."

Megan smiled. "I think you'll like them. They're good quality stock. Some of the best the Triple Diamond has to offer."

"I look forward to seeing them."

"If my father and mother let us." She faced a large painting of Northern California's craggy coastline, her stomach as churned up as the sea splashing against the rocky shore.

"You're a grown woman. Why would they keep you from them?"

"My mother still thinks I'm too fragile to be around such large animals. Even though that's all I've done since I moved to Oklahoma." Megan paced the length of the conference table and paused at the window, staring out at the bright blue sky. "I wish my parents didn't feel like they have to control me."

"No one can control you." Daniel stepped up behind

her and rested his hands on her shoulders, the warmth and firmness helping to steady her nerves. "You're your own individual, with the right to make your own decisions."

She snorted. "Yeah, thus the reason I'm here."

Daniel's hands slid down to her hips and he pulled her back against him, his arms circling her waist. "We'll get through this. Your horses will not be sold."

"I hope you're right." She rested her hands over his and leaned against him. Though she valued her independence, she loved how protected she felt in Daniel's arms. Too bad it was all for show.

The sound of a man clearing his throat made her jump, and she spun out of Daniel's arms to face Mr. Young. Heat suffused her cheeks, and she pushed her hair back from her face.

"I hope I'm not intruding." The attorney smiled and waved toward the conference table. "I took a moment to read through the wording. It seems you will have access to some of your money immediately upon your marriage, and the rest of the trust fund will be transferred over in full upon the six-month anniversary of your wedding."

Megan's heart dipped into her belly. This part she hadn't remembered. If she couldn't get all the money, she might not be able to afford all seven horses. "How much will be released now?"

"One hundred thousand dollars." He pointed to the document.

Megan read it, her chest tightening when she got to the part about being married six months before the remainder of the funds would be released. She couldn't look up and face Daniel without revealing her tears.

A hand slid into her lap and squeezed her knee. Even

with the disappointing news, he was there to reassure her that all would be well. More tears welled up in her eyes.

Mr. Young pushed a box of tissues under her nose.

"Thank you." Megan grabbed a tissue and pressed it to her face.

"Your grandmother loved you very much and wanted to protect you against fortune hunters." Mr. Young held up a hand. "Not that I think your new husband will take advantage of you."

Daniel's hand stilled on her knee. Megan slid hers over his. "My husband doesn't want my money."

Daniel pulled a sheet of paper out of his pocket and handed it to Mr. Young. "Although it hasn't been filed with the courts, I wrote out a prenuptial agreement and had it witnessed by one of the hotel staff in Vegas before our wedding."

Megan frowned. "When did you do that?"

"While you were getting dressed for the ceremony."

"You didn't have to do that."

"Yes. I did." He cupped her cheek. "I didn't want anyone, including you, to think that I wanted anything other than the pleasure of having you as my wife."

She gave him a watery smile and swallowed hard to dislodge the lump in her throat. If only his words were true.

"If you don't mind, I'd like to make a copy of it for our records." Mr. Young took the paper from Daniel and stepped out of the office for a moment, leaving Megan alone with Daniel.

Still reeling from Daniel's words and the fact that she wouldn't have access to all the money in her grandmother's trust fund, Megan stared at the papers in front of her. "One hundred thousand dollars might not be enough to buy all of the horses if they go for auction to other breeders."

"If he plans to sell them to a glue factory, it will be more than enough."

Mr. Young returned, handed the prenuptial agreement to Daniel and turned to Megan. "It will take a couple days to get these documents through the system. Where will you be in the meantime?"

"If her parents will have us, we'll stay at the Triple Diamond Ranch."

"Good. I'll let you know when you can access the money."

Megan stood and held out her hand to the attorney. "My grandmother had a lot of faith in you. Thank you for taking care of her and her assets."

"She was a good woman, and she only wanted the best for you." Mr. Young held out his hand to Daniel. "Take care of her. Her family cares a great deal for her."

"I'll do my very best," Daniel answered, shaking the man's hand.

As Megan stepped out into the sunshine, she drew in a deep breath and let it out. "I'm sorry."

"For what?"

"I'd forgotten about the six-month stipulation. I didn't pay much attention at the reading four years ago."

"I'm sure you were still grieving for your grandmother."

Megan smiled. "She encouraged me to be the person I wanted to be. Not the person my parents thought I should be. It was because of her that I finally moved away from California."

"She sounds like a wonderful woman."

"Just so you know, I don't expect you to stay married

to me for six months. If I can make the money last long enough to purchase my horses and move them somewhere safe, that will be enough for me."

"We'll worry about the six months later. Right now, let's concentrate on getting your horses from your father."

"Are you ready to meet my parents?" She glanced up at him, trying to read his face for any sign that he'd had enough of playing charades.

"I'm ready. I think the real question is, are you ready?" He held out his hand.

She laughed and took his. "As ready as I'll ever be. Let's go to the Triple Diamond Ranch."

CHAPTER TWELVE

DANIEL FOLLOWED THE GPS on his smartphone to the address Megan gave him. Forty-five minutes later, he pulled up to a large stone-and-iron gate with an arched sign over the top indicating the Triple Diamond Ranch.

In the seat beside him, Megan stiffened, her hands clenched in her lap. She gave him the code for the keypad without turning toward him.

After entering the code, Daniel waited as the gate swung open.

Megan leaned forward, her gaze sweeping the pastures to the left and right of the long drive. "I don't see any of the horses."

"Perhaps they have them in another pasture."

"Perhaps." She pulled her bottom lip between her teeth and continued to scan the fields between the stands of trees blocking visibility from the SUV's windows.

The drive curved and angled up an incline lined with tall trees. When they emerged from the forest, a huge, sprawling mansion spread out before them.

"Home, sweet home," Megan muttered, looking anything but excited about the prospect of visiting the beautiful house with the French-vanilla stucco, arched entrance and Roman columns. Surrounded by lush landscaping and bright blue skies, the home was something most people only dreamed of.

"It's beautiful."

"My mother had a hand in the design. They built it when I was a toddler."

Daniel mentally compared the mansion to the single-wide mobile home he and his mother lived in for the first ten years of his life. He had nothing in common with this lifestyle, which made anything permanent between him and Megan even more impossible.

"Did you call ahead to let your parents know what time to expect us?"

"No. They just know it's today. Maybe they will have a prior commitment and we can let ourselves in."

The front door opened, and a woman stepped through. She wore a tailored dress and high heels, and her red hair was twisted into an elegant knot at the back of her head.

She was followed by a man with a shock of neatly combed white hair and smoothly tanned skin.

"Your parents?" Daniel asked.

"That's them."

"You look a lot like your mother."

"I've been told that." Megan glanced around the circular drive. "You can leave the vehicle here. Someone will move it to the garage."

Daniel shifted the SUV into Park, climbed out of the vehicle and rounded the hood to the other side. Thankfully Megan waited for him to open the door. He held out his arm and she accepted it, letting him help her out of the SUV.

She hooked her hand through his elbow and pasted a smile on her face.

Daniel could see the strain in her expression as she faced her parents.

"Megan." Her mother moved forward, her face

wreathed in smiles. She engulfed her daughter in a fierce hug. "I'm so glad you decided to come home."

Her father stood on the top step, his brows angling downward in a V. He was a big man, but not quite as tall as Daniel. His face was lined with experience. Permanent creases were engraved in his brow, probably from years of frowning. Though tanned, his skin had a slightly gray tint to it, and the whites of his eyes were tinged yellow.

Megan hugged her mother and glanced up at her father. "Father."

He nodded. "I shouldn't have to threaten you to get you to return to where you belong."

Megan's frown equaled her father's. "I'm here for now. Can't you be happy?"

The man's scowl deepened. "Your mother has been beside herself."

"Oh, don't let him scare you, dear. I'm just happy you're here." Josephine Talbot clasped her daughter's hand and tugged her toward the house. "Come inside and get unpacked. You must be exhausted."

"No, Mother." Megan pulled her arm from her mother's grasp and leaned into Daniel. "This is Daniel Colton."

"Daniel Colton." Mrs. Talbot's brows wrinkled. "Megan's boss, right?"

"Yes, ma'am."

She pressed her hand to her chest. "How nice of you to see Megan safely home."

"Mother, he's not just my boss anymore." Megan's cheeks reddened.

Daniel felt sorry for her and stepped forward. "What she's trying to tell you is that Megan and I got married two days ago. We're husband and wife." He lifted Megan's hand and pressed a kiss to the backs of her knuckles.

"What the hell do you mean? Married?" Daniel's announcement made Frank Talbot leave his position towering over the rest of them and march down the stairs to confront Daniel and Megan. "Is this true?"

Megan nodded and held up her left hand with the simple ring Daniel had slid onto her finger. Standing in front of a multimillion-dollar mansion, Daniel figured the ring appeared cheap, despite how rich it was in memories and the love his grandmother had shared with his grandfather.

Mrs. Talbot's eyes widened. "You got married?"

Megan nodded. "We did."

"I had such plans for a beautiful wedding for you."

"A wedding with someone we knew," her father grumbled, glaring at Daniel. "Someone suitable."

Megan's back stiffened and she took a step, placing her body between her father and Daniel. "Daniel is more than suitable. He loves me, and I love him. That's all that matters."

"I'm sure he loves you, and every cent you stand to inherit." Her father's face turned ruddy. "I won't stand for this."

Megan threw back her shoulders, her green eyes flashing. "You don't have to stand for it. It was my choice, and I chose Daniel. Besides, he doesn't want my money or yours."

Daniel chuckled at the fierceness of her defense. "Sweetheart, I can stand up for myself." He gripped her shoulders and moved her back to his side. Daniel stuck out his hand. "Mr. Talbot, I'm Daniel Colton, and

I'm happy to make your acquaintance as the father of my bride. If we aren't welcome here, we will be on our way." He stood for a long moment, his hand held out, waiting.

"Frank," Mrs. Talbot said sharply.

Megan's father finally took Daniel's hand and squeezed it with a bone-crunching grip.

Daniel was used to sturdy handshakes, but Frank Talbot was making a point. Pasting a smile on his face, Daniel squeezed back.

Despite the man's recent sickness, he had a killer grip, and he was letting Daniel know he wasn't a wimp.

Though he could swear his bones were breaking, Daniel refused to be the first to release. He bit down on his tongue to keep from yelling out.

Josephine Talbot clucked her tongue. "Come, Megan. Let me help you carry our bags into the house, while those two strut." She rolled her eyes and stepped around her husband. "Men."

Megan cleared her throat. "Father, Daniel. Are you two going to let us carry our things into the house?"

Frank's gaze met Daniel's. "Of course not."

Daniel stared at the man a moment longer and then loosened his grip at the same time as Frank.

He wanted to shake the blood back into his fingers, but he didn't dare show a single sign of weakness in front of Megan's father. Instead, he used his left hand to click the release on the back of the vehicle and unloaded his and Megan's bags.

"You didn't bring much with you," Mrs. Talbot said.

"We're not staying long," Megan announced. "We only stopped by to check on how you and Father are doing. And we wanted to let you know of our marriage."

Her father crossed his arms over his chest. "I haven't approved this union."

"Father, I'm twenty-eight, I don't need your approval to marry whom I want."

Her father's chest puffed out. "As a Talbot, you have certain obligations."

"Well, I'm not a Talbot anymore, now, am I?" She pushed her shoulders back and lifted her chin. "My last name is Colton."

Her father opened his mouth and then snapped it shut, his lips thinning into a straight line. "We'll see."

"Father—" Megan said with a warning frown.

"Megan? Is that you?" a voice called out from the front door. A woman with light blond hair and blue eyes ran down the steps and hugged Megan. "I haven't seen you in forever." She hugged her again and stepped back to examine her. "You look good. Oklahoma sunshine must agree with you."

"Hey, Christine. I didn't know you were here." She looked to Daniel. "This is my cousin."

"Christine has been living at the Triple Diamond for the past month. She apparently cares what happens to us," Frank said.

Megan's green eyes flared. "I care about you, Father. I love you very much, but I won't let you live my life for me."

"Obviously. You moved to Oklahoma without so much as a goodbye, and now this." He waved his hand at Daniel.

"This is my husband. I would hope you'd treat him with some respect."

Daniel almost smiled at how natural the word *hus-*

band rolled off Megan's lips, and he had the sudden urge to pull her into his arms and kiss her.

"Frank," Mrs. Talbot's entreaty pierced the anger in Frank's attack.

A muscle ticked in the older man's jaw. "My apologies."

"Husband?" Christine's eyes widened. "You got married?"

Megan nodded. "We did."

"Let me see the ring." Christine grabbed her hand and lifted it to the light. "Oh, the ring is so pretty and old-fashioned. I simply love it. Aren't you going to introduce me to your hunky husband?"

Megan turned to Daniel. "Daniel Colton, meet my cousin, Christine. She's my father's niece. Christine and I are the last of the Talbots, since our fathers only had one daughter each."

"Oh, don't be so stuffy. All this heritage stuff is silly, anyway." Christine held out her hand and Daniel took it.

"My thoughts exactly," Megan muttered.

"It's just like you to beat me to the draw." Christine laughed. "I thought for sure I'd be next to the altar and here you go and get married." Her cousin raised her left hand, flashing a large marquis diamond. "I'm engaged!"

Daniel's chest tightened at yet another reminder of the difference between his and Megan's worlds.

Megan's smile was tight, but she managed to say, "That's wonderful, Christine. Who is he?"

"Josh Townsend. He's a real estate agent in LA. You'll get to meet him. He'll be here late this afternoon."

"Let's go inside out of the hot sun," Mrs. Talbot said, ushering the group into the cool interior of the mansion.

He'd thought the outside of the house was ostentatious, but the inside outdid the exterior in luxury. White marble floors stretched across the immense foyer. Two carved staircases rose up on either side to the second floor with dark mahogany railings and richly carpeted steps.

The ceiling rose high overhead with bright skylights letting in ample sunlight.

"Where do you want us to put our things?" Megan asked her mother.

"Why, in your old room, of course." Mrs. Talbot waved to a servant. "Let Manny carry them up for you. I'll have our housekeeper, Maggie, bring tea into the sitting room."

"I'd like to wash my hands first," Megan said.

"Me, too." Daniel smiled at Mrs. Talbot. "Thank you."

"You can show Daniel to your room."

Frank Talbot growled beneath his breath.

Mrs. Talbot turned on her husband. "If you can't be nice, go fiddle with your horses or something. I want to spend time with my daughter, even if you don't." She softened her demand with, "But don't push yourself. You're still recovering."

"I'm perfectly fine," Frank insisted.

"For a man who had prostate surgery less than a month ago."

Frank Talbot left the house, grumbling, "Woman has no right to throw my illness around like a weapon."

Mrs. Talbot turned to Daniel and Megan. "Now, you two go on. I'll have something cold to drink waiting for you when you come down."

"If you don't mind, we've been cooped up for a long time in an airplane. After tea, we'd like to stretch our legs."

"Oh, by all means. We can catch up more at supper." Mrs. Talbot smiled. "You can walk in the garden if you like."

"Daniel and I would prefer to go down to the barn and see the horses," Megan said, her gaze following her father out the door. "That is, if they haven't been sold off yet."

Josephine Talbot shook her head. "Your father is all bark."

Megan's lips thinned. "I never know when he will actually bite."

Her mother touched her arm. "Darling, not as often as you think."

Megan turned to face her mother. "Are you saying he was bluffing about selling my horses?"

"Yes and no." Her mother sighed. "He is determined to sell them eventually, and I want him to."

"Mother!" Megan shook her head, her eyes filling with tears. "I love those horses."

"And your father loves you and me. He would do anything to have you closer." Mrs. Talbot touched her daughter's arm. "Please don't hate him."

Daniel's belly tightened. He could see the love and concern in her mother's eyes. The woman was caught between two very independent and stubborn people and was trying to play mediator to keep her family together.

"Go upstairs and wash up. We'll talk in a few minutes." Mrs. Talbot laid a hand on Daniel's shoulder as he walked by. "I promise we're not always this difficult."

Daniel smiled at the woman, liking her in that instant. "I'll reserve judgment."

"That's all I ask." The older Talbot woman nodded and walked away.

Megan paused, halfway up the stairs, her gaze moved from her mother to Daniel. "Are you coming?"

"Just because we're married doesn't mean you get to boss me around." He took the stairs two at a time to catch up with her and patted her on the bottom.

"Hey." She slapped at his hand, her cheeks reddening. "That's mine."

"We're married now. What's mine is yours and what's yours is mine."

"You could have gone along with that rule last night," she muttered.

He grabbed her, cupped the back of her head and nibbled on her ear. "Hey, babe, it's all about the show." Oh, but his body wasn't getting the picture. Holding her this close, touching her bottom and kissing the side of her neck made him forget they were playing a game of charades. He wanted to take her the rest of the way up the stairs, find the nearest bedroom and make use of the bed.

But her mother was waiting, and her father was livid. This game wasn't going to be a dunk.

MEGAN'S BLOOD SIZZLED through her veins, her neck tingling with the touch of Daniel's lips. Once she had him in her room and shut the door behind her, she rounded on him, her hands on her hips. "This is not going to work."

"No? Your parents seem to think it's all real."

"I'm not talking about what my parents are thinking. I'm talking about you touching me, kissing me and patting my butt."

"Liked that added touch of reality?" He winked. "I thought you'd want me to show a little PDA in front of your family."

"PDA?"

"Public display of affection." He entered the bathroom and switched on the water faucet. "Most newlyweds can't keep their hands off each other. We're supposed to be madly in love, thus the quickie wedding in Vegas. That would be one of the two reasons for getting married so fast."

Megan leaned against the bathroom door frame. "And the other?"

"One of us being pregnant." Daniel leaned over the sink and splashed water in his face.

If Megan wasn't mistaken, Daniel was grinning beneath his hands. She grabbed a hand towel from the cabinet and slung it at him. "Well, we both know that isn't going to happen." Her eyes widened. "But my parents don't know that. Crap. Do you think they think we're...you know." The thought of carrying Daniel's baby warmed her insides at the same time it left an empty ache in her womb.

Daniel straightened, wiping his face with a towel. "I have no idea what your parents are thinking, other than my hand hurts and your dad hates me."

"He doesn't hate you. He hates the idea he's not the main man in my life anymore. Did he crush your hand?" Megan shook her head. "He did that to every one of my dates. Scared them off."

"I can see why." Daniel shook his hand.

"How did you keep a straight face and not yell?"

Daniel twirled the towel and popped her with it. "I'm not a teenaged weakling. I work with my hands."

"Sorry. I have nightmares about my father's attitude toward the boys I met."

"You're twenty-eight. You can't tell me he chased away all of them."

"No." Megan didn't offer more. She didn't see a need in enlightening Daniel about her prior engagement. Instead, she raised her brows. "Are you done? Think I might have a chance at that sink?"

"All yours." He tossed the towel on the counter and stepped around her. The doorway was too tight for both of them to fit through at once.

Megan refused to give way. If he wanted by, he'd have to touch her, and to hell with his hands-off approach to their marriage.

Daniel turned sideways and started through the doorway. When his hip touched hers, she stared up into his eyes, challenging him. Yes, she wanted him, and she'd bet her best thong panties he could see it in her eyes.

Daniel paused, his hips pressed to hers. "You're playing with fire, woman."

"Yeah. Unfortunately, there's no one here willing to put out the flame."

For a moment, she thought he'd move past. But his hands shot out and grabbed her wrists, pinning them above her head. Her breath caught in her throat and her breasts jutted out, the nipples hardening against his chest.

"You're making this more difficult than it has to be," he grumbled.

"I know." She swiveled her hips, her pelvis rubbing over the hard evidence of his desire. "That was the idea."

"Damn, woman." He bent, his lips crashing down on hers, stealing her breath away.

His tongue lashed out, darted between her parted lips and claimed her mouth, her tongue and her soul.

She tugged against his hold on her wrists, wanting to wrap her arms around his neck.

Daniel held firm, refusing to release her.

The frustration of not being able to touch him made her even hotter and more desperate to be one with the man. When he finally allowed her to breathe again, she was on fire with a need only he could satisfy.

"Wash up, sweetheart. Your mother is waiting." He turned her toward the bathroom and swatted her behind.

Megan didn't protest. She couldn't. Her mind was in a lust-induced fog, too befuddled to let a coherent thought surface. She'd gotten what she wanted. A kiss to douse the flames. Only it had backfired and fanned the blaze instead, leaving her wanting more of the same.

Megan splashed water on her face and dried off with a towel, staring at herself in the mirror. Her lips were full and swollen from Daniel's kiss. What was she going to do? The more she was with him, the more deeply she fell in love with her husband.

How long would they have to keep up the pretense of a loving marriage? And when it was all over, how would she continue to work with the man knowing what it was like to be married to him?

Megan pulled her hair back, secured it in a loose, messy bun and shook her head. Her mother was a fastidious dresser. Every hair had to be in place and her makeup perfect before she left her room each day. Though her mother tried to instill the same sense of style and confidence in her looks, Megan always fell short, opting out of wearing makeup and refusing to go to great lengths to fix her hair. She could be seen with a ponytail and a clean face most often.

Daniel didn't seem to mind, and the horses didn't care. Why should she?

Megan smoothed the wrinkles out of her dress and left the bathroom.

Daniel held out his arm. "Ready?"

"As ready as I'll ever be." They descended the staircase and entered the sitting room in which her mother had entertained many of the social elite including several political figures and movie stars. The Talbots were as well-known in California as the Coltons were in Oklahoma.

Christine sat on the sofa beside Megan's mother, chattering away about a mutual acquaintance.

"Oh, there you are." Mrs. Talbot rose and waved a hand toward another sofa facing the one she and Christine sat on.

It didn't strike Megan as odd that Christine was so chummy with her mother. Close in age, Megan and Christine had spent quite a few summers together on the Triple Diamond Ranch. They both loved the horses, and they enjoyed the outdoors. Christine's father had taken her and her mother to New York City to live. Not until her mother died of cancer and her father in a car wreck four years ago had she returned to California for good.

Mrs. Talbot took her seat on the sofa and lifted a pitcher of lemonade. "I have hot tea, but I thought as warm as it is outside, you might prefer iced lemonade. And I had the cook make up a tray of sandwiches in case you two are hungry."

"Thank you, Mother. We didn't stop for lunch on the way over."

Daniel helped himself to a triangle of bread and deli meat. "Thank you for thinking of it."

Her mother's smile filled the room. "We're just happy you're finally here."

Megan bit into a sandwich and chewed. She wanted to get outside and check on her horses, but she didn't want her parents to think that was the only reason she'd come home. She didn't want her father to know how much his threat had shaken her.

"Christine was regaling me with stories of her life in LA," Mrs. Talbot said.

"How is your acting career taking off?" Megan asked politely.

Her cousin smiled. "I had a callback from a commercial audition last week. I'm waiting for my agent to contact me."

"Are you going to continue acting after you're married, dear?" Mrs. Talbot asked.

"Yes, of course." Christine glanced at Megan. "Josh is behind me."

"Will he have a decent job to support you while you're pursuing your career?" Megan's mother asked.

"He's in real estate. He's quite good at it. Right now he's on his way back from a convention in Nevada. He should be here for dinner, so you can meet him."

"That will be nice," Megan said, wishing her cousin wasn't there and feeling bad that she had such thoughts. What she wanted was time alone with her mother so she could question her about her father. Alas, Christine was there to stay and completely oblivious to a mother and daughter's need for a private conversation.

Daniel polished off another triangular sandwich and drank a glass of lemonade.

Megan picked at a sandwich and sipped at the lemonade, counting the minutes until she could politely escape.

"Mrs. Talbot, like Megan mentioned, we have been cooped up in a plane for the last few hours. Would you mind if we went outside to stretch our legs?" Daniel asked.

"But of course you should. You can stroll in the garden behind the house or see the horses."

"Megan tells me the Triple Diamond Ranch has some of the best quarter horses in the country," Daniel said.

Her mother shrugged. "That's Frank's pet project. I wish he'd just sell them and concentrate on staying well and healthy."

"Daniel is a horse breeder. He's working on his own breeding program in Oklahoma." Megan rose to her feet, glad of Daniel's segue into getting out of the house. "I'd like to show him the barn."

"Oh, darling, should you be out there? Those horses are so big and spirited."

"I'm a biologist. I work with animals." When Megan's mother wasn't swayed from her fears, Megan sighed and added, "Daniel will be there to protect me, Mother."

Something akin to a snort erupted from Daniel, and a smile tilted his lips upward on the corners.

Megan elbowed him in the side. "Besides, I want to check on Father."

Daniel wiped the smile off his face and offered, "I'll keep your daughter from undue harm caused by the horses, Mrs. Talbot."

"It's just that Megan is our only daughter and, well, I don't want her to be harmed."

"Mother, I'll be fine with Daniel," Megan assured her mother again.

"Oh, let them go." Christine stood beside Mrs. Talbot and slipped an arm around her aunt. "They're newlyweds. They probably just want time alone together."

Megan gave Christine a smile. "That's right. We want

some time alone. And I want to make sure Father is okay."

Megan led Daniel out through the back of the house. They skirted the glistening swimming pool and a pool house and followed a stone path through a rose garden before they emerged on a paved road leading to the stables.

"The last time I was here, my father had been in the hospital for prostate cancer. They think they got all of it, but he's been going through chemotherapy to kill any remaining cells," Megan said.

"I'm sure he's happy to have you here," Daniel said.

She smiled, her chest swelling for the handsome man beside her. He was the kind of man her father couldn't scare easily, and for that she was grateful. "I'm happy you're here with me." Her attention returned to the stable and the surrounding fields. "I don't see any of the horses."

"Don't borrow trouble. They're probably inside or out behind the stable."

"I hope so." She hated to think her father had made good on his threat and sold her horses. Then her marriage to Daniel might still help snag him a deal with the Kennedys, but on her end, it would have been for nothing.

The door to the stable stood wide-open, the interior dark compared with the bright sunshine outside.

Megan stepped through the door and inhaled the familiar scents of hay, horses and manure. A whinny sounded from one of the stalls and another answered, followed by several more.

Daniel leaned close to whisper in her ear, "Seems your horses are here and they remember you."

Joy filled Megan's heart and she ran to the first stall, long ago designated as Misty Rein's. The beautiful bay mare tossed her head above the gate and whinnied again.

Thank God. Her father hadn't sold her horses, yet.

DANIEL FOLLOWED MEGAN to the first stall and ran an appreciative gaze over the animal. She had good conformation, and from what he could see of her teeth and her coat, she was healthy and well taken care of.

His belly tightened at the smile spreading across Megan's face.

She ran her hand along the mare's nose and pressed her tear-stained cheek to the side of the animal's face. "They're still here."

"Of course, they're still here." Her father appeared out of the shadows. "They were my only bargaining chip to get you back to the Triple Diamond."

Megan turned toward her father, color rising in her cheeks. "You tricked me into coming back?"

"I had to do something. You broke your mother's heart when you left."

"I never wanted to hurt you two. I just couldn't live the way you wanted me to. I'm happy in Oklahoma. Happier than I've ever been."

Frank Talbot's eyes narrowed. "Then I guess you didn't come home to stay."

"No. I came home to tell you of my marriage to Daniel." She slipped her arm around Daniel's waist and leaned into him.

Daniel liked the feel of her body next to his. The casual hug warmed his heart and heated other places inside. But mostly, it made him feel good, and he wanted that feeling to go on forever.

Mr. Talbot shook his head. "I wish you had told us before."

Megan tensed. "Before I got married? Why? So that you could talk me out of it?" She reached for her father's hands. "I love Daniel. He understands me, and we have the same dreams."

"And what are those?"

Daniel straightened at the man's challenge. "I'm building a horse-breeding program at the Lucky C Ranch."

"It's hard to make a living with horses."

"Daniel is doing great. His horses are receiving national attention."

Daniel squeezed her arm. "But you're right, sir."

Megan glanced toward him, her brows puckered.

"It is hard to make a living at breeding horses. But I have acquired some excellent stock, and I'm hoping to improve my herd by investing in semen from a national champion stud from Kennedy Farms."

Megan's father's brows rose briefly and then lowered. "You talk the talk, but Kennedy isn't an easy man to work with."

Daniel forced himself to relax. "I've noticed. But I'm working on him. I have a meeting scheduled with him at the Symposium on Equine Reproduction in Reno in a few days."

"He granted you a meeting?" Talbot shot a glance at his daughter. "Are you going?"

Megan nodded. "I am."

Her father scowled. "Your mother never wanted you working around the horses."

Megan gave him a soft smile. "You knew I was all along, didn't you?"

"Someone had to keep an eye on you. You had a mind of your own and a tree far too close to your bedroom window."

Her eyes widened. "You knew I was sneaking out?"

He nodded. "I'd have done it, too."

"Then why didn't you just give me permission to be around the horses?"

"Your mother never knew, and it was better that way." Her father reached out to run his hand along the mare's neck. "Your mother had three miscarriages before she was able to carry a baby almost to full term."

"And I was a preemie." Megan's face softened.

Her father's hand stilled on the horse. "She almost lost you, too. I have to tell you, I don't ever want to see your mother that sad ever again."

Megan's arm tightened around Daniel. "How awful to lose three children and almost the fourth. No wonder she's overprotective. I can't imagine losing even one child." Her eyes misted.

Daniel hugged her close.

"Well, now you know why I had to get you back. Your mother was sad." Frank Talbot shook his head. "I will not allow her to be sad."

"But, Dad, I can't stay. My life is in Oklahoma."

"Now that she knows you are happily married, she might be okay with you living so far away." Mr. Talbot stared hard between Megan and Daniel. "You are happy, aren't you? This man didn't twist your arm to marry him, did he?"

Megan laughed. "Not at all. We're…" She ducked her head, her cheeks suffusing with color.

"I asked Megan to marry me because I couldn't imag-

ine life without her. We love each other," Daniel finished, leaning down to kiss her temple.

For a long moment Mr. Talbot studied them, and then
he nodded. "Okay. But please don't tell your mother
you're working with the horses in Oklahoma. She'll be
hard-pressed to come to grips with the fact that you're
happily married. Sure as I breathe, she'll worry herself
into an early grave if she thinks you're going back to
work with the breeding program."

"But that's what I do," Megan protested. "There's a
bigger chance of my dying in a car wreck than of being
hurt by one of the horses at the Lucky C."

"You let me work it out with your mother. In the
meantime, she wants me to sell all of the horses." He
stroked the mare's neck.

Megan touched her father's arm. "But the horses were
always your project."

"True. But the cancer has taken a lot out of me, and I
can't give the animals as much of my time as I used to."

"I thought the doctor said he got all of the cancer."

"So far, that's what it looks like. But ten horses is a
lot to keep up with. I promised I'd sell seven of the ten,
only keeping a few to ride for pleasure."

"And where will you sell the seven?" Megan's fingers dug into Daniel's shirt and all the way to his skin.

"I hand-selected all of my horses based on their pedigree. They are equal to the ones at Kennedy Farms. If
you have need of more breeding stock in Oklahoma," her
father said, "I'll give them to you for a wedding gift."

Daniel nodded. "From what I see of them, they would
be an excellent addition to the ranch, either as breeders
or as working stock."

Her father glanced at Megan. "Do you want the horses?"

"Yes!" Megan flung her arms around her father's neck. "Thank you, Dad."

Her father's cheeks reddened. "Well, I'd better get back to the house before your mother calls an ambulance."

"Thank you, sir." Daniel held out his hand to Mr. Talbot. "The horses mean a lot to your daughter."

"I wonder if they don't mean more than her family," Talbot groused. He took Daniel's hand and shook it without crushing it this time.

When he let go, Megan grabbed her father's hand and squeezed. "I'll always love you and Mother, but I'm all grown up and want to live my life my way."

Mr. Talbot drew in a deep breath and let it out. "It's hard to let go, not only for your mother but also for me."

"I know." She lifted his hand to her cheek. "You like to control everything around you."

Her father's shoulders sagged. "That has been the hardest thing to learn these past few months. Some things are out of my control."

Megan hugged her father again. "I love you."

He patted her back. "I love you, too. Now, don't be late for dinner. It makes your mother nuts."

Frank Talbot left the barn, and silence reigned for a couple of minutes following his departure. Megan turned to the mare and pressed her forehead to the horse's nose. "You're going to be okay."

Daniel touched her shoulder. "So are you."

She laughed. "I get to keep my horses."

"And you don't have to spend all of your grandmother's inheritance to get them."

"I can use that money to pay for their upkeep."

"You can stable them at the Lucky C."

"I'll pay you for boarding. And if you approve of their bloodlines, we could consider them in your breeding program. I know you are being very selective. I've seen the lineage charts on the horses you have. Mine could be of value to you."

"We'll look into it when we get back to Oklahoma. Hopefully your father won't be in a hurry to get them off his farm."

"I'll speak with him. Perhaps we can use his trailers to transport them." Megan turned to him and wrapped her arms around his waist, burying her face in his chest. "Thank you."

"For what?"

"For suggesting the marriage of convenience. My father would not have been so easily swayed had I come on my own or brought a man he couldn't see eye to eye with."

"Your parents only want you to be happy and cared for."

Megan nodded. "I knew I'd been born premature and spent a month in the hospital before my mother could take me home. But I didn't know she had miscarried three times before me. She must have been heartbroken each time and terrified when I came along." Megan glanced up at Daniel. "I can only imagine how devastating it would be to lose a child."

"You have to appreciate the people in your life while you have them. Tomorrow is never guaranteed." Daniel pressed a kiss to her forehead.

"You lost your mother when you were ten?"

He nodded, his memories going back to the single-wide mobile home he'd shared with his mother. "She did her best to give me a good life. I didn't realize until after she was gone that I had all I needed. I had her love."

"She must have been a wonderful mother." Megan cupped his face, her hand warm against his cheek. "What about Big J? Didn't he love you?"

"He took me in, despite his wife's objection. What man takes in his bastard son and gives him a home and his love? I never felt like his love for me was any less than his love for Abra's children."

"You were fortunate to have him as a father."

"Yes, I was." Abra had been the thorn in his side, never accepting him as one of the family. He fit in nicely with his siblings, but never with Abra. He couldn't blame her. He was the product of her husband's adultery.

"The proof of his love is that you turned out okay. From an orphan to a Colton, you've made a place for yourself at the Lucky C Ranch."

He shook his head. "The horse-breeding program has to prove itself as another way to make the ranch produce. If it doesn't work, I'll have to move out and find a job that will support me and any family that comes along."

"And you don't want to leave the Lucky C?"

He shook his head. "It's my home. The horses have been the one constant in my life. I love working with them."

The mare whinnied beside him as if to add her consensus. She nudged Daniel's shoulder, pushing the two of them off balance.

Megan laughed and held on to Daniel's arms. "Misty agrees. She's usually not so friendly to male strangers."

"Do I pass her test?"

Megan hooked her arm through his. "Yes. You passed

her test and my father's. Now, we'd better get back to the house and dressed for dinner to pass my mother's test."

"Dressed for dinner?"

"She insists on formal attire for dinner."

"I should have packed my tux."

"Not that formal, but slacks and a blazer. Did you bring a blazer?" she asked. "If not, maybe one of my father's will fit you."

"Relax. I brought a jacket." He clasped her hand in his and led her out of the stable and back along the path to the house. "Your family has a beautiful ranch."

"You think so?"

"Yes."

"It's a lot different from the Lucky C." She pointed toward the vineyards and the pastures. "In California, most farms are a mix of cattle, vineyards and orchards, unlike the ranches of Oklahoma."

"I think it's important to diversify."

"Right." She grinned up at him. "Thus the horse-breeding program on a cattle ranch."

"Right." Daniel stopped to stare out over the vine-yard-covered hillside. The setting sun bathed the hills of grapevines in a golden haze.

"You should talk with my father. He's the one who made this place a success."

"I will. Perhaps he has more ideas we can transfer to the Lucky C."

As they neared the house, Christine, wearing a long halter dress in a deep royal blue, rose from a chair beside the pool. "There you are. I'd like to introduce you to my fiancé, Josh."

A man stood from the chair beside her and extended

his hand. "Megan, I've heard a lot about you from Christine and your parents."

"Nice to meet you." Megan shook the man's hand and turned to Daniel. "This is my...husband, Daniel."

Josh turned to Daniel. "Congratulations. You've married into a very special family." Josh curled an arm around Christine. "I look forward to the day Christine and I will be married."

"And when will that be?" Megan asked.

"Soon, I hope." He winked at Christine.

"I'm holding out for a big wedding," Christine said. "Not that eloping to Vegas hasn't crossed my mind. That sounds so romantic."

Josh's handshake was less than firm, and he let go quickly. Daniel had no desire for a repeat performance of Frank's bone-crushing grip, but he had a tendency to gauge a man's character by the way he shook hands.

"I understand you raise horses for a living," Josh said. "How's that working for you?"

Daniel tensed. "Yes, I raise horses." He wanted to tell Josh it was none of his business how it went for him. Instead, he answered with his own question. "What is it you do?"

"I'm into acquiring and selling real property."

"How's that going for you?"

Megan coughed into her hand.

Josh didn't take offense to Daniel's question. Quite the opposite. "I have a knack for finding treasures, tweaking them and reselling for a huge profit. I have a talent for seeing the potential."

"I suppose you could say that's what Daniel does, as well," Megan said. "He can spot an excellent prospect in a horse from a hundred yards away."

"Very interesting." Josh tilted his head. "I would think working with horses would not be very profitable."

Megan hooked Daniel's arm. "Some things aren't about the money but about the passion. Daniel and I love working with horses much more than with people."

"Horses can be very unpredictable and difficult to work with," Josh pointed out.

"With patience and understanding, you learn each animal." Megan's lips twisted. "People can be even more unpredictable than horses at times. And sometimes even less trustworthy."

"You have a point. But most people don't weigh a ton. Seems horses can be a lot more dangerous."

Megan's jaw tightened. "A person with a ton of metal around him can be a lot more dangerous than a horse, especially if that person has an addiction to speed and excitement."

Christine nodded. "Like your former fiancé?"

Megan nodded, her face pale, her lips firming.

Josh turned to Christine. "You mean Chase Buchannan? The Academy Award–winning actor who died in a car wreck a year ago?"

Christine touched his arm. "Yes. Megan was almost killed in that same car accident." Megan's cousin grimaced. "I'm sorry about what happened to you and him."

Megan didn't respond, her body stiff, her green eyes dark.

Daniel hadn't heard this story from her, and it brought home to him just how much he didn't know about Megan Talbot. She'd been engaged to a movie star. His chest tightened.

"Ah, here you all are." Mrs. Talbot appeared in the back entrance to the house. She wore a long dress the color of champagne. Her hair swept up in a twist at the back of her head, the sides sleek. Her ears were adorned with long, shimmering diamond earrings. "Dinner is almost served."

The two couples followed Megan's mother into the house.

Once inside, Daniel turned to Megan's mother. "If you'll excuse us, we'll go change for dinner."

Mrs. Talbot smiled. "Certainly."

Megan took his hand, and they ascended the staircase together. Daniel knew she held his hand for show, but it was warm in his, and he squeezed it reassuringly.

Once in the bedroom, Megan opened a door leading into a huge walk-in closet. "I can dress in here and give you privacy." She handed his suit to him. "You might need this."

"How did it get in there?"

"The maid unpacked your case for you."

He wasn't sure he liked someone unpacking for him. It wasn't something a boy who grew up in a trailer park got used to. Even when he'd moved to the Coltons' main house, he'd insisted on hanging his own clothing and cleaning up after himself.

When Daniel reached for the suit, he caught a glimpse of the closet's interior. It was as big as his bedroom in the Coltons' house. An entire wall filled with dresses. "Holy smokes, you could open your own dress shop."

Megan grimaced, her cheeks reddening. "My mother insisted I have all the latest fashions. She was annoyed when I wore my jeans and boots every day. It's part of the reason she insisted on formal dining. Just to get me into a dress." She closed the door between them. "I'll be ready in a minute."

While she was in the closet, Daniel stripped out of his clothes and slipped into his suit trousers. "I didn't know you were engaged."

"It wasn't relevant when I applied for the job at the Lucky C," she answered through the wood-paneled door.

"What happened to make him wreck his car?"

"He liked going fast," Megan said.

Daniel stuck his arms into the button-up shirt and pulled it over his shoulders, vaguely noticing that the wrinkles had been ironed out of it and the suit. His thoughts were on the car wreck and the fact Megan had almost lost her life. "Why would he drive that fast with you in the vehicle with him?"

Megan opened the door to the closet and stepped out, wearing a long black dress that hugged all her curves like a second skin. "I think he was impressed with his Porsche, and he wanted me to be impressed with the car and his driving skills." She glanced to the side. "I just wanted him to stop and let me out." Megan snorted softly. "He did both by slamming into a telephone pole, which fortunately ejected me, throwing me clear of the vehicle. Unfortunately, it killed him instantly."

Daniel took her hands in his and held them while he stared into her eyes, trying to read the emotion there. "I'm sorry for your loss."

"Yeah, well, it's been almost a year." She pulled her hands free of his. "Are you ready?"

Daniel shook his head. "I can see why your mother wanted you to wear dresses." He swept her from head to toe with his gaze. "You're absolutely stunning."

"Thank you." She dipped her head, color rising up her neck. "You don't have to compliment me when we're in the privacy of my room."

"Yes. I do." Daniel touched a finger to her chin and raised her face so that she was forced to look him in the eye. "You're a beautiful woman. And though I'm not a poet, beauty, whether it's scenery, a painting, a horse or a woman should be recognized. I'm recognizing you."

She stared up at him, her green eyes filling with tears. "That is perhaps the loveliest compliment I've ever received."

For a long moment he stood, enchanted by her shining eyes, her body, the dress—hell, everything about Megan. Then nothing could stop him from lowering his lips and claiming her lush mouth.

At first his kiss was gentle, a skimming of his lips over hers. Within a moment, desire overwhelmed him and his arm slipped around her, bringing her body flush against his. He crushed her mouth with his, his tongue caressing hers in a long, sensual glide.

She tasted so sweet, warm and wet. He could hold her forever and kiss her even longer and it wouldn't be enough. When at last he was forced to draw air into his lungs, he raised his head and pressed his forehead against hers. "We'd better go down before your mother comes up to find us."

"What mother?" She clutched his arms. "You're right. We should go down. My mother has been known to climb the stairs looking for me."

Daniel shrugged into his suit jacket, glad for the extra clothing to hide the evidence of the effect she had on him. The next day or two would be torture. He didn't know how he'd keep his hands off her, but he had to. If not for her protection, then for his. He suspected he was losing his heart to this amazing woman.

MEGAN HOOKED HER arm through Daniel's and walked with him down the curved staircase, wishing they had insisted on staying in a hotel. Then at least they could claim they were still on their honeymoon and wanted their privacy. She'd lock the door and refuse to leave until he made mad, passionate love to her. Oh, hell, once would never be enough.

She was so totally in love with Daniel Colton, there was no going back. At the end of their agreement... She didn't want to think about the end when her emotions were tied up in him already. Megan vowed to take one day at a time. With Chase, she'd learned there might not be more days to follow.

"Oh, good." Her mother appeared in the foyer. "I was about to come up and find you. We're waiting on you two."

"Sorry to keep you, Mrs. Talbot." Daniel kissed Megan's temple. "Your daughter is so gorgeous, I can't seem to stop kissing her. And I can see where she gets her beauty." He lifted the older woman's hand and kissed her knuckles.

Megan's cheeks flamed and her heart warmed.

Her mother smiled at her. "He is a charming man, isn't he?"

"Yes, he is." Megan glanced up at Daniel.

He winked.

"Come into the dining room. I'm sure you're hungry." Her mother led the way into the formal dining room and indicated where they should be seated.

"Thank you, Josh and Christine, for helping to set the table and gather the dishes. I sent Maria home. She wasn't feeling well, and I didn't want her to work when she was sick."

"Anything you need. We appreciate that you're allowing us to stay here for the next few days." Josh laid a hand on Mrs. Talbot's arm. "Your hospitality always makes us feel comfortable and at home."

"It's the least I can do when you've come all the way out here to visit us. And I'm so happy you were able to be here when Megan brought her new husband home."

Daniel nodded. "Thank you for letting us stay, Mrs. Talbot. Especially on such short notice."

Frank appeared in the doorway, dressed in a tailored suit. "What are we waiting for? Let's eat."

Megan and Daniel sat across from Josh and Christine. Frank and Josephine sat at either end of the table.

A servant filled wineglasses around the table, while another placed small bowls of soup in front of each person.

Daniel sipped his soup and played the part of the doting newlywed. Soon the soup dishes were cleared and replaced with plates laden with shrimp scampi smothered in garlic sauce, lobster tails dripping with butter and lush green spears of asparagus.

"Your father has officially retired as CEO of Talbot Enterprises," Megan's mother announced. "He will remain on the board of directors for at least a year until he decides what he wants to do with it after that."

Megan's gaze shot to her father. "I can't imagine you letting anyone else run the company you built from the ground up."

Her father nodded. "Neither could I until my health took a nosedive. I'd rather putter around on the Triple Diamond than spend every waking hour worrying about my business. Perhaps I'll sell it and be completely done with it."

Megan frowned. "I thought you had the cancer licked."

Her father nodded. "For now. But you never know. I didn't want to die with too many regrets."

Her mother sighed. "He's taking me on that trip to Europe I always wanted to go on."

"But you've been to Europe many times," Megan said.

"On business," Frank corrected her. "Your mother was always good to come along and keep me company."

"We never went to explore or enjoy the culture. I was left to wander around on my own. This time your father is going to take me. No phones. No laptops. No business associates. Just the two of us." She smiled at her husband. "Like the honeymoon we never had."

"How very sweet," Christine said. "A toast to the honeymooners." She lifted her glass.

Megan, Daniel and Josh lifted their glasses to her parents.

The look her parents exchanged was one Megan had seldom seen in all the time she'd lived under their roof. Love shone from their eyes, and it warmed Megan's heart.

"Well, I'm glad," Megan said. "I always thought you spent too much time at work."

Her father nodded. "I should have spent more time with you and your mother. I realize that now. I should have been there for your mother more than I was."

Her mother smiled. "We're going to make up for lost time."

"That's right." Her father clapped his hands together. "Don't be surprised if we spend all of your inheritance in the meantime." Then his brows dipped. "But don't worry. We'll keep the Triple Diamond, and it will be yours when your mother and I are gone. You can keep it or sell it. Now that you're married and living in Oklahoma, you might not want the responsibility of owning a ranch in California."

"I would rather you spent all the money you earned. It's yours and Mother's. I'll make my own."

Her father's chest puffed out. "That's my girl."

"And I'll just have to get used to the fact you're working with large animals." Her mother bit her lip. "But please be careful. You are our only child, and we want grandchildren. Lots of grandchildren."

Megan's cheeks heated. "Mother, we only just got married."

Frank nodded from Daniel to Megan. "Of course. But I hope you will at least consider having children."

"We wanted more." Her mother's eyes glazed with moisture. "We were lucky to have Megan. I always wanted grandchildren. Do you two plan on having children?"

Megan shrugged, her gaze going to Daniel. "We haven't thought past our wedding." She didn't even know if Daniel liked children.

"Do you like children, Daniel?" her father asked.

Megan cringed for the man. He'd volunteered to marry her to save her beloved horses. Now he was stuck in an interrogation about his views on children.

"I love children and hope to have half a dozen. You see, I grew up with my half brothers and half sister. I can't imagine my life without them now."

Her mother let out the breath she'd been holding in a nervous laugh. "Thank goodness." A smile spread across her face. "You two seem perfect for each other. Any child would be lucky to have you as parents."

Her heart ached at the joy in her mother's face. Guilt sat like a lead weight in the pit of Megan's belly. The lies they were telling her parents would eventually have to be unraveled into disappointment when she and Daniel announced their divorce. Those grandchildren they so desperately wanted would not happen with Daniel. And at the rate Megan was going with doomed relationships, they'd never have those grandchildren.

Perhaps she'd overreacted to her father's threat to sell her horses. Unfortunately the damage had been done, and now she had to continue the lie or further distress her parents. And with her father just pushing past the danger of cancer, the truth might set him back on his road to recovery.

"Do you two see yourselves moving to California to take over the Triple Diamond Ranch?" Josh asked and popped a bite of shrimp into his mouth.

"Not anytime soon." Megan looked from her mother to her father. "I'm learning so much at the Lucky C Ranch. As long as Daniel will let me, I plan on working with his horse-breeding program."

"Oh, darling." Her mother reached out to touch her arm. "I hope you will reconsider when you become pregnant."

"Josephine, leave her alone. She's a smart woman, and I'm sure she wouldn't put a child of her own in harm's way."

Her mother nodded. "Of course."

Megan could sense her mother wanted to say more, but she didn't. After what her father had revealed in the barn that day, Megan could understand better her mother's overprotectiveness and desire to wrap her only daughter in a protective cocoon.

She wished she'd known this sooner. Knowing wouldn't have made her quit riding horses or sneaking out her window. But it might have made her less inclined to accept Chase's proposal to punish her parents for their stranglehold on her life.

Megan turned to her cousin, shifting the focus off her and Daniel. "So, when is the big day for the two of you?"

Christine blushed. "We haven't actually set a date. I'd like to be married at Christmas. I've always liked the idea of a snowy setting."

"Perhaps we'll be as spontaneous as you and Daniel and elope. Tahoe, perhaps?" Josh smiled at Christine. "A winter wedding at Tahoe." He reached for her hand and raised it to kiss her knuckles.

Christine's eyes glowed. "I'd love that."

"That would be nice," Megan's mother said. "I would have enjoyed throwing a huge wedding for Megan, but I shall be content as long as she promises me some grand-children."

"Mother." Megan shook her head.

"I know. I know." Her mother grinned. "Shall we adjourn to the patio? I can have coffee served there. It's supposed to be a clear night."

Megan pushed to her feet. "That sounds great."

Josh stood. "If you don't mind, I have a few phone calls to make, and then I'll join you."

"Of course." Christine turned to follow Megan's parents out to the patio.

"I'd like to walk off some of that delicious dinner." Daniel held out his arm to Megan. "Care to join me?"

She took his arm. "The garden is pretty at night. Mother had a landscaper commissioned to design it with subtle lighting and smooth paths. I think you'll like it."

"I'm sure I will, as long as I'm with you."

"You two go on. We'll be here when you get back," her father said.

Megan couldn't get away fast enough, her guilt gnawing at her insides. As soon as they were out of earshot, she let go of a long sigh. "I'm sorry you got caught up in the inquisition." They passed through a beautiful rose garden, the roses illuminated by soft white lighting pointed up from the ground.

"What inquisition? Your parents are concerned about their only daughter and living vicariously through you. I think all parents live a little through their children. Even their grown children."

"Since when did you become a philosopher? I didn't even think you liked people. You are always so wrapped up in your horses, I rarely see you interact with other people besides your family."

He slipped his hand down her arm to clasp her fingers in his. "There is a lot you don't know about me, and vice versa."

"You're right." She leaned against his shoulder. "I'm really sorry I got you into this mess. And now that I know why my parents are so overprotective, it makes me feel terrible about lying to them."

They arrived at an arched walkway covered in ivy vines, creating a tunnel through the darkness. Lighting at their feet guided them to the other side and out into the open.

"I know what you mean. The bottom line is that they love you and will do anything to protect you."

"To the point of driving me nuts." She shook her head. "And all it took was telling them I'm married now, and they're backing off. I'm convinced Dad would have sold the horses eventually if I hadn't taken action, though. With my father's health problems, he has had to reposition his life and his involvement in his various interests."

"He has it right. No one goes to his grave saying 'I wish I had spent more time in the office.' Your father might live five, ten, twenty years or more. But there are no guarantees."

"And he finally understands family is more important."

"So does this mean you'll be spending more time with your parents? Possibly moving back to California? Will I be losing my assistant?"

"No, I love Oklahoma. I'm going back. As for this marriage, since my father is giving me the horses, I don't have to stay to arrange for a buyer. I can work with my grandmother's attorney over the phone and fax. We can leave tomorrow."

"I thought you wanted to stay for your family."

"I only came to convince my mother and father that I'm not coming home to stay. I think they get the point."

"What's your hurry to leave?"

"I feel almost as heavily invested in the negotiations with Kennedy Farms as you are. I'd like to be prepared for the meeting with them in Reno, and I'm worried about Halo. She's one of your broodmares. What if the poison had an effect on her kidneys or liver?"

"My brothers are having the vet check her over while we're gone. However, I'd like to get back to find out what poisoned her. Or, God forbid, who."

Megan nodded. "Exactly. I can visit my parents again when we have everything settled."

"What about our marriage?" Daniel asked.

Megan's muscles clenched. "I still need my grandmother's trust fund to support my horses without my father becoming suspicious. If all you're willing to do is the minimum until I get the initial release of funds, I won't hold you to the six months."

"I don't mind holding out for six months. It might get sticky with my family."

"Do we have to tell them?"

"If we want the Kennedys to buy into it, we have to get the Coltons to believe we really did it."

"It's not as if we didn't. We have a certificate to prove it."

"Exactly. But when it's all over, wouldn't you rather come back to California?" He waved his hand. "All of this will one day be yours—a beautiful house, a diversified ranch and servants to take care of you."

Megan shook her head. "My father built this. I want to make it on my own. And as long as my father and mother are here, they would constantly be questioning my involvement with the animals."

"I can see that would be hard to deal with. But it's an easier life than the one you have in Oklahoma."

"I don't want easy. I would be bored and get lazy."

Daniel snorted. "I can't imagine you lazy."

A smile quirked at the corners of her mouth. "If I didn't know better, I'd think you were trying to talk me into staying here. Don't you like me as your assistant?"

He chuckled, the sound warming her heart. "You're the best assistant I've ever had."

She backhanded him gently in the chest, loving how they could tease each other so easily. "I'm the *only* assistant you've ever had. Besides, I love working at the Lucky C with the horses."

"Just the horses?" Daniel stopped and turned her to face him. "What about me?"

Megan's heart lurched, and her breath caught in her throat. "Of course. I love working for you. You've been patient teaching me what you know about breeding horses for their best qualities. You've taught me all the hands-on kinds of things they don't teach in the university labs."

Facing Daniel, Megan couldn't stop talking. Her stomach bunched and her breathing became labored as she stood so close to him without touching him. With moonlight reflecting the darkness of his eyes, a soft breeze blowing through the leaves and the scent of roses in the air, the setting was ripe for love, if only he was so inclined. "It's a lot different working with microscopes and lab rats than with live animals the size of horses," she said, her voice fading, her need to kiss him finally stalling the words.

He pressed a finger to her lips. "Sometimes you talk too much."

"I do. Especially when I'm nervous."

"Why are you nervous?"

"Because I want to kiss you, and I don't know if you want to kiss me back." She swallowed hard and rushed on. "But I've learned that sometimes you have to take matters in your own hands." She leaned up on her toes and cupped her hand around the back of his neck. "I'm taking matters into my own hands."

"I like a woman who knows what she wants."

As she closed the distance between their lips, his arms wrapped around her, pulling her body flush against his, the evidence of his desire nudging her belly.

And she kissed him, her mouth covering his, her

tongue tracing the seam of his lips until he opened to let her in. He tasted of garlic and wine, a heady and delicious combination.

For a long time, Megan stood, locked in Daniel's embrace, wishing she could stay there forever.

A rasping sound broke through the cocoon of passion. She jerked back and glanced around. "Did you hear that?"

"I did," Daniel said.

"It sounded like someone skidding in gravel." Megan called out, "Hello?"

The only sound in response was the thump of her pulse against her eardrums.

Daniel stepped away, his arms falling to his sides. "We should head back."

Kicking herself for being so jumpy, Megan fell in step beside him on the way back through the garden, keeping a lookout for movement. The hair on the back of her neck prickled and stood. She could swear someone was watching her. But every time she shot a glance over her shoulder, all she saw were the lights from the garden and the shadowy images of ornamental trees, bushes and flowers.

As they walked, she convinced herself her guilt was making her paranoid. She'd rather leave the next day than continue to live the lie in front of her parents, afraid she'd reveal something that would expose her and Daniel. Then all the effort they'd gone to for their marriage of convenience would be for nothing. Her father would retract his offer of giving her the horses, and her mother's disappointment at not getting the grandbabies she so desperately wanted would make Megan feel like a complete and utter heel.

"Yes, we should head out tomorrow," she said as they stepped onto the pebbled concrete patio surrounding the pool.

"How was the garden?" her mother asked, smiling at Megan and Daniel as they closed the distance.

"Lovely as ever," Megan responded. "Mother, Father, would you two be terribly disappointed if we left tomorrow?"

Her mother sat forward. "What? So soon?" She turned to her husband. "Did your father say something to make you angry?"

Megan laughed. "No, of course not. It's just that we have a commitment for a symposium in Reno in four days, and we haven't even told Daniel's family of our marriage."

Daniel picked it up from there. "We'd like to go back to Oklahoma and break the happy news. Trust me, they will be excited to welcome Megan into the Colton family. They already love her. And then we will have time to get ready for the symposium."

Her mother wilted. "Oh, well, then, I suppose you should. But I'd hoped you'd stay longer. The last time you were here, we spent so much of our visit in the hospital with your father."

"Which you didn't have to do," her father grumbled. "But I was glad to see you."

"I promise to bring her back soon, and it's easy enough in our ranch airplane."

"Oh, dear." Her mother's hand fluttered to her chest. "I'd forgotten that you'd come in such a small plane. Are you sure you'll be okay flying back? Shouldn't you book flights on a commercial airliner?"

"Mother, I'm more likely to die in a car crash, as I

almost did, than in an airplane crash. Daniel is an excellent pilot."

"Well, then." Mrs. Talbot sighed. "At least have breakfast with the family in the morning before you leave."

"Please do. We'd like to visit one more time," Christine entreated her. "We're rarely in the same place at the same time."

Megan looked to Daniel. "Do we have to leave early?"

"No, as long as we leave by noon. I'd like to clear the mountains in daylight."

"Okay, then. We'll leave after breakfast." Megan pretended to yawn. "If you don't mind, though, I'm tired from all the excitement, and I'm sure Father needs his beauty rest."

"Hey, don't count me off as old and decrepit. I was just temporarily incapacitated."

Megan leaned over and kissed her father's cheek. "I'm glad you're feeling better." She crossed to her mother and kissed her, too. "Good night."

Once she and Daniel left the patio, her heartbeat kicked up a notch. By the time they reached her room, her imagination had her clothes off and Daniel's, too, and she could almost feel his naked skin against hers.

"You can have the first shower," he told her.

She almost asked if he'd like to join her. She might have been forward enough to initiate the kiss in the garden, but hadn't he kissed her back? Though she'd been the instigator for a kiss, she didn't quite have the nerve to initiate making love in the shower. And since he offered to let her go first, she could only hope he'd join her. She left the door to the bathroom open slightly, giving him the option.

After fifteen minutes languishing under the hot water, she got out, dried off and realized he wasn't that into her.

When she left the bathroom, Daniel wasn't anywhere to be seen.

Wearing her T-shirt and jogging shorts, she crawled into her bed and pulled the sheet up over her. Half an hour later, she gave up trying to stay awake and let her eyes drift closed. He wasn't coming to bed with her.

If they stayed married for six months like this, it would be the longest six months of her life.

CHAPTER THIRTEEN

DANIEL WALKED AROUND the grounds until well past midnight, afraid to go back to the room until Megan was soundly asleep. After seeing all she had at the Triple Diamond, he was certain that when she got tired of paying her own way, she'd want to go back to the life of luxury any woman would be happy to live in.

And he couldn't give her that life. Yes, his father would deed him a parcel of land to build a house on. He might even help him pay for a house, but Daniel refused to take any more than what he considered compensation for the work he did on the ranch. Living in the two-bedroom guest cottage was part of what he considered his compensation, and it kept him close to the breeding barn where he concentrated his efforts.

When he finally went back to the bedroom he was sharing with Megan, she was asleep, as he'd hoped. He lay on a chaise longue, his legs and feet dangling off the end. Sleep didn't come to him until somewhere around two-thirty in the morning. He'd have gotten no sleep whatsoever if he'd attempted to lie in the same bed with his new wife. Not after that kiss. His body was wound tighter than a rattlesnake with a new button. Sleep was out of the question.

By the time Megan woke at seven, Daniel was already up, showered, shaved and ready to go.

Megan sat up in the sheets. "Did you even come to bed last night? I wouldn't have bit you if you shared the bed with me."

"I managed on the longue."

Megan's mouth pressed into a thin line as she threw aside the sheets and rose. "I'll only be a few minutes." Her long legs seemed even longer when she wore such short shorts and the baggy T-shirt that did little to hide her sexy form. With her strawberry blond hair rumpled and her face soft from sleep, she was so adorable. More than ever, Daniel wanted to kiss her, take her back to bed and make love to her.

Grabbing her clothes, Megan disappeared into the bathroom and closed the door with a firm click. As promised, she emerged a few minutes later, her face clean and fresh, her hair pulled back into a ponytail. She wore a flowing peach-colored dress that barely came down to the middle of her thighs.

The only thought Daniel could muster in his sleep-deprived brain was how good it would feel to have those long, slender legs wrapped around his waist as he drove into her.

"Ready?" Megan stood in front of him, her brows cocked, a slight smile on her lips.

Daniel sucked in a deep breath and let it out slowly, forcing back his body's natural urge to take her into his arms. He had to remind himself over and over again that this was a marriage of convenience, not a real marriage. Megan was in a class far above his, and he didn't belong in her world. Though the argument had seemed valid only yesterday, it was fading by the minute. "Ready."

She slipped her bare feet into a pair of high-heeled

sandals and straightened. "Breakfast and we're out of here."

Daniel nodded and opened the door for her to step into the hallway.

Christine stood in front of the door, her hand raised to knock. "Oh, good. I was just about to tell you breakfast is served."

Daniel followed Megan, carrying their cases down the stairs. He set them in the hallway by the front door and then entered the formal dining room, where the table had been set with fine porcelain plates, large covered platters and crystal glasses filled with orange juice.

Mr. and Mrs. Talbot stood by their seats and waited for the three of them to join them. As she had the night before, Mrs. Talbot directed Megan and Daniel to the seats they'd been assigned the night before.

"Josh sent his apologies," Christine said. "He ate a quick breakfast a few minutes ago and left for an appointment with a title company in Santa Rosa. He would have loved to have been here to see you off. However, he has a business to run."

"He made his apologies to me in person," Mrs. Talbot said. "I was sure he had an ample breakfast to see him through the day."

As they took their seats, a maid stepped forward, lifted the covers off the platters and helped serve fluffy scrambled eggs, pancakes and toast. Breakfast proceeded in relative silence.

As they finished, Mr. Talbot offered, "I will arrange for the horses to be delivered to the Lucky C Ranch within a couple weeks."

"Thank you, Father." Megan drank the last of her orange juice and pushed back from the table. "Daniel and

I have so much to do back at the Lucky C in preparation for our important meeting with Kennedy Farms."

Her father's brows rose. "I know Marshall Kennedy. I could make a discreet call to him if you'd like."

Megan smiled. "Would you, Father?"

"I'll make that call this afternoon."

Daniel held out his hand. "We appreciate your help. Thank you and Mrs. Talbot for your hospitality. Perhaps next time we come to visit, we can stay longer."

"Good. This was such a short visit, I didn't really get to know you." Mrs. Talbot bypassed his extended hand and hugged him. "Although I should be angry at you for keeping Megan in Oklahoma, welcome to the family. Please take good care of our baby. We love her so very much."

"As soon as we get settled, we'll invite you out for a visit," Daniel said.

Megan gave him an almost imperceptible frown and then smiled up at him. "We should be going. I don't know how you feel, but I don't like flying in the dark."

Mr. Talbot chuckled. "Our Megan can be a bit demanding when she wants to be, but she has a heart of gold."

"I've noticed." Daniel slipped his arm around her waist and pulled Megan to him. "If you want to make it over the mountains before dark, we have to hurry to turn in the rental car and arrange for fuel."

"Mother, Father, I love you. Please take care of each other. I'll see you soon." Megan hugged her parents.

Her mother's eyes glazed. "Don't stay away so long, dear."

Mr. Talbot pulled Megan into a big bear hug. "I'm sorry I had to threaten you to get you to come home.

Had we known you were engaged, we wouldn't have been so insistent."

Her mother hugged her again. "I worry about you so much. But now—" she waved a hand "—now you have a husband to protect you and love you. I suppose I'll get used to it. But it will be hard."

"You don't have to worry," Daniel said. "I'll make sure she's okay."

"And just so you know," Megan said, "Daniel isn't replacing you two."

"We understand. He's an addition to our little family." Her mother reached out to squeeze Daniel's hand. "We have someone else to love. And if Megan loves him, we will love him, as well."

Daniel's stomach knotted around the scrambled eggs. He had been prepared to dislike the Talbots based on Mr. Talbot's threat to sell Megan's horses. The man had never intended to sell them so soon. He'd just wanted Megan back home. Understanding why Mrs. Talbot smothered Megan brought their actions into perspective.

Mr. Talbot crossed his arms. "Megan wouldn't marry someone she didn't love completely." Though he was talking about his daughter, his stare pinned Daniel.

"I'm honored by her love and will do my best to make her happy." Daniel dropped a kiss on Megan's forehead, lingering for a moment, inhaling the scent of her hair and loving the warmth of her skin. He could get used to the feel of her against him.

Megan rested her hand against his chest, her fingers curling into his shirt. "I know you'll make me happy," she said, her gaze rising to lock with his.

Christine hugged Megan and shook hands with Daniel. "It was nice to meet you. I wish you both the best."

Mr. Talbot held out his hand, and Daniel grabbed it. "We look forward to coming out to Oklahoma to visit. Once you get past the honeymoon, let us know."

"I will," Daniel promised, the lie sticking like a sock in his craw.

As he left the house, one of the Talbots' servants appeared behind the wheel of the rental car they'd picked up at the airport in Santa Rosa.

Once Daniel and Megan were driving through the gates of the Triple Diamond Ranch, he let go of the breath he'd been holding.

"Just so you know, I like your parents. And I didn't like lying to them."

Megan stared out the window, her hands twisting the hem of her dress. "I never knew my mother had trouble with her pregnancies. Had she told me, I might have better understood why she was so clingy and why she didn't want me to do anything dangerous."

"You're her only child. Her baby forever."

Megan's lips twisted. "I'm with you. I hated lying to my parents. If I'd known my father was bluffing about selling the horses, none of this charade would have been necessary."

"You heard him, though. He's downsizing his herd."

"I bet if I'd just talked to him about the horses, he'd have come around." Megan cast an apologetic look Daniel's way. "I'm sorry I got you into this."

"You still need the money from your grandmother's estate to support the horses, so this marriage was not a total waste of time." If he was honest with himself, he liked having her as his bride, and he wished it would last longer than it took for the paperwork on her grandmother's estate to be finalized. But when Megan got tired of working for a living, surely she'd want to go back to California and live in comfort.

"Again, we don't have to stay married for the full six months. I can keep the horses a long time on the initial installment of my grandmother's money. I'll figure out how to support them when that money dries up."

"I don't mind committing to the six months. It's not like I've been dating anyone else, and I'd hate to lose my assistant because she had to find a better paying job to support her horses." He winked at her.

She smiled at him, her face solemn but happier than he'd seen it in days. "Thank you for all you've done for me."

Daniel didn't feel like he'd done all that much. In fact, the trip would prove to be more beneficial to him if Mr. Talbot actually made that call and the association with Megan Talbot set him up for a successful business deal with Kennedy Farms.

Once he and Megan had what they wanted, they could annul their wedding or get a quickie divorce and go their separate ways.

The thought of walking away from Megan and their marriage of convenience left a weighted, sour feeling in his gut.

Soon Megan was settled in the plane beside Daniel, and they took off from the Santa Rosa airport into cloudy skies, headed back to Oklahoma. Though the takeoff was smooth, the weightlessness of flying in a small aircraft unsettled her stomach more this time than when they'd left Vegas and Oklahoma.

She leaned back, adjusting the headset over her ears.

"Let me know if I can help you out with anything. Otherwise, I'm going to sleep."

"Sleep," Daniel said, the electronic voice crackling in her ear reassuringly. "It's a long flight in a small plane. You might as well get as comfortable as you can."

Megan closed her eyes and leaned her head against the window, suddenly tired and achy. Hoping she'd feel better after a little rest, she willed herself to sleep.

"Megan, wake up. Megan!" Static rattled in Megan's ears, and she jerked awake.

"Daniel?" she said, her voice hoarse, something warm dripping from her nose. She raised her hand, embarrassed, and brushed away thick liquid. When she stared down at her finger, it had a long streak of blood.

"Sweetheart, are you okay? You were moaning in your sleep." Daniel glanced over at her, his eyes widening. "You have a nosebleed." His brows sank into a V. "There's a tissue in the box behind my seat."

Megan leaned forward and coughed, her breathing a little labored. She figured it was the altitude. "How far are we from home?" she asked, pressing her fingers to her pounding temples.

"An hour. You've been asleep for a while I didn't want to wake you, but you were moaning as if in pain." He shot another glance her way, a worried frown settling on his forehead. "Are you okay? Your face is pale."

"I don't feel so great," she admitted, fumbling for the tissue box, her arms weak and her fingers numb. When she finally managed to grab a tissue, lifting it to her bleeding nose seemed to take all her energy. "I don't usually get nosebleeds from flying."

"I'm going to make an emergency landing." Daniel

glanced at the GPS device on the instrument panel. "We should get you to a doctor."

"How far are we from Tulsa?" she asked, leaning her head back to stop the flow of blood. The movement made her head spin and her vision blur.

"Not too far."

"I can make it," she said. "Please. Don't stop until we get home." Her stomach roiled and her belly cramped. She drew her feet up in the seat and hugged her arms around her knees, willing the cramps to go away.

"Babe, you're not well. I can divert to Oklahoma City."

"No," she moaned. "Just get us to Tulsa. Please." She coughed, the muscles in her belly clenched and she nearly passed out from the pain. Damn it, she didn't want to stop until they got all the way back to Tulsa.

"Are you sure?"

"I think I'll be okay once we land. I just want to go home," she said, her voice fading out, the effort to talk almost too much. She wished she could click her heels and get home in the blink of an eye.

DANIEL PUSHED THE little Mooney as fast as its single engine would take it, but no amount of wishing would make the trip pass any quicker.

Thankfully the flight over the mountains had passed without a storm or any major downdrafts. At first the silence had been welcome, giving him time to think through everything that had happened. Megan slept soundly beside him.

Then Megan became ill, and the last hour in the flight was the longest. Several times her face creased in pain, and she bunched into a tight ball, groaning.

Twice he almost set down. If there had been a decent airport with access to a hospital, he would have. When he came close enough to tune in to the air traffic controller at the Tulsa International Airport, he called for an emergency landing for medical reasons. He asked that an ambulance be waiting on the tarmac.

Fifteen minutes away from the airport, Megan sagged in her seat, her face slack. Her arms around her legs loosened, and her feet fell to the floor of the aircraft.

"Megan!" Daniel called out.

She didn't respond.

He stared at her chest, watching for the rise and fall of steady breathing. For a moment, his heart stopped. Daniel reached out to touch her cheek. It was cool and clammy, and her nose continued to bleed. When her chest rose and fell on a long breath, he nearly cried in relief. "Hang in there, sweetheart. We're almost there."

The air traffic controller gave him clearance. Daniel hit the switch for the landing gear. Nothing happened. His pulse kicked up a notch, but he focused on the training he'd received on this particular plane. He reached for the backup landing gear lever and pulled. The cord should have engaged and let the landing gear down. Instead, the handle and the cord came up in his hand. He pulled the cord again, hoping to engage. The end flew up in his face. It had been severed cleanly.

Daniel had no way of lowering the landing gear. "Mayday, Mayday, Mayday," he said into the radio. He reported the problem and was instructed to perform an emergency landing.

Daniel circled around and came in low and slow. If he tilted even at the slightest angle, he risked touching the tarmac with a wing. If that happened, the plane would cartwheel out of control and disintegrate, killing Megan and him.

Steeling himself for the landing, he gripped the yoke and steadied the wings. The tarmac seemed to rush up at him even as he slowed.

The belly of the craft touched the tarmac, metal scraping concrete in a piercing screech.

Once the plane hit the ground, there was nothing Daniel could do but pray they would come to a smooth halt before the plane shook apart.

Sliding down the runway, the plane eventually slowed to a halt.

Sirens screamed around him. A fire engine pulled up beside them, and an ambulance stopped close by.

Daniel peeled his fingers off the yoke, unclipped his safety straps and bent over Megan to unclip hers.

She moaned and stirred but didn't wake.

Daniel was thankful they'd burned up most of the fuel in flight but didn't trust that the plane wouldn't burst into flame after the crash landing. He opened the door to the plane, gathered Megan in his arms and handed her out to the waiting emergency crew.

They loaded her onto a waiting stretcher and hurried away from the craft. Daniel insisted on going with them. Since he wasn't injured, he was forced to remain behind to answer questions from airport officials.

"Daniel," a voice called out in the confusion.

He turned to face his half brother Ryan wearing his Tulsa PD uniform. "Oh, thank God you're here. Help me get out of here and find Megan."

"I heard over the scanner your plane had crashed and one passenger was taken to the hospital." Ryan asked, "Was Megan injured?"

"Not in the landing. She got sick on the flight over from California. She said she could make it to Tulsa." Daniel shook his head. "I should have insisted on stopping. By the time we were in range of the airport, she'd passed out."

"From what?"

"I don't know." The longer he was away from her, the more worried he became. "I need to go to the hospital."

"Come on. I'll get you through."

Ryan found the airport security guard in charge and cleared Daniel to leave. He led him toward the exit, where his patrol car waited at the curb.

"Sorry, but you'll have to sit in the back. With all the computer equipment we have now, there's no room for a passenger."

"I don't care as long as we get to Megan."

Ryan opened the door for Daniel and closed it once he got in. Then he slid behind the steering wheel and switched on the siren and lights. He radioed to dispatch to find the hospital where Megan was taken. With the correct location, he sped across town.

In minutes they were pulling into the emergency entrance of the hospital.

Ryan had to open the door for Daniel. Once he did, Daniel erupted from the backseat of the vehicle and raced inside, Ryan on his heels.

"Where did they take Megan?" he demanded of the receptionist.

"Megan who?" She stared down at the computer screen in front of her, her fingers poised over the keyboard.

"Megan Talbot," Ryan responded.

"Are you a relation to the patient?" the young woman asked.

"No, she works for our family," Ryan responded.

Daniel touched his brother's arm. "She's more than that," he said. "Megan's my wife. We were married three days ago in Vegas."

CHAPTER FOURTEEN

DANIEL PACED IN the emergency room lobby, waiting for a doctor, anyone, to come out and tell him what was going on with Megan. So far, even after telling them that he was her husband, they wouldn't let him into the room with her.

Ryan stood by, shaking his head. "Married? Why didn't you tell any of us that you were headed to Vegas to get married?"

Daniel shrugged and passed Ryan on another lap across the lobby. "We didn't want a lot of fanfare. We had a simple wedding, just the two of us." *And Elvis.*

Ryan grinned as he keyed a text message into his smartphone. "Wait until the others hear about this. Prepare yourself for some heavy ribbing from the family."

Daniel stopped in front of Ryan, his hands clenched in tight fists. "I don't care what the family does as long as Megan is okay."

Finally a nurse emerged from a door marked Authorized Personnel Only. "Officer Colton," she called out.

Daniel hurried toward her. "How's Megan? Is she going to be all right? May I see her?"

"I'm sorry." She looked around Daniel to Ryan. "I need to talk to Officer Colton."

Anger erupted like a volcano. "I'm her husband. I have the right to see her." He pulled his wallet from his pocket and yanked the marriage certificate from it, whipping it open. "See? She's my wife. We're married. Let me see her."

"The doctor will be out shortly." The nurse snagged Ryan's arm and led him through the doorway. The door shut behind him.

"What the hell is going on?" Daniel asked the empty air.

"Sir, please, take a seat," the receptionist pleaded. "You're scaring the others."

Daniel didn't give a damn about the other people waiting in the lobby. He wanted to see Megan. Then a thought hit him and his heart seized. The only reason he could think of for them to refuse to let him see her yet was that she hadn't made it. A solid block of lead settled in the pit of his stomach, and, for a moment, his heart quit beating.

He took two steps toward the door to the restricted area and raised his fist to bang and demand to see Megan.

Before his knuckles hit the door, it swung open and Ryan stepped out, his face grim. "Daniel, come with me." He grabbed Daniel's arm and turned him toward the exit.

Daniel shook off his hand and spun away. "I'm not going anywhere until I know how Megan is doing."

"They are treating her now and expect her to come through okay."

"Then why won't they let me in to see her?"

"If you'll come with me outside, I'll explain."

"I'm not going anywhere."

Ryan's jaw tightened. "Very well, I'll spell it out here in front of everyone."

"Shoot."

He glanced at the faces of the people waiting to see the on-call doctors. "Preliminary blood tests indicate that Megan had arsenic in her system."

His chest squeezed so tight he could barely breathe. "Oh, God. How?"

"They don't know. There will be questions, like what you had to eat for the last couple of days and where. They might want to do a blood test on you to see if you've been poisoned, as well."

Daniel shoved a hand through his hair. "Anything. Just let me see her."

"The doctor is monitoring her progress with the antidote. They'll let you see her in a few minutes."

"Daniel Colton," a doctor in a white smock called out.

Daniel pushed past Ryan. "I'm Daniel."

"I'm Dr. Baxter." He held out his hand and smiled. "Your wife has been asking for you."

Daniel reached for the man's hand and gripped it. "Where is she?" He looked over the doctor's shoulder as if he could see through the door to where they were keeping Megan. "When can I see her?"

The doctor's smile faded. "She's been moved to a room in the hospital for the night."

"How is she?"

"She's going to be okay," the doctor said, pulling his hand free. "She'll need a few days of rest and plenty of clear liquid. Fortunately, you got her here in time, and the medicine is doing its job."

"How could she have been poisoned?"

The doctor nodded toward Ryan. "The police will have to conduct an investigation. The amount of arsenic in her system was enough to raise red flags."

"I can't imagine where she'd have gotten it. I've been with her for the past two days and eaten what she's eaten. Wouldn't I be sick, as well?"

"Normally, if the poisoning was accidental or the food was tainted. The amount of arsenic in her system was more than what we consider accidental."

"Holy hell." Daniel frowned. "Who would possibly want to poison her?"

The doctor shrugged. "That's for the police to determine. You'll need to list all the places you ate, the people you were with and what you ate to help trace back to the source."

"Sure. But may I see my wife now?"

"Of course." The doctor waved toward a nurse standing nearby. "The nurse will take you back for a blood test and then let you know Megan's room number and floor."

Daniel shook the doctor's hand. "Thank you for helping Megan."

"I understand you two were recently married." The doctor chuckled. "It's not the ideal way to spend your honeymoon. She'll need some extra tender loving care."

"She'll get it. I'll make sure." Daniel went with the nurse into a side room, where she drew a blood sample. She gave Daniel Megan's room number and pointed to the elevator.

Ryan stepped in with him. "Who would want to hurt Megan?"

"I don't know."

"When you were talking to the airport personnel, you said you'd flown in from California, but you were married in Vegas."

"We got married in Vegas and went to California

to inform Megan's parents. We stayed one night at her folks' ranch."

"How is her relationship with her parents?"

"From what I saw, her parents love her. They'd never hurt her."

"I've seen instances where parents loved their children so much, they'd hurt them to keep them dependent on them."

Daniel shook his head. "Megan is their only child. They tried really hard to have that one child. I can't imagine them poisoning her to keep her close. If we had not gotten her to the hospital when we did, she might have died. They wouldn't risk it."

The elevator door opened, and the two Coltons stepped out.

Daniel found the room and knocked gently.

A weak voice answered, "Come in."

His heart hammering against his ribs, Daniel pushed the door open and stepped into a dimly lit room. The curtain was open to the outside, but the sun had slipped below the horizon, casting the room in a dull, dusky light.

Megan lay against crisp white sheets, her face almost as pale as the sheets. "Hey," she said, a smile curling the corners of her lips. "You can turn on a light. It's one of the buttons on this." She handed him the remote control for the bed.

Her hand felt cold to his touch as he took the remote, found a button with a lightbulb on it and clicked it.

The reading light over the bed snapped on, casting a glow over her bright strawberry blond hair.

She raised her hand to her head. "I must be a mess."

He laid the remote on the bed beside her and took her hand in his.

Her freckles stood out against her pale skin, but her green eyes shone, and her bright hair fanned out against the pillow.

"You're beautiful."

She chuckled. "Liar."

"Ryan's here."

She tipped her head to look around Daniel. "Oh, hey. I'm sorry to cause so much trouble."

"Don't be sorry. You didn't cause it," Ryan said.

Megan frowned. "The doctor said I got a hold of arsenic." Her pretty brow furrowed. "How could that be?"

"We don't know. But we need to find out."

She pinched the bridge of her nose. "Did I eat something I shouldn't have?"

Daniel shook his head. "The doctor seemed to think it was more than just tainted food."

Her frown deepened. "He thinks I was poisoned?"

Ryan came to stand beside Daniel. "That's what it looks like."

Her eyes widened and she stared up at Daniel, her hand tightening around his. "Are you okay?"

His chest swelled. It was just like Megan to be more worried about others when she was the one who'd nearly died. "I'm fine. But you have to take it easy for the next couple of days."

A knock sounded on the door.

As Daniel turned, the door opened and Jack's shaggy, dark head stuck around the side, his green eyes shadowed with concern. "Is our best ranch assistant up for visitors?"

Ryan touched Daniel's arm. "I let the family know

about your plane wreck and Megan being taken to the hospital."

"Anything else?" Daniel asked.

His half brother's lips twisted. "I might have mentioned that you two got hitched."

Daniel had forgotten to worry over what the Colton clan would think of his marriage to Megan. Well, he was about to find out.

"So, may we come in?" Jack asked again.

Daniel glanced back at Megan, and she gave a weak smile. "Sure."

"Not for long," Daniel said. "Megan needs rest."

"We won't stay long." Jack entered with his wife, Tracy. He crossed to Daniel and enveloped him in a bear hug. "I don't know whether to congratulate you or give my condolences, brother. Married, plane wrecked and a sick wife. What a combination."

Tracy smiled softly as she pecked Daniel on the cheek and then Megan. "I'm so happy for you both, and I hope you get well soon. However, I have to warn you to be prepared for a Colton gathering. There are more of us waiting outside the door."

Daniel held Megan's hand and stood by her side, bracing himself for the Colton inquisition.

Brett appeared in the doorway after Jack and Tracy moved aside. "Hannah would have come, but her ankles were swollen from being on her feet all day. She sends her love and congrats to the newlyweds." He made his way to Daniel, wrapped his arms around him and pounded him on the back. "You dog! When did you two make the decision to elope? None of us saw it coming."

Daniel was spared from responding when his half brother Eric Colton's broad shoulders filled the doorway. "Daniel, Megan. Sorry, I'm late. I was in surgery and just got the word you were here." He pulled a surgical cap from his head, his buzzed hair shining from perspiration.

"It's okay. Megan is doing much better," Daniel said.

"Good." He shone a penlight into Megan's eyes, then touched his stethoscope to her chest, listened and finally nodded. "You have a good doctor. He was quick to pick up on the symptoms even before the blood test results came back."

"Thank God," Tracy said. "We need more women in the Colton family."

"That's right." Eric stared from Daniel to Megan. "So, you two skipped off to Vegas without letting us all in on the plan?"

"I didn't know I had to get everyone's approval," Daniel countered.

"No, you don't," Ryan said.

"No," Brett said. "But you have to give us a chance to throw you one helluva bachelor party. Don't think that just because you jumped the gun and eloped, you're cheating us out of a chance to roast you."

"Too late. We're already married. No fanfare required." Daniel held up Megan's hand, displaying the ring. "It's done."

Tracy pushed past the men to ogle the ring. "Oh, Megan, how pretty."

Megan's cheeks reddened. "Thank you. It belonged to Daniel's grandmother."

"Then it's extra special." Tracy patted Daniel's arm. "Daniel did good."

"Yes, he did." Megan smiled up at Daniel, the dark smudges beneath her eyes making his heart hurt. The plane crash and the poison had almost killed her. He could have lost her twice in one day. "We need to let Megan sleep. She's been through a lot today."

"From what the news reported, it's probably a good thing I passed out during the landing." Megan frowned up at Daniel. "Why didn't you tell me?"

"I only now got them to let me in to see you."

Ryan chuckled. "Yeah, and he was ready to break down the doors if they didn't let him in. I'm glad you're doing better, Megan."

"Thanks, Ryan." She coughed and closed her eyes.

"That's it. Everyone out," Daniel ordered.

A disturbance at the door heralded the arrival of yet another Colton.

Daniel's father, Big J Colton, his shock of thick white hair standing on end, filled their doorway. "Daniel, what's this I hear about a crash and your assistant taking ill?"

Ryan gave their father the digest version, sparing Daniel the trouble. He ended by saying, "And before all that, the two of them managed to get married in Vegas."

"What?" Big J thundered. "Why wasn't I informed?"

Daniel touched his father's shoulder. "I'm sorry, but we made the decision and moved on it."

"Well, then, I guess there's only one thing I can do," Big J blustered, his frown fierce.

Daniel had seen his father furious, but never for something like one of his sons marrying without his permission. He braced himself, hating to disappoint the man who'd taken him in when his mother had passed.

"What's that, Dad?" Jack asked.

His father's frown disappeared, to be replaced by a big grin. "The only thing a father can do when his son gets married. That's to kiss the bride." He leaned over Megan and kissed her with a loud smack on the cheek. "Welcome to the family, Megan." He turned to Daniel. "Glad you found a good woman. May your lives be filled with love and children."

Daniel's gut clenched. His family had gathered around to wish him well on his marriage, and it was nothing but a big fat lie. What would his father think when they dissolved their vows? He'd be disappointed that Daniel hadn't tried hard enough to keep it together. Daniel couldn't tell his family that it was a farce. Megan's grandmother's trust fund depended on the marriage being legal and valid. And he needed it to make his own deal with the Kennedys.

"As a doctor," Eric spoke up, "I'd say Megan needs rest to recover from her ordeal."

"That's right. We need to get out of here and give the newlyweds a little space." Brett bumped Daniel's shoulder. "You're still on the hook for a bachelor party."

"Really, it's not necessary," Daniel assured him.

"The hell it isn't," Jack stated. "We'll skip the strippers, but there will be beer and football."

Daniel smiled halfheartedly. "Fine. Beer and football. After Megan's well and we've had a chance to figure out what's going on."

"What do you mean?" Big J's smile disappeared.

Daniel regretted opening his mouth. Now he had to explain to the family about Megan's poisoning.

"That's awful!" Tracy pressed a hand to her breast. "Who would want to hurt Megan? She's one of the nicest people I know."

"Exactly."

Big J's frown deepened. "If someone is targeting her,

she's obviously not safe right now." He faced Daniel. "You two will move to the main house until we figure this out."

"No, really, it's not necessary," Megan said.

"It most certainly is." Big J waved aside her protest. "You're going to be resting for a couple days as it is. Knowing Daniel, he'll be out feeding horses at least twice a day. What will you do while he's out puttering in the barn?"

"I can take care of myself." She tried to sit up, but Daniel laid a hand on her shoulder.

"They're right," Daniel said. "I wouldn't feel comfortable leaving you alone in the guesthouse. There's safety in the number of people at the main house. Someone will be around at all times."

"It's not up for discussion." Big J spoke with finality. "You two are moving into the main house for the time being." He bent to peck Megan on the cheek. "We'll see you tomorrow. In the meantime, I hope you feel better."

"Thank you," she said weakly, staring up at Daniel.

Although he really had no desire to move into the main house with the chance of running into his stepmother, Daniel couldn't argue with his father's reasoning.

A nurse entered the room, hitting Brett with the door. Her eyes rounded. "What the heck is going on in here?" Her forehead creased in a deep frown. "Out. All of you, get out. Mrs. Colton needs rest, not a convention."

"We were going," Jack muttered, clutching Tracy's hand as he led her out of the room. He turned at the doorway. "We'll see you guys tomorrow. Congratulations."

The others filed out, leaving Daniel and Ryan as the last men in the room. The nurse checked Megan's vitals and her IV and adjusted her bed down. Then she pointed at Ryan. "You, too. Only her husband can stay the night."

Ryan held up his hands. "I'm going."

The nurse frowned at him again, then left the room.

With a quick peck on Megan's cheek, Ryan said, "Welcome to the family." He turned to Daniel. "Take care of our new sister-in-law. The men still outnumber the women. We could use more good ones like Megan." As he headed toward the door, he tossed over his shoulder, "I'll check on the investigation. As soon as you write down all the particulars of your trip, we'll follow up."

"Thanks, Ryan." Daniel's gaze followed Ryan through the door. When he was gone, the room fell into silence.

"Was that as awkward for you as it was for me?" Megan asked.

Daniel glanced down at her, realizing he still held her hand in his. "I hate to disappoint my family."

"I know." She sighed. "They don't deserve the lies we're feeding them. I'm sorry I got you into this."

"You didn't. I was the one to suggest it in the first place."

"But you wouldn't have if I hadn't handed you my resignation."

"The main thing right now is not to worry about all this. Sleep and let your body recover."

"Yes, sir." She smiled and closed her eyes. "What happened with the plane?"

He'd been wondering that himself. "The landing gear didn't deploy." The manual emergency backup cord had been severed. He didn't mention that.

Her eyes opened, and her brow furrowed. "How did you land without landing gear?"

His lips curled. "Very carefully. On the belly of the plane."

"Oh, Daniel. The plane is ruined?"

He shrugged. "Don't worry about it. That's why we have insurance. We survived the landing and got you to the hospital on time. That's all that matters."

When she opened her mouth to speak again, he held up his hand. "You can ask all the questions you want in the morning. For now, you need to sleep and recover. I have a call to make to Marshall Kennedy to cancel our meeting."

"No." Megan pushed to a sitting position. "I'm feeling better already. You can't cancel the trip to Reno."

"We don't have a plane. It's not worth it to me to go now."

"We're going," she insisted, her voice sounding stronger. "I can arrange for flights to Reno. Or we can rent a plane for the trip. We can't cancel now. We've come too far to give up over a little hiccup in our plans."

Daniel shook his head. "You almost died twice today and you call it a hiccup?" He took her hand in his and lifted it, staring at the ring. "You're an amazing woman, and your father would kill me if he knew what you'd gone through today."

"And that's why you're not going to tell him." She lay back against the pillow and closed her eyes. "Now you can leave and let me sleep. I plan on getting up in the morning and walking out of this hospital."

Daniel chuckled. "Unless you want me to leave, I'm staying. You might have been poisoned once. They might try again. If you want me to leave, I'll sit outside your door. Your choice."

She opened her eyes and gave him a weak smile. "I

really am sorry this is turning out to be more trouble than you bargained for."

"Don't you worry about me. I can take care of myself."

"Good, because I'm too tired to get up." She yawned and rolled onto her side. "See you in the morning." Megan tucked her hand beneath her chin, her hair falling over her face.

Daniel stood for a long time, staring down at her, his heart torn between anger and something else. This woman had left the easy life of the privileged behind, fighting for the freedom to make her own decisions, and ended up poisoned and the target of attacks in Vegas. And yet she was more concerned about being a bother to him. He could easily fall in love with her, and that would never do. Two people couldn't be farther apart in their social realms.

Daniel stepped out of the room and stood in the hallway to make a phone call. Ryan had said he'd check on the status of the airplane and the reason the landing gear had not deployed. Hopefully, the FAA inspector had already taken a cursory look.

Before he could dial his brother's number, his smartphone vibrated in his hand. It was Ryan.

"How's Megan?" he asked without a greeting.

"Better," Daniel replied. "What have you found out?"

"I got word from the FAA inspector. When they moved the plane, they had a chance to look at the landing gear." Ryan paused. "Daniel, it was all chewed up with something that looked like acid, and there was a broken vial strapped to the electrical wires. They think that when you raised the landing gear in Santa Rosa, the vial was crushed and the acid leaked on the wires, causing them to malfunction."

"And someone cut the emergency cord."

"Good thing you two will be staying at the big house. Sounds like someone has it in for Megan, and you could be collateral damage."

CHAPTER FIFTEEN

MEGAN WOKE THE next morning feeling pretty much back to normal, until she got out of the hospital bed and tried to stand on her own two feet. She'd waited until Daniel slipped out for a cup of coffee before she tried to make a run for the bathroom to comb her hair and make herself more presentable to her new husband.

She nearly fell flat on her face, her knees so weak she could barely stand. With concentrated effort, she was determined to make a round trip to the bathroom before Daniel returned.

Dr. Baxter arrived in her room as she settled back on the edge of the bed.

He grinned. "How's my patient?"

Megan straightened, forcing a chipper look. "I feel well enough to leave."

"I'm sure you do." He shook his head. "As good as the food and service are here, no one ever wants to stay." He winked.

After checking her vital signs and flashing a light in her eyes, he declared, "You can go home as long as you have someone with you for the first couple of days." He held up his hand. "Not that I think anything will happen, but just to make sure you don't have a reaction to the medicine or the residual effects of the poison."

"We'll make sure she has someone with her," Daniel

said, stepping into the room, a paper cup of steaming hot coffee in his hand. "She'll be surrounded by family."

"Good, good. I'll have the nurse bring in your discharge papers with instructions. Your stomach might feel a little off for a couple of days, but you should be able to return to work."

Megan glanced at Daniel as she asked the doctor, "We're supposed to go to Reno in two days."

Dr. Baxter folded his stethoscope into his pocket. "There's no reason you shouldn't." He backed toward the door. "Congratulations on your marriage. Hopefully we won't see you again until you come to deliver your first child."

Megan's cheeks flamed and her heart ached. She could imagine a little boy with dark brown hair and bright brown-black eyes like Daniel's.

Once the door closed behind the doctor, she pushed her fantasy to the back of her mind and tilted her chin upward, ready for the battle. "You heard the doctor. We're going to Reno." She eased off the bed and swayed.

Daniel was there to steady her with his empty hand.

She was happy for his warmth and strength, but quickly let go to prove she was capable of standing on her own. "If you will leave me for a few minutes, I'll dress and we can get out of here."

An hour later, they pulled up in front of the main house at the Lucky C Ranch. Megan had been in the house only on a couple of rare occasions, when she'd been invited for a barbecue on the Fourth of July and a birthday party for Big J.

Daniel lifted her out of the truck and carried her up the steps.

"I could have walked," she muttered, trying not to

love the way his arms felt so warm and secure around her. When he set her on her feet, he kept an arm around her middle while he opened the door.

"There she is." Hannah, Brett's wife, hurried toward them in the grand foyer, a smile on her face, her cheeks rosy and her baby bump preceding her.

"I'll be right back with your suitcase." Daniel left her with Hannah and returned to his truck.

"We were so worried about you." Hannah hooked Megan's arm. "Do you need help getting settled in Daniel's old room?"

"If it's all the same to you, I'd rather relax in the living room. I don't feel like I'm sick. Just a little wobbly."

"Well, then, come on in the main living room. There are plenty of seats available to choose from." Hannah led the way to the living room, but she glanced back at Daniel as he entered the house with Megan's case. "And, Daniel, don't worry about the horses. Brett's been out all morning taking care of them."

"If it's all the same to you, Megan, I'd like to go check on Halo."

"Please do. In fact, I'll come with you," Megan said. "I've been concerned about her since we left."

Daniel shook his head. "I'd feel better knowing you were safe in the house, recovering."

"I'm feeling better already." Anxious to get back to normal, doing the job she loved, she spun toward him and swayed.

Daniel's jaw firmed, and he gripped her arms. "If you want to come to Reno with me in two days, rest now." Then he bent to seal her mouth with his in a brief, fierce kiss. "Please," he said when he lifted his head.

Shaken more by the kiss than she cared to admit,

Megan nodded. "Okay. But promise you'll tell me how she is when you get back."

"I will. I won't be gone but a few minutes." He brushed his lips across her forehead and glanced over her shoulder at Hannah. "You'll be with her all the time?"

She smiled. "You bet. The way my ankles have been swelling, I'll be somewhere inside with my feet up."

Daniel left them in the living room.

Megan listened for the sound of the back door closing before she could rest.

"Come have a seat," Hannah urged. "Big J is out with Brett. We have the house to ourselves."

"What I'd really like is a shower." Flying from California, feeling so sick she wanted to die and spending a night in the disinfectant-rich hospital made her yearn for a bar of soap and a hot shower.

"There's one on this floor, if you'll follow me." Hannah led the way to a guest bedroom and bathroom, where Megan dug through her case for her last clean outfit. She'd have to get someone to take her to her apartment soon.

After she took a hot shower, put on clean clothes and brushed the tangles out of her long, wet hair, she felt almost human again.

Megan stepped out of the bathroom and ran into a solid wall of muscle. Her hands rested on Daniel's chest. His curled around her waist and held her tight against him.

"You got back awfully quickly." She smiled up at him and then frowned. "Is Halo all right?"

He nodded. "You smell like honeysuckle."

Megan's heart warmed. The man paid enough attention to know the scent of honeysuckle on her.

"My shampoo."

"You know they're going to expect us to stay in my bedroom upstairs."

"I just made use of this shower for now. I'm sure we can figure out the sleeping arrangements. I can sleep on the floor. It doesn't really matter to me."

Daniel's brows furrowed, his hands tightening around her middle. "You're not sleeping on the floor."

She bit her bottom lip. "I hadn't thought past telling my parents. I kind of assumed that when we got back here, we'd go on living the same as before. You in the cabin. Me in my apartment."

Already shaking his head, Daniel said, "Not possible. Now that the Colton clan knows, we have to keep up the appearance of a newlywed couple."

She sighed and cupped his face. "I guess I really didn't think this through. I'm sorry."

"I'm not." He bent, laid his cheek against her temple and sniffed. "After all that's happened, I feel better having you close enough to keep an eye on. Besides, you smell good."

Megan leaned into him, loving the solidity of his body against hers. She'd have no trouble playing the part of the loving wife in their new role. The problem would be turning off the real feelings.

"Daniel!" A shout jerked her out of the warm haze of loving a man who didn't love her.

Daniel inhaled, his chest moving against her before he set her away from him. "The problem with living in the main house is that you don't have much privacy."

"Daniel!"

"That would be Ryan. We'd better go see if he's got any news for us."

Megan almost opened her mouth to beg him to hold her a little longer. Instead she nodded her head. "Let's go."

With his hand resting at the small of her back, he led her through the guest bedroom and down the hallway to the living room.

Brett, Hannah and Big J stood with Ryan in the living room, their faces drawn. Ryan still wore his uniform from the Tulsa PD.

"No way," Brett was saying. "He would never have done it."

Daniel stepped into the room with Megan. "What's going on?"

Ryan faced Daniel. "Actually, I shouldn't be here, but as your brother, I felt I owed it to you."

Megan's gut knotted, and she braced herself for what she was sure wouldn't be good news.

"Owed me what?" Daniel asked.

"A heads-up." Ryan drew in a long breath. "When they discovered just who Megan Talbot is, and that you'd married her in a quickie Vegas wedding, they put two and two together. Their number one person of interest in Megan's poisoning is the one man who stands to gain the most if Megan dies."

Megan shook her head. "You don't think Daniel poisoned me, do you?" She laughed out loud.

Ryan didn't crack a smile. "I don't think he did, but he has plenty of motive to make him a prime suspect."

Daniel's face hardened, and a muscle ticked in his jaw. "I didn't poison her. I'd never do anything to hurt her."

"I trust Daniel with my life. He wasn't the one who poisoned me. He's the kindest, gentlest man I know." Her eyes widened. "Besides, he wouldn't inherit anything from my death. When my parents pass, and if I pass on as well with no heirs, everything I stand to inherit will go to the next blood relative. My cousin, Christine."

Ryan pulled his smartphone out of his back pocket. "What's her full name?"

Megan reluctantly gave the details about her cousin. "But she wouldn't hurt anyone. She and I grew up together. She's the closest thing I have to a sister."

"Still, if she stands to inherit the Talbot fortune, she's another suspect on the list." Ryan keyed in the data and hit Send to text the information to the Tulsa PD. Then he glanced up. "We have to chase all leads."

A shiver slipped down Megan's spine. She'd spent her young life in the shadow of her father's notoriety, had her own bodyguard at the age of six and thought she'd escaped that life when she'd run away to Oklahoma. No one here should have known about the connection between Megan Talbot and Frank Talbot, the highly successful international businessman from California.

"Why target me?" Megan asked. "My father is still alive. I haven't inherited anything. For all I know, he could have all his money going to one of his favorite charities—the children's hospital, an equine research center, anything."

"According to news accounts, your father's health is already precarious. Am I right?" Ryan asked.

Megan's chest tightened. "Yes, but he's getting better."

"The loss of their only daughter could send your parents into a tailspin. I've seen families fall apart upon the death of their child."

"You think if I died, my father would pass away? That would leave my mother alone." Megan's hand found

Daniel's, and she held on through the pain radiating in her heart. Knowing now how her parents had tried to have children before her, she understood her death could be the fatal blow to her father. And her mother might prefer to join him. "Who would want me and my family dead?" She shook her head, sadness sapping her strength.

"We don't know." Ryan's face softened, and he reached out to touch her arm. "We'll do our best to find out. In the meantime, stick with one of us Coltons. We'll take care of you."

Brett stepped forward. "That's right. We Coltons take care of our own."

"Damn right, we do," Big J said. "You're part of the family now that you're married to Daniel."

Daniel's hand squeezed hers gently. "That's right. You're a Colton now."

"Yes you are. You're one of us, Megan." Brett slid an arm around his pregnant wife.

Feeling only slightly mollified by the show of Colton support, Megan couldn't shake the feeling of impending doom. Someone was after her. But would that someone come all the way to Oklahoma to attack her?

"Come on. You look like you could use some rest." Daniel scooped her off her feet.

"I can walk, thank you very much," she said, her cheeks heating, embarrassed at his masculine manhandling in front of his family.

Brett grinned. "Yeah, we're pretty sure she can walk, Daniel."

Hannah swatted at her husband's arm. "Leave Daniel alone. It's much more romantic to be swept off your feet." She winked at Megan. "Enjoy it now. When you're seven months pregnant, it's a little harder to manage."

"What do you mean?" Brett bent and swept Hannah up in his arms. Then he groaned loudly. "Yeah, you're right. It is a little harder. Packed on a few pounds, sweetheart?"

Hannah glared at him. "Darn right I have."

"And still as beautiful as the day I met you." Brett kissed her soundly and set her on the couch.

Megan watched how Brett and Hannah teased each other, kissed and touched. The love shining from their gazes only made Megan's heart squeeze harder. Safe in Daniel's arms, she couldn't help but wish they were as in love as Brett and Hannah.

Instead of depositing her on the couch in the living room, Daniel carried her up the stairs as if climbing with a full grown woman in his arms was nothing. He pushed open the door to one of the bedrooms and closed it behind him with his foot. They were alone at last. She glanced away from his face, afraid she'd see indifference when what she wanted to see was a love to equal the feelings she had for him.

Daniel set her on her feet, his hand lingering at the small of her back.

A little shy at being alone with him, Megan scanned the clean, crisp lines of the room, from the khaki-colored paint on the walls to the gold, tan and antique-blue comforter on the bed. It didn't say much about the boy he'd been. "No trophies? Pictures from high school? Old guitars?"

"I didn't play guitar. I was outside with the horses most of the time."

She chuckled. "Big surprise."

"My stepmother had this room redecorated as soon as I moved to the cabin. She was glad see me leave her home."

"How sad."

Daniel shrugged. "You can't blame Abra for hating me. My father had an affair with his housekeeper and then brought me to live under his roof. What woman would happily take in a child who wasn't hers?"

"Like a painful reminder of your father's indiscretion." Megan nodded. "I guess I could see her side, but at the same time, it wasn't your fault Big J had an affair."

"No. But Abra couldn't let it go and accept me in her home."

"It must have been uncomfortable for you." Megan frowned. "We don't have to stay here if it's too painful."

"Since Abra was attacked by an intruder back in June, and even while she was in a coma, there have been some other minor accidents on the ranch. Because of this, she's been a little less antagonistic toward me, more vulnerable. I actually think she'd be happy to have more people in the house. She hasn't felt completely safe since that time."

"The Lucky C hasn't been so lucky lately. You'd think by now the police would have all the incidents tied together."

"We thought the hit man after Tracy was the one who attacked Abra, but Ryan assures us the evidence proves otherwise. And that man was caught before the fire." Daniel's brow furrowed. "Perhaps we should hire a bodyguard and get you far away from the Lucky C."

"No." Megan rested a hand on Daniel's chest, liking how solid it was and how safe she felt when she was with him. "I'd rather be closer to you...and the horses."

"Good. Because I'd rather you were close, as well. And don't worry. There are plenty of people around. Hannah's now here with Brett. Big J isn't out and about as often. He's letting my brothers and me run most of the day-to-day operations of the ranch, though he still has a say in the way he likes things."

"Still, I've already put you out so much. I'd feel better if we were at the cabin." She also would have felt more relaxed if it were just the two of them. Keeping up the lie would be more difficult the more people she was around.

He cupped her cheeks in his hands and gazed down into her eyes. "The cabin is too isolated. I can't leave you alone and risk someone making another attempt to take your life." When she opened her mouth to protest, he pressed his finger to her lips. "And don't say it. I know you can take care of yourself, but just this once, let us take care of you."

She nodded, finding herself falling into his incredibly dark, bottomless gaze. She shook her head, bringing herself back to the ground. "Do you suppose the intruder in Vegas was the same person to sabotage the plane and poison me?"

Daniel nodded. "It all makes sense now. When we were in Vegas, the attack seemed like a random event."

"Now it doesn't." She shivered.

Daniel's gaze raked over her. "You should get some rest. You've gone through a lot."

"I am a little tired." She glanced at the big bed. "I'd feel better in my own apartment."

He dragged a finger along her cheek. "Sorry, sweetheart. We're married now. It just won't do to have us sleeping across town from each other."

"I suppose not." She hugged her arms around her middle. "I'm just not comfortable being here."

"Would it help if I stayed until you went to sleep?"

Her lips quirked. "I wouldn't ask you to."

"You're not asking. I'm offering." Once again, he swept her up in his arms and carried her across to the bed.

Megan draped her arm around his neck and sighed. "You're making a habit of carrying me around."

He grinned. "I know. I find that I like it." He laid her in the middle of the bed and pulled her shoes off her feet, dropping them to the floor. His hands lingered on her ankles, and his nostrils flared.

A spark of desire lit a flame at her core, and Megan held her breath, praying he'd take her in his arms and make love to her.

Instead, he toed off his boots and lay on the bed beside her. Pulling her back to his front, he spooned her with his big body. "Sleep," he said, his voice sounding strained.

How in the hell was she going to sleep when all she wanted to do was turn in his arms, strip him naked and force him to see her as a desirable woman? Not just his assistant and the woman he'd entered into a bargain with for a marriage of convenience.

As she lay cocooned in Daniel's arms, Megan couldn't help but think this marriage of convenience was anything but convenient. She wanted so much more. If he couldn't love her, she'd do well to let him go sooner rather than later. The longer she was with him as husband and wife, the harder it would be to let go. To get over him, she'd have to give up her job on the Lucky C and move far away.

Her hand curled around his where it rested against her belly. God, she didn't want to let go.

CHAPTER SIXTEEN

"READY?" DANIEL GLANCED up at the porch where Megan stood wearing a royal blue dress that hugged her curves to perfection. Sleeveless and cinched in the middle with a thick belt, the dress accentuated her narrow waist. The hem came halfway down her long, slender thighs, displaying a healthy amount of her legs while maintaining a conservative appeal.

The black high heels made her seem even taller than she was, and her beautiful burnished gold hair had been artfully piled on top of her head, exposing her long, graceful neck.

Daniel's heart pounded against his ribs as he stared up at the woman he found himself falling deeper and deeper in love with. After he'd brought her home to the main house at the Lucky C Ranch, he'd made it his mission to be there as much as possible and yet to maintain his hands-off approach. He'd given in to his desire to sleep in the same bed with her, but the effort it cost him not to make love to her had nearly been his undoing.

She had been through enough and was still on the road to recovering from being poisoned. The least he could do was let her sleep.

Big J appeared behind her with Abra, who was looking better than she had in a long time, her neatly dyed brown hair cupping her chin in a stylish bob. She gave

Daniel a hint of a smile and patted Megan's shoulder in a minimalist hug. "Please do be careful, Megan. I've enjoyed having you in the house for the past couple of days. I'd hate it if anything happened to you."

"Thank you, Mrs. Colton."

"Oh, please. Call me Abra." She stepped back and waited at the top of the stairs.

Big J offered Megan his arm, descended the steps and he held out a hand to Daniel. "I hope you get the contract you want, son."

Daniel shook his father's hand. "You and me both. It will make all the difference in our horse-breeding operation."

"Son, when you get back, we need to talk about that. I realize the program is a success because of you. Hell, you could be making a lot more money for yourself if you didn't have the Lucky C holding you down."

"I love this ranch and the people on it. It's home."

Big J pulled him into a bear hug. "And we love you, too. When you were a bachelor, that cabin worked out just fine. But now that you're a married man, you need to think of your growing family." Big J draped an arm over Daniel's shoulder and grinned at Megan. "I expect half a dozen grandchildren running around this place."

Megan's face reddened, and her gaze dipped to her feet.

Daniel's gut clenched. He could imagine two or three little girls with strawberry blond hair wearing blue jeans and miniature cowboy boots, whooping and hollering as they ran around the barn. Megan's babies would be adorable. He found himself wanting to be their father and wishing he could give Megan the lifestyle she'd been born into. Even if he took his horse-breeding program out on his own, he'd make good money, but not anywhere near what Frank Talbot brought in.

"You'd better get going. Your plane will be waiting at the airport." Big J clapped a hand on Daniel's shoulder. "Good luck."

Daniel handed Megan into his truck and climbed in the driver's seat.

"We're not flying commercial?" Megan asked.

"No, Big J arranged for a charter airplane."

"Isn't that expensive?"

Daniel nodded. "I tried to talk him out of it, but he insisted. He has the money for it, and he wanted you to be comfortable after your last experience."

"I would have been fine flying commercial," she said, staring straight ahead.

"I still feel as if we should have called off this meeting. With someone trying to hurt you, it's too dangerous to take you out in public."

Megan's lips tightened. "I went along with resting for the past couple of days, but if I'd had to stay inside any longer, I'd have gone completely nutty. Now I know what it feels like to be under house arrest. I left my parents' home because they wouldn't let me breathe."

Daniel nodded. "Fair enough. But please keep close to me. There should be a lot of people in Reno for the symposium. Promise me you'll stay where I can keep an eye on you. If not for you, then do it for my peace of mind."

"Okay. I get it. I'll stick to you like a fly on fly paper." She winked across at him, making his pulse pound and his desire flame.

At the general aviation hangars, Daniel located the charter company and performed the preflight with the contracted pilot, carefully checking the landing gear and the emergency landing gear cord.

Someone had sabotaged his plane before. He'd be damned if the same someone got away with it again. After a thorough once-over, he helped Megan up the steps into the airplane and settled in a seat across from her.

As the plane taxied down the runway, Daniel's gaze slid to the closed door to the cockpit, his fingers digging into the armrest.

"Not used to someone else doing the flying?" Megan asked softly.

Daniel forced himself to relax. "Not really. I've been flying since before I was old enough to drive a car. I prefer to be at the yoke in small planes."

"Flying in big planes doesn't bother you as much?"

"Not as much."

"Think about something else, like what you're going to say to Marshall Kennedy at dinner tonight."

For the rest of the trip, they went over the program Daniel had in place, the pedigrees and lineage. He'd worked so hard to create a firm basis on which to build one of the finest horse-breeding operations in the country.

By the time they landed, he wasn't even thinking much about his sabotaged plane. They touched down without incident in Reno what seemed like only minutes after they'd left Tulsa but had actually been a few hours.

Megan smiled across at him. "You'll have a lot to talk about with Marshall at dinner tonight."

Daniel reached out to take Megan's hand. "What would I do without you? If you hadn't come along when you did, I'd still be digging my way through my filing system."

"You were doing fine without me. But I am glad I could help. Makes me think my degree in biology wasn't a waste."

"Hardly. You're amazing." He stood and pulled her to her feet. "You're not only smart but also look great."

"Let's go seal this deal." She started toward the door. Before she could take a step, he pulled her back into his arms.

"Just so you know, I appreciate everything you and your family have done for me."

She laughed up at him. "Are you kidding? You've saved my life not once, but three times." She stood on her tiptoes and pressed her lips to his in a brief kiss. "I guess that makes you my hero."

The husky tone of her voice sent Daniel all the way over the edge. He crushed her body against his. "I can't decide whether I like you better in that dress or in jeans and boots."

"I'm the same person inside."

"That's why I can't decide. You're amazing no matter what you wear—" his voice dropped to a whisper "—or don't wear." Then his lips met hers, and he forgot everything but kissing her.

Megan sank into him, her mouth opening on a sigh.

He swept in, caressing her tongue in a long, slow glide, his hands skimming along the curve of her waist and downward to the swell of her hips and buttocks.

She made him want so much more of what he couldn't have. Even if she wasn't his employee, and if they didn't have to go back to the way things were before their sham of a marriage, she far outclassed him in every way.

A soft cough sounded over Megan's shoulder. "Sorry, I didn't mean to interrupt."

Daniel stepped back and glanced at the pilot standing by the hatch. His face was red. "I was just going to lower the stairs."

"Please do," Daniel directed him.

"I'll be here when you're ready to return to Oklahoma. You have my number." The pilot spoke as he lowered the stairs into place. Then he stood back. "Take your time disembarking. I'll deliver your luggage to the hotel where we're staying."

Megan's cheeks glowed a pretty pink, and her green eyes danced. "Let's get this show on the road."

She went down the steps first. Daniel followed, wishing they were going straight to their hotel to finish the kiss they'd started, instead of meeting Marshall Kennedy for dinner.

Alas, pleasure would have to wait. He was there on business. He hoped all would go well and they could be on their way back home.

MEGAN SETTLED IN the backseat of the limousine that whisked them from the airport to the convention center, where the symposium would have a meet and greet for the attendees. They were to find Marshall Kennedy there and leave the convention center to have a private dinner with him and whomever he'd brought with him.

"My father said Kennedy was open to dialogue and spoke well of you."

"Remind me to thank your father for placing the call."

"He did say that Mr. Kennedy liked to make up his own mind. But hopefully a little bug in his ear will help smooth the path." Megan reached for Daniel's hand. "Just tell him the truth. You've done your homework, and you excel at choosing quality horses. This is your passion, and that will shine through."

Daniel lifted her hand to his lips and pressed a kiss against the backs of her knuckles. "Best pep talk ever. Thank you."

The rest of the ride was made in silence, Megan's heart nearly bursting with Daniel's praise. He didn't let go of her hand until they got out of the vehicle in front of the convention center.

He alighted first and reached in to take her hand.

She let him help her out and onto her feet. Then, hand in hand, they walked toward the convention center.

Megan was so proud to be with the most handsome man there. He stood a head taller than most men, and he looked so sexy in a crisp white shirt, black jeans and black cowboy boots. He had on his best black cowboy hat and a plain black tie that he tugged at several times. Obviously uncomfortable in the semiformal attire, he squared his shoulders and marched through the door.

"Just so you know," she said, "I think you look pretty darned sexy."

He stopped short, a frown creasing his brow. "You think I should have worn blue jeans instead?"

Megan laughed. "No, I think that if Mrs. Kennedy comes, you'll have someone else batting for you."

"I'm more afraid I won't make it across the room with you at my side. The prettiest woman in the building is bound to cause a riot."

"In this old thing?" She winked. "Let's go make some waves."

Megan strode into the convention hall feeling like a million bucks. She refused to look past the deadline of her marriage. For the moment, she had the man she loved at her side, he thought she was beautiful and that was all that mattered.

The majority of symposium attendees were men in jeans and cowboy boots, nice button-up shirts and cowboy hats. Wives, if they brought them, were dressed in a mix of nice dresses, pantsuits or jeans and cowboy boots. Megan would have preferred her jeans and cowboy boots. But with so much riding on this meeting, she felt more prepared in the blue dress she knew looked good on her.

They made their way around the large room, introducing themselves. Daniel had brought up several pictures of Marshall Kennedy online the night before so they wouldn't miss him. Megan had seen him on only one occasion when he'd visited the Triple Diamond, and that had been when she was more concerned about riding horses than breeding them.

In the crowd, she caught a glimpse of a woman with shiny blond hair and for a moment thought it was Christine. After all that had happened, she had to admit to a case of mild paranoia, the feeling she was being watched. Even at the Coltons' main house. Yet every time she turned around, no one was there. Now was no different. The shiny blond-haired woman she thought was Christine turned out to be a woman with bleach-blond hair in her midfifties.

Megan laughed at herself, her smile growing when she spotted a man fitting the images they'd seen on the internet of Marshall Kennedy.

Kennedy was reportedly tall, like this man, with a head full of strikingly white hair. Dressed in a black button-up shirt, black jeans and a silver bolo tie, he was handsome and commanding, with a crowd of people around him.

Megan leaned toward Daniel and smiled. "In the corner by the bar."

"I see him." Daniel smiled down at her instead of staring hard at his target. "And if I'm not mistaken, he sees you." He lifted his head and nodded. "He's headed this way."

"Daniel Colton?" The white-haired gentleman, surrounded by his entourage, made his way across the room, his hand held out in front of him. "You are Daniel Colton?"

"Yes, sir." Daniel took the hand and shook it.

Megan adopted all her mother's grace and charm from years of sponsoring charitable events. She shone her best smile on the man who could make all the difference to the breeding program Daniel had worked so hard to perfect.

"And you must be his new bride, Megan." He leaned forward and bussed her cheek. "Your father gave me permission to kiss the bride. What a beautiful bride you are. The spitting image of your mother when she was your age." The older man turned to Daniel. "You're a very lucky man. If I'd had a lick of sense thirty years ago, I'd have married Megan's mother instead of chasing horses around the world." Marshall held up both hands. "Don't get me wrong. I married a beautiful, successful woman, and we've been together for the past twenty-five years."

"I'm sure my father is happy to hear that." Megan smiled.

"Colton, you had the good sense to put a ring on Josephine's daughter's finger before you got too caught up in the business. A good woman can help keep you grounded."

Daniel slipped an arm around Megan's waist and smiled down at her. "I am a very lucky man that she chose me. She's not only beautiful but also smart. She has been a huge help to my program already. We work well together."

The heat rose in Megan's cheeks. "He's being too kind. Daniel had the program going strong before I ever showed up at the Lucky C Ranch."

Daniel kissed her temple. "You helped me position it for the next level." He shifted his direct gaze to Kennedy.

The older man nodded, his lips quirking at the corners. "What I've learned from Frank, the internet and the grapevine is that you've done pretty well for yourself, and at a young age."

Daniel tipped his head up. "Thank you, sir. I'm proud of my horse-breeding strategy, and I hope to take it a step further with Kennedy Farm's Striker's Royal Advantage stud services."

Kennedy nodded. "Precisely. We can talk details at dinner." He introduced Daniel and Megan to his ranch manager, Tom Miller, and the head of his breeding program, Gary Callan.

The five of them loaded into Kennedy's waiting Hummer limousine, and they were taken to one of the nicest steak houses in Reno in one of the most prestigious casinos.

"Daniel, are you a gambler?" Mr. Kennedy asked as he took his seat at the table.

Daniel settled in next to Megan and reached for her hand beneath the table. "Only in the sense of weather and crops. However, I like to take what I call educated risks."

Kennedy's eyes narrowed, and he leaned forward. "How's that?"

"I do my homework to find the best solutions to problems. I consult my expert biologist—" Daniel tilted his head toward Megan "—and make the environment as stable as I can when ranching and working with animals before I commit."

The older man sat back, giving Daniel an assessing glance. "Sounds pretty calculated."

"I didn't build my program based on the seat of my pants."

"Have you ever taken an uncalculated risk?"

Daniel squeezed Megan's hand beneath the table. "As a matter of fact, I did. That risk was asking Megan to marry me."

Kennedy chuckled. "How do you figure that as uncalculated?"

"We were in the barn. I'm sure I smelled of horse manure and hay when I asked her."

Megan smiled up at him. "He'd saved me from a runaway horse a few days earlier, I smelled about the same and it was the most romantic proposal I could have imagined. I wouldn't have had it any other way."

Daniel grinned at Mr. Kennedy. "See what I mean? She's perfect."

"Common interests and goals are the keys to a successful merger." Kennedy nodded. "You two will do well together."

"I hadn't met a woman as interested in horses as I am." Daniel gazed at Megan. "Until a pretty redheaded female answered my ad for an assistant. I have to admit, I was hesitant to hire a woman to work with horses. But

she convinced me to give her a try. I was pleasantly surprised that she was more than just a pretty face."

Megan's mouth twisted in a wry grin. "You're sounding pretty chauvinistic, sweetheart." She shifted her
glance to Mr. Kennedy. "I told him I'd been working
around horses all my life. My father bred both quarter
horses and Thoroughbreds. I knew the nose from the
tail and how to manage the records of a much larger
operation."

Daniel's gaze fixed on Megan, giving her a warm
feeling. "She talked the talk."

"How did she convince you?" Kennedy asked.

"I challenged her to ride with me." Daniel crossed
his arms, a grin spreading across his face. "Bareback."

Butterflies fluttered in Megan's belly at the way Daniel's dark eyes danced. He loved telling this story, and it
made her feel special and proud to have passed his test.
Her parents would have been appalled that he'd asked her
to ride bareback. But bareback was how she'd learned
and felt most natural.

Mr. Kennedy laughed out loud.

Daniel's chuckle made Megan's chest swell. "I figured
if she was afraid of horses, she'd refuse to ride bareback,
and she'd know immediately she didn't have the job. I
couldn't have an assistant afraid of horses."

Megan's chin tilted upward. "I'm not afraid of horses.
But I have a healthy respect for them."

Kennedy leaned forward. "Did you ride the horse
bareback?"

A grin spread across her face. "Damn right I did."
Her mother would have washed her mouth out with soap
had she heard her daughter curse in front of anyone.
Megan felt she'd earned the right to be adamant. She

was good with horses, and when her parents refused to give her permission to work with the Triple Diamond breeding stock, she'd been even more determined to prove them wrong.

Daniel's chest puffed out. "Not only did she ride that horse, but she also cleaned her hooves, checked her teeth and gave me advice on what feed was best and how often. She asked questions only someone with an intimate knowledge of horses would ask."

"Now he doesn't know how to live without me," Megan said with a bright smile. She wished her words were true. When the time came for their marriage to end, she knew she wouldn't be able to stay. Daniel already meant so much to her that she couldn't work at his side as just his assistant. What if he fell in love with another woman?

Her heart ached at the thought.

No, she couldn't work alongside him if he had another woman in his life. She'd have to leave the Lucky C Ranch in order to get over him. Seeing him with someone else would tear her apart.

Tom Miller and Gary Callan asked questions.

Megan gave Daniel the lead. It was his program. When she was gone, he'd still be there, raising the finest horses.

Daniel didn't let her sit by, nodding and smiling. He pulled her into the conversation. Soon the five of them were leaning over the table in a lively discussion about studs or mares from other breeders that Kennedy Farms and the Lucky C could benefit from.

Marshall Kennedy finally glanced at his watch. "Good Lord. Is it really eleven o'clock?"

Megan looked around the restaurant. The waitstaff

was hovering around their table, ready to clean up and get out of there. "We shouldn't have kept you so long." She started to stand, but Daniel put a hand on her knee beneath the table.

She waited until he stood and held her chair. Though she hated all the formality of living the lifestyle of the rich and famous, it was nice to be treated like a lady, with respect and care. When it was convenient, Daniel opened doors for her on the Lucky C. There were times that, as an assistant, she opened them for him.

"Tomorrow I would like to show you the stud you were interested in. The symposium arranged for breeders to show their horses at the arena. Will you be available to view him?" Mr. Kennedy asked. "I'll have several of our broodmares, as well."

Daniel slipped an arm around Megan's waist. "We'd be honored."

Outside the restaurant, Kennedy, Miller and Callan shook hands with Daniel and Megan.

"We're staying at this hotel," Kennedy said. "But the limousine is at your disposal. It will drop you off at yours." The older man held out his hand to Daniel. "So that you're not left hanging, I want you to know that I like what I've seen in the way you run your program, the horses you've bred and, of course, your choice of a lifelong assistant." Mr. Kennedy dropped Daniel's hand and lifted Megan's to cup it in both of his. "And you're absolutely right. She is beautiful and intelligent. Your father must be proud."

Megan now knew her father was proud of her, and hearing Kennedy say that he must be made it all the more real. "Thank you for your time, Mr. Kennedy."

"Call me Marshall. I like to be on a first-name basis

with the people I do business with." He winked at Daniel. "Once you've had a chance to see Striker's Royal Advantage, if you're still interested, we'll draw up the papers."

Daniel nodded, his face serious. "Thank you, Mr. Kennedy. I appreciate your confidence in me."

Kennedy clapped a hand on Daniel's shoulder. "You've earned it, son."

Kennedy and his two men returned to the hotel while Daniel handed Megan into the limousine.

Once he was seated, a huge grin split Daniel's face, and he grabbed Megan in a bear hug. "Sweetheart, I could not have done it without you. You were absolutely amazing. I could kiss you."

She stared up into his shining eyes and asked, "What's stopping you?"

Daniel cupped her cheek and tilted her face up, bringing his mouth so close to hers, his warm breath tickling her lips.

"I could so easily fall in love with you," he whispered.

"Again, what's stopping you?"

He brushed her mouth with his, dragging her close against him.

The limousine pulled away from the hotel and was halfway down the road before Daniel broke away to breathe. But only for a minute. Then he kissed and nibbled a trail along her cheek and chin, down the side of her neck to where the pulse beat hard at the base of her throat.

Her body was on fire with need. She couldn't wait to reach the hotel and have this man. Nothing would stop her or get in the way of them making love. Until they broke it off, Megan and Daniel were married. Making love was part of the gig. There was no shame in it and no reason to hold back.

A quick glance at the divider between the driver and the back of the limousine reassured her of their privacy. Megan pushed Daniel to arm's length, grabbed for the buckle cinching the belt around her waist and pulled it free. Then she winked. "Are you afraid to go for a ride, cowboy?"

CHAPTER SEVENTEEN

DANIEL'S EYES FLARED, and his pulse pounded so hard against his eardrums he could barely hear. "Hang on." He fumbled with the buttons on the side of the door and said, "Driver, could you circle Reno for twenty minutes? My wife hasn't seen all the city has to offer."

After the driver responded, Daniel hit the Mute button.

Daniel barely had his finger off the button when Megan reached for the hem of her dress, pulled it up over her head and tossed it to the side.

Daniel froze, and his breath caught in his throat. He reached out to touch the soft skin of her cheeks and then dragged the backs of his knuckles down her neck. He memorized the curves and edges as he crossed her collarbone, smoothed across the muscles of her shoulders and moved downward to the swell of her breasts.

The lace of her bra had an erotic coarseness that set his world on fire. Daniel tweaked the distended nipples through the lace, his mouth watering for a taste of her luscious fruit.

Megan moaned and leaned into his palms.

There would be no stopping him this time. All the best intentions of staying away from her and keeping his hands off this woman were null and void. He had to have her. He wanted her so much he'd make love to her in the backseat of the limousine.

His need for her was like a physical pain in his heart.

Megan reached behind her back and flicked the catches on her bra, freeing herself for him. Then she wove her fingers through his hair and guided his mouth to her nipple. Daniel tugged the straps down her arms and tossed the undergarment away. He palmed a breast in one hand while he tongued the other, angling Megan downward onto the leather seat.

The vehicle slowed for a stop. Daniel wasn't even vaguely aware of the world around him.

Megan reached between them and unbuckled his belt and the top button of his jeans. "I want you. Now." She gripped the zipper and tugged it downward.

"Shh, sweetheart. We have the limousine long enough to do this right."

"I don't want right. I want now." Her fingers slid into his jeans and wrapped around the steely hardness of him.

"At the rate we're going, I won't last long."

"Anyone ever tell you that you talk too much?" She leaned up on her elbow and wrapped her hand around his neck, pulling him down on top of her. Her mouth found his, and she kissed him long and hard.

Daniel hooked his thumb in the elastic of her panties, dragged them down her long legs and tossed them to the side. Then he parted her legs and moved between them, nudging her entrance with his erection.

She pushed his jeans over his buttocks and sank her fingernails into his skin. She gasped, "What about protection?"

"Back pocket," he gritted out, afraid he wouldn't be able to control himself much longer. "In my wallet."

While he balanced over her on his arms, she reached for his wallet, extracted the little foil packet, ripped it open and rolled it down over him. "Now!"

Megan wrapped her legs around his waist and dug her heels into his buttocks.

Daniel drove into her, hard and fast, burying himself deep inside. Her slick channel contracted around him, drawing him deeper.

Holy hell, how was he supposed to make this last when she felt so damned good? He thrust in and out, unable to slow to pleasure her first. The need to have her drove his actions.

Megan let her heels drop against the seat. She pushed off to meet him thrust for thrust, the friction creating an overpowering heat he was sure would light the leather cushion on fire.

Her moans turned into soft mewling cries that sent him rocketing over the edge of reason. He thrust one last time and held steady, deep inside her.

Megan's legs clamped around him, holding him there until his member stopped throbbing and he could redirect the blood flow back to his brain.

He pulled free and handed Megan her clothes, helping her by hooking the bra in the back. Dressing her was almost as sensual as undressing her, and he wished they had more time in the limousine. But they had a room they would share in one of the swanky hotels. "Hey, the sooner we get back to the hotel, the sooner we can resume our negotiations." He tugged the dress over her head and down her torso.

Then he zipped, buttoned and buckled, ready to get on with the night. Alone in their room.

Megan was smoothing her hair and adjusting her

hem when the driver slammed on the brakes and the limousine's tires screeched. Without their seat belts on, Megan and Daniel slid off the backseat and dropped to the floor. Then there was a loud crashing of metal on metal. The limousine was tossed to the side, and they were flung with it.

When all movement stilled, Daniel leaned over Megan. "Are you all right?"

"I think I am," she said, touching her hand to her temple. She'd hit something. A long trail of blood oozed down the side of her face.

"You're hurt." Daniel reached for the door and tried to open it. It had been shoved into the interior three or four inches. The other door was worse.

"Are you two all right back there?" The driver lowered the dividing wall between the front and the back seats.

"Mrs. Colton was injured."

"I'm all right. But can you get us out of here?"

"Both doors have been damaged. You have two choices. Climb through the window between the front and the back or out through the sunroof, if I can get it to open. The electronics aren't working exactly right." A motor whined. The sunroof opened halfway and stopped. After several attempts by the driver, the roof opened.

"I'll go first, then help you out." Daniel pulled himself through the sunroof and reached in to help Megan. The blood on her face made him so angry he could have put his fist through a brick wall.

Once he had her on the roof, he dropped to the ground and held out his hands to help her, sliding her down his body. Then he hugged her tight. "We're going to get you to the hospital."

"No. I'm fine." She turned to the driver. "Are you okay?"

"I'm fine. My seat belt held me, and the air bags deployed. I was more worried about you two."

"What happened?" Daniel demanded.

"It was a hit-and-run. I started through a green light, and a vehicle ran the red and broadsided the limousine, smashing us against a light pole." The driver ran a hand through his gray hair. "Before I could get a license plate number, he was gone."

Several police cars and an ambulance converged on them, blocking traffic on the busy road.

The police took their statements while the emergency medical technicians did their work. They gave Megan and Daniel a once-over, cleaned up Megan's wound and advised her to take a ride in the ambulance to see the ER doctor.

Megan refused. "I really didn't hit that hard, and I'd like to get to bed sometime tonight."

"I think you should let me take you to the hospital," Daniel said.

"No," she said firmly. "Take me to the hotel. I just want a hot shower and a bed."

Short of throwing her over his shoulder and forcing her to go the hospital, Daniel had to concede to her wishes. "Okay, but for the record, I don't like it."

"So noted." Megan leaned against him. "It's been a long day. Let's go."

What had started as a great evening ended on a disturbing note. Daniel called Ryan to let him know what had happened. Ryan would fill the Reno police in on the information the Tulsa PD had collected on the attempts on Megan's life.

When they finally got to bed, Daniel crawled in beside Megan and spooned her body with his. No sexual overtones, just holding her, feeling her body against his.

"Do you think whoever is trying to hurt me crashed into us tonight?" Megan asked, her fingers resting on his arm dug into his skin, her body trembling.

"I don't know." He tightened his arms around her. "Just to be safe, stay close to me tomorrow."

Megan draped her arms over his. For a long moment, silence filled the room.

"Daniel?" she whispered, her voice quivering.

"Yes."

"If someone is after me, you could be collateral damage. I don't want you to be hurt."

"Sweetheart, it's a chance I'm willing to take to keep you safe."

If the person after Megan was in Reno, tomorrow could be more of a challenge than he or Megan originally thought.

Perhaps he should check on security services in Reno. It was time to get some help.

Daniel prayed they'd make it through the following day and return home intact.

WHEN MEGAN WOKE the next morning, she stretched out her arm, searching for Daniel's solid form, only to find an empty bed. On the pillow beside hers, Daniel had left a note explaining he would be back in less than ten minutes with breakfast and coffee.

She sat up and pressed a hand to her head, hoping to get a handle on a mild headache plus alternating feelings of euphoria and impending doom before Daniel returned.

If all went well that day, they'd have a deal with Kennedy Farms, and the marriage of convenience would have fully served its purpose.

Once they sealed the deal with Kennedy Farms, she and Daniel had no reason to stay married. Oh, maybe for a couple of weeks to give the appearance of having at least tried to make it work.

She'd come up with some excuse, maybe throwing a fit over something stupid as a debutante would do. That way Daniel would save face, and Marshall Kennedy wouldn't hold their subsequent divorce against Daniel.

The issue of someone being after her had her equally concerned. Megan didn't want Daniel to be hurt. Perhaps she should hop on a plane, head back to the Triple Diamond and let her father assign a bodyguard to her. Then she wouldn't be putting Daniel in harm's way, and she could start getting over him.

Megan suspected getting over Daniel would take a very long time.

Pushing aside all the thoughts that had whirled through her mind and kept her awake most of the night, she dressed for the day in pressed blue jeans, riding boots and a white blouse. She added a filmy turquoise scarf for a splash of color to cheer her up. As she finished running a brush through her hair, the door to the hotel room opened and Daniel entered, balancing two cups of coffee and a pastry bag.

"You like cream and sugar, right?"

She smiled, happy that he'd remembered. "I do."

"I grabbed a couple of muffins. We meet Marshall in thirty minutes at the arena."

"I don't have to have coffee or a muffin. We can leave now," she said.

"No need."

They ate at the room's tiny table with a view of Reno and sipped their coffee, rehashing the discussion with Kennedy the night before.

When they finished, they brushed their teeth in the bathroom like an old married couple. Megan's headache had disappeared, but a new ache settled in her chest.

She stood at the door to their room without reaching for the knob.

Daniel's hands descended on her shoulders, and he pulled her back against him. "What's wrong?"

"You realize that once we seal the deal with Kennedy, we don't have to continue being married."

Daniel turned her toward him, a frown settling deep on his brow. "We have to stay married for at least six months to fulfill your grandmother's stipulation or you won't get the rest of your trust fund until you're thirty."

She shrugged. "I don't need that money. I only needed the funds we were able to secure to take care of the horses my father is giving me."

He shook his head. "I disagree. You need to have that money for emergencies. You have a couple years before you turn thirty." Daniel smiled. "Tell you what. We can discuss it when we get back to the Lucky C. We'll come up with a timeline if we need to. For today, we're Mr. and Mrs. Colton." He brushed a light kiss over her lips, then bent to seal her mouth with his.

Megan sank into him, loving the way his tongue tasted fresh from the toothpaste.

When he finally raised his head, he stared down at her. "What say you and me skip this meeting? I can think of a dozen other things we could do as newlyweds that don't involve leaving this room."

Megan laughed up at his teasing grin. "I'm in."

He took her hand and tugged her back toward the bedroom.

She started to follow him, but reason kicked in and she dug in her heels. "We can't miss this meeting."

"I don't need this deal. I can find another breeder." Daniel pulled her into his arms. "Stay with me today. Forget the crash last night. Forget the meeting with Kennedy."

Megan cupped his cheek and leaned up on her toes. "We've worked too hard to let this fall through the cracks. If you want to spend the day here with me, let's take care of business first. Then we can come back to our room and attempt all those dozen things we can do without leaving."

Daniel sighed. "You are too smart for my own good." He gripped her hand in his and opened the door to the room. "Come on, let's go make a deal. The sooner we do, the sooner we can start celebrating."

The first real day of the symposium was packed, especially at the arena, where breeders from all over the country had brought horses they had up for stud or for sale.

Daniel and Megan wove through the crowd, searching for the Kennedy Farms stalls with the stud Daniel was most interested in using for his breeding stock.

Daniel nodded toward a group of men gathered around a pen with a black stallion pawing at the sawdust. "There's Marshall."

Megan glanced in the direction Daniel gazed. "He appears to be looking for you. Go on. I'll catch up in just a moment. I need to visit the ladies' room."

"I'll go with you."

"Don't be silly." She batted at him playfully. "You can't go into the ladies' room."

Daniel frowned. "After what happened last night, I'm not leaving you."

"I'll only be a moment. Go on before you lose him in the crowd."

Daniel's gaze switched from Megan to Marshall and back. "No. I can find him again."

"Daniel." Marshall Kennedy waved at Daniel, ending the argument.

"I'll be right back." Megan slipped through the crowd toward the last sign she'd seen indicating bathrooms.

A flash of blond hair made her stop short in the hallway and she stared at the back of a woman wearing jeans and a soft pink blouse, her blond hair hanging loose down to the middle of her back. Something about the way she carried herself struck a chord of familiarity in Megan. When she turned to glance out at the arena, Megan got a clear view of her profile and gasped. "Christine?"

Her cousin ground to a halt and turned toward her. "Megan!" She flung her arms around her and hugged her. "It's so good to see a familiar face in the crowd."

"What are you doing here?"

"When Josh and I get married, we want to start a horse ranch and breed horses. He thought the symposium was a good idea to give us a chance to see what it's all about and how much is involved." Christine's brows rose. "All those years we played at the Triple Diamond, sneaking out to ride, I never knew how much went into the actual operations of a horse-breeding facility."

"There is a lot to it," Megan conceded. "I thought Josh was into real estate."

"He is. But he comes across deals on ranches. He thinks it would be a great investment." Christine glanced over her shoulder. "Are you here with Daniel? Shouldn't you two be on your honeymoon or back in Oklahoma?"

"We'd planned on coming to the symposium before we decided to get married. So, here we are." Megan nodded toward the bathroom. "If you'll excuse me, I had too much coffee this morning. Maybe we can meet up and talk later."

"Sounds good. I can't wait to let Josh know you two are here." Christine waved and stood on her toes, searching the crowd.

Megan left her and entered the ladies' room. No one else was in the facility. She took care of business and washed her hands. When she turned to the exit, a speck of dust landed in her eye and she blinked. The particle felt like sand, scraping across her cornea.

Megan didn't want to keep Daniel waiting and wondering where she was—already, her presence had caused him so many delays and problems. But she couldn't open her eye without tearing. She leaned toward the mirror and lifted her eyelid with her finger. She couldn't see the speck so she blinked several times until the irritation cleared.

With one bloodshot eye, Megan walked out of the restroom, and ran into Josh, Christine's fiancé. "Josh, I was surprised to see you and Christine here."

He gripped her wrist. "No time to talk. Christine told me I could find you here. Daniel's been injured by Kennedy's stud. I was sent to get you and take you to the hospital where they're transporting him."

Megan's heart plummeted to the pit of her belly. "Daniel's hurt? What happened? Where is he?" She pushed past him and would have run out into the arena, but Josh's hand held tight.

"He was kicked in the head. They had an ambulance on standby, and they loaded him up."

"So quickly?" Megan tugged her arm, trying to shake loose of Josh's grip. "I have to go with him."

"That's what I'm telling you. I know which hospital they're taking him to. Come with me."

Her pulse raced through her, her heart thumping against her ribs. Megan nodded. "Okay. Take me there. I have to get to him."

"They went out the back way." Josh held tight to her wrist and half led, half dragged her deeper into the back rooms surrounding the arena.

Megan's breath lodged in her throat. After all that had happened in Oklahoma and Vegas, had someone finally succeeded? Her stomach clenched and she hurried alongside Josh. Daniel was injured. *God, please don't let him die.*

CHAPTER EIGHTEEN

DANIEL STOOD BESIDE Marshall Kennedy at one of the stock panel pens constructed for Kennedy Farms. Inside, Marshall's Striker's Royal Advantage, the black quarter horse stud Daniel had kept his eye on for the past four months, pawed at the sawdust as if impatient to get back to familiar surroundings.

Daniel had wanted this deal so much, he'd married his assistant to make it happen. In the process, he'd come to realize he'd fallen head over heels in love with the beautiful woman, and his priorities had shifted.

If this deal didn't go though…so what? There would be another. But there would not be another Megan.

Kennedy laid a hand on Daniel's shoulder. "My driver told me what happened last night. Are you and Megan all right?"

Daniel turned in the direction Megan had gone, his gaze searching the crowd, hoping she'd emerge. "She got a bump on her head but was too stubborn to rest."

Kennedy chuckled. "She's Frank's daughter, all right." He tilted his head toward the stallion. "So, what do you think?"

Daniel cast a quick glance at the stallion and returned his gaze to the direction Megan should have come from by now. "Mr. Kennedy—"

"Call me Marshall." The man stuck his hand out. "So do we have a deal?"

. "He's exactly what our program needs..." Daniel looked over his shoulder again. "Excuse me, Marshall. I'm worried about my wife. I need to find her. I hope we can finish this discussion later."

"Certainly. A pretty lady like Megan needs a man to watch out for her." The old man waved Daniel away. "Go. We'll be here all of today and tomorrow."

"Thank you," Daniel called out as he trotted back the way he'd come, searching for the bathrooms.

"Daniel!" a female voice called out. "There you are."

Daniel turned toward the sound and found Megan's cousin Christine hurrying toward him. "I ran into Megan a few minutes ago and told her we should get together for dinner. Josh has so many questions about horse ranching, and I know you two are the experts."

Daniel stared at her, trying to wrap his head around the fact Christine was in Reno. "Why are you here?"

"Like I told Megan, Josh has considered purchasing a horse ranch. He wants to start a breeding program like you and Megan have." Christine smiled broadly. "Wouldn't that be wonderful? Megan and I grew up riding together. It gave us lots in common besides being cousins."

Something clicked in Daniel's head. "Christine, where were you the day before we saw you in California?"

"I was staying at the Triple Diamond." She tilted her head. "Why do you ask?"

"Where did you say Josh was the day before we arrived at the Triple Diamond?"

"He was out of town on some real estate training trip."

Daniel gripped her arms. "Where?"

"I don't know." Her pretty brows descended. "He goes on so many."

A lead weight settled in Daniel's gut as he recalled Megan correcting Ryan about who stood to inherit the Talbot fortune should Megan pass away. Not her husband but the next living Talbot descendant. Christine.

And Josh was poised to marry the beautiful Christine. Daniel demanded, "Where is Josh now?"

"I don't know." Christine stared down at Daniel's hands on her arms. "I ran into him a minute ago and told him I'd seen Megan. You're hurting me."

Daniel let go of Christine. "Did you tell him where you'd seen her?"

"Of course. I saw her right here." Christine pointed toward a sign leading to the ladies' room. "She was going into the bathroom."

Daniel ran for the bathroom and burst through the door. A woman stood at the sink, washing her hands. Her eyes widened and she smiled. "I think you have the wrong bathroom. The men's room is next door."

Daniel slammed through the stalls, finding each one empty. When he came out, he stopped by the woman washing her hands. "Did you see a woman with strawberry blond hair leave this room?"

The woman dried her hands on a paper towel, her brow furrowing. "There was a woman headed down the hallway with a man when I entered the bathroom. She looked upset. And yes, she had strawberry blond hair."

"Which way were they going?"

The woman stepped out of the bathroom and pointed. "That way."

Christine stood in the hallway. "Megan wasn't in there?"

"No." Daniel grabbed her arms again. "If you know where Josh might be, tell me now."

Christine's eyes widened. "I don't know. I thought he'd find you." She squirmed under the intensity of Daniel's stare. "You're hurting me."

"Are you the one who has tried more than once to kill Megan?" Daniel shook her. "Are you?"

Christine's eyes widened. She shook her head. "Of course not. I love Megan like a sister. I would never hurt her." She flung her hand in the air. "I didn't even know she was being targeted. Does her father know?"

"Four times already. Someone broke into our room on our honeymoon in Vegas. Then she was poisoned before we left California, and someone sabotaged our plane."

Christine started to cry. "Josh wouldn't do that… would he?"

"Who else other than you stands to gain from Megan's death? You inherit her father's wealth. If Josh is married to you, he benefits."

"I don't believe you."

"Believe what you want, but help me find Megan or your fiancé. I have a feeling he's behind the attempts." Daniel set her to the side and raced down the hallway, ducking into every unlocked room along the way and banging on the ones that were locked. "Megan!" he yelled. Dear God, where was she? If Josh was the one responsible for all of the attempts on Megan's life, he had her and could possibly succeed this time.

Daniel couldn't let that happen.

THE DEEPER JOSH led her into the maintenance corridors of the arena, the more terrified Megan became. Finally she pulled to a stop. "If we're going to the hospital, we should be working our way out of the arena, not deeper into it."

"This is a shortcut," he insisted.

"I don't think so." Megan yanked her hand loose. "I'm going back out the front and catching a taxi to the hospital."

"Sorry, that can't happen. I've spent too much time and money chasing after you." He grabbed her arm and yanked her so close his cologne nearly overpowered her. A scent that sparked a dark memory.

"What do you mean you've been chasing me?" The scent memory of that cologne hit her, and an image of being in the hotel in Vegas with an intruder washed over her. "You!" This was the man who'd attacked her in Vegas.

Despite Josh's boy-next-door good looks with his sandy-blond hair, tailored jeans and white cotton shirt, the glare in his eyes turned Megan's blood to ice.

"Yeah, what about me?" Josh jerked her around and clamped her to him with his arms, dragging her deeper into the darkened corridors.

Megan fought him, twisting and turning, but he had her arms pinned and her body pressed tightly to his. She didn't have room to lever herself free. "You were the one who attacked me in Vegas," she said.

"Says who?"

"I recognize the cologne."

"And you think the scent of cologne will stand up in court?" He dragged her into a room and shut the door behind him. "Look, you've already been enough trouble. We end this now."

"Damn right we do." She stomped on his instep and dug her elbow into his gut.

He loosened his hold long enough for her to break loose and dart past him to the door.

She was twisting the knob when Josh cursed. His low voice cut across the room. "Open the door and I'll shoot you."

Megan glanced over her shoulder.

The man held a small but deadly-looking pistol pointed at her.

"What have I done to make you want to kill me?" she asked, refusing to remove her hand from the knob.

"Call it an accident of birth."

She snorted. "If it's my parents' wealth you want, I never wanted it in the first place. But you'll have to take it up with them."

"I will, once you're out of the picture."

A chill slithered down the back of Megan's neck. The man was insane. To think he could get away with one murder was bad enough. "What makes you think you won't be caught?"

"You're a wealthy man's daughter. Anyone could take a potshot at you."

"The Tulsa and Las Vegas police departments are already searching for the person responsible for the attacks on me. It's only a matter of time."

"I left no trail."

"Are you certain?" She raised her brows, twisting the knob on the door so slowly, she hoped he didn't notice. "They're already looking at Christine as a possible suspect because she stands to inherit my father's wealth if I die." Megan shook her head. "Did you ever really care about her?"

"She's a means to an end."

"The end being that you want my father's fortune."

Megan had the knob twisted around. All she had to do was jerk the door open and dive out into the corridor. "How do you know my father hasn't already changed his will? I told him I didn't want his property and that he could leave it all to the charity of his choice."

"He hasn't changed his will. I've seen it."

Anger shot through her. "My parents trusted you in their home."

"Yeah, and your cousin is gullible enough to marry me. Seems the entire family is too trusting." He shrugged. "Makes it easier."

"You might have gotten away with poisoning me or sabotaging the airplane. But you won't get away with shooting me."

"No? Are you willing to bet your life on that?" His eyes narrowed, and he leveled the gun on her.

If he was going to shoot her, she'd be dead, anyway. Megan threw open the door, dove into the corridor and rolled to the side and onto her feet.

Josh lunged for her, snagging her long hair. He jerked her back and locked an arm around her throat.

Megan bent double, trying to throw him over her. The man was bigger and stronger than she was and had her in his grasp, tightening his hold.

Her vision blurring, Megan knew she couldn't give up. Her parents would be next and then Christine. She wouldn't let this greedy bastard win. But she couldn't quite shake him loose, and her own strength was waning.

A shout down the hall made Josh twist around, still holding her throat.

"Let her go, Josh. You won't get away with it." Daniel stood several feet away, holding his hands up in surrender. "Everyone knows you're behind the attempts on Megan's life."

"If by 'everyone' you mean you, that's hardly a threat." He whipped his gun out and pointed it at Daniel, tightening his arm on Megan's throat.

Her voice cut off with the air to her lungs. Megan could do nothing to help Daniel.

"Oh, Josh." Christine stepped up beside Daniel, tears flowing down her cheeks. "You didn't need my uncle's money. You were doing so well on your own."

"What do you know?" Josh said. "You see what you want to see."

She swiped at her tears. "You're right. I saw a man I thought loved me and wanted to marry me because of me, not my uncle's fortune." She walked toward him. "You were going to kill me, weren't you?"

"Christine, don't." Daniel grabbed her and flung her behind him.

Josh shifted his aim from Christine back to Daniel. "You all deserve to die. You certainly don't deserve to inherit Talbot's millions."

Yeah, and neither do you. Megan did the only thing she could and let her knees buckle so suddenly, Josh didn't suspect it. Her weight tipped him forward along with the aim of his weapon.

Daniel dove at him, knocking the gun from his hand. It hit the floor and slid out of reach. Before Josh could recover, Daniel swung a fist at the man's face, hitting him so hard he fell backward, taking Megan with him. She landed on top of his chest.

His hold loosened. Megan rolled to the side and away from him, the dizziness fading as she filled her lungs with gulps of air.

Daniel yanked Josh up by the collar and slammed his fist into his face again. Josh fought back, but Daniel was bigger, faster and stronger.

Megan crawled across the floor, reaching for the gun.

Christine grabbed it first and pointed it at the two men fighting. "Stop it!" she screamed. "Stop it or I'll shoot." Tears ran down her face.

Daniel rammed his fist into Josh's gut one last time and stood back.

Josh, a hand pressed to his belly, his face a bloody mess, looked across at Christine. "Give me the gun."

"Don't, Christine," Megan said. "He doesn't love you. He only wants your money."

She shook her head. "I trusted you."

He looked up at her, the charming man Megan had first met, a desperate battered face now. "I did it for us." He took a step forward.

Christine pointed the gun at his chest. "You tried to kill the only family I have left." She held the gun out, her finger on the trigger.

Megan's breath caught and held. "Christine, don't shoot the bastard. He's not worth it. It's over. Let the police take him."

"He lied to me."

"He lied to all of us." Megan stood and inched her way toward Christine, sliding an arm around her waist. "What's important is that you still have your family."

"He would have killed you." Christine looked to Megan. "You're the sister I never had."

"I'm okay, sweetie. Let me have the gun."

Her hands shaking, Christine gave Megan the gun and buried her face in Megan's shoulder.

Josh made a fast move toward Christine and Megan.

Daniel grabbed his arm and yanked it up behind his back, between his shoulder blades. "Give it up. This is over."

Within minutes they had the Reno police collect Josh and take him away. Megan called her parents, and her father agreed to fly out to bring Christine back to the Triple Diamond. When the dust cleared and the police assured Megan and Daniel that they were free to leave the arena, Daniel pulled Megan into his arms and held her for a long time.

"I didn't think I'd find you in time."

She laughed, the sound choking on a sob. "I didn't think you would, either."

He set her at arm's length and pushed a strand of her long hair back behind her ear, his touch so gentle it made Megan want to cry. "The attempts on your life made me realize something."

She looked up into his deep brown eyes and gasped at his expression.

"I love you, Megan Talbot Colton." He cupped her cheek and brushed his lips across hers. "I can't give you what your parents can, but I can love you more than I love to breathe."

"How many times do I have to tell people that I don't want what my parents have?" She wrapped her arms around his waist and hugged him. "I have everything I want, as long as I have you."

"Well, it's a good thing, because that's all I can promise. You can have me, and all of my wealth, which isn't much, and my whole heart."

"Then I'd have all I'd need, and I'd still be the richest woman in the world."

His lips descended on hers, and he held her wrapped in his warmth and strength.

A discreet cough brought them back to the arena, and Megan lifted her head.

Marshall Kennedy stood with his arms crossed and a big smile spreading across his face. "I heard what happened, and I'm glad to see you both aren't too worse for the excitement." He stuck out his hand. "I can offer you two a ride back to your hotel or to the hospital."

Daniel tucked Megan in the curve of his arm and shook Mr. Kennedy's hand. "Thank you, sir."

"I also want you to know," Marshall said, "I'm ready to sign whatever deal you want to make. You're the kind of people I want to work with. You're smart and tough and believe in taking care of your family."

"That's right." Daniel grinned down at Megan. "And I want Megan to be part of my family for a very long time."

She stared up at him, butterflies beating in her stomach. "You mean that, don't you?"

He nodded. "Like I promised in front of God and Elvis, I do."

CHAPTER NINETEEN

DANIEL SAT IN the chair of honor, the most comfortable easy chair in Jack's living room, with his feet kicked back and a bowl of popcorn in his lap, happier than he'd been in…well…forever.

"You didn't think you'd get by without letting us throw you a bachelor party, did you?" Brett tossed a piece of popcorn into the air and caught it in his mouth.

"You guys didn't have to go to all this trouble." Daniel glanced around the room at his brothers, gathered in front of the large television screen at the halftime of the football game.

"Now that we're getting so many females in the Colton family, it's nice to have an excuse for a guys' night out," Jack said.

Daniel knew Jack was perfectly content to spend all his evenings with his beautiful wife, Tracy, and his son, Seth.

"It also gives us a chance to impart our wisdom on you without getting slugged," Brett said. "Like, if your wife asks you if the outfit she's wearing makes her look fat, you tell her what you know she wants to hear, or go to bed in the guest room."

"Never go to bed mad," Jack said. "Makeup sex is so much better than a cold shoulder."

Eric dropped onto the end of the couch nearest Daniel's seat. "If you want to make your marriage last, just remember to tell her you love her. A woman never gets tired of hearing that."

Daniel nodded. "I appreciate all the advice. Megan and I are so new to this marriage thing. I don't want to screw it up right out the chute."

"What about you, Ryan?" Brett nudged Ryan with his foot where he lay sprawled on the floor in front of the television. "Got any advice for Dan?"

Ryan shrugged. "Since I'm the lone stag at the stag party, don't go with any advice I've got to say. Apparently my methods aren't working."

"That's right," Jack said. "You're the last single man standing. Tracy and I are hitched, which is a good thing considering she's pregnant."

"No kidding?" Brett grinned. "Hannah will be happy to hear there will be another little one to play with."

Daniel leaned forward and clapped a hand on his older brother's shoulder. "Congratulations." He couldn't wait to start a brood of his own. A couple of strawberry blond-haired girls and strapping boys were what he had in mind. More family to love.

"Well, Ryan, that puts the pressure on you to find a woman to love and marry." Daniel sat back in his chair. "My advice to you is to elope. It's much easier than all the planning and trouble Greta's going through in pulling her wedding together."

"I'd love to skip all the hoopla," Jack admitted. "But I told Tracy that whatever she wanted was fine with me."

"Speaking of Greta." Ryan sat up. "I swear I saw her the other day. Is she back in town and no one bothered to let me know?"

All heads shook.

"Not that I know of," Daniel said. "I'll be glad when her wedding's over. I never would have thought Greta would go for a big wedding. She struck me as a tomboy."

"Well, I guess we can't all go as classy as our man Daniel and get Elvis to officiate." Ryan laughed.

Daniel threw a piece of popcorn at him. "As far as I'm concerned, I wouldn't change a thing. I'm married to a helluva woman, I love her and she loves me."

Jack sat back, staring at the television commercials. "Can't ask for more than that."

Daniel couldn't agree more. He loved Megan so much, he wanted to be with her every waking moment. The party couldn't end soon enough. He pushed to his feet. "Boys, thank you for the party. But I have a beautiful wife waiting for me back at the cabin and…well, she's a lot better looking than the lot of you."

He hurried out the door, climbed into his truck and drove the short distance to the cabin.

Before he could climb out of the vehicle, the door to the cabin opened and Megan stepped out on the porch, her brows knit. "What's wrong? The game's not over yet. I've been watching it."

Daniel strode toward her. "I couldn't concentrate on the game when I knew you were here. Alone. I thought maybe we could make good use of our day off and get a little naked." He swept her up in his arms and carried her across the threshold.

"Sweetheart, you know how to sweep a woman off her feet."

"I'm full of interesting talents," he said, nuzzling the curve of her neck. "Wait until you see what I can do when I get your clothes off."

Megan's laughter was low and sultry, her fingers already working at the buttons on his shirt. "I didn't know I'd be marrying an insatiable man."

With a full heart, he laid her on their bed and kissed her, finally coming home to the start of his very own family. "Darlin', you bring out the beast in me."

* * * * *

Melissa Cutler is a flip-flop-wearing Southern California native living with her husband, two rambunctious kids and two suspicious cats in beautiful San Diego. She divides her time between her dual passions for writing sexy, small-town contemporary romances and edge-of-your-seat romantic suspense. Find out more about Melissa and her books at www.melissacutler.net, or drop her a line at cutlermail@yahoo.com.

Books by Melissa Cutler

Harlequin Romantic Suspense

Seduction Under Fire

ICE: Black Ops Defenders

Tempted into Danger
Secret Agent Secretary
Hot on the Hunt

The Coltons of Wyoming

Colton by Blood

The Coltons of Oklahoma

Colton's Cowboy Code

Visit the Author Profile page at Harlequin.com.

COLTON'S COWBOY CODE

Melissa Cutler

To my husband, who's the most amazing father
I've ever seen. The kids and I are so lucky
to have you as the rock of our family, my darling.

CHAPTER ONE

IN BRETT COLTON'S ears, in his mind, the shrill keening of tornado sirens eclipsed all other sound, despite that he and Outlaw were too far into the backcountry for the sirens to be more than a figment of his imagination—his intuition warning him that this mission was a really stupid plan because there were a hundred ways to die in a storm this angry.

There was no fury in hell or on earth that compared to an Oklahoma thunderstorm when it decided to unleash a twister. The clouds above Tulsa churned, glowing gray green. Golf-ball-sized hail pelted Brett's Stetson and the back of his oiled leather duster. He folded forward, shielding Outlaw's neck and mane from the brunt of the hail's force as best he could, though neither man nor steed were strangers to the elements.

One of these days, Brett's guardian angels would give him up as a lost cause, but, God willing, it wasn't going to be today. Not with so much on the line. Not after everything his family had been through in the past month or the sharp edge of disappointment in his father's and brother's eyes when Brett had broken it to them about the downed fence and the missing cattle. As if Brett had let the herd loose on purpose. As if he was still the same reckless punk he'd been four months ago.

Then again, maybe Brett hadn't completely vanquished the recklessness from his blood, because here he was, racing across the rolling plains of the Lucky C ranch's backcountry, straight toward the deadly funnel forming in the distance. Any minute, a flash flood might come rocketing through, if lightning or a twister didn't hit down first, but he refused to return to the Lucky C homestead without the half dozen pregnant cows that had escaped.

The downed fence was a mystery that Brett would have to contemplate later. He'd checked that line himself the week before. All he knew was that the ranch that he'd once thought of as a fortress was no longer an impenetrable haven for his family, and the decades of peace and prosperity that the Coltons had enjoyed had been shattered beyond repair.

Brett had followed the tracks of the six stampeding cows southwest, keeping them in sight through the rain and the darkening sky, right up until the clouds had let loose with hail. With zero visibility and the cows' hoofprints lost in the churned-up ground and melting balls of ice, he was riding with nothing to guide him but the hunch that the cows had headed toward Vulture Ridge, as the stock on the ranch had done so many times over the years. As long as they'd had enough sense to stop at the ridge instead of going over the edge—*Lord, please don't let them have gone over the edge*—Brett would find a way to get them back to the Lucky C before the twister touched down.

Outlaw expertly cut around scrub trees and boulders without losing speed until Vulture Ridge came into view.

"Gotcha," Brett said, though his words were lost in a crash of thunder.

Four of the cows crowded at the edge of the infamous

gully, their hind hooves pawing at the muddy, disintegrating ledge and baying, clearly terrified. Brett slowed Outlaw to a trot and instead of closing in on the cows head-on, guided the horse in a wide arc. Then he rode along the ridge and came up on the cows from the side. Outlaw knew the drill, imposing his authority to the cattle, crowding and nudging them away from the edge.

Once they complied, Brett craned his neck to scan the expanse of prairie land for the remaining two cows. One, he spotted immediately, huddled against a boulder, but the other was nowhere to be seen. Fearing what he'd find, Brett turned his focus to the gully below Vulture Ridge that had been carved out by centuries of flash floods. The missing cow's ear came into view first, tagged with a green tag that meant she was a heifer—a young first-time mom who was probably beyond freaked out at the moment.

He dismounted and got closer to the edge. The heifer was perched on a narrow outcrop of dirt and rock ten feet below the lip of the ridge, lying on her side, propped against the ridge wall, her massive round belly undulating. She was in labor, and the way she was angled, when the calf was born, it would fall the additional ten feet or so into the gully's basin. That is, if the ledge didn't crumble and the heifer didn't fall herself, first.

This time, Brett's curse was loud enough to be heard over the storm. An older, seasoned cow might have been amenable to Brett's efforts to get her standing and help her pick her way out of the gully, but he already knew this heifer wasn't going to make his life easy like that. He was standing next to Outlaw, debating his options, when a thunderclap sounded so loudly that Brett's teeth rattled.

The four cows they'd gathered immediately spooked and took off along the gully ridge.

Brett swung up into the saddle again. Shaking away the water and ice from his face, he set his teeth on his lower lip and whistled in the same tone he used on the livestock around the ranch, the one that often worked—in normal conditions, anyway—as a command for them to stop. These particular cows weren't interested in commands. If anything, they picked up their pace.

He gave another, different toned whistle command to Outlaw and the horse surged toward the cattle as Brett reached for his lasso. Throwing it in this weather would be a crapshoot at best, but he had to try. He secured the rope in his hands, then drove Outlaw faster, getting in front of the cows and cutting them off.

He waited until they were right up on the beasts to throw the lasso. It caught the neck of the farthest cow, just as it was supposed to, so he cinched it nice and tight and brought all four cows crowded between the lassoed cow and Outlaw's body.

"Thataway, Outlaw," he called over the wind and hail, stroking the gelding's neck. "Thataway."

They maneuvered the cattle to a cluster of shrubs not too far away from where the fifth cow was still huddled by the boulder. Brett swung off the saddle, then looped the other end of the rope around the neck of a second cow. He tied another rope around the necks of the third and fourth cows and hooked all the ropes into the branches of the sturdiest scrub tree. It wasn't all that secure, should another thunderclap spook them again, but it was the best he could do for now.

He left Outlaw standing near them, but refused to tie him to the tree, even if it meant Brett getting stranded should the gelding take off. Because what if the horse needed to flee with good reason? What if Brett didn't make it out of the gully alive? Brett would rather chance getting stranded than put his horse in any unnecessary danger, which was a vital part of the cowboy code he lived by.

Brett threaded his head and an arm through his last bundle of rope from his saddle bag, then stroked Outlaw's neck and got close to his ear. "You stay with the stock. Keep 'em calm for me until I get back." For all he knew, Outlaw understood every word. He liked to imagine that bit of magic, anyway.

It wasn't until he was slogging to the edge of Vulture Ridge that he realized how soaked-to-the-bones he was. The muddy ground sucked at his boots, and his jeans felt as if they weighed twenty pounds. He flapped the tails of his duster around his body, then checked the collar to make sure it was standing on end, but still, bits of hail wormed their way between his collar and his hat to melt against his neck. Sniffing, his eyes downturned and marking each labored step, he put his shoulder to the wind and pressed on.

The heifer was lying on her side still, but didn't seem to have given birth yet. Her hooves hovered in midair over the gully that was rapidly filling with water. The path she'd slid down was steep, but wouldn't be impossible for her to traverse back up over the ridge—if he could get her standing again.

He was debating the merits of risking his life for a single livestock, when the heifer brayed, a pained, fearful cry. Then one of her hind legs and her tail lifted. The water sac was visible already.

"Holy day…" Brett muttered.

The calf was coming.

He slid down the mud wall following the same path the heifer had. There wasn't enough room on the ledge for both of them to fit comfortably. His boot heels cut into the dirt wall as he skirted her body to reach her tail. The calf's tail was crowning first.

"Damn it. This baby's not making it easy on you, is it, girl?" Brett wiped his muddy hands on his coat, then pushed the calf's rump back in. Working by feel, he located the hind legs and positioned them one at a time in the birthing canal.

The heifer brayed and kicked out. If they were at the ranch, Brett would've secured her in a head gate and called for help. All he had now was luck, a single rope and his wits, and he was going to need all three to birth the calf before it died.

He took off his coat and draped it over the heifer's face, hoping the reduction of stimulus from the rain and storm would calm her down. No luck. She kicked harder, and before Brett had gotten back in position near her tail, she tipped over the edge of the outcropping and slid into the rapidly-filling gully.

Brett followed, his rope in his hand. The water was three feet deep and rising. The rain and hail beat down relentlessly as the wind whipped up. Time to get this calf birthed and get the hell out of there before they all lost their lives. The cow, on her side in the gully, strained to keep her head above water. Brett slogged to her backside again, the water and mud caking his legs and seeping into his boots. He wrapped the rope around the calf's legs once, twice, three times.

He wiggled his boots into the riverbed, bracing himself, then got a firm hold of the rope and pulled, growling with the effort. The calf slid another four or five inches out. Panting, Brett adjusted his grip on the rope, then pulled again. This time, the calf came. Brett fell backward in the water, the calf on his chest.

With a laugh of triumph, Brett cleaned the calf's nose out with his finger, then tickled its ear to get it breathing. Then a golf-ball-sized piece of hail smacked Brett hard on his cheek, killing his awe over the miracle of helping birth a new life and reminding him of the danger all around them.

He pushed to his feet, bringing the calf up in his arms. He worked to untie the rope from the calf's hind legs with one eye on the steep side of the gully. The water was above Brett's knees, sloshing at his groin. He couldn't get the rope around the mama cow and keep his hold on the wiggling calf, so he'd have to come back down for her.

He'd pulled himself and the calf a good five feet up the gully wall when he heard it, a roar like no other he'd heard before. Not thunder, not a twister. Something otherworldly that got louder, closer. The gully walls vibrated with the force. A flash flood. Had to be.

In full panic mode, Brett hauled himself to the ledge that the cow had originally slid onto. He grabbed his duster from where the cow had tossed it away from her face. He threw it up to the top of the ridge, then hauled himself and the calf the rest of the way up, his fingers and boot toes digging into the muddy wall, pushing the calf up in front of him with his chest. He heaved the calf over the top of the ridge as a wall of water appeared in the gully, bearing down on their location.

Brett scrambled to safety and got on his knees. As fast as he could, he wound the rope back and set the lasso loop down to the mama cow. Maybe he could anchor her there so she wouldn't get swept away. Maybe the floodwaters weren't as high and fast as they looked.

The flash flood hit her hard, rolling her under. The rope pulled on him as though he was playing tug-of-war with a whole football team. There was nothing to do but let go. He'd heard too many accounts of ranchers getting swept into floodwater and drowning because they were too stubborn to lose their livestock.

Brett's legs were shaky and weak with an adrenaline crash as he stood, following with his gaze the glimpse of the cow's head in the water until she disappeared. The floodwaters gurgled and spit at the edge of the gully wall. He stared at the water, trying not to think of the loss as a failure. After all, he'd saved the calf, five pregnant cows and his own life.

He swung his attention to the boulder where he'd left the other cows and Outlaw. Outlaw was still there, but none of the cows. Damn it.

He pulled his drenched, muddy coat on, then lifted the calf into his arms again and trudged to his horse, his eyes on the storm front that looked to be moving away from them. At least one thing had gone his way today.

Outlaw nuzzled his cheek.

"Thanks for waiting for me," Brett said. "Happen to see which direction those cows went?"

Could've been his imagination, but Outlaw snorted in reply.

He scratched the horse's neck. "Good. How about you lead me to them so we can call it a day?"

He lifted the calf onto the saddle first, then hoisted himself up, the weight of the water and mud making him feel a good fifty pounds heavier than he had when he'd left the stable. The orphaned calf looked up at him, helpless and trusting. Brett usually didn't think of the livestock as cute, but this one surely was, with long lashes, a soft buttercream-colored coat and a pink nose. He wrapped his coat around it and held it close.

"We'll get you home soon and make you up a bottle as soon as we find your mama's friends. I do believe we're gonna name you Twister. How does that sound?"

The calf's tongue came out to lick a pebble of hail from its nose, the cutest thing Brett might've ever seen besides his nephew, Seth.

Jack, Brett's oldest brother, was going to be furious about the loss of the cow. Already, he didn't trust Brett, and this wasn't going to help. But Brett was tired of working under his brother like some hired hand, getting his butt chewed for every perceived misstep. He was ready to redeem his reputation and earn his slice of the Colton legacy—and he had just the plan to make it work. All he needed now was to hire a financial whiz to help him crunch the numbers and profit projections he'd need to help Jack see his point of view.

With a whistle and a nudge of Brett's boots, Outlaw burst into motion back through the storm toward home while Brett's mind churned, plotting and planning his next move to seize a hold of his bright future once and for all.

BEING A POSTER girl for the perils of sin had gotten Hannah Grayson nowhere fast. For as much mileage as her family's church had gotten out of using Hannah's accidental pregnancy as a cautionary tale, they could have at least provided her with a small stipend to ease the sting of being disowned by her parents, fired from her job and evicted from her apartment, all while battling a nasty case of morning sickness.

From her pocket, she withdrew the help-wanted ads she'd printed from *Tulsa World* newspaper's online classifieds. Every lead on the papers but one had been crossed out as a dead end. She'd been counting on her newly minted accounting degree from Tulsa United On-line University to help her land on her feet, but every employer she'd met with had taken one look at the now-obvious swell of her belly and decided she wasn't quali-fied for the job.

With her meager savings running out, she'd made a deal with herself to explore this one last lead before giv-ing up on accounting in favor of a retail or a fast-food position, but it was a long shot at best.

Tulsa businessman in need of an accountant for a temporary project, discretion a must.

No name or company name given, no phone num-ber or address. Just a generic email address of "okla-homa45678" that could belong to anybody. Including a psychopath. Which was why she'd created a new, ge-neric email address of her own to reply to the ad and had refused to give out even her name to the individual when she agreed to meet him at a window booth in the Armadillo Diner & Pie Company.

Replacing the classified ad in her purse, she paused at the window of the Fluff and Fold to check herself in the window reflection. Wisps of her pencil-straight black hair lifted in the wind that had hung around Tulsa since the previous week's storm. She smoothed them into place and used the pad of her thumb to sharpen the line of her light pink lip gloss on her bottom lip.

The gray slacks were a clearance-rack find from a couple months earlier, when they'd been a loose fit. Now, the waist sat below the swell of her belly, which she'd covered with a form-fitting pale pink blouse. She could have de-emphasized the evidence of her pregnancy with another outfit, but all that had done in the past was delay the inevitable disinterest from the prospective employers that came when she disclosed the truth, and wasted everyone's time. Better to put her condition out in the open right up front, before a single word was exchanged.

With her eyes on her reflection, she stood tall and proud, rubbing a hand over her belly. "Something's going to work out, little guy. Or girl. If this opportunity isn't it, then we'll keep trying. I'm not going to let you down."

She squared her shoulders and strode toward the diner door, harnessing her pride and owning her power. She was a terrific accountant and a good person. That had to count for something. Maybe Mr. Anonymous Businessman would be the first person to see her for the workplace asset she could be.

Inside the Armadillo, the smell of old, burned coffee and cooking eggs rushed up on Hannah, making her stomach lurch. She ground to a stop in the waiting area. Hands on her hips, she raised her face to the ceiling and breathed through her mouth as the wave of nausea passed. When she'd selected the diner as a meeting place, she'd been hoping for a free meal, not the possibility of the diner smells triggering her morning sickness.

"You okay, darlin'?"

Hannah lowered her gaze to see a middle-aged waitress eyeing her with concern from behind blue-tinted eyelashes, tapping a laminated menu against her palm.

"I think so. Food smells, you know?" She rubbed her baby bump and offered a smile to Janice, or so the waitress's name tag read.

"Oh, I know. Try working here while pregnant, with the omelets in the morning and the liver-platter special at dinner. I spent the first half of each of my pregnancies serving the food, then running to the can. How far along are you?"

The mention of eggs and liver had Hannah raising her face to the ceiling again. "Nineteen weeks."

"Ah. Well, the worst of it should be about over. You want a table near the air vent, I bet."

After another fortifying breath through her mouth, Hannah lowered her face and smiled at Janice. "Actually, I'm meeting someone here. Job interview."

Her curiosity about Mr. Anonymous's identity had her shifting her gaze from Janice to the row of window booths. There was only one man at a booth by the window. Brett Colton, and he was standing up next to the table, his napkin in his hand, nailing her with a gaze of utter shock.

Gasping, Hannah wrenched her face away. *Crap on a cracker. This can't be happening.*

Janice's voice floated over the air as though from a great distance. "Well, bless your heart, looking for work in your condition. What does your baby daddy have to say about that?"

Her baby daddy was about to say a whole lot because, judging by his expression, he'd heard the whole exchange with Janice and was really good at doing fast math in his head.

"Excuse me," Hannah muttered. Then she pivoted in place and marched back out the door.

She paced the sidewalk in front of the diner, garnering her courage because she knew with 100 percent certainty that Brett was going to follow her out and demand the answers he deserved. Over the past few months, she'd played this moment in her head a dozen different ways, but it never looked anything like this. She never planned to leave him in the dark about the baby. All she'd wanted to do was hold off on telling him until she had a job and a permanent place to stay.

"Anna, wasn't it?" The growl of Brett Colton's sexy-as-sin voice had her freezing in her tracks. She squeezed her eyes closed as mortification set in that the father of her child didn't even remember her name correctly. Then again, what did she expect from Tulsa's most notorious playboy? She bet he seduced a different girl every night of the week, or so the rumors would have her believe.

She fluttered her eyes open and caught sight of her reflection in the Fluff and Fold window again, surprised at the sight of a meek girl hanging her head, dread and guilt etched in her features. What happened to the proud, confident woman she'd been only a few minutes earlier? She'd done nothing wrong and broken no rules. There was no official timetable on telling a man you were pregnant with his child.

Clinging to that truth, she straightened up, smoothed her features, and then spun to face Brett. "It's Hannah, actually."

He winced at that, and then those soulful green eyes turned sheepish—a reaction that Hannah found absurdly comforting. "Sorry. Hannah." He closed and opened his mouth, his eyes flitting from her belly to her face, as though he was in the same clueless state of communication as she was. "I, uh…you're, um…nineteen weeks. That's about when we, uh…"

"Yes. I know. It's yours," she blurted. And cue her turn to wince. So much for breaking the news to him gently.

The sheepishness vanished from his face, along with the color. "That's impossible."

She schooled her features to mask a sudden flare of irritation. "Really? Ya think?" Okay, so maybe she hadn't done that terrific a job concealing her feelings.

"We used protection, so how is that possible?"

She'd asked herself that same question a million times. "Yes, we did. We used protection that you supplied, in fact. So maybe you should be the one explaining to me how it happened."

His eyes narrowed. "Moving on. You're going to have to work pretty hard to convince me of the reason you kept this from me. When were you planning on telling me, anyway? Or did you?"

The accusation dripping from his words got her back up. "So you didn't remember my name correctly, yet you expected me to remember yours and know where to find you? Narcissistic much?"

His mouth fell open at that and the color returned to his face in full force. "I'm sorry. You're right. I…"

He looked so abashed and sincerely apologetic that all the fight rushed out of her. "That wasn't fair of me. I'm sorry. The truth is, I did remember your name and I fully planned to tell you. I was looking to get my life in order first."

The ranching community of Tulsa was an *everybody's in everybody's business* kind of town, and Hannah couldn't bear for her baby to be born under a cloud of suspicion and rumors that his or her mother was a gold digger, getting pregnant on purpose to get at the Colton fortune. It would be bad enough for her baby having its mama's reputation run through the mud in the church community.

His mouth screwed up as though he didn't buy what she was selling. "By answering a sketchy classified ad for temporary work? I've been in your car and to your apartment. Your life is the opposite of screwed up. Try again."

She smoothed a hand over her stomach out of habit. If he wanted to hear the whole pathetic story, then who was she to deny him?

"That's the truth, whether you believe it or not. When my parents found out I was pregnant, they relieved me of the burden of being their daughter, which included firing me from managing the feed-supply store they own. And, because I'd sunk all my money into getting my accounting degree, I had nothing in savings. So I sold my car to pay my doctor bills, which then got me evicted from my apartment.

"I'm trying to get my life back on track, but nothing I've tried is working. I can't just snap my fingers and fix my life. All I wanted to do is land on my feet before coming to you. A job. And a place to live." She'd wanted to tell him truthfully that she was doing fine and didn't need his financial support or—God forbid—a mercy proposal of marriage. She'd seen enough of her parents' own unhappy marriage to know that wasn't the life she wanted for her or her child.

"The only trouble is," she continued, "who's going to hire a pregnant lady for any kind of real job, with health insurance and maternity leave? Nobody, as it turns out, because I've looked. I've scoured this whole darn city looking for work that would help my baby—" Emotion tightened her throat. She was exhausted and nauseous and so tired of being judged unfairly. She swallowed and took a breath. "I've been looking for work that would help my baby have a good life."

Grimacing, he wrenched his face to the street, his hands on his hips, his eyes distant.

Hannah did a whole bunch more swallowing, reining in her hormone-fueled emotional fireworks as she studied his profile. He really was a stunning specimen of a man—his face perfection with those masculine cheekbones and that fit cowboy's body that had brought her so much wicked pleasure that night. He kept his light brown hair disheveled just so, adding a rakish quality to his charm. No wonder he turned the head of every woman in Tulsa when he walked down the street.

He deserved better than to find out he was going to be a father on the side of the road outside a Laundromat, not with a woman he loved, but with a virtual stranger.

When she was sure she could speak calmly, she said, "I'm not trying to get at your family's money, Brett."

He jerked his face in her direction, his face a stone mask now. Gone was any trace of the smile he'd wooed her with nineteen weeks ago at the Tulsa club where she'd decided to let her hair down after her college graduation.

"You still need to pay your bill, hon," called a female voice.

Hannah and Brett both turned to see Janice standing at the Armadillo's door, waving a slip of paper.

"I'll be right there," Brett called to Janice, his voice

tight with harnessed emotion. To Hannah, he added, "I need to take care of this, and then we're going to go somewhere private to talk."

Hannah nodded, even as her stomach ached, empty. She'd been counting on the interviewer's promise in his email to buy her breakfast. She wrapped her arms around her ribs and battled a fresh round of pathetic tears. "I'll wait here."

He huffed, his hardened, distant expression not really seeing her when he looked her way and took her arm. "I don't think so. You're coming inside with me while I pay the bill. I don't want you disappearing on me before I get some answers. I don't even know your last name." He swept his hand in front of him. "After you."

CHAPTER TWO

BRETT WAS PRETTY sure he'd never been so blindsided by anything as seeing the woman he'd slept with a few months earlier appear at the diner where he was waiting to interview a temporary accountant—and learning that she was pregnant with his child.

His child. Good God, what had he done?

He'd already come to think of that bender of a weekend as life-changing because he'd nearly gotten himself killed, not because he'd knocked up the girl he slept with, the one whose last name or phone number he hadn't even bothered to ask, he was so drunk and self-destructive. He was lucky he remembered her face at all, given the state he'd been in, but she held the dubious honor of being his last conquest before he'd gotten right with himself and had given up partying, drinking and women cold turkey.

He held the diner door open for Hannah, who marched past him, her feathers clearly ruffled. "I know you're upset, but you don't get to treat me like a criminal."

He wasn't trying to, but he also wasn't taking a chance on her sneaking away before he got some answers. All he had was the email address she'd contacted him with about the job, and he doubted that was anything but a shell account. He didn't even know her last name, and hadn't even recalled her first name correctly. Didn't that just say it all about how severely he'd screwed up his life?

At the hostess desk, he paid for his coffee and left a generous tip. That's when he heard it. Hannah's stomach growled. Loudly.

He froze, his change halfway in his wallet.

"Shoot," she muttered. "You didn't hear that."

In his periphery, he watched her arms wrap around her middle, protective and proud. His attention slid to the scuffed black flats she wore. They were old, worn. The edges of the material fraying. Yet she'd worn them to the job interview so they had to be the best pair she owned. She'd lost her job, her car and her apartment. Where was she living now? Was she getting the medical care she and the baby needed?

That's when it hit him that the answers to those questions didn't matter yet. All that mattered at that moment was that she was clearly hungry. She was also too thin, now that he thought about it. Hungry. Jobless. Homeless—and she was having his baby. Damn.

"Change of plans." His words came out as a croak. He cleared his throat, then met the waitress's confused gaze. "Could you seat us again? Turns out I'm hungry for breakfast after all."

Hannah stiffened. "I don't need your charity."

Judging by her growling stomach, she did, but she was far too proud to accept it. She hadn't come to him for help when she first found out she was pregnant or when she'd lost her job. She'd made of point of telling him that she wasn't after his money. Other than her dancing skills—both of the club variety and the horizontally-in-bed variety—her sense of pride and honor were just about all he knew about her. That, and the fact that she was an accountant, which he would have never pegged her as.

Proud, dancing Hannah the accountant didn't follow the waitress, but stood stock-still, giving him a stink-eye that even his mother would admire. She didn't want help or charity and didn't seem to trust his breakfast offer, but Brett did have one thing he could offer her that he bet she wouldn't refuse.

"You came here today to interview for a job and I need an accountant, so I say we get on with the reason for our appointment."

She held him with a searching gaze as though testing his intentions, then gave a terse nod.

He fought against letting his relief show on his face as he ushered her ahead of him to follow the waitress to a booth.

The waitress handed them menus. "I'm glad you came back for some food, darlin'. I was worried that your morning sickness got the better of you."

Hannah offered the woman a warm, genuine smile that held Brett riveted, his memory jogged. He remembered that smile from the night they'd hooked up and what it felt like to have it directed at him.

"Wait," he said as the waitress turned to leave. "Janice, I'm really hungry. I think we'd better get that food on order right now. Hannah, you ready?"

"I'll have the oatmeal and a fruit cup."

That wasn't enough. Not nearly. When his brother's now ex-wife had been pregnant, she ate her weight in food every day. "I'll have the Paul Bunyan flapjack stack, the sausage omelet with the cheese grits, and a side of bacon." He winked at Hannah, whose eyebrows were pinched as though she were onto his plan. "Working on the ranch builds up quite an appetite."

When the waitress left, he folded his hands on the

table. "Let's get right to this interview. Lucky C—that's the name of my family's ranch—needs a new accountant."

"I know what your family's ranch is named. Everybody round these parts knows the Coltons, which is why it doesn't make any sense for you to post the help wanted ad the way you did, anonymously, discretion required."

On top of everything else, she was smart as a whip. Smart, proud, stubborn and a great dancer. Her list of attributes was getting unwieldy.

"What are you smiling about?" she asked.

He shook his head. "You're quick. I can already see you'll do a great job for the Lucky C."

She frowned at his compliment. "You're patronizing me. You don't even know my qualifications." From her massive purse, she pulled a page of substantial, pricey stationery from a folder. Her résumé.

"I'm not patronizing you. I put the ad in the classifieds because I need an accountant. You answered the ad and I'm a pretty good judge of character. Something tells me that you're perfect for the job."

"I am, but first, tell me why you did what you did, with the anonymous classified ad. Your family's ranch is huge and prosperous. If you need an accountant, you could have the best in Oklahoma, none of this cloak-and-dagger baloney."

He could tell she wasn't going to let him off the hook. "My father's getting up there in years and his memory isn't what it used to be. I've done what I can to help him—we all have—but it's time we bring in a qualified professional. I made the ad anonymous because my father's in denial about what's happening to him and I didn't want to alert the Tulsa gossip hounds, not after everything our family went through last month."

That was only a half-truth, but the real reason he'd wanted to hire an accountant wasn't going to cut through her pride, so he had no remorse for feeding her a line, not when her and their baby's well-beings were at stake. The real reason he'd put the anonymous ad in the paper was because he'd been planning to hire an accountant to take a look at the ranch's books on the sly, without his father and brothers' knowledge, and to help him crunch the numbers for the horse breeding business plan he was going to lay out for his family to consider investing in. But Hannah needed more than a part-time temporary job on the sly.

She set a hand on his forearm, her face pinched with worry. Her nails were trimmed to a short, practical length but were well-manicured and glossy, as though she'd used clear polish on them. "What happened last month? Is everyone okay?"

That surprised him all over again. The local news had done a thorough job raking his family through the public eye. "You mean you didn't hear?"

Her concerned look deepened, darkening her eyes. "No. Last month was the worst of my life. I was just trying to survive."

She was just trying to survive. He gripped his knees hard, holding himself back from scolding her. *You should have contacted me. I would have taken care of you. I would have taken care of everything.*

Brett wasn't ready for fatherhood, and truth was, it'd take some time for that change in his life to sink in, but nothing was going to stop him from doing the right thing by Hannah and the baby. That's what Colton men did and that's what Brett was going to do—for the rest of their lives.

Marriage? Maybe. If that's what Hannah wanted, what she needed in the long run, then his code of honor depended on making that offer to her. But not yet. Not when he wasn't sure she'd even agree to come live at the ranch once she heard what happened there the month before. He'd just have to find a way to convince her despite everything, because there was no getting around the truth about the trouble at the Lucky C. She'd find out soon enough. "Our house was robbed and my mother was attacked."

Hannah gasped. Her grip on his forearm tightened. "Is she…?"

He set a hand over hers and squeezed. "She's alive. In a coma. The doctors aren't sure she's going to make it, but we have to hold out hope."

Brett's relationship with his mother was the most complicated in his life. They'd never seen eye to eye and clashed more often than they were at peace. His deepest regret was that their last words to each other were angry, cruel. She wasn't an easy person to love, but she was the only mother he had and the thought of losing her hurt him something awful.

Hannah turned her hand over and threaded her fingers with his. "I'm so sorry. Did they catch the man who did that to her?"

"Yes. They have a suspect in custody. If you accept my job offer, and I sincerely hope you will, I want you to know that the ranch is safe. You don't have to worry about that." God, he hoped that was true. But there was no need to worry Hannah with his private doubts that the police had captured the man responsible for the assault, not when there was no evidence beyond his gut telling him that there was more to the robbery and attempted murder than everyone else thought.

Mistrust—or was that her pride rearing its head again?—pushed through her worried expression. "I don't remember you making me an official offer yet."

Their food arrived in a clatter of plates on Janice's massive serving tray, the smell so delicious that Hannah's stomach gurgled like crazy.

"I was just about to. Come work for the Lucky C, Hannah. It's what the ranch needs, and it's what you need, too. I'm prepared to compensate you with a competitive salary, health insurance, housing—"

"Housing? Isn't that a little unusual?"

She was a hard nut to crack, this one. Far harder than her sweet, soft voice and kind smile suggested. He summoned his most charming smile onto his lips, hoping that a little buttering up would help his cause. "Maybe, but then again, I've never met an accountant as pretty as you, so I'd say this situation is mighty unusual any way you cut it."

Sure enough, the mistrust in Hannah's eyes softened. And was that a hint of a smile on her lips? She poked her spoon through the air in his direction. "You can't flirt with me if you're going to be my boss."

"Then you're accepting my offer?"

"I said *if.*"

He slid the plate of bacon toward her. When charming failed, bacon often had a way of coming to the rescue. "Eat."

Desire shone in her eyes, jogging another memory of the lust he remembered seeing on her face that night at the club, then later, at her apartment. He remembered the way her every emotion played on her face without artifice or pretense. At the time, he'd appreciated that quality of hers only because it had made her easier to seduce, then easier to bring pleasure to in bed. He supposed what he was doing this morning still counted as seduction, but now, he was wholly focused on her needs instead of his.

To his relief, her fingers closed around a crispy slice of bacon. "I wasn't going to eat your food, given your enormous rancher's appetite, but that smells too darn good to resist. One little piece…" She crunched into the bacon, her eyes closing with the bliss of it.

He watched her face, riveted anew by the ever-shifting nuances in her expression.

Yet he forced his wayward thoughts aside. There would be time enough to marvel over Hannah, but he was a man on a mission, and he would not be deterred for anything. "Our chef cures and smokes her own bacon, harvested from our ranch's livestock. I wake to the smell of it frying in the kitchen every single morning. You could, too."

Her eyes jolted open. "I'm not moving in with you."

Time for the next step in his seduction. He liberally spread butter on his stack of flapjacks, then drizzled it with warm maple syrup. He sliced off a hearty wedge, then held his forkful across the table for her.

She backed her face up, eying the flapjack bite suspiciously.

"When was the last time you had pure maple syrup and real butter?" he crooned.

She reached a finger out to his plate and swiped at a drop of syrup, then brought it to her tongue.

Mercy. Just like that, Brett felt every one of the nineteen weeks of his self-inflicted abstinence.

"You, Brett Colton, are as slippery as a snake-oil salesman."

He brandished the fork under her nose. "I prefer to think of myself as stubborn and single-minded. Not so different from you."

The suspicion on her face melted away a little bit more. She guided his hand toward her and closed her lips around the fork in a way that gave Brett some ideas too filthy for his own good.

He cleared his throat, snapping his focus back to the task at hand. "When my parents remodeled the big house, they designed separate wings for each of their six children, but I'm the only one of the six who lives there full-time. Me and my father. My younger sister passes through sometimes, but you would have your own wing, your own bathroom with a big old tub, and plenty of privacy."

For the first time, she seemed to be seriously considering his offer. Time to go for broke. He handed her another slice of bacon, which she accepted without a word.

"Where are you living now?" he said. "Can you look me in the eye and tell me it's a good, long-term situation for you and the baby?"

She snapped a tiny bit of bacon off and popped it into her mouth. "It's not like I'm living in some abandoned building. I'm staying with my best friend, Lori, and her boyfriend, Drew. It's not ideal. Actually it's far from ideal—I mean, I'm sleeping on the sofa—but with the money from this job, I'll be able to afford my own place."

"And until that first paycheck, you'll live at the

ranch." He pressed his lips together. That had come out a smidge more demanding than he'd wanted it to.

Their gazes met and held. "Are you mandating that? Will the job offer depend on me accepting the temporary housing?"

Oh, how he wanted to say yes to that. "No. But you should agree to it, anyway. Your own bed, regular meals made by a top-rated personal chef, and your commute to work is down a set of stairs and along a short dirt road to the ranch office. The only traffic you might run into would be some overly excitable ranch dogs."

She popped the rest of the bacon slice into her mouth, then washed it down with orange juice. "I know why you're doing all this, and I still don't fully believe you about the reason you're hiring an accountant on the sly, but I really am grateful for all you're offering—the job and the accommodations. In all honesty, this went a lot better than I thought it would."

"The job interview?"

"No, telling you about the baby. I thought you'd either hate me or propose to me."

Brett didn't miss a beat. "I still might."

"Which one, hate me?"

Leaning forward, he gave her a look full of commitment and honor. "Ask you to marry me. I haven't taken that option off the table yet, either." At the flush of pink to her skin, he added with a knowing smile, "For the record, I don't think there's a person on the planet who could hate you."

"There's a whole congregation of them over on Grand Avenue and Fourth Street."

"That's your church?"

"The Congregation of the Second Coming. My parents' church, not mine. And it's more like a cult than a church, truth be told. Even before they excommunicated me because of the pregnancy, I was done with that place. I'm still a Christian, but I doubt there's room for that church's closed-minded judgment in the kingdom of heaven."

"Then you're better off without them."

She drew herself up tall. "Thank you. Yes, I am."

"Take my offer, Hannah. Let me take care of you." He clamped his teeth together, cursing himself for adding that last part. A strong, proud woman like her would chafe at such an old-fashioned notion.

She picked up her butter knife and made swirls in the bottom of her oatmeal bowl. Brett held his breath, watching her.

"I accept the job and the housing, even though 'Pregnant with the Boss's Baby' sounds like a bad soap opera plot." A conciliatory smile graced her lips.

Relief swept through his system with the force of last week's flash flood. "I don't know, I think it has a nice ring to it." Even as he said that, the truth in her jest hit him with a fresh dose of clarity. He was going to be a father. His future was going to include diaper changes, first steps, scraped knees and sleepless nights. Everything in his life was about to change, and he and Hannah would forever be linked by the life they'd created together.

His attention raked over the mother of his child, who was worrying the edge of her napkin. "What's bothering you now?"

"What about your family?" she said. "You took all this so well, but what if they hate me? Or worse, what if they think I got pregnant on purpose to get at your money?"

As much as he wished that her worry had no merit, she'd brought up an excellent point, because his family had no shortage of closed-minded judgmental attitudes, too. He'd been fighting for months to get them to see him in a new light, to prove to his brothers and father that he had turned over a new, more responsible leaf, so that they'd finally support the big plans he had for the family business. The last thing Brett needed was to add fuel to his brothers' and father's belief that he wasn't fit to help run the Lucky C, and nothing said *screwed-up, irresponsible rich boy* better than getting a girl pregnant during a one-night stand.

But facing the consequences of his misspent years and terrible choices was his problem, not Hannah's, so he squelched the grimace he felt coming on at the thought of breaking the news to his father and siblings. "Leave them to me."

CHAPTER THREE

BRETT STOOD AT the edge of Vulture Ridge, at the very place where he'd watched the cow get swept away in the flash flood, his gaze absorbing the land that he loved, despite Mother Nature's occasional cruelty. Today the sky was clear, but they'd had afternoon thundershowers every day lately, and this afternoon's forecast was no different. Even now, at a few minutes to noon, the clouds were stacking up on the horizon.

His eyeballs ached from a sleepless night of self-torment, with his conscience replaying every mistake he'd ever made. Every whiskey-soaked night, every morning of work he'd slept through—his past was littered with so much waste of money, time and opportunity that he could hardly believe that he kept being given more chances to get it right. That same life-changing bender of a weekend that had resulted in his car accident was now changing his life all over again. From this point forward and for the rest of his days, he would be beholden to a woman and, soon, a child. Somehow, he was going to become a man worthy of the charge—that he knew with absolute certainty.

Before dawn, he'd walked out of his house determined to stop looking back, ready to face his future with eyes wide-open. With a straight spine and determination coursing through his veins, he'd saddled Outlaw and had taken off to the backcountry, long before Jack and the ranch hands had arrived for their workdays.

He'd watched the sun rise over the prairie with an appreciation that reminded him of how he'd felt returning to the ranch after being released from the hospital after his accident—full of gratitude and hope. The longer he soaked in the views and scents of the backcountry, the land he adored, the more at peace he became with the new direction his life was going. Becoming a father was going to change a lot, but it wasn't going to change everything. He would always have this land, this Colton legacy. And now he had someone to pass it to. The realization brought a smile to his lips.

The irony wasn't lost on him that the very reason he couldn't give up fighting for his rightful place in the Colton legacy was the very reason he was about to be back to square one with his family on that very topic. When his dad and brothers learned about Brett's impending fatherhood resulting from a one-night stand, he was going to lose their trust all over again, along with whatever leverage he'd fought for over the past four months.

When the alarm on his phone chimed, alerting him that it was almost time for the family meeting that his older brother Ryan, a detective with the Tulsa PD, had called in order to share the latest developments in their mother's assault case, Brett's resolve faltered for a split second. Nerves settled in his gut like stones. Ryan wasn't the only one with news to share.

A click of his tongue and a slight wiggle of a rein was all the direction Outlaw needed to turn away from the ridge and trot in the direction of the ranch buildings. Brett urged him faster, relishing the feel of unadulterated power in Outlaw's muscles and stride. Brett knew that Outlaw loved this part, too, the wind in their faces and the open range at their feet as they shot across the plains, the sensations of speed and freedom potent enough for Brett to almost imagine it possible to outrun his past and his reputation.

The circular driveway in front of Brett's family home—the Big House, as it'd been called since long before Brett's birth, and where now only he and his dad lived, and his mom before her attack—was crowded with vehicles, including his half brother Daniel's truck and the farm truck that Jack's fiancée, Tracy, liked to drive around the place. Even his brother Eric had deigned to make a rare appearance, by the looks of it. Greta, they'd already been informed, couldn't break away from her job until the next day, when she planned to swing through the Big House for a short stay.

Brett walked around to the back of the house, then climbed the four steps up to the wraparound porch. The stones in his stomach that had been sitting there since seeing Hannah yesterday seemed to double in size with every step. He swallowed hard, then opened the door and entered through the mudroom attached to the kitchen.

The aroma of onions and garlic and roasting beef wafted past his nose as he removed his hat and boots. Maria, the chef, must be slow-cooking a roast for supper, if he had to hazard a guess. For Hannah's first meal there, he'd requested something hearty and homey that showcased the ranch's prized steer, and judging by the mouthwatering smells, Maria was going to knock it out of the park.

A smile worked its way onto his lips at the sudden vision of the look on Hannah's face when she'd crunched into that first slice of bacon the previous morning. Oh, man, he couldn't wait to watch her reaction to Maria's cooking. The anticipation of it was almost enough to quell his nerves over coming clean to his family about the many ways his life was about to get turned upside down.

From the kitchen, he crossed the foyer to the living room on the east side of the house, where a collection of male voices could be heard. As opposed to the kitchen, the foyer invariably smelled of fresh flowers from the arrangement that graced the circular marble table at the center of the grand entrance, which his mother insisted on having delivered weekly. To her warped way of thinking, the flowers were a display of power and wealth, but since Brett's brush with death, he'd come to think of the arrangements as reminders of how beautiful and fragile life was.

Even after his mom's attack, Edith had maintained the fresh flowers in the house. The only change was that the smaller arrangements that used to grace his mom's room got sent to her room at Tulsa General Hospital.

He'd taken no more than three steps through the foyer when a blond ball of little-boy energy bounded toward him, squealing his name. Despite Brett's nerves, he felt another grin coming on. Nobody made Brett feel like a rock star more than his five-year-old nephew, Seth, Jack's only son. The two were fast friends, and had been since the day Brett first held Seth in his arms when he was nothing more than a red-faced potato head wrapped in a hospital blanket. He opened his arms as Seth launched himself into them.

"Hey, cowpoke."

"Hiya, Uncle Brett!"

"Wait, what's this in your armpit?" With that, Brett dug his thumbs into Seth's prime tickle spot under his armpits. Seth squealed with delight, writhing and arching.

Brett redoubled his efforts. "Just a sec, I think I've almost got it," he teased. "Lemme just dig in there a little deeper."

Seth's legs kicked out, and one of his feet accidentally nudged the marble table. The flower arrangement's vase wobbled. Brett lunged for it as best he could while being careful not to drop Seth, but Jack was quicker.

Jack steadied the vase, casting his signature stern look at Brett that got right under his skin, as it always did. "Careful, you two. Edith works too hard to keep this place up to have you messing it up by roughhousing."

As though Brett needed to be scolded like a child. He was about to say as much when Tracy appeared. She wore her dark blond hair pulled into a ponytail and a dark shirt and jeans that emphasized her pale, slim figure.

"Oh, now, Jack, they were just having a little fun. No harm done." She rubbed his shoulder and offered him a sweet smile. Jack instantly relaxed, a phenomenon that Tracy got full credit for cultivating. Truth be told, Brett was fascinated by the soothing and centering effect she'd had on Jack since coming into his life the month before.

"Seth, why don't you go outside and play so the grown-ups can talk?" she said to her soon-to-be stepson. "See if you can find your kitty friend, Sleekie, in the barn."

Brett managed to ruffle the little guy's hair before he bounded outside, half skipping and half jumping.

Brett followed Jack and Tracy to the living room that

doubled as a library of sorts. When he'd been a kid, this had been a place of fascination for him in the house, the one room his parents had forbidden the kids from entering, not just because of all the breakable trinkets and pieces of art, but because it was where they retired with their guests for cocktails after the occasional dinner parties his dad was so fond of hosting.

His dad, Big J, was seated in his usual chair near the fireplace, chatting up Brett's older brothers Ryan and Eric. Daniel sat apart from the others, bent over his smartphone and keeping to himself as usual.

Dad was still fit and youthful, even after a lifetime of working the ranch and raising six kids, largely on his own when Brett's mother, Abra, decided to check out and skip town, which was a lot. Brett saw a little bit of all his siblings in Dad. They shared the same nose and same shape of their face, but Brett was the only one of the Colton kids who'd inherited his dad's boisterous laugh and love of good times, or so Edith, their housekeeper, was fond of saying.

Dad gave Brett a wave and his signature beaming smile. "I saw you race out of here this morning before dawn. You get some kind of sticker in your paw about something?"

Brett most certainly did have a sticker in his paw, but his big announcement could wait until after they learned more from Ryan about the search for his mom's attacker. He dropped into the center cushion of the sofa between Eric and Ryan. "Checking the fences. Can't be too careful after that one was tampered with during last week's storm."

Dad harrumphed as though he didn't buy Brett's pat response. Brett just smiled serenely at him.

"Losing one pregnant cow was enough for a lifetime," Jack grouched.

"She wasn't pregnant when she was swept away in the flash flood," Brett corrected.

"Yeah, what'd you name that calf you birthed in the gully?"

"Twister, and she's doing just fine, thank you very much. And now that you mention it, what do you say we focus on Twister and the five pregnant cows I saved, rather than the one we lost, Jack? Maybe you could take a hiatus from busting my chops all the damn time."

Jack scowled at him. "Maybe you could start giving me reason to trust you."

"All right you two, that's enough. Don't forget that your mother is lying unconscious in a hospital bed," Dad barked. "Ryan, let's get to it. What's the latest on the investigation into her attacker?"

"Right, okay," Ryan said, scooting to the edge of the sofa. With his elbows propped on his knees, he flipped through the small notebook that was an ever-present accessory of his shirt pocket. "I don't know an easy way to break this to y'all, but you know how some of you were doubting that the hit man who tried to kill Tracy last month was the same perp who attacked Abra and robbed her room? Well, those same doubts have arisen among my investigative team. And we have some proof of that."

Brett had been among the earliest to voice his doubt that the hit man had also targeted their mom, but convincing the police to drop that lead and concentrate their efforts on an unknown perpetrator had been like trying to herd a group of pregnant cows in a thunderstorm—which he knew since he'd had the honor of attempting both feats. "What kind of proof?"

Ryan gave a look around, as though some interloper might be eavesdropping on their meeting. Not that there were interlopers to be found, but he still lowered his voice. "The gold locket with Greta's picture in it that was stolen on the night of Abra's attack turned up at a pawnshop. Greta's picture had the eyes gouged out, making her likeness unrecognizable, but the inscription on the back was a dead match."

Dad cursed under his breath. Jack scrubbed a hand over his chin, his eyes narrow and his expression distant.

"Pawnshops have security cameras, right? So this is great news," Brett said.

"Yes and no. We were, indeed, able to identify the suspect using the pawnshop's external security camera to identify the man's car's license plate, and we brought him in for questioning last night."

"And this is the first we're hearing about it?" Dad grumbled.

"Who is he?" Eric asked.

"A dead end. The guy's name is Dell Cortaline, a small-time oxy addict we've seen before. He's not our guy, though. There's no way. He's not smart enough to get in and out of this house without leaving fingerprints or some other trail of evidence."

"Then how did he get the locket?" Brett asked.

Ryan rolled his tongue around the inside of his bottom lip. His gaze locked onto Dad. "He claimed to have found it in the bushes outside Tulsa General Hospital."

Brett leaped to his feet before he knew what he was doing. "What? That's…"

Jack stood and joined Brett behind the sofa to pace. "What that is is a new threat. Someone's trying to get at Mother in the hospital."

"That was my thought, too," Ryan said grimly.

"I'm assuming your boss agreed to put an armed guard outside her room? To make sure she's safe?" Dad said.

Ryan rubbed the back of his neck. "That's easier said than done. This isn't a big enough red flag to justify putting an armed guard outside her hospital room door 24/7, but I have put the hospital on alert. Abra's in intensive care, which is highly monitored by the staff, anyway, both with door locks and cameras. Visitors don't have easy access to the rooms in the ICU. I really believe she's safe in there."

"I'm there a lot, too," Eric said. "I'll keep a closer eye. But I agree with Ryan. The ICU is practically impenetrable."

Dad shook his head. "I don't understand. Abra wasn't the kind of person who'd have a target on her back. But if her attacker went to the hospital where she's at, then that makes it personal, doesn't it?"

"Maybe, maybe not. It's possible that Abra saw the perp's face and he's afraid she'll be able to identify him. Could be that when he discovered how difficult it would be to get to her inside the ICU, he abandoned his plan and tossed the jewelry. That theory leaves me with more questions, but that's one of the more solid theories we're considering at this point."

"Any news about the possible DNA the police tech found under Mom's fingernails from the attacker?"

"Detective Howard is doing her best to expedite the results, but DNA testing is notoriously slow. As soon I know, I'll let y'all know, and that's a promise."

"This is an attempted murder case," Dad said. "It's got to count for something that we might have an attempted murderer on the loose in Tulsa. Can't you push them harder?"

Ryan pocketed the notepad again. "No, I can't. I know we're all in a hurry, but this isn't the only unsolved violent crime the Oklahoma State Bureau of Investigation is running DNA tests on. I'm doing the best I can. As far as we can tell, the ranch is safe."

"It is if you don't count the downed fence lines. Last week was the third occurrence since Mother's attack of our fences being tampered with."

"Maybe that's the ghost that Maria keeps swearing she sees walking the fields at night," Jack said, a gallows humor grin on his face.

With a huff, Dad shook his head. "I swear, Maria is the most superstitious person I've ever met."

"Even still," Daniel said, "I think Brett's right. And I think we need to take action."

Being that this was the first time Daniel had seen fit to open his mouth that day, the chatter in the room died instantly as everyone gave him their full attention.

Jack dropped back down to the sofa. "What do you propose?"

"While the police do their thing, we circle the wagons. No more vandalism. No more hit men or violent robberies. We need to protect the ranch and the people in it."

"Agreed," Brett said. He'd promised Hannah that she'd be safe here, and he planned on delivering. "I vote for nightly patrols in groups of two."

"That works for me," Daniel said. "And we should consider installing alarm systems to every house and motion sensor lights in the yard, and running background checks of every Lucky C employee."

"This ranch employs a lot of people," Dad said. "We can't account for everyone, all the time."

"Well, we sure as hell better start trying," Brett said. "Daniel's right. It's time to cowboy up and take care of our own. No one hurts the Coltons and gets away with it."

"I'll help as much as I can," Ryan said. "Meanwhile, my theory is that since we found one piece of Abra's jewelry, there's got to be more. I'll get some uniforms in our department to search local pawnshops again. I've already got a techie going through the hospital's external security footage."

"I'll take first patrol tonight," Jack said.

Dad stood. "I'll join you. This old house is too quiet these days without Abra."

Nobody argued with that, even though their mother was a nonentity in the house most days. She and Dad hadn't slept in the same quarters as long as Brett could remember, and she rarely left her bedroom suite, especially in the evenings.

In the awkward silence that descended over the room, Daniel stood and set his empty coffee mug on the tray. Eric followed suit, busing his mug then checking his phone.

Brett drew a deep breath. The mood wasn't even close to relaxed and jovial, but it was time to get this next conversation over with. "Wait, everyone. Eric, Daniel. I have something big I need to tell you."

"You're gay," Daniel deadpanned under his breath, quiet enough that Brett was probably the only person who heard him.

"What? Yeah. Exactly." He slapped Daniel on the back. "Way to call it, bro."

Daniel shrugged, flashing a hint of a devilish smile that was gone just as fast. He might be Brett's funniest sibling, if only he'd let his guard down around the rest of the family.

Jack released a deep sigh. "This better not be any more of your harebrained schemes to make changes around the ranch. I already agreed to purchase a stud horse, so don't push your luck."

"It's not about the business. Well, I mean it is, but not like that." He bit his lip to stop his blathering while everyone resettled.

Edith chose that moment to bustle in and beelined for the coffee service. "Are you done with the coffee, everyone?"

"That depends," Dad said. "Brett, is this going to be quick or should I pour myself another cuppa?"

Brett checked the time out of habit. He was scheduled to pick Hannah up in ninety minutes, give or take. "Have another cup, Pops. And Edith, you might as well stick around to hear this, too."

In no time, all eyes were on him. Last night and that morning, he'd visualized broaching the topic of his impending fatherhood from dozens of different angles, but the only conclusion he'd reached was that there was no good, easy way to reveal the news.

"I hired an accountant for the ranch." He shook his head and nearly smacked it. *What the heck was that, stupid? That's how you're going to tell your family you're going to be a father?*

Jack scowled at him, his mouth agape. "How do you figure you have a right to make a decision like that without consulting us?"

No backing down now, especially with Jack in full

jackass older-brother mode again. "Number one—because we could use the help. Pops, you spend half your time at the hospital tending to Mom, as you should be, and you have enough to worry about without messing with a bunch of ledgers and spreadsheets."

"That's my call," Dad said. "Don't tell me what I can and can't handle. I'll retire when I'm good and ready, and I'm not expecting to anytime soon. I'm with Jack. What were you thinking, making such a huge decision like that on your own?"

A wave of panic hit Brett. He'd expected his dad to stubbornly cling to his job, but not to be so fundamentally offended by the idea of Brett hiring help. A part of him had held out hope that his dad would be relieved to have the burden taken off his shoulders.

"With all the new tax laws and corporate regulations this country is levying on small farms, the ranch's books have become a helluva lot more complicated than simple addition and subtraction," Brett said. "If we want this ranch to thrive in the future, then we have to modernize every aspect of the business in a competitive, forward-thinking way—our breeding programs, our business model and our financial plan."

Jack groaned. "Here we go again. I thought you agreed to lay off the 'futuristic business' talk until we see how that goes."

"I know, and you'll see that I'm right, but hiring an accountant is different. Tax planning, retirement planning, workers comp insurance," Brett enumerated on his fingers. "Pops, you don't want to have to deal with all that, do you? Furthermore, you're not qualified to. None of us are."

Jack set his mug on the coffee table hard enough that

the spoons on the tray rattled. "I'll give you that, but I still don't understand why you saw it as your right to go behind our backs to do the hiring. Even if you are right about us needing a full-time accountant."

Brett squelched a look of utter shock. Jack conceding a point to Brett? It was inconceivable. He was afraid to look outside, lest he see the ranch's hogs taking to the skies upon wings. "You won't regret it. She's highly qualified."

Ryan and Jack both threw up their hands as though they'd choreographed their disgust. "She. Okay, I get it now, hotshot," Ryan said. "So by *highly qualified* you mean she's young and hot."

Hannah was young and hot, but he kept that part to himself.

Jack stabbed the air with his index finger. "We are not—I repeat, *not*—hiring your good-timing girl of the week to be responsible for our ranch's financial health. Deal off."

Well, this is going about as well as I expected, Brett thought grimly. *Time to solidify their stellar opinion of me*. At least Hannah wasn't around yet to witness the ass chewing he was about to get.

He slid her résumé onto the table. "She's not my good-timing girl of the week." She had been exactly that give or take nineteen weeks earlier, but that was beside the point. "Her name is Hannah Grayson. She has a bachelor's degree in accounting from Tulsa United's online program, from which she graduated summa cum laude."

Dad slid his glasses on and took a closer look at her résumé. "This looks reasonable. She seems to have quite a head on her shoulders and, since she's a new graduate, we could hire her at an entry-level salary, which would be affordable enough. Make her part-time so we don't have to pay benefits and I'll agree to it."

Brett barreled ahead, suddenly eager to get to the real point of his announcement. "I already offered her a full-time position with benefits and a competitive salary because she's pregnant."

Jack's whole face turned red, his head of steam going like gangbusters. "You just keep pushing and pushing, don't you? The Lucky C isn't a charity organiz—"

"With my child," Brett added, cutting him off. "I'm going to be a father in about twenty weeks, give or take."

CHAPTER FOUR

THE ROOM WENT dead quiet. Dad stared at Brett, disappointment dragging at his features. Jack's mouth flopped open while Tracy rubbed his arm. Eric and Daniel stared out the window, their expressions shuttered.

Brett sipped his coffee, though he couldn't even taste it, giving them time to get over their shock.

In the gaping silence, a hard, patronizing laugh burst out of Jack. "You really did it this time. How in the world did you get yourself into a mess like that?"

Jack's laughter, even more than the disappointment in the rest of his family's eyes, snapped Brett's patience. He was done with being a whipping boy. "Let me see if I can spell it out for you. When a man and a woman are attracted to each other, sometimes they express that attraction by doing a mommy-and-daddy grown-up dance with all their clothes off—"

Jack sneered at him. "And you wanted me to give you more responsibilities around here. Unbelievable."

Dad scrubbed a hand over his mouth and chin. "Like I always say, the apple don't fall far from the tree," he murmured, his eyes shifting briefly to Daniel.

Just once, Brett wanted his father to tell him that with pride in his voice instead of disappointment. Just once in his damn life. Brett had grown up idolizing his dad, from his larger-than-life presence and joviality that made him the life of every party to the bullheaded conviction that had led him to forge the Lucky C ranch from the earth and transform it into a profitable enterprise.

On the surface, yes, Brett's getting a girl pregnant out of wedlock seemed similar to his dad's screwups, but the situation with Hannah wasn't at all like the extramarital affair his dad had that resulted in Daniel's conception. Brett hadn't broken any marriage vows. Not that Brett or any of them would point out the differences aloud and risk making Daniel uncomfortable. He might only be their half brother by blood, but he was a full brother in their hearts—the only place it mattered.

He didn't think Dad meant to be callous with the comment. Over the years, his dad had made it clear that he'd separated in his mind the sin of his affair from the love he felt for the son he'd gained from it. Still, Brett chanced a look in Daniel's direction to see him staring out the window, as though he'd shuttered himself from the conversation.

Brett wished his sister, Greta, had been there. She had the kindest and most forgiving heart of all of them and, because of that, been the glue of the family since she'd been a child. She would've known what to say to ease the tension in the room and remind Daniel that their dad didn't mean any harm.

With his eyes on Daniel's profile, Brett cleared his throat and tried to imagine what Greta would've said had she been present. "Then it's a good thing we grew up understanding that family is family and that a baby is a blessing, no matter what."

Edith gave Brett an affectionate rub on the back. "Well said."

Eric refilled his coffee mug. "I'm with you on that

sentiment, but this is a lot to take in. I'd like more details about what happened. Forgive my bluntness, but I've gotten the impression that you've slept with plenty of women over the years, and you managed not to knock any of them up—I feel safe in saying. So how did a mistake like this come about? I mean, assuming it *was* an accident and she didn't do this on purpose to get at our money. Because something smells fishy to me."

Brett looked from Eric to Ryan and the rest of the family, all of whom wore expressions of surprise and concern and, as opposed to his dad and Jack, they looked as if they were ready to listen to what Brett had to say instead of merely pelting him with insults. Even Edith perched on the edge of a chair, her arms crossed and a sympathetic smile on her lips.

Brett shifted toward them, putting a cold shoulder to Jack. "She's not trying to get at our family money, and you're just going to have to trust me on that until you meet her." Behind him, Jack chuffed, but Brett pressed on. "Here's what happened. You remember that day, four months ago, when I wrapped my truck around the tree? That was the moment that made me turn my life around and get a clue about the kind of man I wanted to be and the kind of life I wanted to lead."

"Of course we remember that," Ryan said. "You tattered that truck and you're lucky to be alive."

"I am. I know. Leading up to that moment, I'd had a hell of a weekend, a real bender after Mom and I had argued. About what, I can't even remember. Anyway, I'd gone out clubbing the night before the truck accident, which was where I met Hannah and slept with her. We used a condom—" Eric opened his mouth, probably to suggest that Hannah had sabotaged the condom, so Brett held a finger up to quiet him and added, "A condom that I provided, so get that out of your mind. Yesterday was the first time I'd seen her since that night. Needless to say, we had a long, serious talk. Neither one of us has any idea why the condom didn't work."

Jack templed his hands in front of his mouth. "Wait. She's nineteen weeks pregnant, yet she didn't tell you until yesterday? I'm with Eric. Something smells fishy to me."

"Hate to beat a dead horse," Ryan said, drumming his fingers on his knee, "and maybe you're right and our suspicions will be laid to rest when we meet her, but this wouldn't be the first time a desperate, misguided young woman tried to get at our family money. And with your less-than-monogamous lifestyle, you'd be the perfect target for a scam. My advice is for you to get a paternity test before this goes any further."

Less-than-monogamous lifestyle. That would have been the understatement of the century a few months ago. Nevertheless, Hannah had called it correctly. On the surface, her being desperately hard-up for money and pregnant with a Colton's child looked bad from every angle—except one. "No paternity test necessary. I'm going to take her word for it that I'm the father, and when you meet her, you'll take her word for it, too."

Dad snickered. "She's that homely?"

"What? No. She's that honest. Honest and smart and stubborn to a fault. You'll see." Because he knew that everything would change in their minds the moment they laid eyes on her. She'd win them all over with a single smile, of that he was certain.

His family still looked unconvinced, so Brett continued. "The reason she waited so long to tell me about the baby was that she wanted to get back on her feet first. Because she knows exactly how suspicious this looks from the outside. Hannah's parents disowned her and fired her from their family business when they found out she was pregnant. She spent the last of her savings on medical care for her pregnancy and has been crashing on her friend's sofa ever since. This solution, her moving here and working for us as an accountant, was my idea. And believe me, it took some convincing."

"Wait, she's not only going to work for us, but you're moving her in here, without a paternity test, background check, nothing?" Jack said.

"I'll run a background check on her, no problem." Ryan whipped his phone out and peered at Hannah's résumé, mouthing the letters of her name as he typed.

Brett grabbed the résumé away from Ryan's gaze. "Not necessary. I went by her family's store yesterday after I dropped Hannah off at her friend's house and I talked to her parents. I didn't tell them who I was or why I was there, but I asked them where Hannah was and congratulated them on her pregnancy, and let me tell you, they're even nuttier and filled with more hate than I expected."

Just picturing the fury in their expressions when they told him their heathen daughter was dead to them put Brett in a fighting mood. "What's more, Hannah hadn't told them I was the father. I don't think she's told any-body. Does that sound like the actions of someone try-ing to scam me?"

"A background check still wouldn't hurt," Ryan mut-tered.

Brett shook his head, ignoring Ryan, his attention on Jack. "So, to answer your question, yes, I am moving her in here. She's homeless, jobless, out of money—and she's having my baby. And she's too stubborn to agree to anything that has the whiff of charity, which was why I offered her a job. Full-time with benefits so I can make sure she and the baby get the proper health care they need."

He could tell he was breaking through their judgmental walls because they'd started to squirm, their eyes averted. Time to drive the nail the rest of the way in. He stood and tossed his napkin on the table. "Y'all keep banging on me about being irresponsible, and I'm the first to admit that I used to be. But even if you can't see it, I've changed. This is me being responsible, doing the right thing and living up to our family's code of honor. Ask yourself—what would you do if you were in my shoes?"

That shut them down, all but his dad. "Did you at least offer to make her an honest woman?"

The head of steam Brett had built up diffused a little. If they were moving on to questions like that, then perhaps his family was ready to accept Brett's new reality. "This is the twenty-first century, Pops. A woman doesn't have to be married to be considered honest."

Dad chuffed at that, clearly a nonbeliever in that vein of modern-day feminism. "When's this Hannah woman coming to the ranch?"

"I'm going into town to get her as soon as we're done here."

A car engine sounded outside. Everyone craned their necks to look out the windows. Brett took a few steps in that direction in time to watch a yellow taxi disappear along the road leading away from the house.

"Something tells me Ms. Hannah Grayson has saved you from having to make a trip into town," Ryan said.

Jack clapped his hands together as he stood. "Let's get this introduction over with."

The somber resignation in Jack's tone set Brett's teeth on edge again. He whirled around, a warning on his tongue for everyone to behave themselves and show Hannah the respect she deserved, but Edith saved him from it.

"I have a better idea," she said brightly from the doorway, where she stood with the rolling coffee cart in front of her, blocking passage. "Let's give our new houseguest a chance to settle in first, before she has to contend with a household of grouchy men. Let Brett help her get acclimated first. Greta will be here tomorrow, and I can't think of a better way to celebrate a new baby than with a big family dinner."

Thank you, Edith. She was a commanding force in the house, not because she was pushy or overbearing, but because of her kindness and levelheaded management of the household since before Brett was born. The family respected her too much to defy her will. It was all he could do to keep himself from throwing his arms around her.

"That's a perfect idea," Brett said. "Hannah's skittish enough about being here."

Dad pushed himself out of his easy chair. "I like that plan. That'll give me some time to get used to the idea."

"You can eat at our house tonight, Big J," Tracy said. "We can let Brett and Hannah have a private dinner together. It sounds like they still have a lot to talk about, if they just connected yesterday."

That was a perfect idea. He'd have to talk to Edith

about arranging for a multicourse dinner for the two of them, a meal they could really linger over while they got to know each other. "Thank you, Tracy."

Eric rattled his car keys and inched toward the exit that Edith was still blocking. "I'll try to make it tomorrow night, but I have a late shift at the hospital." In other words, he was begging out of the event, as usual, because there was no way he drew so many short straws for late shifts at the hospital, coincidentally any time the rest of the Coltons planned a get-together.

"If we wait until tomorrow, then Tracy and Seth can meet Hannah at the same time, too."

"I'll plan a big dinner. Brett, you figure out what she likes and dislikes. Maybe there's something she's been craving."

"Thank you," Brett said. So relieved.

She stepped to the side and swept her hand toward the rear of the house. "Out the back entrance, all of you. No sense in intimidating her in the first five minutes she gets here with a big group of strapping, foul-tempered cowboys."

"Yes, ma'am," Ryan mumbled in an exaggerated drawl. He kissed Edith's cheek as he passed, as they each did, in a show of respect to the woman who'd played a fundamental part of their upbringing and daily lives for decades.

When the last of them had filed out of the room, she smiled lovingly at Brett. "I'll talk to the staff and make sure you get the space you need to do this your way. And I'll send Mavis up to the guest suite next to yours and have it fixed up for Hannah in no time. Fresh linens and the works."

He gathered all hundred pounds of her in a tight hug,

lifting her off her feet. "You're a lifesaver. How do you always know the exact right thing to say?"

She blushed and swatted her hand through the air, dismissing the praise. "Hush, now. Go on and find Hannah before she gets cold feet and calls that taxi back."

HANNAH CREPT ALONG the wraparound porch of Brett's massive house, away from the window where she'd been eavesdropping. Not that she'd set out with the idea of listening in on Brett's family's conversation, but once she'd stumbled into hearing range, she'd been powerless to resist.

A case of cold feet had compelled her to ask the taxi driver to wait there until she gave him the all-clear to leave, just in case she had a change of heart or she'd accidentally come to the wrong house or she'd misunderstood Brett's desire for her to move in that day. The driver hadn't been too keen on waiting, but she'd promised him he could leave the meter running and after a bit more begging, he'd acquiesced.

After climbing the tall staircase leading from the circular driveway up to the mansion sitting on the highest and most central part of the ranch, she'd knocked and pressed the doorbell, but no one had answered. The longer she stood there, the more nervous she got and the more she doubted her decision to show up early.

Thinking that the house was so big that it was entirely possible that no one had heard the doorbell ring, she'd followed the porch around to the side of the house, which was when she'd heard voices. More specifically, she'd heard one of the men in the room explain his theory that their mother's attacker was still on the loose and, potentially, had been lurking around the ranch.

Wait, what? That wasn't what the local news had been reporting. Last night, she'd used Lori's computer to research Brett's mother's attack. What she'd learned had made her heart break for Brett and his family. His mother had been attacked in her bedroom and left for dead, her belongings ransacked and her jewelry stolen by—according to the news report—a hit man who'd been hired to off Brett's older brother's fiancée. The main suspect had been gunned down, or so the police and the newspaper had indicated.

She continued to listen to Brett's family talk, justifying the eavesdropping because she deserved to know if she was safe at the ranch or not, or if Brett had glossed over his family's troubles in his fervor to get her to agree to his plan. If there was any chance that she was in danger at the ranch, she could turn right around and leave.

But the more she listened, the more affected she was by the hurt in each man's voice over their mother's assault and their frustration that her investigation had stalled. And then, one minute turned into the next, and before she knew it, she was listening to Brett tell his family that he'd hired an accountant.

She was touched by his approach, and that he'd opened the conversation with a discussion of her accounting skills. For whatever reason, that mattered to her. A lot. He'd stood up for her, and complimented her abilities and qualifications. She'd been held entranced by his praise…right up until one of the other men in the room had labeled her as Brett's good-time girl of the week.

She'd winced at that, even though she agreed with the term, if not the negative judgment implied by it. She'd been Brett's good-time girl as much as he'd been her good-time guy for the night. While she refused to be shamed for enjoying her sexuality, even if Brett's family turned out to judge her as harshly as her own family had, it still smarted to realize that, as she'd expected might happen, Brett's family assumed she was trying to get at their money. It wasn't a shock that they didn't trust her. The surprise was that they didn't seem to trust Brett, either. And that frosted Hannah something fierce because she'd suffered the same mistrust at the hands of her own family.

Probably, her relationship with Brett's family would go a lot more smoothly if she weren't aware of their candid feelings about her and Brett, because those assumptions didn't matter in the grand scheme of things. All that mattered was that she believed in herself and knew in her heart that she was a good and honest person. Which meant it was high time for her to get the heck out of earshot again.

She tiptoed back to the front of the house and down the stairs, her eye on the taxi. Nothing was stopping her from jumping back in it and taking off. Except that there kind of was, now that she was considering it. Brett was being judged by his family the same as she'd been by hers. They were about to become parents together, and if she stayed with him, if she gave him a chance, then she would spare him from her same fate of having to face his family's negativity alone.

And Brett had told her the day before that his father was slipping mentally. Not only that, but Brett's dad shouldn't be working so hard around the ranch when his wife lay in a coma. Brett's father deserved better and the ranch deserved better, too, because Brett was also right about them needing an actual financial specialist to help them with long-term tax planning, one of her specialties. No matter how negatively Brett's family judged her for getting pregnant, her conscience couldn't just walk away from that situation.

Her two measly pieces of luggage sat in the driveway next to the cab. She'd packed light because, one, she had no idea how long she was staying, and, two, she didn't actually own that much stuff anymore, having sold most of it to afford the business of living. She navigated around the suitcases and handed the taxi driver his rate plus a generous tip through the open driver's side window. "Thank you for waiting. Have a nice—"

"Back up so I can turn around."

Gee, what a sweet guy. So deserving of my last bit of cash as a tip—not. She stepped back and tripped over her suitcases, planting her rear end hard on the one she'd knocked over.

Her face growing hot with embarrassment, she took a furtive glance around for witnesses. Not seeing any, she stood and brushed off her dress in time to watch the taxi hauling butt in a cloud of dust as it disappeared along the dirt road.

She took a moment to catch her breath, marveling at the endless string of awkward moments that her life had become since graduating from college. What was her next move? Should she try knocking again? Call Brett's cell phone? Settle in on the porch and wait for Brett's family to find her after they finished their meeting?

"If you're here looking for a handout from Mr. Colton, then you'd best be leaving before I call the police," called a female voice.

Hannah turned to see a familiar, if unexpected, face. Her defenses immediately went on red alert, as they did every time she saw someone from the Congregation of the Second Coming. "Mavis?"

Mavis Turnbolt was dressed in what could only be described as a maid's uniform. Her brown hair was constrained in a tight braid that had been coiled into a bun from which no wild hairs had escaped. She was only a year older than Hannah, and over the years, their mothers had made valiant, yet fruitless, attempts to push them into friendship. She could've lived the rest of her life without needing to see any member of the Turnbolt family again, but after all she'd been through, another piece of bad luck didn't even faze her.

Then again, it wasn't fair of Hannah to be critical of Mavis in exactly the same way she hated to be judged. Hannah hadn't been to the church in years, not since her eighteenth birthday, so for all she knew, Mavis had broken the hold that the church had over her, just as Hannah had.

"It's nice to see a friendly face. I had no idea you worked here," Hannah said, offering her hand for a handshake. "I work here now, too."

Mavis eyed Hannah's hand as if it were a snake. "I will not be associating with jezebels, so you'd best take that hand back."

So much for that fair chance. "And you'd best watch your attitude. Neither my baby nor I deserves your scorn."

"Scorn is the only thing a sinner like you deserves. Wait until the Coltons learn they've hired one of Satan's newest disciples."

Hannah wrapped a protective arm around her belly. "First of all, this baby *is* a Colton, thank you very much. And second, can you even hear yourself? Satan's newest disciple? Really?" She cringed inwardly, wishing she'd thought twice before engaging with someone who was so filled with hate. It wasn't as though she stood a chance of changing Mavis's mind.

Mavis's face broke out in a hard smile. "I guess I have a whole lot of news to share with our church, then. We'll be praying for the Coltons to cast you out of their lives before you sink your claws of sin any deeper into their family."

Oh, brother. "Sounds like a good plan, Mavis. Y'all just go ahead and get busy praying. In fact, with all that prayin' you need to do, I doubt you'll have time to work in a den of depravity like the Lucky C. What if our sinning ways brush off on you? If I were you, I'd quit right now."

"You'd love that, wouldn't you?"

"Honestly, I really would."

"The devil has no power over me." Her face screwed up as if she was going to sneeze, except that she didn't sneeze—she spit on Hannah's shoe.

Hannah was too shocked to do anything more than gasp as Mavis hurried away. Who went around spitting on other people's shoes? How was that even a thing that people did in the twenty-first century?

She dug through her purse in search of a tissue.

"The Lucky C is a den of depravity? Well, how about that. I had no idea," a drawling male voice said.

She glanced up to see a handsome man wearing a white Stetson pull a handkerchief from his jeans pocket. He looked to be about Brett's age, with a friendly smile and dancing blue eyes, one of which he used to wink at her right before he knelt and wiped off her shoe.

"Thank you," she said to his flannel-shirted back and hat.

He stood and pocketed the handkerchief again. "Pleasure's all mine." He stuck his hand out. "Name's Rafe Sinclair."

She shook his offered hand. "I'm Hannah Grayson."

"Pleasure to make your acquaintance. Now, I have to be honest here. I saw you tiptoeing around the big house, so I hope you don't mind if I inquire about what or who you're looking for. Maybe I can help you on your way."

"I was just having a look around. This is my first day at my new job here at the Lucky C and it's quite impressive."

He touched the brim of his hat. "A new job and you're expecting? My goodness, you're a busy bee. What kind of work were you hired for? Because I bet the ranch is gonna need a new laundress now that you've affronted Mavis."

Note to self—stay away from the laundry room, and Mavis. "I'm the new accountant."

A look of confusion flickered over his face, just for a moment, replaced anew by his smile. "How in the world is a pretty little thing like you going to handle the complexities of the accounting needs of the Lucky C?"

So much for her intuition that Rafe might be one of her friends at the ranch. She bristled inwardly at the derogatory implications dripping from his words, but fought to keep her outward demeanor cool. "Oh, I'm sure I'll manage just fine, but your concern is noted."

Noted and dismissed as useless drivel. A lot of men in ranch country shared Rafe's views, and he probably thought he'd done nothing wrong. She'd let her skills as an accountant prove him wrong and maybe open up his mind a little bit.

"Hannah?"

Brett's voice carried across the yard. She turned her back to Rafe and found Brett striding toward her. And dang it all if her heart didn't skip a beat at the sight of him. He was dressed in a light gray cotton T-shirt that was a shade too form-fitting, with the outline of his pectorals clearly defined and the sleeves pushed up above his biceps, tucked into snug Wranglers. His long legs ended in scuffed brown leather boots. With that look, and the ranch backdrop, he looked every inch the consummate cowboy. All he needed now was a cowboy hat, and she bet her bottom dollar he had one nearby. Thank goodness he wasn't wearing it now because turning into a puddle of hormonal lust wasn't the first impression she wanted to make with Brett's family.

"You didn't need to spring for a taxi. I was going to pick you up in a couple hours."

Clipped to his belt was what looked like a ranch radio, as though she'd caught him in the middle of his workday. Which she had, now that she thought about it. In her haste to prove herself self-sufficient, she hadn't considered that she'd be interrupting his duties at the ranch. "I didn't want you to have to, but it looks like I disrupted your day, anyway. I'm sorry about that."

He nodded past her, in greeting to Rafe, then leaned in close, his shoulder brushing hers, and got his lips close to her ears, whispering, "I told you I'd take care of you, and I know you're not used to that, but you have to give me a chance to try."

Behind the aroma of dirt and honest ranching work, she caught the scent of his soap or shaving cream, masculine and fresh. That was when her hormones decided it was their turn to take the wheel.

Wicked, red-hot need kicked up inside her. It hadn't been the first time since she'd hit her second trimester that lust had slapped her upside the head—or her nether regions, as it were—but this was the first time it'd happened while she was touching an honest-to-goodness man—a handsome one at that. One she knew from experience was an expert when it came to wringing pleasure from a woman's body.

A memory surfaced of his hands on her, pinning her wrists above her head, his mouth plundering hers with rough, wicked kisses. A hum of pleasure bubbled out of her before she knew what she was doing.

Brett eyed her curiously.

Mortified, she shook the image out of her mind. At least Rafe had wandered away, out of earshot. "And you have to give me a chance to prove that I'm not helpless."

Her gaze traced Brett's strong, clean-shaven jawline from his ear to red, luscious lips quirked into a teasing smile. "You don't have to prove anything to me, but for what it's worth, I believe that your general lack of helplessness was one of the bullet points on your résumé, if memory serves."

She returned his smile. "Sounds like we have a lot to learn about working together since we're going to be parent partners."

"Parent partners. I like the sound of that."

In her periphery, she spied Rafe leaning against a beat-up white ranch truck, watching them. Beyond him, Mavis's face was visible in the doorway of a long, low-ceilinged building toward the stables. A few other workers had stopped what they were doing to watch, their gazes transfixed on Brett and Hannah. "There are a lot of people watching us."

"New arrivals always draw the workers' curiosity. Little do they knew that they're seeing the latest member of the Colton family."

"The baby's not going to be here for five more months."

His expression turned solemn. He rubbed a tendril of her hair between his fingertips. "I was talking about you. Doesn't matter what happens between you and me from this point on, because like you said, we're parent partners from here on out. Like it or not, we're bound for life. You're a permanent part of the Colton family now."

She'd never thought about it that way, but the idea wrapped around her like a quilt. She'd always longed to be a part of a big family, even if they took a while to warm up to her. She was going to hold out hope that they got over their misgivings and that everything would turn out all right.

"Speaking of your family, where is everyone?"

He nodded toward the house. "Edith, who you'll meet in a minute, had the idea that tomorrow night would be soon enough to meet everyone. She thought you might appreciate getting settled here first and she shooed everyone out the back door."

Hannah loved Edith already, whoever she was. "Yes, a night to settle in first would be heaven-sent. I'm looking forward to meeting her so I can thank her myself."

"I saw that you already met Rafe. He's an indispensable member of the Lucky C operation. Has been for a couple years now."

"What exactly is it that he does for the ranch?" *Besides insult women's intelligence and capability?*

"He's a jack-of-all-trades, but mostly, he helps run the day-to-day operations of the cattle-breeding program."

Then she probably wouldn't have much contact with him. "And I saw Mavis Turnbolt, too, before you found me. She and I go way back, but I didn't know she worked for your family as a maid."

"What a small world. I'm glad you got to see a familiar face."

"She's a member of my parents' church," she said drily.

"Ah. Tulsa really is a small world. I had no idea, but I guess I'd better make sure Mavis isn't let into the kitchen before meals so she doesn't spit in our food."

She couldn't help but smile at his support, as well as his spot-on prediction. "Gross, and I wouldn't put it past her to try."

The light in his face changed. He brushed his thumb across her cheek. "You are aware of the effect those dimples have on a man, right?"

Oh, this man was smooth. For all she knew, he'd used that same line on dozens of women. The trouble was, the more she fought against a smile, the wider it grew and the deeper her dimples probably got right along with it.

"I was not aware of that, actually." The only time her dimples were ever mentioned was by customers at her parents' store by lonely old grandfatherly and grandmotherly types that she didn't pay any mind to.

He cupped her cheek in his hand, his eyes growing dark. "No, I reckon you wouldn't be."

Brett's light touch sent a shiver skittering over her skin, evoking the memory of every delicious detail of their one wicked night together. From out of nowhere, an all-consuming hunger came over her, to be touched, cherished. Most likely, it was a product of her haywire pregnancy hormones as she recalled, or maybe it was just because she'd been really lonely lately. She pressed her cheek into his palm, her eyes closing and her lips parting.

At the realization that she was barely fighting the wild urge to turn her lips into his hand to taste his skin, she pulled away from his touch and gave herself a vigorous mental smack.

He swallowed hard and stuffed his hands in his pockets. "Seriously, though, if she gives you any hassle—if anyone here or in town gives you any hassle at all—you let me know and I'll handle it. Deal?"

She was tempted to reiterate that she wasn't helpless, but she could tell how important it was to him that he take on the role of her protector. Besides, she was warming to the idea of him in that role, too, as long as he didn't turn into a chauvinist about it like his employee Rafe. "Deal."

A crack of thunder pulled their attention to the gray clouds piling up in the sky beyond the smattering of barns and buildings to the west.

Brett tipped his head toward her suitcases. "Where's the rest of your stuff? Do we need to take a trip back into town today to get it all? I have time this afternoon and a big ol' truck you can fill."

"This is it," she said. "I've got a couple boxes of mementos and books at Lori's apartment, but I'm pretty low-maintenance when it comes to shoes and fashion, and after I got evicted from my apartment, I sold just about everything but the essentials."

He frowned at that, which rubbed her wrong. "Don't go reading into that too much or feeling sorry for me. I'm fine and I have everything I need. Material goods aren't important to me—they never were. It's no big deal."

His frowning lips twitched into a grudging smile. His eyes glowed, not with fire but affection. "Yes, ma'am. My mistake." He nodded at the house. "Let's get you indoors before today's afternoon shower hits."

CHAPTER FIVE

THERE WAS NO other word to describe Brett's house besides *mansion*. Certainly, it was the largest and most elegantly appointed home that Hannah had ever been in, with a marble-floored grand entrance that extended up to a vaulted ceiling and had as its focal point a circular table in the center of the space boasting a massive floral arrangement that oozed the word *rich*.

The formal sitting room on the far side of the foyer was too stiff and stuffy to look lived in, with sparse furniture and a glass fireplace that seemed more for show than warmth. Every room and hall that she could see was decked out in marble and white decor, and the light palette should have brightened the place up, but there was a heavy weight to the overt grandiosity. As if a person could never get fully comfortable there or kick off her shoes and relax.

Then again, perhaps the weight and gravity in the house were side effects of the violence that had occurred there the month before and the heartbreaking reality that, even as Hannah stood in the home casting judgment on the place, Brett's mom was fighting for her life in the hospital. That had to be taking a toll on everyone who lived and worked there.

Two women waited at the far end of the foyer near the base of a grand staircase. The taller, slimmer of the two had silvery hair pulled into a tight bun and the shorter one looked to be about Hannah's age, with brown hair and eyes, an olive complexion and a curvy build.

The taller woman stepped forward with her hand extended in greeting and a bright smile lighting up her face and accentuating her abundant laugh lines. "You must be Hannah. I'm Edith, the Coltons' housekeeper."

From her firm, confident handshake to her perfect posture, Edith exuded efficiency and poise. Hannah bet she never missed a beat, but in the best, most genuine way.

Brett leaned in and gave Edith a kiss on the cheek in greeting. "You're a lot more than just a housekeeper."

She waved off the praise. "Oh, pish. The title suits me."

"Edith is in charge around here. Anything you need or any questions you have, she's the one to ask. And this," he said, nodding at the other woman, "is Maria, our talented chef. We were lucky to steal her away from the New York City restaurant scene a few years ago."

Maria's eyes glowed with warmth. "The luck was all mine." She enveloped Hannah's offered hand in both of hers. Her hands were rough, calloused, and her nails trimmed short. "I was ready for a change from those long, late nights in New York kitchens, and since my parents live in Tulsa and they're getting older, it was the right move to come home to be near to them. Managing the Coltons' kitchen has been an honor."

Brett draped his arm across Maria's shoulders. "I'll have you know that I was only able to lure Hannah here by tempting her with the promise of your signature, small-batch cured bacon every morning."

Maria seemed delighted. "Consider it done."

Hannah gave him a chiding look. "I didn't agree to this arrangement because of bacon."

"So you're saying it was the real maple syrup and butter I plied you with that reeled you in?"

The preposterous idea tickled her funny bone, and before she knew what hit her, she was back to smiling like a lovesick fool. How did he do that? How did he make her so instantly comfortable and joyous? He had the gift of charm, for sure, but not with the artifice of a snake-oil salesman, as she'd originally compared him to. More like a gifted leader.

"You're going to give Maria and Edith the mistaken impression that all I care about is food."

Edith's eyes twinkled. "Well, you *are* pregnant, if you don't mind me mentioning. So a healthy preoccupation with food is perfectly permissible, you know."

"And if Edith says it's okay, then you're good to go. I learned that growing up," Brett said.

"You're going to love the dinner I'm making for you tonight," Maria said. "And tomorrow night, the whole family will get to meet you. I'm planning a feast in celebration."

Hannah drew a fortifying breath at the idea of being the center of attention in a room full of Brett's whole family—the same people who were eager to run a background check on her. Then again, if she could confess to her parents that she was pregnant out of wedlock and resist their attempts to cajole the father's name from her, then she could handle meeting Brett's family all at once—her family, too, now.

There was just one problem—Brett's mother, the family matriarch, wouldn't be there. "Thank you. Both of you. But I wonder if perhaps now isn't the right time for a celebration, given that Brett's mother is in the hospital."

Edith didn't miss a beat. "The way I see it, the Coltons could use a little uplifting, and what better way to inspire hope in this family than by celebrating the news of a new Colton coming into this world?"

As Brett said, if Edith deemed it so, then there was no salient counterargument to be had.

"Then I look forward to it. Thank you both for making me feel so welcome."

"Our pleasure. We're going to let Brett show you to your bedroom suite. Brett, you let me know about tonight." Edith's smiling eyes darted between Hannah and Brett before both women walked away on silent feet.

Brett picked up Hannah's suitcases and they started up the stairs. After a particularly powerful crack of thunder, lightning flickered outside the window, casting long shadows of the grand stairway's ornate chandelier onto the walls as they climbed to the second floor.

"Edith and Maria are very nice," Hannah said.

"Most of the people here are. We consider it a job requirement," he added with a wink.

Hannah thought about Mavis Turnbolt. Maybe not all the employees were as nice as Brett seemed to think. He did seem to see the best in everyone, which was a quality of his she found endlessly attractive—yet another one on her growing list of them.

"What did Edith mean with her question about tonight? If she's wondering about your dad, because I know he lives here, too, then I don't mind meeting him tonight at dinner. I don't want him to dine alone."

"No, it's not that. My dad already made plans to eat at Jack's house tonight. Maria thought you might prefer to

eat a low-key meal in the kitchen or your suite tonight."
They crested the top of the stairs. Brett stopped and set
her suitcases down. His hand, big and strong and sure,
slid over her arm as his gaze met hers. "But if you're
amenable to the idea, I'd like to have you all to myself
in the dining room. A dinner date, if you will."

Oh. She felt heat rising on her cheeks, even as her
lusty hormones started clamoring for attention again.
"You really are a smooth operator, aren't you?"

"Is that a bad thing?"

She smoothed her hands over his chest, letting her fingers bump over the ridges of muscle beneath it, muscles
she remembered quite well from their night together.
Mmm. Her hormones definitely approved. "No, it's not
a bad thing—as long as you use your powers for good
and not evil."

He chuckled. "'With great power comes great responsibility'?"

"Exactly."

His smile turned contemplative. "Please say you'll
have dinner with me tonight. I want to get to know you,
Hannah. You're carrying my child—"

"Our child."

His focus dipped to her belly. "Yes, *our* child." His
gaze turned distant, but only for the span of a few heart-
beats. Then he cleared his throat. "So dinner seems like
a good place to start to get to know each other better.
Like, middle name, birthday, favorite dessert. You know,
the important stuff."

"Bernice, October twenty-second and red-velvet cupcakes."

A smile lightened his features. With her suitcases in
hand once more, he led her over thick burgundy car-

pet through a dimly lit hallway. "Cupcakes rather than cake?"

"Yes. Only cupcakes will do."

"I'll be sure to inform Maria."

The hallway ended with a floor-to-ceiling window, but this afternoon, with the sun gone behind a curtain of darkening clouds, the hall was dim. With the quiet and the shadows, Hannah's thoughts drifted once more to the tragedies that had befallen the family the month before. She scanned the doors they passed, wondering behind which one Abra's attack had occurred.

"Your mom, she was attacked in your parents' bedroom, right?"

Brett froze midstep. His face went pale.

Hannah regretted the question instantly. "I'm sorry I asked. I didn't mean—"

"No. It's a fair question. She and my father sleep in separate quarters. She was attacked in her suite, which is adjacent to his on the other end of this hall. Listen, Hannah, you're safe here at the ranch. On my word."

"The police think your mother's attacker is still on the loose." She cringed inwardly at the slip. She'd come by that information by eavesdropping and wasn't eager for Brett to find out.

Brett's lips flattened into a straight line. "You're right. Some of her jewelry that was stolen the night of the attack turned up in a Tulsa pawnshop this week so the police are investigating, but that would have to be one stupid criminal to come back here again. If it makes you feel any better, we're starting nightly patrols around the perimeter of our acreage to make sure everything's as it should be, starting with my brother Jack and my dad tonight—not because of what happened to my mother, but because we've had some fences tampered with recently. You're safe. I promise. Just do me a favor and don't go walking around after dark by yourself, okay?"

Another crack of thunder shook the house, followed by the sound of rain pelting the windows. Dread tightened Hannah's chest as she thought back to the conversation she'd overheard just minutes ago in the sitting room. What had she gotten herself into?

He took hold of both her shoulders. "Hey. There's nothing to worry about. You're safe. I wouldn't have asked you here if you weren't. We're just taking extra precautions."

"Okay. I can accept that answer."

"Good, because it's the truth."

She drew her shoulders up and rubbed her arms. "I just… I can sense the heaviness and heartbreak in this place. Despite Edith's optimism, I know it couldn't have been easy to spring the news of the baby on your family, with everything else you're all going through. I know it doesn't sound like it with my questions about your mom, but I'm glad I'm here. I'm going to do a great job as your bookkeeper."

His expression softened. "As if there was ever any doubt about that." They set off again along the hallway. He stopped next to an open door and ushered her in ahead of him. "Your suite."

Forget comparisons to her apartment—the suite was bigger than her parents' *house*. Like the rest of Brett's house, the sitting room of the suite and what she could see of the bedroom beyond it had no shortage of windows. Tall ones that showed off the uninhibited view of the Oklahoma landscape—rolling hills of grassland and scrub trees that had been turned to a quilt of deep greens and mustard yellows by the rain and dark gray clouds that served as a foil for the rich colors.

The rectangular sitting room was decked out in blue-and-gold shabby-chic decor, including royal blue, gold and white embroidered curtains framing every window and delicate whitewashed wooden furniture with artfully distressed flair. The whole suite looked as if it belonged in a magazine and was the most luxuriously appointed space Hannah had ever been in.

"This suite is incredible. I love it."

"My mother's handiwork. It's always struck me as ironic that she could decorate rooms to look so warm and inviting."

He didn't elaborate on the odd comment, but disappeared with her suitcase through the double doors that opened into a bedroom. She made to follow him to check out the next room when a mouthwatering aroma caught her attention. There was no mistaking the smell of chocolate chip cookies. Inhaling deeply, she followed the scent to a cozy sitting area near the balcony doors composed of a sofa and chairs clustered around a spindly-legged coffee table.

Eureka. On the table sat a tray loaded with cookies and a carafe of milk set in a small ice bucket. Edith and Maria's loving touch, no doubt. The chocolate chips on the cookies shimmered. Could it be that they were fresh from the oven?

She lifted one from the plate. It was warm to the touch. She took a decadent bite, barely stifling a moan of pleasure as the melty chocolate hit her tongue. She had the rest of the cookie gone in the next bite, then strolled to the bedroom in search of Brett, blissed out on the sugary, chocolaty goodness.

She found Brett arranging her suitcase on a luggage rack near the wall of windows in the bedroom and devoted a few moments to properly appreciate his backside as he leaned over. When he glanced over his shoulder at her, she wrenched her gaze away, feeling positively lascivious, though not at all remorseful about it. Her attention landed on the bed in the center of the room and she nearly choked on her last bite of cookie.

The bed was enormous.

"You okay?"

"I don't think I've ever seen a bed that big."

"Yeah, it's nice, huh?" He walked to her side at the foot of the bed, smiling at her. He tapped his lip. "You have something on your lower lip."

"Oops. I found chocolate chip cookies in the sitting room. I couldn't help myself from indulging in one already. And I'm glad I did because it was melt-in-your-mouth delicious."

She darted her tongue out and licked the bit of chocolate off.

His gaze lingered on her mouth until with a grunt, he wrenched his gaze away, not unlike she had when she'd been caught staring at his backside. What a pair they made, pretending not to be affected by each other. But there was a reason that the two of them had fallen into bed together that night four months ago, an attraction that had crackled between them from the first moment that their eyes linked.

He cleared his throat, his focus on the wall. "Uh, anyway, as I was saying. Guests who've stayed in this room have said the mattress is great, so you should be really comfortable here."

"How could I not be comfortable in a bed this size?

I bet I could lie in the middle of it, spread-eagle, and neither my feet nor my hands would touch the edge."

Really, Hannah? Spread-eagle? Could you make any bigger a fool out of yourself?

He said nothing to that, nor did he look her way, but his lips went flat. With a sharp intake of breath, he spun on his heel and fast-walked out the bedroom door.

Way to go, champ. Huffing in frustration at herself, she gave him a minute of space before joining him in the sitting room once more.

He was at the windows, pushing the curtains all the way open. "As soon as the afternoon storm passes, it'll brighten up in here. There's a great view of the ranch from your balcony."

She seized on the topic change with gusto. "There already is a great view. Your ranch is beautiful. Where's your suite? What kind of view does it have?"

He tipped his head left. "Mine is right next to yours. You could knock on the wall behind your bed and I'd hear it in my sitting area."

So they were back to talking about her bed. Right. Okay. Maybe she wasn't the only one navigating a minefield of Freudian slips.

Shaking his head, he hooked his thumb toward the main suite door. "I'd better go. I'll come by your room tonight at seven to escort you down to dinner."

"Brett?" she called to his retreating form.

He paused halfway out the door.

"Thank you. For all of this. You're being really great for a person who found out his life just got permanently turned upside down."

His posture straightened. Trust and strength radiated from his eyes. "Your life did, too," he said. "We're in this together, Hannah. More than anything, that's what I want you to know. I'm not sure it's fully sunk in yet that I'm going to be a father or how my life is going to change, but it will and it's going to be fine. I'm going to do right by you and by the baby. I promise."

She loved that he got that, how they were in the same boat and that lamenting their life changes or having a negative attitude wouldn't do anybody any good, especially their child. Right then and there, she knew he was going to make a magnificent father. "I'm going to do right by you and the baby, too."

A warm, genuine smile tugged at his lips, the kind that made her knees go weak all over again. "Then it sounds like we've got the makings of a great partnership."

HANNAH PROWLED HER suite, looking in drawers and cabinets and under the bed, getting a feel for the place. After that, she unpacked, which took about two seconds, then prowled some more, restless. She couldn't stop thinking about Brett's room on the other side of the wall from her bed. She couldn't stop thinking about how he'd smelled and the feel of his body close to hers. She'd been at Lucky C for less than an hour and already she was stir-crazy and man-crazy all at the same time.

There was only one solution to an emergency situation like that. From her purse, she found her phone and hit the first speed-dial number for the one person who knew her inside and out and loved her unconditionally— her best friend.

"Hey there," Lori said. "Are you calling from your new digs?"

"New *temporary* digs."

Lori clicked her tongue in protest. "Maybe."

Hannah rolled her eyes.

"I can hear that eye roll," Lori said, bringing a smile to Hannah's face. "I didn't expect to hear from you so soon. Is everything going okay?"

"More than okay, but I need to do a *pros and cons*." One thing she loved about Lori was how great a sounding board she was, and *pros and cons* with Lori was Hannah's favorite way of navigating difficult decisions.

"All right, let's do it. What's the topic this time?"

Hannah took a deep breath and locked gazes with her reflection in the vanity mirror. "Sleeping with Brett Colton."

"Whoa, whoa, whoa. Back up. You just moved in to his family's house this afternoon—and he's already coming on to you again? Damn. That man is as much of a horndog as we'd always heard."

"No, he hasn't come on to me. *I'm* the horndog. My hormones are so out of whack right now, I've got whiplash. I vacillate between wanting to hurl because of my morning sickness, resisting the urge to weep uncontrollably, wanting to shovel cookies into my piehole, and fantasizing about doing naughty, naked things with my baby daddy."

"Dang, sweetie. You're a hot mess."

"Tell me about it. I'm like a one-woman soap opera. For the foreseeable future, my bedroom suite shares a wall with Brett, and he's so charming—like, pantie-melting charming—and he arranged for us to have a private dinner tonight. A dinner date, he called it. And you should see what his butt looks like in the jeans he's wearing. I'm dying over here."

"Wait—you don't just have a bedroom, you have a *suite*? How rich are the Coltons?"

"I have no idea, but now that I'm their accountant, I wouldn't tell you even if I knew."

"That's no fun."

Hannah snapped her fingers. "Back to my problem."

"You mean your sex problem," Lori teased.

"Yes, Lori. Thank you. My sex problem." Geez, she hoped Brett wasn't listening on the other side of the door. Cringing at the idea, she walked into the bathroom and pushed the door mostly shut.

"Continue," Lori said.

Hannah lowered her voice. "Okay, so, I pretty much want to throw myself at him tonight at dinner. I mean, I'm already pregnant with his child, so what's the harm? And you know me, that's *so* not my personality."

"You're the good girl," Lori offered.

"Yes, exactly. I'm the good girl. Except now I'm the jezebel who got pregnant from a one-night stand, so maybe I should just own it and embrace my inner slut."

"First of all, take a breath, Hannah."

She braced her hand on the bathroom's marble countertop. "Trying."

"And second of all, I hate the word *slut*. That's your parents' shame culture talking through you, so knock it off."

That was another thing she loved about her bestie; she told it like it was and didn't let Hannah get away with any defeatist self-talk. "Okay. You're right."

"Of course I am. Third of all—"

Despite herself, Hannah grinned. "There's no such term as 'third of all.'"

"In this case, there is. Third of all, what's up with the

word *jezebel*? Where the heck did you come up with that ancient insult?"

Hannah allowed herself a sound of disgust, even though her run-in with Mavis would also make a juicy bit of gossip to share with her best friend. "Remind me to tell you that story some other time. For now, we need to focus on the pros and cons."

"Right. Okay. I'll start," Lori said. "Pro—he's hot."

"Con—he knows how hot he is."

Lori chuffed. "How is that a con?"

"Hello? Pantie-melting charm is not selective. It works on all panties."

Lori chuckled. "Sorry. That's funny. Plus, I got an awesome visual there." She cleared her throat. "All right, continue."

"He's a player, but because of this baby, we're bound together for life, which he reminded me of this afternoon."

Lori whistled and muttered some silly innuendo about bondage and Brett.

Hannah ignored her and pressed on. "So, there's no such thing as casual sex between us anymore. Our relationship will always be complicated, but having a fling with the baby daddy who also happens to be my boss and my housemate is the most complicated scenario I can imagine, especially when it wouldn't lead to anything more than a temporary affair."

"How do you know it wouldn't lead to anything more?"

Hannah gave the phone a skeptical sidelong glance, as if Lori could see it. "Hello? He's a player. He's *the* Brett Colton."

"I'm getting the picture now. You're worried about

falling for him and him breaking your heart because he's not the type of guy who settles down with one woman."

Hannah wanted to resist the idea. Because it was crazy and stupid. Falling in love in a forever way with anyone in this huge, gonzo world carried a one-in-a-billion probability, much less doing so with the random guy she met in a nightclub who got her pregnant. She didn't even want to think about calculating those odds.

"Brett and I have spent exactly five hours in each other's company, total. I know next to nothing about him and he knows next to nothing about me. That's not a foundation for love."

"You're worried about falling for him and him breaking your heart," Lori repeated, more adamantly this time.

Hannah gave the phone the evil eye again. What the heck was a best friend good for if she wouldn't let you hide behind your denial? "Of course I'm worried about falling for him and him breaking my heart. Have you met the man?"

"Nope."

Suddenly claustrophobic, she stomped out of the bathroom and straight to the balcony door. She was annoyed that Brett was so attractive and charming, and annoyed at herself for being a hot mess. But mostly, she was annoyed that she was light-years away from being financially independent so that she and Brett could tackle the issue of parenthood and their relationship on even footing. "We'll fix that soon because I want you to meet him. Let me get my bearings around here and get started in my new job first, and then I'll have you over, okay?"

"Can't wait. In the meantime, I have another *pro* and *con* for you," Lori said.

"I don't think I'm in the mood for that anymore."

Lori ignored her protest and forged ahead. "Pro—you should sleep with him because you've had a crappy few months and you deserve to blow off steam with a hot guy who's into you."

True, that. A bit of Hannah's bluster deflated. "And the con?"

"Don't take this the wrong way because you know I love you, but the con is that you're a neurotic math geek who overanalyzes everything and I know you're going to overanalyze this decision to the point that you might not be able to properly blow off steam and relax."

"That is true, too. So what am I supposed to do?"

"Have dinner with him tonight. Maybe after spending some time in each other's company doing something other than screwing, which is how you two have spent almost all the hours you've clocked together so far, you'll realize that your attraction to him isn't as potent as you thought it was."

Hannah considered herself to be an eternal optimist, but even she knew that the odds that having dinner with Brett would snuff out her lust for him were dire, indeed. The man had a gift for words and when he looked at Hannah, he really looked at her, in a way that was both sincere and maddeningly flirty. She seriously doubted that spending more time with him would quell her lust. Still, she said, "That is sound advice. Thank you."

"You're welcome. Call me tomorrow, okay? I want to hear how this turns out."

After they ended the call, Hannah stood at the glass French doors, looking out at the ranch and the vistas beyond. The land was beautiful, with the dark clouds and rain turning the grass a vibrant green and the fences surrounding the corrals and fields a brilliant shock of white. On a whim, she lifted her phone and took a picture.

From behind a line of single-wide trailers near the barn that were probably offices, something white caught her eye. She took a second look.

A young woman wearing a white dress was standing in the rain and watching a group of ranch workers guiding cattle through a series of chutes toward a large fenced-in area. The woman didn't hold an umbrella or move to shelter herself from the storm, so her dress was soaking wet and her brown hair was plastered to her cheeks. None of the workers seemed to notice the woman.

A flash of lighting zinged through the sky in the distance. A few moments later, a loud crack of thunder sounded and the rain turned into a deluge.

The woman didn't move. She didn't lift her hands or sidestep under the nearest roof eave.

Hannah zoomed her camera phone in on her and took another photograph. Now that she was looking through the zoom lens, she would swear that the woman was trembling, though the summer rainstorm was warm, the air humid. Through the lens, she could just barely make out something in the woman's left hand. She zoomed in as tight as the camera would allow, but couldn't make out what exactly the long, sticklike object dangling from her hand was. A baseball bat? A cane? *An ax?*

Yeah, right. Ridiculous, Hannah. She was letting the eerie feel of the mansion and the lightning and thunder send her imagination on a wild adventure. She shook her head to clear it, refusing to add hallucinating to her list of pregnant quirks.

Lori was right. She was overthinking everything instead of relaxing into the idea that maybe it would be okay to let down her guard around Brett and his family. Maybe bringing her to this heaven on earth at the Lucky C was God's way of letting her know that everything was going to be okay for her and her baby if she'd just open her heart to the possibilities He'd set before her.

She dropped onto the sofa and lifted another cookie from the plate. It wasn't warm anymore, and the chocolate wasn't melty, but it was almost as delicious as the first one she'd eaten. Unable to resist another look, she stood again and returned to the French doors, curious if the rain-loving mystery woman was still enjoying the foul weather. Hannah scanned every inch of the ranch that she could see, looking for the shock of white fabric against the browns and grays and greens, but the mystery woman was gone.

CHAPTER SIX

Brett had never been a fan of the Big House's dining room, which sat at the back end of the ground floor and boasted a semicircle of glass French doors that opened to a veranda and overlooked the pool and the Coltons' pastoral domain beyond. The space reminded him too much of itchy formal wear he'd been forced to stuff himself into as a kid when his parents hosted dinner parties for other cattle-breeding bigwigs and state senators and the like.

The room itself had been decked out with tasteful, high-end decor. A smattering of white candles surrounded by bud vases of wildflowers graced the center of a massive, dark-stained wood table and the heavy burgundy drapes had been pulled back to reveal a darkening horizon, the lingering glow of the now-absent sun turning the prairie into a sea of indigo shadows.

Edith had set up two place settings at the corner of the table nearest the veranda. Brett had offered Hannah the chair with the best view in the room, and they'd dug into course after course of delectable plates from the kitchen. From a spinach salad with warm bacon dressing to seared shrimp canapés, Maria presented each of the first two courses as though they were entertaining the queen of England.

As Hannah sipped the sparkling apple cider that had

been set up in an ice bucket next to the table and ate heartily of Maria's offerings, she seemed entranced by the view as much as Maria's culinary talent or Brett, which suited him just fine. He wanted her to grow to love the ranch as he did.

"I can't stop looking outside. Your ranch is incredible," she said.

Brett took a drink of his beer, his gaze fixated on a whole different kind of beautiful view—his luminous dinner companion. "Every time I think you're looking at me, your attention slips over my shoulder to the windows."

He touched his shoe to hers to let her know he was merely teasing her.

"I've been looking at you plenty. I've just been sneaky about it." She winked at that and Brett's heart did a heavy *ba-dum* in his chest. "But honestly, I grew up in a postage-stamp-sized house in town, where you'd look out the window and all you'd see was the peeling paint and dirty windows of the house next door. I can't imagine what it must have been like growing up here with the prairie as your playground."

He flashed a bright smile. "That was the best part. I was the fourth child, yet another boy in my father's quest for a girl, so I was on my own a lot, exploring the ranch, following my big brothers around." He almost added, *it was the perfect setting for children to grow up in, like it will be for our child*. But that might have been overkill for day number one of their arrangement.

"Just your father?"

"My mother's not exactly maternal. Pops wanted a big family and for reasons that I certainly don't understand, she obliged him, but in between pregnancies, she'd take off for parts unknown. Spas in Europe, cruises and all manner of escapes."

She set a hand on his forearm, her smile dimming, which was a shame. "No wonder you're so close to Edith."

To counter the conversation's turn for the serious, Brett smiled wider and sat up a little straighter. "Edith is going to spoil our baby rotten, just like she did my nephew, Seth. I can't wait to watch."

Maria buzzed in, a covered plate in each hand. "Your main course. Braised beef tenderloin from an award-winning steer right here at the Lucky C and accented with a Cabernet mushroom reduction."

Hannah patted her belly. "Speaking of being spoiled rotten, you're so talented, Maria. I can't believe the Coltons' luck to get to eat your cooking every day."

"Your luck, too, now." Dang it. There he went skirting the line of overkill again.

"You're very kind, both of you. I'm glad you're finding the meal pleasing." Then, as fast as Maria had breezed in, she was gone again, leaving Brett and Hannah to each other's company.

They dug into the beef, with Hannah making blissed-out moans that sent Brett's thoughts right into the gutter, not that it'd been out of the gutter since they'd stood in the driveway that afternoon and she'd turned her dimpled smile on him. Being with her in her bedroom suite had damn near killed him—long before she'd invited the visual of her lying spread-eagle on the bed.

He cleared his throat, desperate for a distraction. "What were we talking about before Maria came in?"

"You, growing up."

"Ah." And now that he was recalling it, their conversation had taken a turn for the somber, talking about his mother's depression-fueled negligence. He wasn't crazy about continuing that topic, but it was a little late to worry about that.

"What was it like growing up with three older brothers? I'm an only child, and I can't get enough of stories about what it's like being a sibling. What a glorious feeling that must have been to have playmates 24/7. My house was so quiet all the time."

Grateful that she'd spared them from delving into a painful topic, he sat forward, all smiles. "Ours definitely wasn't. Oh, the stories I could tell you…"

She laughed at that, the sound echoing in the vast room. "I bet you could. Were your brothers good to you? Or is it like a lot of stories you hear about, with big brothers tormenting little brothers?"

"If you asked them, they'd claim they were angels." He spread his arms wide. "Shepherds who taught me the ways of the world and kept me safe from danger."

The sidelong gaze she gave him put those heart-stopping dimples of hers on full display. "But…"

"But they're all full of horse pucky because the truth is that there was a fair bit of torment involved. The way I usually put it is to say that they designated me the proverbial royal taster."

"Royal taster?"

"Yeah, you know like in medieval days, with kings and queens, how servants would have to taste the king's food first to make sure it wasn't poisoned? That's what I was for my brothers, except about more than food. 'See if there are leeches in that creek,' they'd say. 'Go find out if that's poison ivy or not. I can't remember what it looks like.' Or 'You go inside first and see how mad Dad is that we're two hours late for supper.'"

She chuckled. "Oh, no! And you fell for that?"

"Every time. I ate it up. I suppose the messes they got me into could've made me cynical, but I liked the attention. With every bit of trouble I got in, the more attention I got, both from my parents and my brothers, which just fueled my bad behavior. Call it 'fourth child syndrome.'"

"Did things change when Greta came around? Did she become the royal taster?"

"No way. That girl was treated like a princess from the moment my father found out he'd finally managed to sire a girl." He refilled her flute with sparkling cider. "But that didn't stop us from doing our brotherly duty of tormenting her every chance we got, despite the punishments we subjected ourselves to with our rowdiness."

"What did your punishments usually entail?"

"Switches were a popular choice with my mom, but my dad preferred the firm application of his palm to our backsides."

She rubbed her arm. "My father preferred a belt."

After meeting her father at the family's store the day before, he had a good idea why she seemed rattled at the memory. He touched her arm. "Just so we're clear, I don't believe in using those kinds of methods. There are more constructive ways to discipline a child than hurting them physically. I've learned a lot by watching my brother Jack with his son, Seth."

Her shoulders relaxed. "I'm glad we agree on that. I've been worried, wondering if our parenting styles and life philosophies will mesh. I know so little about you."

"That's why we're having this dinner." He covered

her hand with his and squeezed. "And many more to come, I hope."

Then Maria was back again, clearing their plates. "I'll be back in a few minutes with dessert, hot from the oven. It'll be worth the wait."

Hannah's attention slid to the darkening ranch beyond the artfully lit pool and patio. "This has been wonderful tonight. I'm absolutely taken with the Lucky C."

"I'm glad to hear that. So am I, actually. And I have a vision for this place, for the future," he said. "The original reason I put that job ad in the classifieds."

"We're finally getting around to that, then. I was wondering if you'd ever come clean with the truth about why you placed that job ad."

He felt a wince coming on and let it happen, poker face be damned, because he was ready to own up to his white lie. He shouldn't have been surprised that she'd known all along he was fudging the truth with his job offer, as smart as she was. He'd told only Jack and their dad about his vision, and neither had been exactly encouraging. But if he wanted Hannah's help, if he wanted her trust, then he had to trust her, too.

"Yes, I am ready to own up to it, because the truth is that I still need your help with it, if you're willing," he said.

"I'm willing."

"Hear me out first."

Maria hustled into the room, the scent of baked chocolate preceding her. In front of them, she set two bowls. "Brownies à la mode."

Brett didn't recall Hannah's orgasm face from their one-night stand, but he was willing to bet it looked a whole lot like the face she was making at that moment, looking down at her dessert. Of its own accord, his body stirred to life. Ignoring his physical response, he dug into his dessert.

"You gonna be able to listen to my plan for the ranch or would I be better off waiting until your brownie-gasm ends?"

"Brownie-gasm is right. I've had a lot of chocolate-gasms today, actually, between this and the cookies in my room. A girl could get used to that kind of twice-daily pleasure."

He was just starting to wrap his brain around the double entendre when she slapped both her hands over her face and groaned. "I didn't mean that. I mean, I did." She shook her head. "I mean, a girl *could* get used to—" She winced. "I'm going to shut up now. Please continue your story. Tell me your plans for the ranch's future while I sit here and die of embarrassment."

He bit the inside of his cheek, fighting the urge to tease her. Or kiss her. Maybe both.

He cleared his throat. "The majority of Lucky C's revenue comes from cattle breeding, but it isn't the lucrative industry it once was. The Lucky C needs to diversify if the business is going to stay strong for generations of Coltons to come." His attention darted to her belly for an instant. "The way I see it, the future of this ranch is in horse breeding and training."

"I don't know that much about either industry. What kind would you breed?"

"Cutting horses. My brother Daniel—well, half brother, technically—he's the resident horse whisperer of the family. He runs a horse-training program on our property, renting the land from us. The Lucky C also gets a cut of his profit, so we've been able to watch that profit double every year he's been in business.

"This year, the demand for his horses has exploded, and my gut's telling me that he's going to outgrow the arrangement very soon. He's already been approached by other horse-breeding ranches to come work for them. They're wooing him with blank checks to buy the DNA for any prizewinning stud he wants.

"Jack, my oldest brother, who runs the Lucky C, gave me the green light to buy a highly rated stallion named Geronimo for Daniel to breed, with the Lucky C splitting the profits with him as a way of testing the waters for getting the Lucky C into the horse-breeding business, but that's not enough. If we want to keep Daniel and his profits at the Lucky C, then we're going to have to play ball, big-time. One stallion's not going to cut it. My plan is to set up a new arm of the Lucky C Corporation with Daniel and me as comanagers so we can finally give him the budget he needs to grow his breeding business. And I'd like your help in setting up that business plan to present to Jack and my dad."

She took his hand securely in hers. "Of course I can help with that. We'll knock their socks off."

"That's the plan."

They shared a smile, which brought Brett's mind right back around to imagining what it would feel like to kiss those lips. He slipped his hand out from under hers and picked up his fork again.

"Why isn't Daniel already a part of the Lucky C Corporation?" Hannah asked. "I can already tell how important the idea of family is to you, and Daniel's family, so why wouldn't your dad and brothers invite him to be a part of the family business?"

If she could already tell how important family was to Brett, then that was a very good sign, even though she was asking a minefield of a question. "It's complicated. My mother isn't Daniel's biggest fan, to put it mildly. She sees him as a constant reminder of my father's infidelity."

"Ouch."

"Yeah. But my dad's terrible choices aren't Daniel's fault. None of the rest of us would ever hold that against him, but he feels it all the same. Add to that the fact that Jack doesn't want to shift the ranch in a new business direction, especially a direction that's my idea. He sees cattle breeding as our brand and he wants to keep with the old ways."

"Why would Jack oppose an idea just because it's yours? Is that a sibling-rivalry thing?"

"No. That's not it. Until a few months ago, I wasn't worthy of Jack's trust." He found her hand under the table and gave it a squeeze. "Or yours, either, for that matter."

"Hard on yourself much?"

"With good reason. My father used to joke that the Colton family DNA ran out of ambition genes by the time I was born. All I got was the cowboying ones that revolved around whiskey, women and horses."

She eyed him skeptically. "I find that hard to believe. And that's terrible that your father made you feel that way."

"It was the truth, as hard as it is to come clean to you about that. Growing up in the shadow of four smart, successful, career-driven older brothers, I never felt like I could live up to the lofty bar they set. By the time I hit high school, I realized just how easy it was to skate by on my looks and family money, so I stopped trying. In no time flat, I became my own worst enemy, hard drinking and partying all the time, nearly flunking out of school, and taking so many stupid risks."

Her look of skepticism gave way to a slow nod. "That I do remember. There were some girls from my high school who were sweet on you, even though you were in a school across town. Every Monday, it seemed, students whispered about the hell-raising you got into over the weekend."

Damn, this was rough. It made no common sense to be attempting to prove himself worthy of protecting and caring for Hannah and the baby by coming clean about what an entitled, shallow jerk he'd grown into, but there was no way around this guts-spilling to the mother of his child. "My hell-raising didn't stop at high school. I went to college, but dropped out. I just couldn't see past the moment-to-moment fun to the bigger picture of my life."

He paused, taking a long, slow swig of beer, fortifying himself to continue to the hardest, darkest, bleakest days of his life.

She threaded their fingers together. "I'm not judging you, just so you know. Nobody's perfect and it seems like you've been hard enough on yourself as it is. Too hard."

He really wasn't being too hard. Maybe not hard enough. "The weekend that you and I met in the club, I was in the middle of a bender. The next night, I was at a different club, coming on to a different girl—or, rather, three girls."

Her expression shuttered and her fingers went stiff, though she left them twined with his. But what had he expected? It was such an ugly truth. She'd meant nothing to him that night but a moment's pleasure—a terrible beginning for their child. All he could do now was keep telling her the story so she'd understand how much he'd changed, and why he couldn't seem to shake his reputation with his family.

He rubbed her knee. "Hear me out, okay? There's a happy ending to this story. I promise."

Her gaze rolled up to meet his. In her eyes, he saw stubbornness, the same look that had made him instantly smitten with her in the diner the morning before. "I appreciate you telling me all this, but I already know all about the kind of man you were. I knew it when we slept together, too. Just like I now know that's not who you are anymore."

Brett closed his eyes, overcome with a potent cocktail of relief and shame and affection for Hannah, his throat constricting painfully. He had to swallow before saying, "No, it's not."

Hannah partially stood and scooted her chair around the corner of the table, flush with his chair. She snuggled in tight against his side and took his hand again. Then she set her head on his shoulder. "Keep going with your story. I want to get to that happy ending you promised."

He kissed her hair and left his nose buried in it, it smelled so sweet and feminine. "That night, those three girls followed me back to the ranch for an after-party. I never should have gotten behind the wheel, I was so drunk out of my mind, but thank goodness I was alone because, just past the entrance to our property, I drove my truck off the road and flipped it. It rolled twice, or so the girls said. I have no memory after leaving the club. I barely have any memory of that weekend at all.

"The girls witnessed the whole accident. They left one person with me while the rest drove on to the Big House and got my dad. Dad called my brothers and an ambulance, and thankfully I was only bruised and banged up. No major injuries. The seat belt and airbags saved my life."

"Thank God for that," she said.

"It took me almost dying to realize that I was wasting my life. I wasn't contributing to my family's legacy or living by the code I'd been raised to follow. I was only hurting my family and myself."

"That was one heck of a strongly worded message that God sent you."

He pulled his arm out from between their bodies and wrapped it around her back, holding her close. "And effective."

They were quiet for a long time, staring at the shadows of the French doors on the wall in the moonlight and the flicker of the candles on the table. Hannah felt good in his arms. Good in a way that reminded him that he'd never really held a woman just for the sake of being close to her, for the sake of contact—and now that he had, he loved it. The heat of their bodies together, a woman's soft curves melting into him, Hannah's sweet scent, the feel of her breathing and moving and simply being. What a simple, yet vital, pleasure his previous lifestyle had prevented him from experiencing.

That cocktail of relief and humility and affection rippled through him again. He had to be the luckiest man alive to have been given a second chance at life. It wasn't everyone who could claim to be living proof that people could change for the better and turn their lives around by sheer determination.

Hannah's hand spread over his chest in a lazy exploration until her fingers took to worrying a button on his shirt. "I was always so envious of you and your life," she said in a dreamy, faraway voice. "You seemed so free and happy, while my parents were so strict. Growing up, I never felt like I wasn't suffocating to some degree or another. It took coming of age and moving out for me to finally catch my breath."

"Given that your parents are the type of people who would disown their only child over one mistake, then I can imagine that your life was no picnic growing up."

"No picnic, indeed. I wasn't allowed to go to any high school dances or mixers, or go on any dates in high school. According to my parents, I was always in danger of being snared by the devil's slippery slope of sin." She patted her belly. "I'm still reeling from the notion that, in the end, I proved my mother right about forbidden fruit leading to many jams."

He kissed her hair again, just because he could and she didn't seem to mind it. "I've never been referred to as forbidden fruit before. It has a certain ring to it." Then a horrible thought occurred to him and it took all his mental wrangling not to bolt upright and ruin their cuddly moment.

Carefully modulating his voice, he said, "Please tell me you weren't a virgin that night. I'd never forgive myself for tarnishing a memory that's supposed to be beautiful by being drunk and careless with you."

She gave a soft laugh. "No, so you can relax again. I tarnished that memory all on my own, giving that gift away to a different boy who didn't deserve it when I was eighteen. I was so starved for experience when I got out from under my parents' thumb after I turned eighteen that I kinda went crazy. My friends called it my own personal Rumspringa, after the Amish tradition. True, I'd never had a bona fide one-night stand before I hooked up with you—or after that night, for that matter—but I don't regret it. I was due for some fun. That was the day I graduated from college."

"I didn't deserve your gift, either. For the record."

Her hand found his chest again. "I'm sorry you don't remember much about that night, because you were quite good, actually. You lived up to your reputation."

The performance review was so unexpected, he couldn't stop a surprised bark of laughter. "Good to know I did something right by you that night. Still, I'm sorry that I put you in this monumental jam."

The hand on his chest moved higher until it hit the skin of his neck. Chill bumps raced over his body at the contact as her fingers explored his neck and jaw and ear. "You didn't do anything *to* me." Her words came out as a purr, husky, seductive. "We got into this jam together. I was the one who suggested we take our conversation back to my place."

His hand slid from her shoulder down her ribs and lower still. He had no idea what the hell he was thinking, getting handsy with her when he'd sworn off sex until he got his life on track, but that logical place in his brain had gone radio silent. When she shifted her weight toward the leg nearest him, of its own accord his hand slipped even lower, cupping her backside.

He splayed his fingers over her curves and turned his face into hers, brushing his lips over her temple. "If you're calling what we did that night a conversation, then what do you call this right now?"

Her fingers deftly popped open the top button on his shirt. "This is your pantie-melting charm mixing with my dangerously out-of-control hormones."

A chuckle rumbled up from his chest. He'd never thought about pregnancy hormones as lusty, but then again, he'd never given much thought to pregnancy hormones at all. All he knew was, he wanted to kiss Hannah in a bad way and there was nothing or no one to stop him.

Hannah's fingers were talented in the button-popping department. She had half his shirt undone before Brett knew what hit him, probably because she was distracting him from logical reasoning by smoothing her parted lips along his jawline.

He tucked his chin in, his lips reaching for contact with hers, his hands itching to haul her up onto his lap. Brett had never wanted to kiss someone so desperately, but then his arm brushed her belly and he remembered who they were and why they were there. With a growl of frustration, he wrenched his face and hands away from her body. Though his body and heart protested, he pushed up to his feet and paced to the French doors, breathing hard.

"I'm a changed man from the one who hooked up with you in that club." He had a plan for his life now, and it didn't involve taking advantage of the mother of his child on her first night at the ranch. He dropped his forehead to the window, relishing the sting of cold on his skin. "I didn't bring you to the ranch so I could seduce you. I asked you to stay here so I could take care of you and the baby, not take advantage of you."

He felt her eyes on his back. "That's a shame," she whispered, breathless.

He rolled his forehead along the glass, twisting to look over his shoulder at her. Her lips were parted and dewy, and even in the dim lighting, he could see the color staining her cheeks. With that good-girl conservative blouse she wore clashing wildly with her parted lips, dark eyes and mussed-up hair, she was a sight to behold. And he wanted her in a bad, bad way.

As he watched, she stood and sauntered toward him—a seductress intent on the object of her desire. In a flash of memory, he saw her the night they'd hooked up, that same wicked gleam in her eye. Clearly, she was not a woman who demurred, and damn, if that didn't just make him rock-hard and desperate to give her what she wanted.

He braced for impact, but she didn't touch him. She stood next to him and pressed her forehead and palms to the glass, her gaze searching the dark ranch grounds beyond the window.

"Are your dangerously out-of-control hormones going to keep testing my resolve for the rest of your pregnancy?" He'd meant it as a jest, to break the tension, but his voice was still thick with need.

"Probably. But if you're expecting an apology, you're going to be sorely disappointed."

He chuffed at that. What else could he do? One of these times, he had no doubt he'd cave and give Wicked Seductress Hannah what she wanted, but it wasn't going to be tonight. "Let's get out of here so Maria and the staff can do their thing cleaning up."

"Should we help with that?"

"On a normal night, sure. But I wanted this dinner to be special, and how's it going to feel like a proper date if we have to bus the table ourselves?"

They strolled through the foyer to the grand staircase. "How's it going to feel like a proper date if you don't kiss me good-night?" she said in quiet purr of a voice as they mounted the stairs.

Oh, man, she wasn't making this easy on him. Then again, she hadn't pretended that she was going to. "Your hormones again?"

A mischievous grin graced her lips. "No. That was all me."

He fought a grin, way too turned on by her good-girl/bad-girl dual personae. "Hannah, we talked about that. I don't think getting physically involved with each other is the best plan."

"It's not the worst plan, either."

In loaded silence, he walked her to her suite door, then kissed her lightly on the cheek. "Sweet dreams, Hannah. I'll see you in the morning."

CHAPTER SEVEN

THAT NIGHT, NOT even Hannah's teeth-gnashing frustration at Brett for leaving her as an unsatisfied puddle of need at her bedroom door kept her awake for long. After a good stomp around her suite, cursing Brett's level-headed logic, she'd thrown herself onto the expensive, luxurious bed calling to her from the other room, figuring she could at least fume in comfort. But, being that it was her first time lying on a real bed in three months, she fell into a fast, deep slumber. She'd slept so soundly that she didn't wake until long after the sun had risen on Friday morning, despite that she'd never so much as taken off her shoes or crawled under the covers.

She had no idea what the day was going to bring or which of Brett's family members she'd be meeting, but, despite Brett's insistence that she wait to start work on Monday, she hoped to convince him otherwise. So she took a nice shower, blow-dried her hair and dressed for the career in a pair of black slacks that fit under her belly and a long, fitted blue cotton dress shirt that stretched over her belly, showing it off. With a touch of cosmetics, she felt fit, pregnant and ready for her first day on the job—right up until her stomach lurched.

"Oh, boy." She braced her hands on the vanity and breathed. The pregnancy book said that she should be getting over her morning sickness any day now, but apparently her stomach didn't give a whit what the book said.

She took a sip of water, then blotted her now perspiring face with a tissue. So much for fit, pregnant and ready for her job. With her ghostly pallor and clammy sweat, she only matched one of those three descriptors anymore. Maybe once she got to work, she'd be too busy to think about her nausea.

She threw open the doors of her suite and marched through the hall to the stairs. The first scent she detected was bacon. That was a good start. Some nice salty bacon might do her stomach some good. She was nearly to the ground floor when she caught a whiff of coffee and—oh, heck, no—scrambled eggs.

She barely made it to the powder room on the first floor in time, and didn't manage to get the door closed or the fan on before the water she'd had to drink decided to come back up.

"Oh, dear. Morning sickness?"

Hannah didn't yet trust herself to raise her face from over the toilet, but she recognized Edith's kind voice.

"It's more about the food than the time of day, but yes. That's exactly it."

"Brett specifically requested bacon in this morning's meal because you like it, so I'm assuming that's not what made you queasy."

"Not the bacon. It was the eggs and coffee." She gagged again at the thought, then pressed a tissue over her nose and mouth.

A hand stroked her hair. "Poor dear. From now on, you can rest assured I won't be fixing eggs again. The Coltons do love their coffee, but I'll figure out a way to prepare it somewhere you won't be able to smell it."

Hannah sat back on her heels. "I'll get some crackers for my room to eat first thing in the morning so I'm not walking around with an empty stomach. That's helped in the past. There's no need to put you and the Coltons out like that by moving breakfast."

"Nonsense. We don't mind," Brett said, hovering in the doorway behind Edith. "Are you okay, Hannah?"

Hannah hid her face, wishing Brett wouldn't see her in such a pathetic state. Edith must have sensed her unease because she shooed Brett away.

Edith sidestepped, shielding Hannah from view. "She's just fine. Morning sickness is all. Perfectly normal. All we need is a few minutes of girl time and then I'll bring her out."

"Are you sure, Hannah? There isn't anything I can help with in here? A glass of water or something?"

Hannah watched Edith corral him out the door. "Bless your heart. We've got everything under control in here, but you know what you can do? Tell the others that you've all got about three minutes to finish your eggs and coffee, then we'll have the rest of breakfast on the porch. No eggs or coffee or else you'll have to answer to me."

"But—"

The door shut with a decisive *click*, leaving no time for Brett to question the order.

"He's so sweet," Hannah said, sounding as miserable as she felt.

"Yes, he is. Don't let word get around, but between you, me and the wallpaper, I've always had a particular soft spot for Brett."

It was official. Next to Brett, Edith was Hannah's favorite person on the ranch.

Edith retrieved a washcloth from the cabinet under the sink and wet it. "Usually, I set up a breakfast buffet in the kitchen so the Coltons and their employees can eat when they get the chance. The Lucky C is a working ranch, so most everyone is up before the sun." She pressed the washcloth to Hannah's forehead. "But this morning, Brett didn't want you dining alone, so he stuck around the house. And I've got to warn you, Big J and Jack, Brett's brother, have let their curiosity get the better of them. They're out there, too."

"I'm not fit to meet anybody right now."

"Nonsense. We'll have you fixed up in no time. And to avoid the bad smells, we'll move breakfast out to the porch."

"I don't want to put you and the Coltons out by changing their breakfast routine."

With a *tsk* of protest at Hannah's comment, she gathered Hannah's hair, then moved the washcloth to the back of her neck. "Brett told me yesterday that your comfort and needs are my first priorities. Not that I needed him to tell me that, because I'd already arrived at that conclusion on my own."

With Edith's aid, Hannah stood. She blew her nose, then brushed off her knees.

Edith smoothed Hannah's hair, then reached for a tissue. "For your eyes. Your mascara's running."

From seemingly out of thin air, Edith produced a compact of powder and a brush, then doted on Hannah's face and hair for another few minutes, making her feel thoroughly cared for. *Like a good mom*, she thought with a private smile. Like the kind of mom Hannah wanted to be. So full of love that her children would never doubt that they were the center of Hannah's universe, or that her love for them was unconditional.

"Thank you for all your kindness. I've been kind of lost lately."

"Then it's a good thing Brett found you and brought you home."

Home. Hannah had been at the Lucky C for less than a day, but she already knew that this home was nothing like the house she grew up in. Her baby was going to thrive here, and Hannah would, too.

"Brett told me you had a big part in raising him and his brothers and sister. I can see how you're like a mother to everyone around here. And I bet you're going to be a great honorary grandma for this baby." Realizing how dismissive that sounded about Brett's actual mother, she added, "No offense to Abra, of course."

Edith took to fussing over Hannah's outfit. "Oh, I don't think Abra would take offense. She was the first to admit to her delicate constitution and her inability to tolerate children."

The assessment of Abra had been given in a matter-of-fact tone that left no room for questions. After the hints that Brett had dropped about his strained relationship with his mother, it came as no surprise that his mother had neglected the family when he was growing up, or that Edith had filled that role for the Colton kids. In fact, she was certain that Edith got a lot of credit for Brett's turning out to be such a good man.

"As for me," Edith continued, "I never had children or a family of my own, and being a part of the Colton family has brought me so much happiness. I can't wait to meet your little bundle of joy. Being considered one of his grandmothers would be an honor, indeed."

Linked arm in arm, Edith and Hannah walked from the powder room, skirting the foyer in the direction of a short hall, with Hannah holding her breath.

"Another five steps and we'll be at the nearest exit. You've got this," Edith whispered.

Edith walked her to a service hall and through a door that opened onto the wraparound porch. Hannah gulped in a huge breath of fresh air, not minding the singular aromas of the ranch's livestock and dried grasses and dust. The scents reminded her of her parents' shop when she first unlocked the doors in the morning, when the scent of livestock feed and the lemony soap she used to mop the hardwood floors the night before hung heavy and concentrated in the stuffy room.

Good thing those didn't activate her morning sickness or she'd be plumb out of luck. She released her grip on Edith and straightened. Her stomach was still unsettled, but the nausea was manageable.

"Better?" Edith asked.

"Much. Thank you."

The two women walked along the porch to the front of the house where Brett sat with two men who looked strikingly like the ones she'd seen from the dining room the night before. Brett's father—whom she guessed was the man who looked as she imagined Brett would in thirty years—and his older brother Jack, who was maybe ten years Brett's senior, and had the same proud jaw and shape of his nose as Brett and his father.

Brett stood upon seeing them, looking concerned.

Hannah waved away his worry. "Just morning sickness."

"I'm glad that's all it is, but that still stinks." He offered her the chair next to his.

nah. "Especially one who's got a bat in the cave. Am I right, Jack?"

It got Hannah's defenses up to have Rafe interrupting breakfast, though she wasn't sure why. He wasn't exactly lecherous, but he rubbed her the wrong way, and not just because he was impeded by a sexist state of mind.

"A bat in the cave?" Jack said through a chuckle. "That's a new one. How's it going, Rafe?" The two men shook like old friends.

Rafe turned his attention back to Hannah, tipping his hat. "Morning, Miz Grayson."

"You two have met?" Big J said.

Hannah couldn't bring herself to smile, per se. "Yesterday. He was a member of the welcoming committee."

Big J tipped back in his chair and chuckled. "Rafe here is smart enough to greet a pretty lady when she comes around, aren't you, Rafe?"

Rafe's gaze flickered over Hannah's body. "Yes, sir."

Brett's arm settled on Hannah's shoulders, not possessively, per se, but protective, as though Rafe put his defenses on alert, too.

"Unlike your 'bat cave' reference, Rafe, I prefer the term 'bun in the oven,'" Big J said with a wink to Hannah that was light-years different from the wink Rafe had sent her.

Edith set a plate of bacon, toast and fruit in front of Hannah. "I was a candy striper at a hospital before coming to work here, and one of the obstetricians who also worked there was from England. She called it being 'in the pudding club.'"

Hannah smiled, though she was still unsettled by Rafe's presence. "That's ridiculous."

Big J gave a hoot of a laugh. "Yeah, but I can see

the merits of organizing a club of like-minded pudding lovers."

"How about 'pea in the pod'?" Brett said. "That's my favorite, except that our baby is way bigger than a pea already." It could have been Hannah's imagination, but Brett had seemed to stress the words *our baby*. Another subtle warning to Rafe?

Whether it was or not, Rafe pushed off from the rail. "I'll let y'all get back to your breakfast." To Big J, he added, "I just swung by to see if you needed me today, boss."

Big J scratched his neck, considering. "I reckon I don't, but thanks all the same. Look here—our Hannah is a bona fide accountant now. This little lady's gonna have everything under control in a flash, aren't you, darlin'? Better than you or I could manage, I can tell already."

Rafe's eyebrows flickered and he gave a mild nod, probably still trying to assimilate the idea in his Neanderthal mind that a woman was capable of reading spreadsheets. "Congratulations again on your new job, Miz Grayson. And good luck. Don't let Big J boss you around too much." With a tip of his hat, he set off with a cowboy swagger along the dirt road.

With Rafe gone, Hannah dug into her breakfast with unapologetic zeal. As Edith had said the day before, she had a pregnancy pass to indulge in a temporary food obsession.

"What's your plan for today, Hannah?" Big J said. "Is Brett gonna give you the grand tour of this place or am I gonna get you set up in the office?"

"My vote's on *tour*. You deserve a little R & R," Brett said. Hannah gave him a chiding smile. "The tour can wait until this weekend. I'm used to keeping busy and these past few months without work have been maddening. Nothing but R & R. Besides, the reason I'm here at the Lucky C is to work, right?"

"Right," Brett said, his expression shuttered and his tone flat. "Exactly."

Brett and Big J flickered a look at each other that Hannah had no problem interpreting. Her accountant job wasn't the reason she was at the ranch, and everybody knew it, including Hannah. She was smart enough to be aware that her excellent qualifications as a CPA weren't the reason Brett hadn't offered her the job. Just like she was smart enough to know that housing wasn't a typical perk that came with most of the jobs at the Lucky C.

Brett might be determined to provide for her and the baby, but she was equally determined to earn her keep, quash rumors of her being a gold digger and help the Coltons out while she was at it. Before she could second-guess herself, she was turning to Brett's father. "Brett told me that you've been handling the ranch's finances, but I can help free up your time to be with your wife and your grandson. I'm truly grateful for this opportunity to put the accounting degree I broke the bank to get to good use."

Big J chuffed at that. "Opportunity? My son knocked you up."

"Pops, please," Brett growled.

Hannah set a hand on Mr. Colton's arm. "There were two of us there that night to share the responsibility, so don't be so hard on Brett."

"Or else what?" They were fighting words, save for the twinkle in Big J's eyes and the benevolent way he patted her hand.

She decided to assume he was teasing her and run with it. "Or else I'm going to be forced to defend Brett's honor. And I don't think you want to be messing with the likes of me. I can be pretty ferocious, bat in my cave and all."

Everyone at the table chuckled at that, just as she'd hoped.

One of Big J's dinner-plate-sized hands closed over hers. He tipped back in his chair to meet Brett's gaze, his eyes dancing. "I like this one."

One side of Brett's lips kicked up in a lopsided smile that turned her legs to rubber every time. "Me, too."

Big J stood and tossed his napkin on the table. "And since the books at the ranch are my job—or, were—then I say, if you want to work, then let's go get to work." He offered Hannah his arm.

Hannah stood, grinning and so darned relieved to have been accepted by Brett's dad that she didn't care what happened the rest of the day. Even Jack seemed lighter and less judgy than when she'd first walked onto the porch. "I'd be delighted."

As THE CHORUS of voices chatting downstairs grew louder with each Colton family member who arrived for dinner, Brett's nerves kicked up. Really, there was no good reason to be nervous about introducing Hannah to the rest of his family, not after her introduction to his dad and Jack had gone a lot better than he'd anticipated. In general, Jack was by far the most critical of Brett's choices, and he'd thought Jack would be the slowest person to warm to Hannah, but she'd made short work of winning both him and Dad over.

Even still, his stomach was full of butterflies when he knocked on the door of Hannah's bedroom suite.

She opened it wearing a blue dress that accentuated her creamy skin and black hair and had him doing a double take, she looked so pretty.

"You look fantastic. I like that dress."

She patted the fancy braid in her hair self-consciously. "I swear, Maria and Edith are like a pair of fairy godmothers. Edith helped me with my hair and Maria brought me a huge bin of maternity clothes that'd belonged to her cousin."

He hadn't meant to touch her, not after their conversation the night before and the now-constant battle he was waging with himself to keep from kissing her, but before he could stop himself, he molded his hand to the curve of her waist and bussed her cheek. "I'm glad they're taking good care of you. I want to make sure you feel safe and happy here."

She ran her palms along the collar of his slate-gray dress shirt. "I'm sure you say that to all the accountants you hire."

She fluttered her eyelashes and her lips parted. He had no idea if she consciously meant to invite a kiss to those sweet lips or not, but the effect was the same. Just like that, the urge to take her face in his hands and kiss her until her toes curled returned with a vengeance. Truth be told, he'd thought of little else since their dinner the night before besides touching her, kissing her. About finding out if the experience was as decadent as he recalled in his fuzzy memory of their one-night stand.

Drawing a sharp breath, he peeled away from her touch and walked to the balcony door, his back to her and his hands in his pants pockets. "Not every accountant, no. Just to the mothers of my children." He cringed. So much for that smooth charm of his that she kept pointing out. "That didn't come out right."

Her footsteps sounded in approach. "Maybe we're both a little anxious about dinner with your family."

Actually, he'd forgotten all about that when he'd had her in his arms. "That must be it, but there's no reason for you to be nervous. Because of course they're going to be taken with you, like my dad and Jack already are."

Then her hand was on his shoulder blade. He flinched and locked his knees, lest he spin around and take her in his arms once more. Actually, forget taking her in his arms. He wanted to seize hold of her hips and push her up against the wall, caging her between his arms as he plundered her mouth with his tongue and lips. She was so bold and so full of passion, he had a feeling she preferred her lovemaking with an edge of roughness, even if he could only give it to her like that just a little, because of the baby.

"Your dad's so sweet and funny," she said, cutting into his wayward thoughts. "I had a great time at the office with him today, learning the job."

Shaking off the vision in his imagination of the two of them locked together as he took her against the wall, he turned to face her, not sure how he'd stop himself from enacting his vision if she had that come-hither look on her face again. "I just hope my brothers can keep their inappropriate jokes to a minimum. Sometimes, when we all get together, things get a little rowdy."

She chuckled at that.

"What?"

"It makes me smile to imagine a rowdy, happy family get-together. My own family dinners were always such solemn affairs. My mom used to say we had to be quiet because it was easier to hear God that way. But I always had the sinking suspicion that their marriage was so unhappy that they preferred the quiet to having conversations with each other."

"Sounds like my parents' dysfunctional marriage."

"I don't want that for myself," she said. "That was a promise I made to myself a long time ago. Never to get trapped in a loveless marriage like them."

"Same with me. Life's too precious to spend it with the wrong person." He hesitated for a moment, then added, "I do have to warn you that my dad will probably bring it up tonight that you and I should get married."

Her smile turned impish. "He already asked me about it today."

Brett rolled his eyes. "Sorry about that."

"It's okay. You and I have a plan to be parenting partners, and it's none of anybody else's business how we go about that."

Smart, funny, bold, proud, sweet, sexy... Brett's head was swimming with adjectives to describe the inimitable Hannah Grayson. She was strong in a way that made him feel stronger, and so funny and generous of spirit that he didn't think he'd ever smiled so much in his life. *Get a grip, man.* She might be strong, but she was also vulnerable—pregnant and depending on him for a roof over her head, a job and support—and he was hell-bent on sticking to the role of her protector and partner, rather than her seducer.

He reached for her hand and tucked it in the crook of his elbow. "Let's get going. Edith isn't a fan of tardiness."

CHAPTER EIGHT

THE DINING ROOM had been transformed from a mood of soft, candlelit romance the previous night into a bright, festive party atmosphere, the lights turned up, the table decked out in teal, silver and black, from the tablecloth to place settings to the artistically scattered baubles and candles adorning the center.

From Hannah's hasty count as she and Brett entered, six members of the family were already present, including a little boy who had to be Brett's nephew, Seth, Jack and Big J.

"There she is, my new accounting wizard!" Big J's boisterous voice hushed all other conversations. "Hannah, get on over here so I can gush to my boys about what an asset you're going to be to our business."

Brett's head cocked to the side to send her a look full of warmth and pride as he guided her to Big J and the circle of people around him.

Hannah blushed, of course, a ridiculous reflex to praise, and one she'd tried hard to shake. Clearly, she had some work to do on that front. But even she could admit that Big J was right. She *was* going to be an asset to their business because it'd taken her about two-point-one seconds in the office to figure out that the ranch's books were in disarray and that they were bleeding money every quarter due to a lack of tax planning. She had her work cut out for her, but that was fine. Nothing wrong with a little job security—even though the baby in her belly was probably all the job security she needed with the Coltons.

Brett let Big J go on and on about how he'd gotten Hannah up to speed before interrupting him in order to introduce Hannah around. Brett's brother Ryan, a Tulsa police detective, looked so much like Brett that she did a double take. They boasted a similar muscular yet slim build and shared the same brown hair, cut short, and vibrant green eyes. But where Brett's eyes sparkled with an unending well of charm, Ryan's were serious, contemplative.

Daniel, Brett's half-brother, shared a Colton essence in his facial features, but his hair was nearly as black as Hannah's and his skin was darker. He was quiet, distant even, and stood apart from the others. It wasn't until Brett gathered him in a hug and slapped his back that Daniel's brown eyes warmed.

The mood in the room shifted when they heard the sound of the front door closing.

Big J clapped his hands together and gave a whoop. "Got to be my princess!"

Sure enough, women's voices sounded, and then a young woman appeared. Hannah was hit with a surprise moment of déjà vu, Greta looked so familiar. And it wasn't just that Colton essence or her eyes that mirrored Brett's and the rest of the family. Hannah couldn't quite put her finger on what it was about her. Behind Greta stood a handsome young man that Hannah assumed was her fiancé.

Big J greeted them at the entrance to the room, beaming, his arms spread wide. "Greta, Mark. Now my night is complete." He hugged Greta, rocking a little. "I'm so glad you two made it."

Greta kissed his cheek. "Of course we did, Daddy. Sorry we're late. We stopped by the hospital to see Mom first. Eric was there. He sends his regrets."

"Ah, well, he's a busy man. So much responsibility. Any news on Abra? How did she look today?"

Greta moved farther into the room and hooked her purse over the back of a chair near the center of the table. Mark, whom Hannah assumed was her fiancé, trailed her, quiet, and looking thoroughly out of place. It wasn't lost on Hannah that Big J didn't greet his future son-in-law with more than a nod, and save for a handshake from Ryan, nobody else really did, either. Clearly, Greta was the star of the show.

"Eric had some good news. He said that Mom had an increase in brain activity today. That's a really good sign, he said. He said it increases the odds of her waking up from the coma and not having brain damage."

Big J raised his hands to heaven. "Thank goodness. We'll take all the good news we can get."

Greta's eyebrows knit together as her eyes scanned the room. "Speaking of good news." Her gaze landed on Hannah and she strode forward, her hand extended in greeting. "You must be Hannah. I'm Greta. Congratulations on the baby and on snagging Tulsa's most eligible bachelor."

Greta slugged Brett in the shoulder, and that's when it hit Hannah where she'd seen Greta before. The previous afternoon, the woman in the white dress standing in the rain near the ranch office. Except that Greta and Mark had just come into town tonight, so Hannah had to be mistaken. There were a lot of workers at the ranch, so surely some of them would have a slight resemblance to Greta from that distance and in such foul weather. She shook off the thought, though made a note to check the photograph on her phone the first chance she got.

Maria and Edith chose that moment to walk in, each pushing a tray loaded with platters of food. "Go ahead and take your seats, everyone," Edith said. "Dinner is served."

Big J assumed the seat at the head of the table and tucked the silver napkin into his shirt collar. When Maria set a plate of salad in front of him, he picked up a piece of lettuce and let it flutter back to the table. "This isn't all we get, right? I know you've had me on a diet lately, but a man can't survive on lettuce alone."

Maria patted his shoulder. "I made your favorite tonight, so be patient and eat your vegetables."

"I swear, between you, Edith and Abra, it's like I've got three wives henpeckin' me all the time. I don't know how them polygamous fellers with all those wives stay sane."

Brett showed Hannah to a pair of seats across from Greta and next to Daniel, leaning in as he pulled her seat out. "Pops is in rare form tonight. He loves having the whole family around."

Hannah gave a quiet giggle. She loved how gregarious Big J was.

Edith and Maria served the remainder of the salads and were on their way out when Big J called to them. "Edith, Maria, pour yourself some champagne. I have a couple toasts to make and since you two are part of our family, you might as well stick around."

Once Maria and Edith had full flutes in hand, Big J held up his. "First, I'd like to make a toast to the Coltons.

We've had a rough summer so far, but I know in my heart that Abra is going to pull through and be back at this table soon. And what better news for her to wake up to than the discovery that not only is she about to be a grandmother again, but she'll soon be having a new daughter-in-law, too, if Brett cowboys up and marries—"

Brett squirmed. "Pops, please."

"Sorry," he said, though his cat-eating-a-canary grin didn't look the least bit sorry. "As I was saying, the Colton clan is about to be two more strong. Hannah, welcome to the family. And we can't wait to meet Baby Colton come this November. Cheers."

They clinked glasses. Hannah was filled with so much affection for this family, who'd embraced her wholeheartedly. It was everything she'd never had in her life but always wanted. Her eyes clouded with unshed tears of happiness and she leaned a little closer to Brett as she sipped her sparkling cider.

"Don't put those glasses down yet," Big J warned. "I have a second toast to make, this one to my lovely daughter, Greta, and her fiancé, Mark. Your engagement party didn't go as planned, but I know your mother would want you to carry on with the wedding. Nothing is more important in this world than love. And—"

"Actually, Dad, let me stop you there," Greta said.

Big J snorted and lowered his glass. "Can't a man toast his family without getting interrupted these days?"

Greta set her hand over Mark's. "We have a tough announcement to make, something we've given a lot of thought. We've decided to postpone wedding preparations until Mom is awake and better. She's been so excited about the wedding and helping me plan it that I can't imagine forging ahead without her."

The room was quiet. That had to be so hard, thinking about getting married while her mother lay in a coma. Hannah didn't blame her one bit, but Big J's face fell.

"I don't think that's what your mother would want," he said.

"I do," Greta said gently. "And maybe knowing that I'm waiting for her will inspire her to wake up."

Brett was the next to speak. "We understand, sis. And I'm sorry for both of you that what's supposed to be the happiest day of your lives has become anything but."

Greta threaded her fingers with Mark's. "It *will* be the happiest day of our lives, because we're going to wait until Mom is with us again. All that matters to us now is her waking up and making a full recovery."

Hannah offered Greta a smile. "She will wake up. I'm sure of it. There's so much love in this family, how could she not want to rush back into your lives as quickly as possible?"

She felt Brett stiffen. Yes, he'd told her the night before that his mother hadn't been there for him growing up, but that didn't mean she couldn't change. After all, Brett's near-death experience had opened his eyes to what was important in life. Perhaps her brush with death would do the same.

Greta dabbed her eyes with her napkin. "Thank you, Hannah. And that's enough sadness for tonight. I want to hear more about you and Brett. How did you two meet? Dad didn't say over the phone. I didn't even know you were dating someone, bro."

Brett rubbed the back of his neck. "Yeah, about that. I take the full blame for—"

"We met at Avid, a nightclub in downtown Tulsa," Hannah said, cutting him off and sparing him from trying to dance around her reputation, as he'd seemed poised to do. "I'd just graduated from college and wanted to blow off steam and celebrate getting my degree. I wasn't looking for anything more than a single night of fun and neither was Brett, so it was good that we found each other there. I know that's not a pretty story, or sweet, but it's real. As Big J said in his toast, you're our baby's family, so we have nothing to hide."

A chill settled over the table. Brett's backbone was ramrod straight. His hand tapped the hilt of his steak knife against the table as his narrowed gaze roved over each person there, as though daring them to say something disrespectful. They didn't, but then again, they didn't have to. The unmistakable disappointment in their expressions as they returned Brett's stare got their message across loud and clear.

Hannah held her head high and kept a smile painted on her face. She was so dang tired of being judged that she'd lost all her tolerance for it. True, all the disappointment tonight was wholly directed at Brett, but even still, watching Brett's family regard him with that same negativity that she'd suffered at the hands of her parents and their church friends—albeit to a much lesser degree— made her spitting mad. She and Brett hadn't done anything wrong. Searching for a human connection in this crazy, harsh world, even a temporary one, was not a sin. Sex between two consenting adults was not a sin.

She covered Brett's hand with hers, stilling the knife tapping. "This baby is going to be the happiest mistake ever. I have no regrets." And, feeling as brazen and strong as a mother bear, she looked every one of Brett's family members in the eye, smiling her challenge to them to be happy right along with her.

Brett gave her a sidelong glance. She wouldn't have thought it possible, but his backbone grew even taller. His chest even puffed a little, if she wasn't mistaken. "Neither do I," he said with a tinge of wonderment, as though he was arriving at that conclusion as he said the words.

Tracy's smile broadened. "As Brett reminded us a couple days ago, every baby is a blessing. We're so excited for you two."

"Then one more toast," Big J said. "If you'll keep your traps shut without interrupting me, I'll keep it short." He raised his flute. "To happy mistakes."

Brett's posture relaxed. He brought Hannah's hand to his lips and kissed it, then took up his glass in his other hand. "To happy mistakes and new beginnings."

THE *CLOMP* OF footsteps mounting the stairs that led up to the office told Hannah that her evening with Brett was over, which was a shame. They'd been poring over a draft of the horse-breeding proposal for hours, and Hannah had enjoyed every moment of it.

She and Brett worked great as a team, bouncing ideas off each other and molding his vision for the ranch into a fleshed-out business proposal. There was no way his dad and Jack could look at the projected figures that she and Brett had come up with, as well as the concrete business plan they'd articulated, and tell him no. She was sure of it.

When the door opened, they looked up from where they were sitting on either side of the desk, even though they both knew full well who would be standing there. Sure enough, Daniel tipped his hat in greeting to Hannah, then turned his attention to Brett. "Ready? I got the horses saddled."

Hannah tapped her pen, frustrated. "I wish you two didn't have to ride patrol tonight. The ranch has been quiet for the entire week I've been here."

Brett stood and replaced his hat on his head. "Maybe that's because the patrol is working."

Hannah followed them to the door. "Stay safe, okay?"

"No worries there. Like you said, the ranch has been quiet."

Sleekie, the black barn cat who'd taken a shine to her, appeared almost instantly, demanding to be petted with a series of loud meows. Hannah knelt to stroke her.

"Even still," she called to Brett and Daniel as they walked away. "Daniel, look out for him."

Daniel glanced at her over his shoulder as they walked toward the two saddled horses near the stable. "Always." And for a man of few words as he seemed to be, that was as much promise as she could hope for.

She remained at the office door, letting out an appreciative hum as she watched Brett swing into the saddle. "That is one fine specimen of a man, Sleekie."

But all Sleekie did was wind around Hannah's legs, purring.

Hannah scooped the cat up and stood, her attention on Brett and Daniel as they cantered along a dirt road headed west, into the setting sun. Despite having to bid Brett goodbye and her worry about him staying safe, evenings were her favorite time on the ranch. After near-daily afternoon rainstorms, the world seemed to hush in reverence to the setting sun amid the lingering storm clouds. The prairie glowed warm with oranges and purples and deep, dark greens. The ranch itself turned peaceful and sleepy. Even the cows and other livestock seemed to understand the coming of night.

After Brett and Daniel disappeared from view, she lingered on the front steps of the office, absentmindedly petting Sleekie and watching the sunset over the piece of land she was growing attached to. The moment the sun dipped below the horizon, she closed her eyes and said a prayer for Brett, for their baby, and to thank God for providing such a good life for her. She hadn't understood why He'd taken her life on such a difficult path, but she was starting to see the plan for her at the Lucky C with the Coltons and she definitely approved.

When Sleekie started to squirm, she set the cat down and returned to the office. Flipping all the lights on, she got back to business. After setting aside Brett's horse-breeding proposal, she opened the spreadsheet for the Lucky C. The numbers weren't adding up the way she would've hoped. Every month for the past year, the ranch's account was coming up short by several thousand dollars.

The errors were probably a result of Big J's haphazard style, compounded by his occasional forgetfulness Brett had mentioned to her on the sly. Whatever the cause, the result was the same. She had her work cut out for her. Tonight's plan involved cross-checking deposit receipts with the hand-printed ledgers and the computerized spreadsheets that Big J had created, then inputting the real numbers in the brand-new spreadsheet that she'd created earlier that week.

Sleekie leaped onto the desk and sat herself down right on top of the open ledger.

Hannah scratched her behind the ears before moving her to the side. "Well, Sleekie, since you don't have fingers, how about you cross your paws that I'm right about these shortages being typos? Otherwise that means someone's stealing money from the Coltons and we can't have that, can we? Not after everything they've been through."

The mere thought of someone stealing money from the Coltons made Hannah spitting mad. She really hoped she was able to find the nearly twenty thousand dollars that looked to be missing.

Sleekie gave a meow, then tipped on her side and got down to her own business of giving herself a bath, unconcerned with the missing money.

Not ten minutes later, Hannah cursed under her breath and shot to her feet, angry and shocked at what she'd found. She picked up the check stub that she'd cross-referenced with a bank statement and gave the two a second look. In her hands she held the first clue about what had happened to the money. "Sleekie, it's not a typo."

Footsteps sounded, coming up the steps. Sleekie dived off the desk, but Hannah didn't have time to do more than wedge the check and the bank statement into the open ledger she'd been working with and flip it closed before the door opened.

Rafe seemed as surprised to see her as she was to see him.

"Oh," he said, backing up a step. He removed his hat and pressed it to his chest. "Evening, Miz Grayson. I didn't expect you to be here so late."

"Then what are you doing here?" Too late, she realized how rude that had come out. "Sorry. You startled me and that came out wrong. I mean, how can I help you tonight?"

He moved farther into the room. "My apologies for

giving you a start. I saw the light and thought it'd been left on accidentally. Thought I'd do my part for the environment and the Coltons' electric bill and come turn it off."

He propped one hip on her desk, his broad grin revealing a row of straight white teeth. "But come to find out, it's just purdy little Hannah making herself useful."

It struck her then that she'd once teased Brett that he was as slippery as a snake-oil salesman. She hadn't met Rafe Sinclair yet. With one eye on him, she reached a hand to the keyboard. One hit of a button and the computer monitor went into sleep mode.

"Yep. It's just me, trying to get these books figured out." She tried out a smile, but she had trouble making it happen. She'd seen the man nearly every day since arriving at the ranch, and so far he hadn't been guilty of anything except misogyny, but still, Rafe made her uncomfortable. He didn't seem to understand the concept of personal space and his gazes at her lingered a little too long and were a little too studious.

He picked up the ledger she'd closed. "I've got a good mind for numbers and I'd be happy to help you. In fact, I can see it now, the two of us working together, me helping you make heads and tails of this complicated business so you can get back to your evening and relax, maybe sneak some of Maria's strawberry jam, like you do."

Since when had he seen her eating jam? She only did that in her suite. Then again, she was so addicted to the stuff that there was a chance she'd had a spoonful at breakfast on the porch without remembering it. "That's sweet of you to offer to help, but I've got a good handle on my job." She eased her hands around the ledger and gave a tug, but Rafe's grip held firm.

"Doesn't mean you couldn't use a man's help."

Oh, brother. "Sorry to break it to you, but that's exactly what that diploma on the wall behind me means."

His attention slid past her to the wall. She took his momentary distraction as an opportunity and tugged on the ledger again, harder this time. He released it with a low chuckle.

"So it does, Miz Hannah."

She didn't want to remain in Rafe's company for a second longer. Men who felt entitled to come on to women no matter how uncomfortable they became and who paid no mind to personal boundaries made her skin crawl. There'd been men like that in the Congregation of the Second Coming, men like that at her college campus library, and there would always be men like that the world over. But that didn't mean she had to suffer in their company.

She slipped around the side of the desk, affording him a wide berth, strode to the door and opened it. "I'm afraid I have to ask you to leave so I can keep working. Thank you for understanding."

After a long pause, he stood and replaced his hat on his head. "Forgive me for interrupting your work. Have a safe night, Miz Hannah." When he reached the door, he gave the handle a jiggle. "And be sure to lock this door behind me so the bogeyman can't get in."

What a slimeball, shrouding his threats in disingenuous charm and implications, giving her no concrete grievances to share with Brett, should she choose, except for the way he creeped her out.

She certainly did lock the door behind her and pulled

the curtains closed, but she couldn't concentrate on her work anymore. Rafe had gotten in her head. She locked the ledgers, bank statements and other evidence into the desk's largest drawer. On a gut instinct, she backed up the ranch's accounting files to a portable drive and pocketed it. Then she added a password to the computer's launch page before logging out—a version of her due date using random capital letters—just in case.

The whole time, she couldn't shake the sensation that someone was watching her. Of course, that was just her imagination being ridiculous, because the curtains were closed.

"Must be that bogeyman Rafe mentioned. Huh, Sleekie?" But the comment she'd meant as sarcastic, as a means to point out how silly she was being getting so freaked out, hovered in the stillness.

She hadn't seen Sleekie since Rafe's visit, so the smart cat must have hightailed it out of the room. To make sure she didn't accidentally lock the cat in overnight, she checked every nook and cranny of the office, under chairs and tables and behind the curtains.

She had one hand on the doorknob when she thought twice about leaving the ledgers and other possible evidence behind. Yes, she'd locked them up, but her gut was talking again and this time it was telling her to take it all with her back to her room for safekeeping.

After stuffing the loose papers and files into a manila envelope, she stepped outside, locked the office and set off across the grounds to the Big House. She still couldn't shake the notion that there were eyes on her, and her pulse pounded faster with every step she took. Thankfully, she was spared from walking in total darkness by floodlights gracing the eaves of the stables, the feed shed and just about every other building on the grounds. Her path was lit and out in the open and just about as safe as could be. There were no bogeymen, no ghosts, and no one was going to get her on this short walk home in the middle of the Coltons' property.

CHAPTER NINE

ON THE PORCH of the Big House, Hannah glanced over her shoulder in the direction that she'd felt someone's eyes on her throughout the evening. Movement, a splash of white, caught her eye near the bunkhouse. The skin on her neck prickled. She stood still, watching the night, but saw nothing else. It had to have been a curtain blowing in the breeze because someone left a window open. Had to be.

She flung the main door of the Big House open a little too hard. It banged against the wall, the sound echoing in the silence within. She didn't draw a full breath again until she'd locked the front door and flipped on every light operated from the switch panel in the foyer.

"Hello, Edith? Are you still around?"

Nothing. As usual, Edith had retired for the night with the setting sun. Maria must have left already, too. Knowing that Edith and Big J were somewhere in the house should have proven a comfort to Hannah, but her unease only ratcheted up. So silly. She was freaking herself out for no reason.

She made it up the stairs in record time. Subdued lighting glowed throughout the hall from wall sconces. The floor-to-ceiling window at the end of the hall was nothing more than a black rectangle, showing the darkness of the ranch's land. Brett and his brother were out

there in the night, patrolling to keep her safe. She had
nothing to worry about, tucked away inside a perfectly
secure home.

Her attention pulled toward the hallway that led to
Abra's suite. The crime scene.

Stop thinking about it, Hannah. For real.

She hugged the envelope to her chest and scuttled to
her room. As usual, Edith and Maria had left a light on
for her inside.

She opened the door and at the first glimpse of movement, yelped and stumbled back. Someone was in her
room. She pressed herself to the hallway wall on weak
knees, breathing and wondering what the heck she
should do next.

Maria appeared in the doorway. "Oh, my God, Hannah. I'm so sorry I scared you."

Hannah sagged against the wall and let her hand holding the envelope flop to her side. "It's just you." She let
out a peal of nervous laughter. "Oh, God. My heart."

"Are you okay?" Maria asked.

"I think so."

Maria disappeared into the room again, then reap-
peared holding a glass of water. "I knew you were working hard and I thought you might like a late-night snack
when you got home. I'm sorry I scared you."

Hannah accepted the water and drank deeply from
it, feeling her heart beat in her throat as she swallowed.
"Truthfully, I was already spooked before I opened the
door. Got myself all worked up over something I thought
I saw on the walk back here. Of course, it was nothing."

"Was it the ghost? A woman?"

Hannah clutched the glass and gaped at Maria.
"You've seen her, too?" she whispered.

Maria nodded. She wrapped an arm around Hannah and led her into a chair in the suite's sitting area. "So have some of the ranch workers. I think she might be the woman whose baby's bones were found at the Coltons' family cemetery last month." She made the sign of the cross on her chest.

Hannah's head was spinning. "Excuse me?"

"You didn't know?"

"Uh, no."

"Jack found them in the family cemetery, like I said. They don't know who the bones belong to or where they came from, but the police think they were planted there. Ryan said that they didn't look like they'd been there long. Soon after they were discovered, we started seeing the ghost. I think the mother still walks the prairie, looking for her baby."

"That's horrible." Not just because a baby had died, which was unbearably sad in its own right, but that someone had disrespected the bones by moving them. And if they'd planted some poor, sweet baby's bones at the Lucky C on purpose for the sake of scaring the family or confusing the investigation against Abra's attacker, then that was a despicable excuse for a human being.

Hannah shook her head, pushing away the thought that someone could stoop to such depravity. Though she was aghast about the bones, and frustrated on the Coltons' behalf, she didn't believe in ghosts. Did she? Then again, she sure had believed in the possibility a few minutes earlier. She thought about the photograph she'd taken on her phone. Ready to share the photograph with Maria, she looked around for her purse, but realized almost immediately that she'd forgotten it in the office.

"I hope I didn't frighten you all over again," Maria

said. "I can't imagine anything else bad happening at the Lucky C. Not with so many people patrolling the grounds and the police investigating the crimes against the family. I'm sure the worst is behind us all."

"I'm sure you're right," she said instead. Hopefully Maria didn't hear the lie in Hannah's words. She clutched the envelope tightly to her chest—the possible proof that not all the worst was behind the Coltons. She hated the idea of breaking it to Brett that his family may have yet another crime to weather.

After Maria left, Hannah locked the suite door, then prowled the rooms, looking for the perfect hiding place for the folder of evidence. Before she'd found one, she saw a Bible she didn't recognize lying open on the vanity.

Even from a distance, she could see a circle of red marker ink on one page. Baffled, she moved in for a closer look. What she discovered had her huffing in disbelief. Guess her first semilogical explanation that Maria had left it behind had been wrong.

"Mavis, you crazy girl."

The Bible was open to Deuteronomy, the circled verse commanding the righteous to stone unmarried fornicators as a way of purging evil—one of the most popular passages misappropriated by the Congregation of the Second Coming.

Shaking her head at Mavis's nerve, she slid the folder of evidence between the vanity and the wall, out of sight. Then she flipped the pages of the Bible to her favorite psalm about forgiveness. *Let's see you try to twist that verse into something hurtful, Mavis.*

Smiling now, she rummaged through the desk for a pen and circled the verse over and over again until she's created a thick blue frame for the exalted words. Just because her parents' cult could twist the word of God for their own agenda didn't make them right or true. Forget creeps like Rafe and religious fanatics like Mavis; Hannah was above them all. She knew in her heart who she was and what she stood for.

And what she stood for right now was indulging in the late-night snacks that Maria had left for her. Tonight's choices were a plate of fruit, nuts and crackers, as well as a bottle of sparkling apple cider. God bless Maria. She flounced onto the sofa and popped a nut in her mouth.

Inevitably, her thoughts shifted to Brett. He might have rejected her every advance and refused to consider the possibility of them as a couple, but he'd made all this possible for her—the comfy bedroom, the great job, the pampering from Maria and Edith, and, most importantly, the sense of security he'd brought to her life. No matter how jumbled up her feelings were for him, or how unconventional their arrangement, she knew she could count on him, no matter what, even if she hadn't felt very secure on the ranch itself that night. She glanced at the curtained windows, hoping his night had been more peaceful than hers.

THE RANCH WAS quiet and the night air was balmy and pleasant, neither of which explained Outlaw's restlessness one bit.

Brett and Daniel sat astride their horses on the far reaches of the ranch's epicenter, keeping one eye on the backcountry and the other on their homestead. The Big House glowed like a beacon in the distance, while the bunkhouse and barns stood like a line of matchsticks. Windows were lit and clusters of men sat outside smoking and shooting the breeze. One ranch hand whom Brett didn't recognize in the dim light strummed a guitar. Every now and then, he caught a chord on the breeze.

When Outlaw whinnied and stamped the ground for the hundredth time, Daniel tipped his head towards Brett's horse. "My horses have been on edge lately, too. Their appetites are low and they're nipping at each other. Something's in the air."

"We're feeling it at our end of the ranch with the workers. A few of them swear they've seen a ghost in the field. A woman."

"What do you think?" Daniel asked.

Brett swung his attention away from the homestead and toward the darkness. "Like you said, something's in the air. All I know is that it sure wasn't a ghost who put my mother in the hospital or tampered with our fences."

"Not to mention the bones in the cemetery last month."

"Man, that was terrible. Disturbing." Even now, the memory of those bones haunted Brett's mind in Technicolor detail. "What I don't get is why the perpetrator would still be skulking around the ranch. And the hospital, if we believe that druggie who tried to sell Mother's locket to a pawnshop."

Daniel's gaze went distant. "Secrets."

"I don't follow."

Daniel shrugged. "Maybe the perp accidentally left something behind around here. Or he didn't find what he was looking for in Abra's room. There would be lots of reasons to come back, which is why you and I are killing a perfectly good night sitting out here in the dark."

Damn, Brett prayed that neither of those motives held true, because if that were the case, then no one on the ranch was safe. "I hope you're wrong. But I still don't get what you meant by *secrets*."

"The ranch is too far off the beaten path for a small-time crook to risk, so I don't think jewelry was the main point of the break-in. Not for the relatively low-value items that were stolen, and not given that photo albums were also taken. So if money wasn't the motivation, then that means secrets are involved."

Yeah, right. "That's a nice theory and all, except for one thing. My mother doesn't have any secrets. She's a depressed, bitter socialite." Saying the words dredged up all the frustration and pain of their combative relationship. He would forever regret his last words to her before her attack, and when—he refused to think of it as an *if*—she woke, he'd be the first in line at her bedside to tell her that he forgave her and ask for her forgiveness in return, but that didn't mean he was obligated to transform her into a saint in his mind.

Daniel gave him a look. "Everybody and every place has secrets, bro." He spurred his mount into motion, headed away from the homestead to the fence line in the distance.

Brett gave a long look at Daniel's back, at the shoulders that were unmistakably Colton DNA. Daniel's mother had been Brett's father's mistress—his father's secret. Maybe Daniel was onto something with his theory.

Brett urged Outlaw to catch up, his mind chewing over the possibility that his mother could have brought the attack on herself through keeping a secret of her own. No way. Not Abra Colton. If she'd gotten herself in hot water, she would've come racing to Brett's dad for help.

As fast as Daniel had taken off, he brought his horse to a stop. Brett instructed Outlaw to do the same.

Daniel brought his rifle up, aiming it to his right. "Did you see that?"

Brett scanned the countryside in the direction that Daniel's rifle was pointed, but saw only tall grasses and scrub trees in the last lingering indigo glow of daylight. "No. What?"

Daniel nodded to his right. "Three o'clock. I saw movement."

"Coyote?"

"Not sure. Probably, but it looked bigger to me."

They stood still and quiet. Brett strained his eyes. Then he saw it, a glimpse of movement more than two football fields away. With the gait and the shape, it had to be the head or back of a large animal or a small man, its form black against the night and moving quickly away from them on top of a small rise.

Brett took up his rifle and whispered, "Come on. Let's see what, or who, we've found."

They proceeded forward with caution, letting their horses pick their way quiet and steady over the land. Brett's senses were on high alert now. He heard every crunch of grass under the horses' hooves, every rustle of leaves in the breeze. He was keenly aware of his own loud, fast heartbeat and the twitchy urge of his trigger finger where he held it straight against his .22.

How long had it been since he'd shot a gun? Several months, at least. It was one of those skills that never left a man completely, but he sure hoped he wouldn't need to pull the trigger tonight.

They were nearly to the top of the rise where they'd seen the movement when a flare of light burst to life on the far side of the rise and reflected off the clouds. Brett and Daniel stopped their horses and exchanged a nervous glance. Brett adjusted his shotgun against his shoulder, his eyes locked on the glow coming from the other side of the hill.

That's when he saw it—a flicker that could only be one thing.

"Fire," Brett said, urging Outlaw back into motion.

With a curse, Daniel sped to join him. They raced over the hill. The hunting shed they sometimes used when there was evidence in the area of bobcats, coyotes or mountain lions was fully engulfed in flames.

"I'll radio for help," Daniel said. "You keep looking and I'll catch up with you. We've got to catch whoever did this and I'm guessing they're not going to hang around to watch us put the fire out."

Brett and Outlaw took off into the prairie, cutting a wide path around the burning building. He kept his head on a swivel, straining for a glimpse of movement in the darkness, but the light of the fire hindered his night vision. It took a long time for his eyes to adjust enough to see anything but the silhouettes of trees, boulders and the horizon.

Then, he saw it again. Movement. At first glimpse of something making haste across the prairie a good fifty yards to his left, Brett sucked in a breath in shock. He slowed Outlaw while his eyes got a read on the motion again. Something or someone was definitely out there with him, something as big as a person, rustling the underbrush and running on foot fast away from him. Contrary to Maria's imagination, this was no prairie ghost, so it'd only be a matter of seconds before Outlaw caught up to him. Or it.

Gun at the ready, he nudged Outlaw's flank.

Then, somewhere nearby, a gunshot fired.

CHAPTER TEN

THE DARKNESS WAS disorienting, but the gunshot seemed to have come from the direction of the outbuilding. Out on the prairie, there were few places a man and horse could hide that would shield them from gunfire. Brett briefly considered pulling his flashlight from his saddlebag because the dark was so frustrating in its limitations, but that would do little more than blind him to the world beyond the limited scope of the beam. Listening for sounds of movement was still his best choice.

He held his breath, held Outlaw perfectly still, and opened his ears. Nothing but the hollow, droning whistle of wind across the grass and the faint crackle of burning wood in the distance. To his right, a twig snapped, followed by a rustling sound. Brett swung his attention and rifle in that direction.

"Freeze! Or I'm going to blow your head off," he bellowed.

He would never shoot without first having a visual on his target, but maybe his threat would inspire the trespasser to speak up. More rustling sounded, getting farther away. Brett gave a slight tug of pressure to Outlaw's rein, commanding him forward a few steps.

A howl cut through the breeze. Outlaw stiffened and stopped moving, his ears tall. Brett couldn't make sense of the sound, higher pitched than a dog's wail or the keening of tornado sirens. It was the kind of sound that crawled under your skin and came back out in nightmares, or when your mind was in the twilight zone between sleep and waking.

Brett kept up his visual scan of the surrounding prairie, but saw nothing.

Then the sound cut off as though someone had hit Stop on a stereo, though it echoed in Brett's ears for several moments longer until it was eclipsed by the sounds of Brett's pounding heart and his panting breaths.

The next gust of wind carried with it the noxious odor of burning wood laced with chemicals. The fire.

He pulled his phone from his pocket and called Daniel. "Did you hear that sound? That howl?"

"Huh? No, but I thought I heard a gunshot. Are you okay?"

"Fine. I heard the shot, too, but I lost the trail. Whoever set that fire and shot at us is long gone," Brett said.

"A crew's on their way from the ranch, bringing the water tank."

"Police? Fire department?"

"I haven't called them yet. I figured we'd see what we've got first. They might just get in the way of our investigation."

Ryan would be ticked off beyond belief if they didn't clue him in, but he agreed with Daniel's plan to wait and see. He gave a wiggle of the rein with his right hand, turning Outlaw in the direction of the fire. "I'm headed back your way."

"Keep your eyes open and your gun ready."

Brett gave one last look over his shoulder. "Copy that."

At the site of the fire, Daniel, along with Rafe, Jack

and at least a half dozen ranch workers had already doused the flames with water from the tanker truck, which idled nearby, its headlights illuminating the scene. The men stood around the burned-out shell of the hunting blind, hands on hips, pointing and talking.

Brett dismounted a fair distance away, hoping to spare Outlaw from breathing the most concentrated levels of residual smoke and fumes. He walked toward the men, his gaze still scanning the horizon for movement, though he felt in his bones that the perpetrator had vanished.

Ash and carbon scattered in the breeze, kicking around Brett's boots as he walked. A particularly large piece of ash tumbled across the ground in his direction. Brett bent forward and plucked it up. He knew the moment his fingers touched it that it wasn't ash, but a photograph. He angled it into the light from the tanker's headlights.

It was from a Christmas card from years and years ago. He, his brothers and sister, and his parents posed in front of a beige studio backdrop, all dressed in Sunday finery. Every set of their eyes had been gouged out.

THE PARKING LOT of the Tulsa police precinct that Ryan worked in was packed. Brett found a spot on the street, then texted Ryan about his arrival as he trekked to the main entrance. The lobby was mostly full. Behind the front desk, uniformed and plainclothes officers carried on with their busy morning, most anchored to their desks with their fingers busy at keyboards.

A bony woman with frizzy gray hair and a variety of tattered bags and purses slung over her right shoulder stood at the front desk, demanding answers about why her next-door neighbor hadn't yet been arrested for spying on her, despite the numerous police reports that the woman had filed. The receptionist had patient eyes and a serious expression, as though she earnestly valued every opinion and complaint lobbed at her throughout her shift.

A jingle of keys preceded Ryan's arrival in the lobby. He was dressed in beige slacks and a blue dress shirt unbuttoned at the collar. He'd rolled the sleeves up over his forearms and had affixed his badge to his brown leather belt, right next to his holstered firearm. Nobody exuded effortless confidence like his brother Ryan.

"Thanks for meeting with me," Brett said, standing.

"I've been at my desk this morning, drowning in paperwork, so I appreciate the break." The frizzy-haired woman at the front desk slapped her palm on the counter, her voice turning shrill. Ryan eyed her for a beat, then turned his attention back to Brett. "Let's go to my office. I just made a fresh pot of coffee."

He followed Ryan through the maze of hallways. The mention of coffee conjured a vision of Hannah in Brett's mind and brought a smile to his lips as he recalled her first morning at the ranch. She'd tried hard to tough it out that morning at breakfast, but he wasn't sure he'd ever seen anyone so green around the gills. Thankfully, her morning sickness seemed to be fading. Even still, she'd rallied like a trouper every morning, insisting on getting right to work—highlighting a one-two punch of moxie and self-deprecating charm that had—

He shook his head. There he went again, damn it all. Daydreaming like a smitten schoolboy. It was hightime he knocked that nonsense off because his wayward thoughts were making it harder and harder to think clearly when it came to protecting the woman and child in his charge. Now, more than ever, he needed to stay focused on what mattered most—keeping them safe.

Ryan stopped at his office door and ushered Brett in. "Don't try to tell me that smile is because I'm offering you coffee."

"Nah. Just thinkin'."

Ryan gave him a poke in the ribs as he passed. "About your baby mama, I bet."

"Lucky guess."

"No way. That was me using my advanced detective skills. How are the two of you doing?" He pushed the door to his office closed with his shoe, then made a beeline to the coffeepot on the table in the corner.

Brett took a seat in front of the desk. "She's already proved to be a major asset to the business, and she's helping me come up with a horse-breeding proposal to present to Jack and Pops, which is invaluable."

Filling two mugs with coffee, Ryan frowned. "That's a cop-out answer."

"How do you figure that?"

He handed Brett a mug. "What I asked was, how are you two getting along? I mean, you'd only met her twice before she moved in with you, right? So, how's it going? Do you like her?"

"Don't you ever get tired of interrogating people?"

Ryan assumed his seat behind the desk. "Nope."

Brett sipped his coffee. "Well, she won over the whole house within the first five minutes of them laying eyes on her, just like I knew she would, and she's been charming the socks off everyone ever since. And at least once a day, she gets this look in her eyes like she wants me to kiss her, and every single time, I come about this close

to caving. And there's nothing sayin' I'd be able to stop
with just a kiss. So I'm pretty miserable."

Ryan snorted. "How would making out with her be
a bad thing?"

"Because I'm ninety-nine percent sure that would've
been the wrong move. Her pregnancy hormones tend to
make her rather…passionate, you might say. But there's
no getting around the fact that she's in a vulnerable position. No matter what Little Brett is telling me to do,
sleeping with her is not the right move. She and the baby
are my responsibility and I'm not going to muck all that
up by overstepping my boundaries."

Ryan raised his mug in a salute. "Mature."

"Precisely. Thank you." That was exactly what he was
determined to be—no matter how kissable she looked
or how ardently she tried to seduce him. "Thankfully,
most of our evenings together are cut short by my patrol shifts."

"That's a helluva thing, that fire last night. I'm glad
you and Daniel called me in. I can't figure out why anyone would be motivated to start a fire all the way out in
the back fields."

"The fire marshal had just arrived at the ranch before
I left to come here."

"Good," Ryan said. "He should have some answers
for us soon about the cause and origin point. But I'm
fairly certain that you haven't come all the way here
for advice on your love life or to talk any more about
the fire, since we just saw each other a few short hours
ago." He threaded his hands together behind his head
and leaned back in his chair. "So, to what do I owe this
visit?"

"I might have some insight as to the motivation of

our arsonist." Brett slid the defaced Christmas photo across the desk. He'd taken the precaution of sealing it in a plastic ziplock bag, hanging his hope on the chance that the police would be able to salvage fingerprints or DNA from it. "I found this at the scene of the fire, but I haven't shared it with anyone yet. I wanted to talk with you first."

Ryan left the photograph on his desk and stared at it for a long time, his expression inscrutable. Then he scrubbed a hand over his mouth. He picked the bag up and held it close to his face while he took a slow drink of coffee.

"I'm pretty sure that's from one of the photo albums stolen from Mom's room," Brett said into the stretching silence. "And it's defaced in the same way as Greta's photograph in the stolen locket the police found outside the hospital."

Ryan set the photograph on the desk again and leveled a somber look at Brett. "Well, holy hell. If there was any doubt before, there won't be now. This makes it personal."

"My thoughts exactly. This confirms our suspicion that the hit man who went after Tracy last month wasn't Mom's attacker and that her attack wasn't a random robbery gone bad. Whoever it was, they knew where her room was, where she kept her jewelry and her photo albums, and—" he speared a finger onto the desk near the photograph "—they cared enough to deface our family memories. Multiple times."

"And they set that building on fire knowing you'd find it, along with the photograph. It was a plant. Just like the locket."

Brett nodded. "I hate the way this is shaping up."

"Me, too. Who knew where you and Daniel were patrolling last night?" Ryan asked.

"No one. We decided which direction we'd go after he came to the office to get me. But anyone who was at the ranch could've seen which direction we left in."

"That's what I'm afraid of."

"What?"

Ryan rolled his gaze up from the photograph to pin Brett with a grave look. "That whoever's behind all this damage and Abra's attack works at the ranch."

A chill crawled under Brett's skin. How could he keep Hannah safe if the danger was right under their noses, invisible in plain sight? "Like I said, I hate the direction this is going."

"You said you didn't show this photograph to anyone else? Not even Daniel or Hannah?"

"No one. Not Daniel, and definitely not Hannah. I don't want her to worry unnecessarily."

Ryan nodded. "Let's keep it that way for now, until I've had a chance to think this through. If whoever's doing this lives and works at the ranch, then the fewer people who're aware of the evidence, the better. Someone wants to hurt our family. Not just Mom, but all of us."

Brett was too agitated to sit. He pushed up from the chair and paced to the door, staring blankly through the glass into the hall. "Why would someone do all this? What do they have against our family?"

Daniel's theory about secrets popped into Brett's head. But secrets about whom? And what?

"No idea what the motive is," Ryan said. "None of it makes sense yet, but it's going to very soon because I'm not going to rest until it does."

"I just moved the mother of my child onto the ranch. I told her I would take care of her and the baby and keep them safe, but how can I do that if Mom's attacker is right under our noses?" He pivoted and pinned Ryan with a stare. "I have a family to protect now, damn it."

Ryan pressed his hands into the desk and stood. "We're going to get this guy. I promise you that." He took the bag holding the defaced photograph in hand. "Follow me."

He strode out of his office and down the hall. Brett followed. They stopped in front of a partially open office door. Ryan gave a little wave through the glass, then entered. Brett hovered in the hall, reading the name plate next to the door. Detective Susan Howard—Forensic Investigator.

Detective Howard was sitting behind her desk, working on her computer. She didn't look older than thirty, with blond hair pulled into a tight bun and a no-nonsense air about her that oozed competence and intelligence.

When she noticed Ryan, she rose. "Ryan. Hi. It's nice to see you." She rushed to stack files on her desk and toss some trash in the wastebasket. "I, um, wasn't expecting to see you today."

Once upon a time, Brett had fancied himself an expert on women, so he felt confident in his assessment that the good detective was flustered to see Ryan in her office. She also looked like the kind of woman Brett would've hit on in a heartbeat before his car accident, with a fit, curvy body that would make any man with a pulse do a double take, right up until he realized that she was armed and could probably kick his butt to Mexico, should she get it in her mind to.

"Hey. Yeah, sorry to bother you," Ryan said. "I need a favor."

She came around the side of her desk and propped a hip on the corner of it. "Everything okay?"

"Not sure. More trouble at my family's ranch."

She strummed her fingers on the desk. "You should let me help you more often, Ryan. It's my job. Just because you and I didn't—"

"Have you met my brother Brett yet? Brett, this is Detective Howard, our forensics investigator." Ryan practically dragged Brett into the room by the arm.

A flash of surprise crossed the detective's face, as though she'd assumed until that point that she and Ryan were alone. "Oh. Hello."

Brett held his hand out in greeting. "Pleased to meet you, Detective."

"I'm sorry for all your family's gone through lately." All business now, she folded her arms in front of her, tapping her fingertip against her elbow. "What's this favor that you need?"

Ryan held the photograph up. "A rush job on fingerprints."

She took the bag from him and perused the photo. "This is your family?"

"It is. Hard to tell with the eyes scratched out, I know."

She twisted to reach for a pair of reading glasses on the desk. Then, as Ryan had, she held the photograph up close to her face and studied it in silence. "Where did you find it? In a fire?"

"How'd you guess?"

"I see bits of ash." Her eyes tracked from one end of the photograph to the other as though she were reading a book. "Am I going to find a police report about this fire?"

Ryan's posture went stiff. "No. Not yet. It happened last night. But the fire marshal was sent to investigate today, so the report's coming."

She walked to a cabinet, unlocked the combination lock, then set the photograph inside and relocked it. "I've got another rush job to finish right now for that murder case that came in last week, but I'll process the photograph for you tonight."

"Thank you. You're a lifesaver. If I'm not here at the office, then text me the results."

She tossed a notepad at him. "You'll have to give me your number again, because it's not in my phone anymore."

Brett detected the slightest hint of a sharp edge to her tone and took a step back, deciding he might be better off waiting in the hall while Ryan finished up.

Ryan jotted on the pad and handed it back to her, then shifted his weight, looking uncomfortable. He hooked his thumb toward the door. "Thank you. We should go. But, uh, thanks again."

Back in Ryan's office, Brett had planned on heading out to let Ryan get back to work, but then Ryan topped off Brett's coffee cup, so Brett took a seat to enjoy it.

Ryan sat next to Brett and sipped from his own cup. "Hey, by the way, I like her."

"Who? Detective Howard?"

A bit of coffee sloshed over the rim of Ryan's mug when he jolted. "Huh? No, I mean. Susie's great, and I…uh. I was talking about Hannah. Earlier, we got side-tracked talking about the fire, so I didn't have a chance to tell you that. At the family meeting last week, you told us to wait until we met Hannah before casting judgment and you were right. She's pretty great."

The vindication felt good. He'd learned to endure their disappointment, but Hannah deserved better. "Thank you for saying so. You're right. She's incredible." He felt a stupid smile coming on and let it shape his lips without a fight. "She's got Dad wrapped around her little finger and he's loving it. Edith and Maria, Hannah's started calling those two her fairy godmothers because all they do is fuss over her, like the rest of us are chopped liver. I can't imagine what it's going to be like when the baby comes. We're all going to be invisible to Edith and Maria."

"You don't look like you mind that so much."

Brett shook his head. "It's been a heck of a year for me. It seemed like everything that could go wrong did, except I'm excited about the baby—now that I've had time to adjust to the idea—and I like Hannah. A lot. Too much."

Ryan's lips twitched into a grin. "For what it's worth, I think you're going to be a great father."

"Thank you. Seriously. It's nice to inspire confidence for a change."

But as Brett finished is coffee and stood, the truth came back to him about why he was at the police precinct that morning.

"You look like you're plotting a murder. What's going on inside your brain now?" Ryan said.

"It doesn't matter how great of a father you think I'm going to be, or how blown away everyone is by Hannah. Because the fact remains that someone has it out for us and our ranch. Someone violent and ruthless, with inscrutable motives that are anyone's guess. How do we catch a guy like that? With patrols and fingerprinting and constantly playing defense? That's the best we can do to keep our family safe?"

Ryan squeezed his shoulder. "Like I told you, we'll get this guy. I've got officers on the scene of the fire gathering evidence. With all the rain we've had lately, whoever did this had to have left tracks on the ground, coming and going. And the fire marshal is doing his thing, too. If he can pinpoint the accelerant the perp used, then maybe we have our first lead."

Brett breathed through his frustration until he'd collected himself. "You should know that I'm going to do everything in my power to catch this guy myself."

Ryan's eyes narrowed. "Within the purview of the law, is what you meant, right? You're not going to go vigilante on me, are you?"

Brett leveled a hard look at his brother. "I'm going to do whatever it takes to keep the mother of my child safe, so if you're worried about my methods, then I suggest you and the law find this bastard before I do."

CHAPTER ELEVEN

HANNAH WOKE FROM another restless night's sleep. The baby's flutters of movement had morphed into full-blown soccer matches in her belly, and he or she was quite fond of midnight game times—just in time for her to hear Brett arrive in his room after the nearly nightly patrols around the grounds that he continued to volunteer for.

She couldn't decide if the ranch was really in that much danger or if he was trying to avoid her. Maybe he just loved riding around the ranch in the dark, for all she knew. Either way, the effect was the same: she was rarely ever alone with him anymore. But once she heard him enter his room after midnight each night, she couldn't go back to sleep because she was too busy listening.

It was torture on her overactive libido to hear his shower water start, and to imagine him stripping down, his muscles sore from a long night of riding. So many times, she'd knelt in her bed facing the wall, her fist up and ready to knock…right up until she thought better of it. Ever since their near-kiss that first night, he'd been polite and attentive, but emotionally distant. That was probably for the better because the more she'd gotten to know him, the more those same fears that Lori had guessed during their *pros and cons* game that first day at the ranch came rushing back to her in full force.

Not fears about Brett's indiscriminate pantie-melting charm, because she knew better now that he was no longer a partying womanizer. She had complete trust in him and in his assertion that his priorities and attitude had permanently changed from the man she'd hooked up with in the club. True, her physical attraction to him was even more potent than the night they'd slept together, but beyond that, she genuinely *liked* him. And that, in a nutshell, was her fear. It would be so easy for her fall for Brett Colton—and fall hard and fast in a forever kind of way.

His bedroom was silent this morning, which probably meant he'd caught only a few hours' sleep before rising to tackle the daily ranch chores. She pressed her palm to the wall, sending him a silent greeting, then emerged from her bedroom to find a tray holding a fresh biscuit, jam and a carafe of milk. Edith's doing. Ever since Hannah's first morning at the Lucky C and the terrible morning sickness she'd experienced, Edith had gone out of her way to make sure Hannah was comfortable and nausea-free.

No more eggs, ever, and coffee was now prepared on the front porch, which had turned out to be a welcome improvement for the ranch workers and Coltons, Edith had told her, because they no longer had to take off their boots to refill their mugs. And every morning, Hannah woke to find a tray of stomach-settling food in her sitting room. Whether it was from Edith and Maria's ministrations, or because her morning sickness was finally subsiding as the pregnancy books professed, Hannah was feeling stronger and less sick with every passing morning. She could proudly say she hadn't thrown up in a whole week, since her second day at the ranch.

As she nibbled the biscuit, she looked out over the ranch and watched the men and women work—cattle being moved, big machines moving alfalfa and feed. She gave a little gasp of surprise when Brett appeared in her field of view. Dressed in a black cowboy hat, a camo-green T-shirt and jeans, he strode over the grounds talking into a radio, a clipboard in his other hand and Rafe walking by his side, consulting his own clipboard.

She stood at the balcony door, eating jam right out of the jar, her eyes on Brett, studying, yearning. Probably, he was right that they should leave well enough alone. Sex and romance would overcomplicate their relationship, damage it, even, because relationship statistics weren't on their side. The odds of them starting a romantic relationship that was lasting were minuscule. Who did that? Who met at a club, had wicked animal sex, didn't bother exchanging phone numbers, got pregnant, and then ended up falling in love? That was crazy talk.

With her mind on Brett and their future, she emerged from her suite in search of breakfast. The door to Greta's suite was open. She'd been staying at the ranch on weekends, to give her dad moral support. When Hannah passed her door, she saw Greta standing in the sitting room of her suite, holding a paper, a hand over her mouth and a worried expression weighing in her eyes.

Hannah paused midstep. "Greta? You okay?"

With a gasp, Greta jumped, her hands flying up and the envelope fluttering to the ground along with what looked like a newspaper clipping.

Hannah rushed forward to pick up the fallen papers. "Sorry. I didn't mean to startle you."

Greta swooped down and snatched up the papers before Hannah could. "It's okay. I just… I got something in the mail that rattled me."

Hannah angled her face to look at the newspaper clipping Greta held. It was a copy of Greta and Mark's engagement announcement. The photograph was circled in a red pen and a large red X crossed out Greta's face. Her eyes were gouged out.

"What the…" Hannah said.

Greta pressed the clipping to her chest, hiding it from view. "I'm sure it's nothing."

"This isn't nothing, Greta. Are there any indications of who sent it?"

Greta walked to the sofa and sank onto it. "Probably one of Mark's ex-girlfriends. He has a lot of them."

Hannah wasn't sure where to start—at the pain dripping from Greta's admission that Mark had a lot of ex-girlfriends, or the fact that one of them might be crazy enough to send an anonymous threatening letter to Greta, despite how much she and the Coltons had gone through in the past month.

Hannah assumed a seat next to Greta. "Whoever did this, why would they send it here and not your apartment or Mark's apartment?"

She gestured to a tall chest of drawers near the door where it looked like a stack of mail sat. "I still get a fair amount of mail here. Edith collects it and puts it in here for when I pass through. The postmark is the downtown Tulsa post office."

"You should show Ryan. If someone has it out for you, then it's best to start an official paper trail now."

Instead of heeding Hannah's advice, she crumpled the newspaper clipping up and tossed it in the wastepaper bin by the bed. "Like I said. It's probably just a jealous ex-girlfriend."

"Do you really believe that? I don't think there are as many crazy ex-girlfriends floating around this world as television shows and movies make there out to be."

At that moment, Mavis chose to walk by, a laundry basket on her hip. Could she have done this? After planting that Bible in Hannah's room, she wouldn't put it past Mavis to do something like this to Greta if she got it in her head that Greta was a sinner, too. The thought of it made Hannah spitting mad.

"Maybe not, but who else could it be?" Greta said. "Regardless, something this minor isn't worth worrying my brothers or dad over. They have enough on their minds."

After a deep breath, Greta gave a whole body shake, as if sloughing off her worry.

"You should at least talk to Mark," Hannah said.

Greta winced. "Maybe. But until I decide what to do, don't tell anyone, okay?"

Hannah gathered her in a hug. They hadn't spent much time together or been able to bond since Hannah came to live at the ranch, but Greta was clearly rattled and a hug seemed like the perfect gesture to let her know she wasn't alone. "If you want to talk more, I'm here. Even if it's just about Mark and his exes. I mean, I can relate. Look at the man in my life right now. Brett and I aren't even romantically involved and I still don't want to know how many exes he has."

A halfhearted smile spread on Greta's face. "That's an easy answer—zero. He never dated anyone long enough to consider them exes."

Hannah chuckled. "Comforting. Thank you. I feel

so much better now about the odds of convincing him to give a relationship with me a try." Hannah's face instantly heated. "I didn't mean that. I mean, I did. I do, because he's amazing, but—"

Greta braced her arms on Hannah's shoulders. "Your secret's safe with me. And here's some advice—give Brett some time. The accident he was in four months ago really scared him. He hasn't been the same since. I know my dad and brothers are hard on him, but he's trying his best to turn his life around. He's a good man."

"I agree. A very good man. Thank you."

They shared a smile.

"No, thank *you* for poking your head in here," Greta said. "We should go out together sometime. Maybe you'd like to go shopping one day? We could look at baby clothes, and maybe register for your baby shower."

Hannah leaned back and stared at the ceiling. "Oh, goodness, I haven't given any thought to that at all."

"I'd love to plan one for you. It'd help take my mind off my worries about Mom and postponing my wedding. Please say you'll let me."

Hannah hugged her again, because she looked as if she needed as many hugs as she could get. Hannah couldn't imagine how difficult the past month had been on Greta. For as distant and strained as Brett's relationship was with their mother, she and Greta had clearly been close.

"I'd love for you to do that. And I'd love to go shopping with you. Just name the day and time."

Greta sniffed. "Thank you for giving me something to look forward to."

After another round of hugs, Hannah gave an excuse of being hungry for breakfast, then stomped down the grand staircase, through the formal living room, through the servants' wing and down the stairs to the basement where the laundry room was located.

"Mavis Turnbolt, are you down here?"

She was greeted with nothing but silence, save for the hums and rattles of the running washer and dryer from the laundry room tucked under the stairs. She poked her head around every corner of the basement, but found no one. Back up the stairs and through the house she went, room by room, angry and determined not to let Mavis get away with any more passive-aggressive threats.

Before today, Hannah hadn't yet ventured into the wing of the house where Big J's and Abra's suites were, nor had she seen the crime scene yet, but that was exactly where she found Mavis—in the sitting room of Abra's suite, threading a gauzy, pale fabric through a long white curtain rod and muttering to herself. Bible verses from the sounds of it.

Abra's suite was awash in sand, cream and silver tones that could have graced a suite at a luxury resort in a desert oasis, from the simple, tight-looped pale rugs that looked as though they'd never been walked on to the elegant chaise lounge and potted palm tree near where Mavis was working.

Hannah surveyed the room, marveling at its beauty though it had been the scene of such a violent act a mere few weeks earlier. The family must have taken great pains to restore the room quickly, with the hope that Abra would return to it soon.

Thinking about everything the Coltons had suffered and that Mavis had poured salt into their wounds with her egregious behavior got Hannah's back up all over again. She barreled into the room, guns blazing. "Turn around and face me, Mavis."

Mavis gave a squeak and whirled around, the curtain rod in hand as though defending herself. "You frightened me," she seethed.

"It's time for you to own up to your own sins, Miss High-and-Mighty. I know it was you who sent that newspaper clipping to Greta."

She kicked at the curtain fabric pooling on the floor over her shoes. "Excuse me?"

Hannah strode closer. "Don't play innocent. You know exactly what I mean."

"I don't, but you'd best keep your distance from me. I don't suffer unrepentant whores well."

Oh, the nerve of this one. Hannah jerked the curtain rod out of her hand. "Is that another threat? What are you going to do, attack me?"

The moment the words left her mouth, a chill came over Hannah. Brett's mother was viciously attacked and left for dead within the very room in which Hannah stood. The carpet was a light cream color and looked brand-new, as though it'd been replaced since the attack. Probably because it'd had Abra's blood on it.

Mavis certainly didn't seem to mind being in Abra's room. Could it be that Mavis was far more sinister than circling Bible verses that threatened death and mailing defaced engagement photographs? Was she capable of assaulting Abra? Hannah wasn't afraid of facing off against Mavis, even physically, but she also had a baby to think about.

Confronting a possible attempted murderer wouldn't be the safest plan, but the more she considered it, the less likely it seemed that Mavis was capable of such an overt act as physically attacking one of her employers. The Congregation of the Second Coming preferred threats and passive judgment. They preferred to leave the actual punishment to God.

"You'd better explain what business you have coming after me. Right now."

Hannah tossed the curtain rod behind her. "The business I'm talking about is the mutilated engagement announcement you sent to Greta. Was that some sort of sick and twisted threat or condemnation of her 'sinful ways'? Well, congratulations, you only succeeded in making yourself look like a petty, vindictive fool."

She speared a finger at Hannah. "I didn't send nothing to Greta, and you'd better stop spreading lies. You had better stop harassing me or I'll—"

"Or you'll what? Leave another Bible for me in my room with more circled verses implying I should be stoned to death for my sins?"

Mavis huffed, indignant, then hoisted a plastic laundry basket onto her hips. "The thought crossed my mind. Heathens need all the divine help they can get. Especially one of Satan's disciples who's carrying a bastard in her womb."

With that, Mavis brushed past Hannah, bumping her belly hard with the laundry basket.

Hannah leaped back, her arms around her belly, protective. Though she knew better than to let herself be drawn in to Mavis's vitriol, the last shreds of Hannah's control snapped at the rough treatment. Nobody physically trespassed against her growing baby and got away with it. She stormed after Mavis, seeing red.

"Don't use that term in this house. And while you're at it, don't you ever speak of my baby again."

Mavis sniggered and pushed out a side entrance of the house, onto the wraparound porch. "And why not? This house is a den of sin. Do you think it's an accident that so much tragedy has befallen this place? God punishes sin, and you'd best not forget it."

Hannah raised her open hand, ready to slap Mavis before she thought better of it. Instead she curled her fingers into a fist at her side. "Not my God," she said through clenched teeth.

Mavis whirled to face Hannah, an ugly sneer on her lips. "My point exactly. Maybe your parents ought to follow through with their plan to hire an exorcist to rid you of that demon you're hosting."

Of all the things. An exorcist? They wouldn't dare. The final threads of her composure snapped. She marched off the porch, hot on Mavis's heels. "Why would you accept income from a place that's a den of sin? What are you doing here, anyway?"

"I thought it was my duty to evangelize here, to get you all to see that sin and the Devil are not the way, but I'm done with that. There's no helping you or this cursed family and I'm not giving any more of the Coltons' dirty money to the church." She untied her apron and threw it on the ground. "When you're ready to repent, you know where to find salvation."

Big J strode up as Mavis stomped away. "What was that about?"

"Mavis Turnbolt just quit."

"Hmph. Never did like that sourpuss." He swiped the discarded apron from the ground and put it over his neck. "Well, now that you're doing the ranch's books, I suppose I'm in search of a new job around here. I think I'm going to need a bigger apron, though."

Despite herself, Hannah smiled; he looked so silly and the thought of a big old burly cowboy like him fussing over the laundry was so outrageous. "I don't think you'd last a day. Better leave the laundry to me and Edith while you undertake the task of finding someone new. Just don't hire anybody else from my parents' cult, like Mavis is."

They strolled together toward the office, Big J still with that silly apron on. "Your parents belong to a cult?"

"I used to call it a church, but I know better now. I struck out on my own the day I turned eighteen, without any real knowledge of how the world worked. I got a job at a drugstore and then another at a diner, just to make ends meet. My parents weren't pleased by my life choices, but when my father was forced to retire from working the feed store that he and my mother own, due to his arthritis, I sucked up my pride and took over management of the store. I figured when my mother retired, too, I'd buy it from them and I went to college so I could learn how to be a good business owner and manage the store's finances properly."

"And then you got pregnant."

They'd stopped in front of the steps that led to the office. "Yes. Everything changed."

He set a hand on her shoulder, then leaned in and kissed her cheek. "For the better. Because now we have you here."

She untwisted the apron string around Big J's neck. "Agreed. One hundred percent. I love it here."

And though she'd originally planned to move away as soon as she got her first paycheck, she couldn't imagine leaving now.

"Has my son asked you to marry him yet?"

Big J had asked her that same question a few times already. Brett had said his father was increasingly forgetful, but this was the first evidence Hannah had seen of it. "No. And I'm glad he hasn't because I'd turn him down. The only reason I would ever marry is for love."

And even though she was half in love with the man already, it wasn't enough to build a marriage on. Especially not when he didn't return her feelings.

"Ah. Well, he's got time to persuade you before the baby gets here. Say, is it a boy or a girl? I can't remember if Brett told me."

Another red flag went up in her mind. "We talked about that last night at dinner. We're not sure if it's a boy or a girl yet. We'll find out later this month at the ultrasound appointment."

"That's right. We did talk about it. Riding patrol last night with Brett dulled my mind, I'm afraid."

Hannah made a mental note to talk to Brett about his father. Perhaps letting Big J go out on patrol was too taxing a job. She was definitely going to caution Edith against letting him get anywhere near the laundry chores. "It's okay. It was a long night for me, too, worrying about you all out there in the dark."

"You don't need to worry about us. We'd welcome the chance to meet up with the attacker on our land again. Teach them about the consequences of doing harm to the Colton family."

His words chilled Hannah. What if they did confront the attacker? What would they do? Certainly not vigilante justice. She had to hope.

He gestured toward the office. "How's the job going? You making do all right? Do you have any questions?"

"I'm loving my new job. Thank you. The books are

complicated, but I'm getting my system in place one step at a time." She debated mentioning to him about the discrepancy, then decided to wait until she'd talked to Brett.

He patted her hand. "You're a good girl. I think I'm going to go grab some coffee. You want any?"

She couldn't decide if he was merely having a bad morning, or if his memory lapses were something his children needed to worry about. She hated to add to Brett's burden, not when so much else was as stake around the ranch. "No, thanks."

"Say, I'm headed to the hospital this afternoon. What would you say about joining me? I know Abra's not conscious, but I'd like to think she can hear us. Meeting you, hearing about the baby, it might give her more of a reason to wake up and come back to us."

If Big J thought it would help Abra wake up, and would give her a reason to keep fighting to stay alive, then it was the least Hannah could do.

"I'd be honored."

CHAPTER TWELVE

THE THIN, FRAIL woman in the ICU bed didn't look a thing like Brett, nor Eric, who'd walked Big J and Hannah to Abra's room, nor any of her other children, really. Not only that, but she didn't *look* like she was capable of giving birth to five children, she was so bony and fragile-looking beneath the purple-and-cream-colored quilt covering her bed. Her skin was as translucent as tissue paper and her dark brown hair was going gray at the roots.

The room itself was peaceful. Little loving touches were all over, including the quilt, which looked homemade, innumerable cards and a large vase of flowers that adorned the table near the window. Hannah hung back with Eric at the door as Big J assumed the seat near Abra's head and took her hand.

"Honey, you've got a special visitor today and we've got something big to tell you. You're going to be so happy, just like we all are. We found out that Brett's going to be a father. The mother of his child is here to meet you. Hannah is her name. You're going to love her as much as we all do, I can guarantee it."

At Big J's urging, Hannah pulled a seat around to the other side of the bed and took Abra's hand. It was warm and full of life, yet smooth, as though she'd never worked a day of manual labor, despite living on a ranch for several decades. "Hello, Abra. It's so wonderful to meet you. I wish it was under different circumstances, but I want you to know that you're going to be a grandma again, in about eighteen weeks."

"We just want you to wake up, honey. The family isn't the same without you. Greta's putting her wedding plans on hold, waiting for her momma to help her out again." His voice caught on the last word. He brought a handkerchief out from his pocket and swabbed his eyes. "And we can't be disappointing Greta, not after all the trouble I went through to get us that baby girl."

Hannah cringed inwardly. No wonder Brett felt like a perpetual disappointment to his parents, with his dad talking about him as though he was nothing but a hindrance to them in their quest to have a daughter.

"What's going on here?"

Eric was gone and in his place at the door stood Brett, his eyes glinting with irritation.

Hannah's heart sank. He must have heard his father's unfortunate choice of words. Though she wished she could wrap her arms around him and soothe his torment, he didn't welcome her touch, and she'd do well to remember that.

She stood, feeling her own sudden surge of defensiveness.

"Your dad asked me to come with him, to tell your mom about the baby."

Her explanation did nothing to diffuse his defensiveness. If anything, his scowl intensified as he held his father's gaze. "I already have. I came and told her the day I found out."

Big J stroked a hand over Abra's hair. "Oh, well, now, that's even better. We've got to keep reminding her of all she has to live for until she wakes up. What are you doing in town, Brett? It's a surprise to see you here."

"I was in town getting a contract notarized for Geronimo's sale, and I thought, since I was already nearby, I'd stop by the hospital. Could I talk to you in the hall, please, Hannah?"

"Sure. Of course."

With a stiff stride, she followed him down the hall. He looked like she felt, his shoulders and back tight, radiating frustration. He couldn't possibly be that upset with her for coming to see his mother, could he?

As soon as they were out of earshot from his mother's room, she said to his back, "My coming here means a lot to your dad," she said. "There was no way I was going to tell him no when he asked." When he kept walking she snagged his arm. "Don't be upset with me. Please."

Brett spun to face her. "I'm not angry with you. I just…" He shook his head, his gaze on the floor. "I can't believe my dad keeps saying stuff like that. You'd think, after all these years, they'd stop thinking about me and my brothers as 'everything they went through' in order to have a girl. That's so screwed up. Just once, I'd like to hear my dad say he's happy to have me as his son. Just once."

Well, that explained that. She stroked a hand over his hair. "He does love you. I can see it in his eyes, and in the way he's showing me such kindness. He loves you and your brothers, but I know what you mean. I cringed when he said that, too."

He glanced up at her. "They have the most miserable marriage. I've never understood it. He loves her so much, and he would've never divorced her, yet he had at least one affair. Who knows how many? It's like the two of them are doomed to be locked in an eternally dysfunctional bond."

He sighed, his shoulders slumping. "I hate how angry I am at her. The last words we spoke before she was attacked were said in anger. I don't know how to forgive her for the years she neglected us all, as though we meant nothing to her. After she had Jack, my dad wanted a girl, and for whatever twisted reason that I don't understand, because she loathed being a mother, she kept popping out babies for him, trying for that little princess. Eric, then Ryan, and you can imagine how distraught they both were when they had me. I've been a disappointment since the day I came out of her womb and they've never let me forget it."

"Why didn't you move away from the ranch, or at least to another house on the property?"

"My mother was gone more than she was home. She only came home from her travels abroad in Europe because of Greta's engagement party because she had to keep up appearances. I lived at the Big House so my dad wouldn't be alone. And the less noble part of me—the me before my car accident—felt like my parents owed me, that I was entitled to this huge house and a chef and a housekeeper and a laundress."

Hannah nodded. She could see how he'd feel that way, especially before his life-changing accident. "Whoever attacked your mom chose the perfect time because she was rarely ever home. The attacker knew about the engagement party."

"The police thought about that, too. The only problem is that everybody knew about it. It was in the newspapers and local society pages. My mom made sure to splash it everywhere that her little girl, her precious only daughter, was getting married."

"I've only known Greta for a little while, but I bet she didn't appreciate being put up on a pedestal like that."

A bit of the fight drained out of him. "Got that right. But she and Mother were still close, anyway, especially as Greta got older."

She touched his hand. "You're still full of a lot of resentment. That's a heavy burden to be carrying in your heart."

He cocked his head and looked at her for a long time. "I've forgiven both my parents. My dad, especially, a long time ago, but my mother, too. You would think that choosing to forgive someone would take away the anger, but it doesn't. Not completely. I'm not sure I can ever let go of it all. I just hope my mother wakes up so she and I can keep working toward finding peace with each other. This can't be how it ends between us."

She wrapped her arms around him and squeezed, burying her face in his chest. "She will wake up, Brett. We just have to keep praying."

She knew exactly what he meant about the difference between forgiveness and acceptance, because she was struggling in the same way with her parents. If one of her parents were grievously injured and she had to live with the possibility that they might never reconcile, she'd be just as torn up as Brett was.

His dropped his face and nuzzled the top of her head. "I'm sorry I snapped at you earlier. Seeing her here, hearing my dad go on about Greta, leaves me feeling so raw. I just want to be a better parent than my parents were to me."

Standing in a shadowy corner of the hallway, locked

in an embrace with the man who'd shared his deepest, rawest feelings and fears with her, she'd never felt closer to another person before. "You will be. And I'm going to be right by your side, trying my best, too. We're a team, you and me."

After a long, quiet moment of connection, of breathing and being in each other's arms, Brett lifted his face and kissed Hannah's cheek. His hand stroked her hair. "I hope this comes out the way I intend it to in my head, but forgive me if it doesn't. I can't believe how lucky I am that when I made the biggest mistake of my life and knocked up a random girl I hooked up with in a club, that it turned out to be you. I mean, of all the women in the world, I can't imagine going through all this with anybody else. It blows my mind, how lucky a man that makes me. We are going to give this baby such an incredible life."

Her eyes crowded with tears that slipped down her cheek and soaked into the fabric of Brett's shirt. "It's the same for me, you know. I had no idea that the man I picked up at a club because he had a killer smile and a tight butt would turn out to be my own personal hero."

"Hero?"

She smoothed her nose along his jaw. "You swooped in and rescued me exactly when I needed it most."

He *tsk*ed, his puff of breath tickling her ear. "It doesn't count as rescuing for a man to take care of the mother of his child, as he's supposed to do, anyway."

"It felt like rescuing, all the same."

She angled her face up to kiss his cheek, but as her lips touched his skin, he turned and captured her mouth with a tender kiss. Her whole body lit up with sensation. She wound her arms around his neck and kissed him back, reverently, trying to let him know without words that he really was her hero.

This kiss was different from their kisses during their first encounter. Those had been reckless and sloppy—a means to satisfying a wholly selfish pleasure. That first kiss hadn't carried any of the connection they'd now forged. She wasn't kissing a hot guy from the nightclub. She was kissing the father of her child.

His hands came up to cradle her face. With a hum of approval, she swept her tongue over his closed lips, wanting more. His body went rigid, and then, as if something had snapped inside him, he pressed her to the wall with a growl, his kiss turning wicked, needful. When she opened her mouth for him, he took it, plundering her with his tongue. Her body came alive with a hunger so potent, so desperate, that it was all she could do to cling to him and let him take from her what he demanded.

As abruptly as he'd initiated the kiss, he stopped it. Still cradling her head, he kept his face close, breathing hard through parted lips as he met her searching gaze. "We can't do this. I can't do this."

"Of course we can."

He dropped his hands and peeled away from her.

She pressed her palms to the wall behind her, finding her footing and relearning how to breathe.

He propped a forearm on the wall opposite her, his head bent, and let out a sigh that seemed to well up from the deepest, darkest depths of his soul. "I shouldn't have done that. I'm sorry. It's just that I'm finding you harder and harder to resist."

Her heart gave a painful squeeze. She wished he hadn't apologized for doing what they both wanted. "That's a good thing."

His gaze shot up to lock with hers. Gone was the raw need and open heart he'd shared with her only a few moments ago, and it its place was a mask that might as well have been made of iron. "No, it really isn't. Tell me how starting a physical relationship helps us, long term, as coparents? We're in such a good place right now, why would we risk ruining everything?"

"Sometimes risk is worth it."

"Okay, yes, but not in this case. Because what if things don't work out between us, which is practically a statistical inevitability, and you leave the ranch? Then what happens when the baby's born—I get weekend visitation rights? You already made up your mind to move out as soon as you have the money to afford it. At least if we stay friends, I have a better chance of convincing you to live at Lucky C permanently. We can be a family. It might be unconventional, but it's the best-case scenario to allow me to be a full-time father to my child."

She hated that he was right about so many points, but she couldn't shake the idea that this was a time to think with their hearts, not their brains. "Your whole life, your family's made you feel like you're not good enough, and you let that seep into your thinking and your self-worth. You know how I know that? Because the same happened to me, growing up, and then with this pregnancy. I've never been holy enough or repentant enough. I've never lived up to others' standards."

"You're more than enough, Hannah."

"You're more than enough for me, too. These past few weeks, I've come to care about you. A lot. The more time I spend around you, the more I want to spend. You make me laugh. You make me feel cherished. You make me feel like I'm where I'm supposed to be. I'm not leaving the ranch, Brett. I'm here for good."

The iron mask remained steadfastly in place. "That's easy for you to say today, but how about in a year or two? What happens if we don't work out romantically, and in a couple years down the road you want to start dating again? Are you still going to live with me then? Think about it, Hannah."

She touched his chest, but she may as well have been touching a statue. "I don't want to be afraid to try."

He sidestepped out of reach. "It's not about fear. It's about doing the right thing, the smart thing. Doesn't matter what your hormones or my hormones are telling us to do, I have a responsibility to you and the baby and I'm not going to go mucking it up by taking advantage of you when you're in a vulnerable state. That's something the old Brett would've done, but I'm not that loser anymore."

And with that, he strode away, down the hall, past the open door to his mother's room, and disappeared from view.

THE WAY HANNAH saw it, there were only two possible reasons that Brett was killing himself to protect the ranch by patrolling the ranch's eleven thousand acres at all hours of the day and night except for the time he spent mounting security cameras and motion-sensor lights on every building, and changing locks on all the doors of the Big House. Either he wasn't being honest with her and the others about what had happened the night of the hunting blind fire in the backcountry or he was desperate to avoid Hannah.

In the days since their kiss at the hospital, she'd barely

seen him except for glimpses of him stolen from her balcony. He was strung out and on edge all the time. She longed to reach out to him, to soothe his worries and get to the heart of what was bothering him, but getting him alone had proved impossible. Even if she could, she wasn't sure she'd try to kiss him again, he was so deadset on the two of them not getting involved romantically.

Rather than succumb to sleep only to have the baby wake her with its midnight soccer practice, she'd taken to staying up late and using the time to sift through the previous year's bank statements, checks and ledgers, doing as much as she could without the benefit of the computer spreadsheets she'd created. If only she hadn't sold her laptop to pay her student loan, she might be able to avoid the ranch office altogether, thereby avoiding the threat of Rafe stopping by to leer at her under the auspices of offering help.

As midnight neared, her eyes started to burn. She removed her reading glasses and rubbed her eyes. She hadn't finished going through the entire previous year's finances, but she'd gone through another two months' worth of data and had discovered another two thousand dollars to be missing, which put the total close to twenty thousand dollars and change.

She hadn't talked to Brett about the accounting discrepancies because she still wasn't sure if there really was something illegal happening or if she was overthinking the situation. After all, of the two possible scenarios—embezzlement or bad math and typos courtesy of Big J's lack of formal business training—it didn't take a genius to figure out which would, statistically, be the more likely truth. Until she had unequivocal proof of wrongdoing, she refused to burden Brett with her suspicions.

She was gathering the papers into the manila envelope when the baby started in with a thump-thump-flutter rhythm against her ribs. She rubbed the top of her growing baby bump as she hauled herself up from the floor using the sofa arm as support. "A bit early, isn't it, little one?"

She tucked the envelope in the hiding spot behind the vanity, debating how to kill time until the baby simmered down and she dared to attempt sleep. She had a hand on the television remote control when she spotted her phone. Tonight was Lori's night to close at the café.

Can you talk? she texted.

As she waited for a reply, she grabbed the jam jar and a spoon from the tray on the coffee table. Tonight's late-night snack had been a lemon-poppy-seed scone. The scone was long gone but the jar of Maria's homemade strawberry jam was still half full. Her eyes rolled back in her head as the first bite hit her tongue.

Her phone chimed. Sure. I just got home. Call me.

Lori picked up on the first ring. "What are you still doing awake?" she said.

Hannah swallowed another bite of jam and paced to the balcony door, looking out at the night. "Can't sleep. Baby's a midnight acrobat."

"How fun, though, right? To feel it move."

The ranch was quiet, though one of the motion-sensor lights on the barn had turned on. "I do love it."

"So then why don't you sound happier? Is everything okay with your baby daddy?"

How could she explain it to Lori? Her relationship

with Brett was so complicated. "He's a great guy. Really great."

"What about that pantie-melting charm you were so worried about?"

"He really is charming, but he's not a player anymore. He's so committed to his family and to being a father. Almost to a fault. He's taking great care of me."

"And by taking care of you, you mean he's bringing you to screaming orgasms every night, right?"

"No. Not that. Not yet."

"His call or yours?"

"His."

Lori groaned. "Don't tell me he's an overthinker like you."

Of all the attributes she was discovering that she and Brett shared, she'd hadn't considered that one, but Lori had a point. "Little bit, yeah. But I've only been here a few weeks. There's time."

"Yes, except that you're a walking, breathing ball of lusty hormones who clearly has a mad crush on your baby daddy. Who happens to sleep *one wall away from you*."

Hannah swirled the spoon in her mouth, her lips kicking up in a smile. "There is that."

"Could you knock on the wall right now and wake him up? Or better yet, burst into his room wearing nothing but sexy lingerie?"

"I don't actually own any sexy lingerie, but I couldn't do that, anyway, because he's out."

"Uh-oh."

"Not like that. Some vandal's been tampering with the fences around the ranch, so he and some of the other men on the ranch have been conducting nightly patrols of the grounds."

"Oh, wow. That's not good. First his mother was attacked during a robbery the month before and now this. Hannah, sweetie, are you safe there?"

Wasn't that the million-dollar question? "I think so. Brett keeps telling me I am."

"I hear a *but*."

"But I don't know. Sometimes I get the weirdest vibes that someone's watching me."

"Creepy."

"Yeah, I know. I think I'm just psyching myself out because…" She debated the merits of sharing the accounting discrepancies with Lori, then decided against it. No need for her to worry.

"Because what?"

Hannah pressed her hand to the window, thinking fast for a reason that would satisfy Lori's curiosity. "A few of the workers swear they've seen ghosts on the prairie."

Lori snorted. "Remember, you're an overthinker. Of course you're psyching yourself out. You're staying in a new home where someone's been attacked and people are talking about ghost sightings. I'd be wigged out, too."

"That's my thought." She mindlessly scooped another spoonful of jam. It wasn't until she'd put the spoon in her mouth that she realized there hadn't been any jam on it. The jar was empty. Disgusted with her lack of self-control, she dropped the spoon into the jar and set it back on the tray.

"But if you ever start to feel unsafe for real, you know we've always got room for you here."

Hannah had briefly considered moving off the ranch until the culprit had been caught, but she'd dismissed the idea almost immediately, knowing that Brett would consider that a personal failure of his to be her and the baby's provider. Moving away would damage their fledgling partnership. Besides, she didn't yet own a car and had no idea how she'd get to and from the ranch every day to work if she moved back in with Lori.

"Thank you," Hannah said. "I'll keep that in mind, but every day I'm more sure I belong here."

"Okay, well, my offer stands."

"I love you, sweetie."

"Love you, too. Now start planning how you're going to seduce this new, gentlemanly Brett Colton before he steals your heart completely."

He already has. "I'll give it some more thought. And thanks for the sexual pep talk, as usual."

"That's what I'm here for."

When their call ended, Hannah navigated the touch screen of her phone to her photographs and checked out the shot she'd taken of the mystery woman. Really, it could be anyone. The daughter of one of the ranch workers, a girlfriend, one of the maids who worked for Jack. Anyone. But it looked an awful lot like Greta. Same length and color of hair, a similar build and same shape of her face.

If there had been a strange woman lurking about in broad daylight, then Hannah wouldn't have been the only person to spot her. *Others have spotted her. They think she's a ghost.*

With a shiver, Hannah dropped her phone back to the table where it was charging and walked to the balcony. After belting the robe she wore, she flung the French doors open and stepped outside. There were no ghosts in sight tonight, no lurking young women or would-be robbers. Just the balmy July night. The sky was cloudy, the half moon shrouded and casting only a faint gray glow over the roofs of the ranch buildings and the tips of the wild grasses.

The longer she stood outside, taking deep breaths, the stillness and peace of the ranch seeped into her bones. Then, in the distance, she spied movement, all shadows and darkness silhouetted in the moonlight. A tingle of fear crept up her spine.

That had to be Brett and Daniel coming home from patrol, didn't it? But what if it wasn't? What would she do if that was the perpetrator? She backed into a shadow on the balcony, hiding in plain sight from whoever it was who was approaching the ranch.

Then the clouds moved from in front of the moon and she saw that the movement was two horses, with men on them. That had to be Brett and Daniel. She strained her eyes, watching. When the riders crested a short rise, she made out their identities clearly. Her heart gave a flutter. She stepped from the shadows again and walked to the balcony railing.

It wasn't long after Hannah stepped to the rail that Daniel noticed her. He said something to Brett and gestured with his head. Brett's face shot up. His gaze locked onto Hannah. She raised a hand in a wave that he didn't return.

Daniel said something else to him, then tugged the reins of his horse and took off in a gallop toward the stable. Brett continued on a direct path to her. He cut such a fine figure on the horse, a rifle slung across his back on a strap.

The closer he got, the more she realized that he wasn't happy to see her. She kept a smile on her face and affection warming her features, but he looked worn to the bone, with dark circles under his eyes and a permanent frown on his lips.

He pulled his horse to a stop below her balcony, his gaze roving her body before settling on her face.

"Hi," she called, letting her hair cascade around her like she was some princess in a tower, greeting the knight who'd come to rescue her. "Long night?"

He shook his head and looked away. His lips parted, then closed again, as though he couldn't find the words to reply. "You shouldn't be out here."

She ignored his sour mood, clinging to her princess fantasy out of sheer stubbornness.

His horse sidestepped restlessly. He shifted the reins and made a clicking sound with his lips, bringing the horse back to standing still. "Your horse isn't nearly as tired as you are."

The next time he looked at Hannah, he wore a slight smile, his gaze still tired, but warmer. "This is Outlaw. And he's definitely as tired as I am. He's ready to get back to the stable, get cleaned up and go to sleep. A lot like me."

"Then go ahead and get Outlaw tucked in bed," she said. "I just wanted to say hello."

"You shouldn't be outside this late," he repeated.

She crossed her arms and swung a hip out in mock defiance. "Who's going to get to me all the way up here?"

She hadn't meant to say that as a challenge, but the moment the words fell from her lips, she got the craziest vision of him swinging off his horse and scaling the wall to reach her.

Frustration flashed across his face. "I don't know and that's what I'm afraid of."

His words and his concern were a reminder of why he and the others patrolled the property every night, and it wasn't because they enjoyed the sleepless nights. She wrapped her robe more tightly around her. He looked so beat down, and was working so darn hard to make sure everyone in his care was safe. It should be her climbing down the wall to reach him and be a balm for his troubles.

Her concern must have shown on her face because his expression softened. "Go on inside, Hannah. Get some rest. I didn't mean to make you worry."

He was right that she was worried, but more about him than anything else at the moment. This huge house, these thick walls, and the aura of family and love made her feel safer than she ever had before. Yes, Abra had been attacked in that same house only a month earlier, but whoever had done so had to be long gone.

He didn't wait for her reply before nudging his horse into motion again. Defying his command, she watched his proud, strong back move in the saddle until he reached the stable.

It only took her a moment of deliberation for her to decide what her next move was. She stopped by the bathroom in her suite, brushed her teeth and her hair, then stole from her room on quiet feet.

She really wasn't a fan of the dark house. It was eerie as all get-out, probably because she didn't yet feel 100 percent at home there. She didn't know the sounds or what every shadow meant. But she blocked the creepiness from her mind, flipped lights on as she moved from room to room, until she got to the kitchen.

Of all the spaces in the house, she loved the kitchen most of all. With its earth-tone color palette and cluttered counters and good smells and worn wood table in the corner, it felt like love. Like a big hug from Maria and Edith.

Grooming and settling his horse in for the night would take time, so she made herself a cup of tea and waited, imagining her child in this kitchen. She could see Maria and Edith doting on him or her, sneaking them tastes of the sweets they were making, chiding him for eating jam straight out of the jar like his mama. Such a comforting vision. Maybe Hannah would be there, too, doting and laughing and loving.

More than anything, she wanted to give her and Brett a chance at something real. Even if he wasn't ready to entertain the idea right now, they had all the time in the world. All she needed was a hefty dose of patience, of which she was in short supply at the moment.

When she heard the door open in the mudroom that sat between the kitchen and the back porch steps, she stood, her tea forgotten. Though she wanted to rush to him and throw her arms around his neck, she waited by the table until he'd come in the house and locked the door behind him.

When he saw her, one side of his lips kicked up in a tired smile. "I should've guessed a stubborn woman like you wouldn't take my advice and get some rest."

"Did you eat dinner?" she asked.

The last time they'd shared a meal was the night of the hunting blind fire. She loved dining with Big J, Edith and Maria, and sometimes Jack, Tracy and little Seth, but she missed Brett's conversation. She missed his smiles and levity.

"No. Not hungry."

To be fair, he didn't look hungry. He looked exhausted. But there was no better cure for that than some TLC. She poured him a glass of water as he emptied a flashlight, keys and a pocketknife from his pockets onto the counter.

Then she stepped close and held the glass out to him. "You're not taking care of yourself."

His lips pressed together, pulling into a straight line. "I'm managing fine, but thank you for caring." Still, he took the offered glass and drained it in a few gulps.

Anticipation and nerves made her heart pound as she inched closer. She slid an arm around his middle, her hand smoothing over the soft, worn flannel of his shirt. He gripped the empty glass hard, his knuckles going white. Then she set her cheek on his shoulder.

"You're a good man, Brett Colton."

With an incredulous huff, he averted his gaze.

Affection bloomed in her heart. She lifted the glass from his hand, though it took some coaxing to get his grip to ease, and set it on the counter. Then she cradled his cheek in her palm, her thumb scraping over thick stubble. Before she could overthink it, she angled her face up and let her nose brush along his jaw.

He wrenched his face away. "Woman, you're going to be the death of me," he growled.

Undeterred, she took his hand and pressed it to the curve of her flesh where her hip met her backside. "But what a way to go."

His fingers tightened over her flesh, gripping her with purpose. Even through the layers of fabric from her robe and nightgown, she felt his warmth, his strength. It was all she could do not to moan at the pleasure of finally—*finally, damn it*—feeling his hand on her body. Their kiss in the hospital hallway felt like a lifetime ago.

Chancing another bold move, she brought her hands to his shirt collar and slid the top button through the hole, releasing it. She moved to the next button.

"Hannah, please. We've been over this." His hand left her backside and clamped around her wrist, stilling her progress, but her mind crowded with memories of their one-night stand.

He'd cuffed his hands around her wrists that night, too. He'd pinned them over her head, positioned her against the wall in her living room and ripped her underwear off. He'd actually ripped them away from her body as though the idea of having her had turned him into a madman. She'd loved every second of it.

She allowed herself a quiet pant of arousal through her open mouth. The flesh between her thighs turned sensitive and tingly. She squeezed her inner muscles, wallowing in the tender, needy feeling the action evoked.

In one abrupt motion, he released her wrist and backed away from her, as though he'd noticed her reaction. He prowled to the sink and braced his hands against the counter. His jaw was tight, his eyes hard as he gazed on the darkness beyond the window.

"Would it be so bad for me to take care of you for once? Since you're doing such a good job taking care of me?"

"We're having a child together. We can't afford to be careless with our relationship." His words were clipped, his tone little more than a growl.

And there they were again, back to that same circular argument they seemed doomed to have for all of eternity. Careless or not, she was determined to be the kind of person who took chances—and there was nothing she wanted more than to take a chance on her and

Brett. "We can't just ignore what we want from each other indefinitely."

"I'm not willing to jeopardize everything because I want you in my bed."

Heat and need raged through her body with the force of a wildfire. There was no way she was giving up this midnight seduction after that admission. *You're going down, cowboy. You just don't know it yet.*

With her eyes on his back and the stiff set of his shoulders, she untied the belt of her robe. It fell open, cool air swirling over her body, tightening her nipples.

"So you think this is just going to go away on its own?" She shrugged the robe off her shoulders. The silken fabric licked at her legs as it pooled on the floor.

His grip on the counter turned his knuckles white. His jaw, his gaze, everything about him was stone. "This?"

As if he hadn't just admitted that he wanted her. As if the air around them didn't crackle with lust, with the urgent hunger to get their hands on each other, to connect on the most intimate level a man and woman could— hearts, bodies and minds.

"The need, Brett." Her whisper came out strained, as though the desire implicit in her words were a visceral thing, jagged and coarse. "The need."

Her body quivered with the craving to press her nude body against his back and wrap her hands around his waist, feeling that hard, male body beneath her palms. It would be so easy to wrap her arms around his waist and unlatch his belt, then set her fingers to work on the button and zipper of his jeans. It would be so easy to show him exactly what she meant in a few short moves.

Instead, she stayed the course of her seduction and pulled her nightdress over her head, then added it to the pile on the floor. Cool air swirled around her breasts. But either Brett hadn't heard the rustle of her clothes being shed or he was choosing to ignore it because he didn't flinch, nor turn his focus from the window.

Though every molecule in her body was straining for contact, she pivoted on the ball of her foot. She stepped over the pile of clothes, leaving them on the floor for him to trip on, and walked with silent, measured steps toward the hall that led to the stairs.

She didn't speak until she was in the hall, far enough away that if he turned, he'd see flesh, but only a glimpse before she vanished around the corner. "Good night, Brett. Sweet dreams."

She felt him watching her mount the stairs and added a little sway to her hips. His footsteps stopped at the base of the staircase, but she forced herself to keep her face pointed straight ahead, and forced her legs to keep moving. *Come on, cowboy. Follow me...*

CHAPTER THIRTEEN

HANNAH HELD HER breath as she turned the doorknob to her suite, straining to hear the sound of his footsteps, but the house was silent. Was he really going to let her walk away? Was he really so determined to keep her at arm's length that her naked body didn't provoke him to action? How depressing.

She cast a final look down the hallway, but all she saw was darkness. Fine, then. Okay. Maybe her seduction technique hadn't been as effective as she'd thought. There was plenty of time to prove to him that their relationship was worth taking a chance on. Her heart giving a painful squeeze, she stepped into her room and closed the door behind her.

At a loss for what to do next, she stood for a moment in the middle of the room in the darkness, then walked to the nearest window, her attention on the moon. Pressing her palm to the cool glass, she allowed her mind to go blank, to think of nothing but how vast the world was and how breathtaking the moon looked shining down on all of creation.

The suite door flew open and banged against the wall. With a gasp of surprise, she spun around. Brett's silhouette filled the threshold. In his hand, he gripped the bunched-up wad of her clothes. "Do you have any idea how crazy you're making me?"

"What?" she breathed.

He kicked the door closed again, then prowled in her direction, tossing her clothes on a chair as he moved. "Do you have any idea how badly I want you right now? How badly I've been wanting you since that first night you came to the ranch?"

"I…"

And then he was before her, his face a savage cut of shadows and moonlight. "I've been working so hard to resist you, but while I was fighting to stay strong and trying to put our baby's needs before my own, you were stripping off your clothes behind my back."

He crowded against her, pressing her against the glass door, his eyes dark and volatile. She shivered at the first contact of the cold against her warm skin, but all thoughts of discomfort vanished at the feel of his jean-clad erection pressing into her belly.

One of his hands came up to cup her neck. The other gripped her hip. "You're making it so damn hard for me to do the right thing."

She opened her mouth to protest, but his lips descended over hers, hot and demanding. His hands gripped her hips, locking her body against his. She threaded her fingers into his hair. The rush of getting what she'd been longing for made her knees weak. She opened her mouth for him, mating her tongue with his.

While his mouth plundered hers, his hand slid over her backside, then down to her thigh. He cupped the back of her knee and jerked her leg up against his hip. The metal latch of his belt poked into her, rough and unforgiving against the stretched, tender skin of her belly. She reached her hands between them and unlatched the belt, the sides of her hands rubbing against the impressive erection that even twenty weeks later was still emblazoned in her mind. Her body's center pulsed at the memory.

She pushed the buckle off to the side, then closed her fingers around the button of his jeans. A flick of her fingers and a tug of the zipper made his pants gape open, his erection pressing against dark cotton. She curled her fingers around it.

He broke off the kiss, growling out as his hands closed around her wrists and pinned her hands against the glass near her shoulders, such a similar movement to that first time that she cried out with satisfaction.

Breathing hard through flared nostrils, he gazed down at her. "You need to know something first."

She remembered this with perfect clarity, too—the way he took control in the bedroom, rough but not too rough, brazenly confident right to the edge of smugness. The perfect mix of wicked and kind. She struggled against his hold on her wrists just for the pleasure of him tightening his grip. He pinned her lower body with his hips and slid her hands higher against the glass until her body was stretched out and utterly at his mercy.

She heard the surprise in his throaty growl when he said, "You like that, don't you?"

The question proved that he hadn't been exaggerating when he'd admitted to not remembering much about their one-night stand, because that night she'd proved to him over and over again how much she got off on his proclivity for dominance, for making a woman submit to his will. For her answer tonight, she strained her neck to brush her lips against his, though she could barely make contact and he made no move to get closer.

Before she could catch her breath, he took her mouth

in an aggressive kiss, his tongue a hard, wet instrument of his mastery. This time, when he wrenched his face away, breaking the kiss, he was breathing as hard as she was.

"If we do this, then you'd better be ready for me to fight for you." His voice was low and harsh, as though he was speaking through clenched teeth. "Because I'm warning you right now, Hannah, that I don't take my responsibility to you lightly. And despite the carelessness of the first time we slept together, I don't take this lightly, either. Not anymore."

"Neither do I."

He nodded. "I want you and the baby here at the ranch with me and I'm going to fight for that, even if sleeping together proves to be one complication too many. You get in bed with me tonight, then I'm expecting you to fight for us, too. Do you understand? Can you accept those terms?"

His words wrapped around her, carrying with them the unmistakable weight of his fear and his determination, and so much honor that it made her heart burst with love. She met his hard gaze. "This is me fighting for us, and I plan to keep fighting. You know how stubborn I am."

This time when he kissed her, his aggression was laced with tenderness. "I love the sound of that." He brought her arms around his neck, then moved his hands over her back. "There's one more thing we need to discuss first," he said.

She tipped her head back, battling a sudden rush of frustration. "I'm going to self-combust pretty soon if we keep talking. This pregnant lady needs some action, cowboy."

His lips twitched, as though he was battling a smile. His hand moved between her thighs to cup her mound. "You mean, this kind of action?"

She whimpered. Bracing a hand on the back of his neck, she spread her legs wider. "That's a good start."

One of his fingers pushed between her folds. "You're so wet for me, and so on edge." His finger made a lazy swirl around her most sensitive flesh, rendering her limbs weak and trembling. She squeezed her eyes closed and rode out the sensation. "Do you need to come right now so you can relax and enjoy everything else I'm going to do to you?"

Without waiting for a reply, he added a second finger and pushed them inside her.

Her fingernails dug into his neck. All she could manage was another whimper.

"I'm gonna take that as a yes."

He braced an arm around her waist as his right hand worked a relentless pattern of thrusts and swirls that shattered any last vestiges of her composure. She threw her head back, arching, rocking her body in time with his movements.

"That's it. Take what you need."

But she was incapable of taking anything. All she could do was cling to him and feel and reach for the relief he offered against the near-painful pressure building inside her.

He bathed her neck and shoulders with kisses and nips of his teeth. When she was panting and desperate and so, so close, he sucked her earlobe, then said in a gravely whisper, "I want every inch of you."

Her whole body rippled with pleasure at the idea.

And she thought she'd been ready to combust before. Her body turned into molten heat.

"Yes," she said between labored breaths.

She rose onto tiptoes, the balls of her feet pushing, pressed her back against the wall, her shoulders rising. Everything she was, inside and outside, lifting and tensing and building. Here it came, closer, closer...

Her mouth opened with the beginning of a whimper that died in her throat when he slipped a third finger inside her. Clamping his other hand on her hip, he pulled her down and thrust his fingers up with a force that tipped her right over the edge.

He stabilized her body between his own and the wall, his teeth grazing her neck, as she lost herself to the release and succumbed to pulse after pulse of ecstasy.

When she'd recovered her wits, he removed his fingers from her body. His lips lingered on her shoulder, kissing and soothing. "That better?" he murmured.

She threaded her fingers into his hair and held him tight. "You have no idea how badly I needed that."

Raising his head, he gave her a wolfish smile. "Oh, I had a pretty good idea." His hand cupped her breast, toying with her nipple. She hooked a hand around the back of his neck and pulled his face to hers, kissing him hard and wet, stroking her tongue against his in his mouth.

Tired of having her access to his skin hindered by his clothes when he had full access to her body, she made short work of his shirt buttons and pushed the shirt off his shoulders. He let her work the rest of his clothes off as he explored her body with his hands and lips.

"Anything we can't do, with you being pregnant? I don't know much about that stuff."

"Me, neither. We're both new at this. I think we can

do whatever we want, as long as you don't put much pressure on my belly."

"Got it. I'll be gentle."

"Not too gentle, I hope. I might be pregnant, but I'm not breakable."

He wrapped his hand around her leg and jerked it up against his thigh, his lips near hers. "Have I been treating you like you're breakable?"

"No. Just making sure."

His free hand cupped her breast, plumping her nipple as his mouth descended over it. He sucked her good and hard, getting his teeth involved until she cried out. "Who would've thought that my sweet little Hannah likes it a little rough?" he crooned against her skin.

Holding back a teasing comment about his terrible memory of their one-night stand, knowing he might take it wrong and feel guilty, she took hold of his erection and gave him a long, slow tug that twisted his mouth into a crooked scowl. "Sweet little Hannah needs this. Now."

He took her by the wrist and pulled her behind him to the sofa. When they arrived, he guided her in front of him, facing the sofa. "Climb up. On your knees."

She obeyed his command, kneeling on the cushions. He pressed his hand between her shoulder blades, pushing her gently down until her chest rested on the sofa back.

His next touch was his lips against her spine, kissing a path down.

"You ready for me?" His words were thick and raspy. He might have complete command over her body and her pleasure, but she could tell he was hanging on to that careful control by only a tenuous thread.

"Yes," she whispered. "Take me, please, Brett."

But rather than what she expected, his lips found her body's center. Tender from her first orgasm, she cried out at the first touch of his tongue to her swollen flesh. He was relentless in his pursuit of her pleasure, working her body with his mouth and tongue until she was trembling and sweaty. Her chest had sunk down into the cushions and her hips reached for the ceiling, obscene and shameless, giving him unfettered access to her body.

When at last she felt first tremors signaling the inevitability of another release, he ceased his ministrations.

"Brett, I need…" she gasped.

He surged into her with a groan. His hand smoothed up her sweat-slick back, then took hold of her shoulder. He lifted her torso until it'd cleared the cushions and her hands were braced on the sofa back, then his hand closed around her neck. He brought her body up close, her face near his.

Her arms flew back and grasped at his head and his hair as her body exploded in a fierce, swift shock wave of bliss. His thrusts had grown harder, creating an aftershock of energy that rippled through her flesh every time their bodies collided. He turned her face sideways, then kissed her, as sloppy and wet and wicked as he had during their one-night stand.

The hand on her neck shifted to her breast. His other hand moved from her hip around to her front. He tucked his arm between her hip bone and her belly, hooking his hand around to her pleasure center. At the first touch of his fingertip, her cry filled the room.

He nipped her ear. "You're going to come again."

"I can't."

He pinched her nipple between his finger and thumb and tugged. "Yes, you can."

His touch was as insistent as his words.

"Give it to me, baby. Give me one more release from your hot body. Come on."

His teeth bit down on her shoulder, a lightning bolt of the perfect storm he'd created within her. Ignition. Lost to the sweet agony of Brett's total command over her body, she threw her head back and shattered again. He crooned his approval as he buckled forward, spending himself inside her with a roar of release.

CHAPTER FOURTEEN

BRETT WOKE DISORIENTED by the brightness of the room. Ranchers' schedules meant a lifetime of waking in the dark. He had, in fact, woken around 5:00 a.m., but had forced himself to stay in bed, not wanting Hannah to wake up alone and wonder why he'd left. Guess he'd drifted back off, because now her room was as bright as the middle of the day. His eyes, behind his eyelids, ached from the light.

He peeled one eye open. The sun was shining through the open windows. Sleeping next to Hannah had felt like heaven. He'd been so tired lately. He hadn't realized how on edge he'd been—about the ranch, about Hannah. But somehow, knowing that she was going to stay at the ranch, that she was going to fight for a future with him, lifted a huge rock from his chest. He was more determined than ever to make the ranch a safe place for her and their child.

"Good morning," she croaked.

"Did I wake you?"

"No. Our little guy—or girl—did. Baby's crazy active right now. I think he's learning how to play soccer." She took his hand and set it over her belly. "He or she has no respect for its mama's need for sleep. So rude."

He heard the love in her every word and snuggled back into the pillow, no longer in a hurry to get to work.

It wasn't long before something thumped against his palm. He couldn't speak, it was such a miracle. He buried his face in Hannah's hair, gritting his teeth against a wave of emotion. That was his child in there. His healthy, growing child that he'd get to meet in only a few months.

What a thin line he was walking, sleeping with her, risking losing full-time fatherhood if he and Hannah's relationship crashed and burned. Last night, that risk had paled in comparison to his blinding need to claim Hannah's body, but with the light of day and the feel of his child moving beneath his palm came a clarity of perspective about everything he stood to lose.

"When's that ultrasound appointment?" he croaked. She'd wanted to wait until her Lucky C health insurance kicked in at the turn of the month, but Brett had been insistent that they spare no cost.

"On Friday."

"I can't wait. Is it too soon to talk about names?"

She drew a circle over the back of his hand where it still sat on her belly. "I'd figured we'd wait until we found out the sex of the baby, but there's nothing stopping us from throwing some names around. I was thinking, if it's a boy, we should consider naming him John after your dad. If you're open to that idea."

Brett rolled to his back. "Oooh, doggie. My dad would be the proudest grandpa in all Oklahoma. I don't think his feet would ever touch the ground again."

"Then that settles it. John Colton it is, if it's a boy. But I have no ideas if it's a girl."

Brett hadn't spent a single second considering names before this moment, but the perfect one popped into his head. It was time to fight for what he wanted instead of being paralyzed by fear. It was time to have faith in himself and in Hannah, just as he was asking her to have faith in him. "Faith."

"Why Faith?"

He took her hand and threaded their fingers together. "Because that's what you had to have in me to come to this ranch like you did. And to keep the baby, in the first place."

She rolled over to face him, which was no easy task given the size of her belly, and kissed him. "I love that idea. Faith Colton. It has a ring to it."

They lay in contented silence. Brett's mind spun out in all different directions. About his future with Hannah and his legacy with the ranch, about the crimes that had been happening lately, about which room they'd transform into the nursery if he could convince her to stay by his side to raise their child at the ranch. After a while, he realized Hannah's breathing had evened out. Her eyes were closed.

As much as he hated to leave her, he really did need to get to work. Jack was probably impatiently waiting to ream him for sleeping in.

When he eased out of the bed, her eyes fluttered open. "Are you going?"

"Gotta work. You go back to sleep."

"If the baby will let me, then I'm going to try. I'm sleepy this morning."

He nuzzled her cheek. "Gee, I can't imagine why."

They hadn't fallen asleep until the wee hours of morning, and even though he didn't know much about pregnant women, he figured they needed as much sleep as they could get. She hummed and snuggled more deeply into the pillow. He smoothed a hand over her hair, then tiptoed from the bedroom in search of his pants and underwear. He'd gotten his boxers on when the suite's main door opened.

Brett didn't have time to do more than put on his underwear and hold his jeans up in front of him.

"Oh!" Edith stood in the doorway holding a tray of food, her face beet red.

"Oh is right." After a moment's hesitation while he processed Edith's presence in the room and his state of undress, he decided he didn't care. He was relatively decent and she was like a mom to him. "Come on in. Sorry to embarrass you like that."

He pulled his pants on, then walked to the bedroom door and eased it closed.

Edith set the tray on the coffee table. "She gets queasy in the morning. Biscuits and tea help," she said in a quiet voice.

He nodded. "Then thank you. I'm late for work, but I didn't want her to wake up alone and wonder why I'd left without…" He shook his head, letting his voice trail off. And the *why* didn't explain why he was talking about it to Edith.

"A wise call, if you're interested in this wrinkled old lady's opinion."

He poured himself a glass of water from the pitcher atop a table near the door. "You're too young to be calling yourself an old lady. I don't see a single wrinkle on your pretty face."

She swatted away his comment, but blushed all the same. "Jack stopped through about an hour ago asking after you. I called your room, and when you didn't answer, I suggested to him that you'd probably gone off to the backcountry early. You've been doing that a lot lately."

"I've had a lot on my mind."

"I imagine you have." She nodded toward the bedroom door, her hands clasped behind her back. "Are you going to marry her?"

He choked on the water he was sipping. After a coughing fit, he said, "You sound like my dad."

"Well, are you?"

He swirled the water in his glass, considering his best, most diplomatic response. "It's come up on and off since the day I found out she was pregnant. She and I have discussed it at length and neither of us want to end up in a loveless marriage like our parents have. Hers, too."

Edith crossed her arms over her chest. "All right, that's a good plan. So are you going to marry her?"

Brett gave a quiet chuckle. "I wish it was that simple, but first I've got to get her to fall in love with me."

"And what about you?"

He set the water down and grinned at her because that was an easy question to answer. Hannah was smart and resourceful and sweet. She got him in a fundamental way and when she looked at him, she saw his best self, the man he'd worked so hard to become. She got along with his family and she had the most remarkable way of laughing with her whole face, eyes and cheeks and lips, that socked him in the heart every time. He loved talking with her, he loved working with her and he loved sex with her.

"The truth? I'm already gone."

READY FOR ANOTHER long evening of patrol, Brett bounded downstairs to grab a quick dinner with his dad and Hannah before heading out. It'd been a good week. The sale of Geronimo had gone through and the horse was settling down and getting used to his new digs at Daniel's stable, which made Daniel and Jack happy. And Hannah's morning sickness had subsided completely, which was one worry off his mind. Best of all, after he got home near midnight every night, instead of dragging his butt into a cold, lonely bed, he got to snuggle in close to Hannah.

Adding to his peace of mind, there hadn't been any more crimes or suspicious incidents around the ranch since the fire the week before. Sure, the police didn't have any new leads, but he'd take the respite from trouble as the gift that it was.

When he reached the dining room, he found his dad there, but not Hannah. Pops looked old tonight. And lonely. Not that Brett's mom had been good company for him, but she'd been somebody, and her absence had a palpable effect on the feel of the house. Even Hannah had felt it her first day there. And for a man who'd fathered and raised six kids, it had to have been difficult on his dad to watch them grow up and leave to start their own lives, all but Brett.

Brett absolutely could not wait to fill the house with the cries and laughter of a baby. The thought of it almost made him laugh, the thought filled him with so much joy.

He rubbed his dad's shoulder as he passed, then dropped into the chair next to him. "Hey, Pops. How are you tonight?"

"Oh, fair to middling."

Brett nodded at the untouched place setting and empty chair where Hannah usually sat. "Where is she?"

"Who, Abra? I don't know where that woman goes when she disappears."

Alarm bells sounded in Brett's mind. If his dad was confused about where Abra was, then they needed to get him evaluated by a doctor pronto because he was far worse off than they all believed.

He studied Dad's face, looking for signs of his usually sharp wit, proof that he was merely making some kind of inappropriate joke. But all he saw was the faraway look in Dad's eyes, his slightly slack-jawed mouth and the tremors in his hands. With all that had happened recently, the transformation from the robust, charming man to a senior battling dementia gave Brett a sinking feeling in his stomach. It was all he could do not to grab Dad in a bear hug.

"Mom's still at the hospital," he corrected, taking care to keep his tone patient and free of the worry that now plagued him. "I meant Hannah. Have you seen her?"

He gripped his thighs, bracing himself for Dad not to remember who Hannah was, but to his great relief, Dad's eyes sharpened and he seemed to fully inhabit his body again. "Huh? No. Not since this morning when I checked in at the office and she had her nose in the books. She's a go-getter, that one. You should think about marrying her."

He patted Dad's arm, his heart sinking all over again because his dad had given him that same advice almost daily since Hannah had arrived at the ranch. The only difference now was Brett's response. "I am, Pops. Trust me on that."

A clatter of silverware and dishes preceded Edith's arrival in the room. She slid a tray onto the table. "Good evening, Brett."

Brett bussed her cheek. "Good evening to you, too. Where's Maria?"

"She asked for a night off to be with her parents, which I was more than happy to oblige. How's that new horse of yours?"

"Looking good. Now we just need to give Daniel some time and space to breed Geronimo, and I think we're going to have the start of a great new direction for the ranch."

She served Dad a plate of lasagna. "Jack on board with you yet?"

"Not yet." With all the turmoil around the ranch, he'd decided to put off showing Jack the business plan that he and Hannah had created until things settled down. "But even Jack was as excited as a kid on Christmas when Geronimo walked down the trailer ramp."

Dad chuckled. "Attaboy. You'll bring your brother around soon enough."

Edith set a plate of lasagna in front of Brett. "Is Hannah still at the office?"

"That's what we think," Brett said. "She probably lost track of time."

"Shall I call her?" Edith asked.

"Nah, I'll run over and get her." He loved catching her in the act of working. That look on her face of singular concentration, her reading glasses perched on the tip of her nose. Maybe he'd get to steal a kiss or two while he had her alone. "Don't wait on dinner for us. We might be a while."

Edith's eyes twinkled with delight. Geez. Hannah must've been rubbing off on him, that was such an obvious Freudian slip. "I meant because she might be in the middle of something. She's been working magic with the ranch's books and I'm not going to pull her away until she's at a good stopping point. Not that we'd be late for dinner because I plan on holding her up."

"Mmm-hmm," Edith said.

"If that's the case, then you're not as smart as I thought," Pops said.

Shaking his head and grinning like a fool, Brett swatted the air behind him as he left, dismissing the teasing.

"Hold on," Edith said. "I'll make you a tray. You two can eat dinner in private at the office. You're riding patrol tonight with Ryan, correct? I thought I heard Jack say something to that effect this morning."

"I am, but Hannah and I'll come back here for dinner. I don't want Pops to eat alone."

Dad craned his head around to glare at Brett. "Pshaw. I'm not some decrepit old geezer. I can entertain myself. Maybe there's a game on TV."

Edith winked at Brett. "I'll keep him company."

A few minutes later, loaded with plates of lasagna and red velvet cupcakes, he made his way along the dirt path to the office, anticipation speeding him along. He hadn't seen Hannah all day, and though they'd texted each other a few times, he couldn't wait to be near her again.

Evening was descending on the ranch. It was bound to be a beautiful night, weather-wise. The sunset turned the whole sky orange and purple. The colors and clouds reflected off the office windows as Brett mounted the stairs to the office. He turned and watched the dark orange sun appear below a fluffy purple cloud above an expanse of deep green rolling hills as far as the eye could see. Brett defied any man to find a more breathtaking view than the Lucky C at sunset.

He was nearly to the office when Ryan drove up in his

unmarked police car. Damn. Guess he'd have to make his visit to Hannah faster than he'd wanted to.

"You're early!" Brett called.

Ryan unfolded from the car and a grabbed a jacket from the backseat. "Been a while since I've been on a horse. Thought I'd brush up on my skills before we get going."

Like the rest of the Colton kids, Ryan had learned how to ride before he'd learned to walk, which meant he'd arrived at the ranch early for some other reason that he wasn't keen on broadcasting. Something having to do with the investigation, Brett guessed. They'd have plenty of time that night to discuss the investigation. But for the next half hour or so, Ryan was on his own because Hannah was the only thing Brett wanted to think about.

Brett held the tray of food aloft. "I'm going to go eat dinner with Hannah in the office. I'm sure there's plenty of lasagna in the house if you're hungry."

"I'm good. Take your time. Like I said, I've got some rust to brush off the old brain when it comes to riding."

Sure he did. Hopefully, when they were out on the range, Ryan would come clean about his true reason for poking around the ranch.

Brett pushed open the unlatched office door, but Hannah had the radio on, tuned to a country station, and she didn't seem to hear him. She was sitting at the desk just as he'd imagined, with those glasses on her nose, her lips silently mouthing the numbers she was reading, and her hair wound around a pencil to form a disheveled bun on her head. He leaned his weight against the door frame and drank her in.

"I take it back," he murmured.

She startled just a little, dropping her pencil as her

face shot up. When she realized it was only him, she smiled in a way that hit him straight in the heart. "Take what back?"

"There is such a thing that's prettier than an Oklahoma sunset."

Her expression turned demure at the compliment. "You've got to stop that."

He made some room on the desk, then set the tray down. "Why?"

She removed her reading glasses, looking bashful. "Because I don't know what to do with it."

He leaned over the desk and cupped her cheek in his hand. "I'd take a smile in response in the future, but right now, I'm going to go crazy if I can't kiss you."

He leaned across the desk and angled his lips over hers. He kept it tender and light and full of love. When the kiss ended, he stroked his thumb along her cheekbone. "That's what I've been looking forward to all day."

Hannah rose from her chair and licked her lips, her eyes appraising his belt buckle. "Really? Because that's not what I've been looking forward to."

Her gaze was hungry, as if he hadn't wrung several epic orgasms from her body the night before.

He eyed the room. There was a lock on the door, curtains on the windows and plenty of options on where to get comfortable while he satisfied her. Besides, what kind of decent provider would he be if he didn't give his woman what she needed? "You want to eat first, while it's hot."

She walked around the desk and hooked her hand down the front of his pants. "Unless that's a euphemism, then no."

He laughed out loud at that. "Let me lock the door."

"I'll close the curtains."

They came together again in the middle of the room, their kisses desperate. This was going to have to be a quickie because Ryan was waiting, but with the way she was ripping at his clothes right now, she wasn't interested in taking her time.

He smoothed a hand over her breasts. "You are so sexy."

"I was just thinking the same about you."

He cleared off the desk, stacking files and papers onto chairs, returning pens to their holder.

"You know," he said as he removed the last of the items from the desktop. "I was born a cowboy. Never been much into staying indoors or being fenced in, and office work, that's my idea of hell, but tonight, I'm suddenly inspired to perform some desk work."

He wrapped his arms around her. His hands grabbing hold of her backside, he lifted her onto the desk.

"Is that so?" she purred, onto his game. "You're going to put in a little overtime on the job?"

He stripped her shirt off over her head, then laid her back like an offering on an altar. "You see, I have a very demanding boss with a lot of desperate needs that are my duty to address."

The leggings she wore pulled off easily. He added them to the chair where he'd tossed her shirt. It'd been too dark last night for him to see much of her body, but tonight he drank his fill of her in the full light of the office. Beyond lust and the urgency to brand her body with his touch, the sight of her belly swollen with his child brought forth a surge of possessiveness and ego. He was a modern guy, but damn, it brought out the inner caveman in him to see his beautiful, brilliant Hannah pregnant with his child.

"What a burden, to be so needed," she said. "Maybe she's just trying to help you live up to your full potential on the job."

With a wry huff of laughter at her words, he brought her ankle to his mouth. He dragged his lips and tongue along her leg, reveling in the scent and taste of her skin and the way her breath hitched when he reached her inner thigh.

If his true potential as her man was to screw her brains out whenever need took a hold of her, then that was one element of his job description that he was fully on board with now. He pulled the nearest chair toward the desk, right between her legs, and propped her feet on the chair arms. With his arms wrapped around her hips, he scooted her backside to the edge. She squirmed and whimpered at the first gentle swipe of his tongue.

"You drive me crazy, Brett."

He slid his hand up her side until he found her hand and twined his fingers with hers. "You ain't seen nothin' yet."

Then he put his lips and tongue to work, feasting on her wet, hot flesh until her cries bounced off the office walls and her thighs tightened around his head.

When her release had subsided, she sat and stroked her hands over his hair. Her cheeks were flushed and she wore a languid smile. "My turn now. You want to get up on the desk or stay in the chair?"

He swiped his thumb over his mouth, then kissed her. "I'm going to take a rain check on that until tonight, after patrol. Knowing I get to come home to you is going to keep me going tonight while we're on the range."

He helped her off the desk and back into her clothes. In his periphery, he caught sight of the tray of food. "I'm afraid dinner's cold. Sorry."

She straightened her shirt. "Worth it and then some."

"Agreed."

He slid the tray back onto her desk, then reached for the papers he'd cleared from it. Now that he wasn't distracted by lusty thoughts, he realized that the paperwork she'd been poring over had been the previous year's ledgers as well as a stack of check stubs and invoices. "What're you doing with these invoices? They're dated last November."

She eased the stack of papers from his hands. "It's nothing."

She set the stack off to the side on the far end of the desk as though she didn't want him looking too closely at them.

"You're not acting like it's nothing. Is everything all right?"

"Yes." She worried her lower lip and sank into her desk chair. "No, actually. I wasn't going to say anything to you until I was sure there's an issue, but the truth is that I can't get the monthly balances right, not for any month in the past year."

He pulled his face in surprise. His dad was a great businessman with a head for numbers. Then again... "My dad's mind is going. Could he have done the math wrong?"

"That was my hunch, too. At first look, the numbers that were incorrect looked like easy mistakes, numbers transposed and things like that. Except that the weekly totals are off by about the same amount every time. Five hundred dollars, give or take some change. So far the account seems to be short about twenty-three thousand dollars."

Brett cursed. "That's a lot of money to go unnoticed."

"It is. I wasn't going to say anything to you until I was sure, but I think somebody's skimming money from the Lucky C."

Brett walked to the window and flipped the curtain open, looking outside. He wished he didn't have to go on patrol that night. His instincts were telling him that something bad was brewing, and Ryan's ambiguous reasons for being on the ranch early weren't helping him feel secure about leaving Hannah alone.

"That's a serious allegation."

"Which is why I hadn't said anything to you yet." She touched his shoulder. "Don't worry yet and don't mention the discrepancies to anyone, okay? Let me triple-check my math first. There's no need in upsetting your dad and brothers unnecessarily."

Before anything else happened, he needed to talk to Ryan. They'd stick close to the homestead tonight, but there was no way he was leaving her alone and vulnerable in the office. "I have to go. Ryan's waiting on me. But I'd feel better if you were safe and sound inside with Dad and Edith."

"That's fine with me. I'm not crazy about the idea of working here after dark, either. Rafe stops by the office sometimes, especially if you're not around, and every time he does, he makes me feel a little uncomfortable. Okay, a lot uncomfortable."

Okay, that was a name he hadn't expected to hear tonight. "Wait. Rafe comes by the office to see you?"

"Almost every time I'm alone."

"For what purpose?"

Hannah shrugged. "I'm not sure. He's flirty and... I don't know. I get a weird vibe from him, but it's nothing to worry about, especially right now. I'm going to pack up and get to the Big House."

He rubbed his temple, his head spinning with all these new revelations. "How long has that been happening?"

"Since the afternoon I arrived, but it's just a gut feeling. He hasn't done anything, really. Just hangs around too much, stands too close, looks at me a little too intensely, and he's always slipping sexist remarks into the conversation. He's a bit of an ass, honestly. I'm not a fan."

"You should have told me."

She wrapped her arms around him again. "You've had enough on your mind, and there really isn't anything specific to tell."

"Hannah, you can tell me anything. Especially if a man is making you feel uncomfortable."

"You really are my hero, you know that?"

He kissed her head. "I'm trying. How about you let me walk you home?"

"Not necessary. I'll finish eating and get my stuff together so I can work in my room. I promise to be in the Big House by dark."

He tipped her chin up and gave her a lingering kiss. "Good. Thank you. That'll be a load off my mind. You and I can talk more tomorrow about the discrepancies with the books. I'll help you get to the bottom of it. And I'll be paying Rafe a visit, too. You won't have to worry about him anymore."

"Thank you." She walked him to the door. "Stay safe out there. I couldn't bear it if something happened to you."

"I will. Same goes with you, okay?"

A rumble of thunder caught him off guard as he stepped outside. He'd forgotten about the weatherman's prediction of a storm that night. Wouldn't be the first time he and Outlaw had been out in weather. He pulled the brim of his hat lower, his eyes scanning the ranch grounds for any sign of Rafe. Not seeing any, he looked toward the bunkhouse. The light in Rafe's corner bedroom was on.

He had half a mind to go give the man a dressing-down right then and there—and half a mind to fire his sorry ass—but Ryan was waiting. After one last look, he turned away from the bunkhouses and headed across the grounds to the stable where Ryan sat astride his horse, waiting for him and wearing a teasing grin.

"When I told you to take your time, I didn't mean I wanted to stand here counting the cattle while you got your rocks off. I guess you decided to help your baby mama work through her pregnancy hormones after all."

Brett bit the inside of his cheek against a smile. "We were that subtle, huh?"

"Oh, yeah, real subtle, what with the way you slammed all the windows shut and closed the curtains at lightning speed. I think I actually saw the trailer rocking."

"Hannah and I are happy. Get over it."

Ryan shook his head, his smile firmly in place. "Get Outlaw saddled so we can get out of here."

"Something's up with you. Can you talk about it here or should we wait?"

Ryan's smile fell. He glanced back and forth as though checking to make sure no one was in earshot, then dismounted and got close to Bret. "You know that rush job we asked Susie to do? She found a set of prints, but she wasn't able to identify who they belonged to. They don't match any of the prints we have on record from the Lucky C. And believe me, we printed everyone after Abra's attack."

"Then why were you here early?"

Ryan gave another look around, then stepped closer. "The accelerant that the fire marshal determined was used in the fire was an ammonium nitrate compound common in the same agricultural fertilizer the Lucky C uses."

Brett's ribs gave a squeeze as all the pieces fit together. "You were here early to take samples. Even though the prints don't match, you still think someone got the accelerant here at the ranch. Is that part of the message they're sending us?"

"I don't know about the message, but it sure looks like it's shaping up that way. The samples I took are off the record. Susie's going to see if there's any truth to our hunch before we show our cards. Just about every ranch and farm in Tulsa uses some similar combination of the same agricultural products, so it's a long shot. Especially with that unidentified fingerprint. The important part is that the clues are stacking up. It won't be long now."

Brett looked toward the office. Inside it sat his whole world, his new family. "It better not be. I'm getting itchy for some justice to be served so we can get on with our lives."

"Come on. Let's get out of here. I'd like to take a look at the hunting blind again before this rain hits."

The hunting blind was out in the backcountry much farther than Brett had wanted to travel that night, given the warnings that his instincts were niggling him about, but they were starting early and he couldn't think of a solid reason to refuse Ryan's request. With a nudge to Outlaw's flanks, they got their patrol under way, riding straight into the gathering clouds.

CHAPTER FIFTEEN

As the last glow of daylight succumbed to the encroaching storm clouds, Hannah walked to the Big House, carrying the food tray with the manila envelope of possible embezzling evidence tucked under her arm. She was nearly there when Big J burst out the main door and practically flew down the porch steps.

Hannah quickened her stride and met him in the driveway. "Big J, are you okay?"

"Hannah, there you are." He was pale and anxious, his sweater misbuttoned, as though he'd thrown it on in haste. "I just got a call from the hospital. Abra's taken a turn for the worse."

"Oh, no. Let me set this stuff down and then I'll drive you."

"That's okay. Jack's meeting me here. He's going to drive me to the hospital."

"I'll go with you."

"Actually, Edith already retired for the evening and I don't want to bother her, but I couldn't get either Brett or Ryan on the phone—they must be out of range—and I don't want them to come back to find us all gone. Would you stay here and tell them what's happening? You can drive over with Brett."

"Of course." She made to hug Big J, but he was too

jittery to hold still. The minute they heard the sound of a truck, he seemed to forget about her existence.

Hannah set the tray and the envelope on a step and followed him to the edge of the driveway. She gave a small wave to Jack, who was behind the wheel of a big black truck. "I'll be praying for your mom."

Jack's lips were a thin line as he nodded.

Hugging herself, she watched their taillights disappear along the long road leading off the property. That was it. She was alone again at night on the ranch, exactly in the position she'd promised Brett not to get in. The breeze kicked up, splattering her with the first raindrops of the storm that had been threatening all afternoon.

Lights shone from the bunkhouse, reminding her that she wasn't actually alone. The ranch had lots of people on it at any given time. And somewhere out there in the night, Brett and Ryan were patrolling for the express purpose of keeping everyone safe. Time to call them and give them the tough news about their mom.

She turned back toward the house, picked up the tray and envelope, and walked the rest of the way to the house. From the phone in the kitchen, she dialed Brett's cell phone. It flipped to voice mail without ringing. So did Ryan's, which probably meant they were out of range.

She closed her eyes and said a quick prayer for Abra, then reached for the envelope. She'd get that hidden behind the vanity, then keep trying to reach Brett. A roar of thunder shifted her focus to the window. The rain was really coming down now. Poor Brett and Ryan.

With a heart heavy with worry, she turned toward the stairs. She was halfway up them when the lights flickered once, twice. The house went dark.

Hannah gripped the rail, startling as a flash of lightning strobed through the house. No two ways around it—it was going to be a long, troubled night and she had a sinking feeling about how it was going to end.

BRETT WAS MISERABLE. The last time it'd rained this hard, he'd found himself in the backcountry, that time chasing pregnant cows. What a wet July this had been. Great for local farmers, but not so good for a rancher trying to keep his family and his livestock safe.

Tonight's storm had arrived earlier than the weather forecasters had predicted, but at least Brett and Ryan had reached the hunting blind before the rain hit, for all the good it'd done them. All they'd done is determine that there was no new evidence to find. No more photographs lodged in the scrub bushes or grass and no unusual footprints or tracks indicating how the arsonist had traveled so far into the backcountry—bicycle or truck or horse. Nothing.

Soaked to the bone, Brett hunched into his jacket and pulled his cell phone from his pocket. It'd been more than an hour since he'd checked it last, not wanting it to short-circuit from the rain.

He'd missed nearly twenty phone calls. A handful from his dad and the rest from Hannah.

"Ryan, something's not right."

He dialed Hannah's number. "Hannah called a lot. Dad, too."

Ryan pulled his own phone out as Hannah's voice mail message kicked on.

"Damn it." Brett's hands were trembling now, but he was afraid to get the horses moving, lest they lose the signal.

"I missed a bunch of calls from them, too. Them and Jack," Ryan said.

"Hannah didn't answer her cell phone," Brett said. "I'm trying the house."

The answering machine didn't even answer the phone at the house. It merely rang and rang until Brett grew impatient.

"Nothing?" Ryan asked.

Brett shook his head.

Ryan frowned. "I'm calling Dad now. It's dial— Hey, Dad. Is everything okay? Looks like we missed some calls." Ryan paused, listening. "Just a sec, Dad. Brett's here, too. Let me get this on speakerphone."

When the speakerphone clicked through, Ryan gave Brett a thumbs-up.

"Hey, Pops, it's Brett. How's Mom?"

"Hannah didn't tell you?" He sounded absolutely defeated.

"She's not with you?" Brett asked.

"No. I asked her to stay at the ranch so she could tell you about your mom. The docs think it might be time for us all to say goodbye to her." His voice hitched.

Brett's and Ryan's gazes met. Brett's own dread and heartache reflected back at him in his brother's eyes.

In all of this time, since she'd been attacked, worry of her death had been distant. Once the doctors stabilized her condition and brain scans revealed that she still had a lot of healthy brain activity, he'd pushed the idea of her dying to the back of his mind. But now, what if she really did die before the two of them could make amends? What if he was about to lose his mother forever?

It was too much. Brett closed his eyes. "Tell me Mom's not dying. Please."

He barely recognized his voice for the strain in it. Suddenly, he was back to being a kid again, watching his mother stack luggage in the trunk of a taxi and driving away. This was how abandonment felt. *As though you should have done more, you should have been better or sweeter. You shouldn't have back-talked, then maybe she would've stayed home instead of taking another extended trip abroad.* Maybe she would've fought harder to live, to come out of the coma, if they'd all been more understanding of her depression...

A squeeze on his shoulder had him opening his eyes to find Ryan next to him, sharing his strength. Probably he was going through his own emotional roller coaster of bitter memories and what-ifs about their mother.

"Oh, son. I'm so sorry," Dad said.

"Hang in there, Dad," Ryan said, his voice strained. "We're out in the backcountry on patrol, but we're on our way. We'll be there as soon as we can."

"I love you, Pops," Brett said. "Hang in there, okay?"

"Love you both, too, Brett, Ryan. See you soon."

They galloped at full speed back to the ranch, neither attempting to talk over the wind and rain and their own troubled thoughts and feelings. All was quiet around the homestead. The Big House was lit, a golden beacon in the bleak night as it ever was.

"I'll take care of the horses after I figure out where Hannah is," Brett said, dismounting. "You go on and we'll meet you at the hospital."

"Roger that. Thanks."

They embraced, sharing each other's strength.

"See you in a few," Ryan said. Then he jogged to his car and took off like a bullet down the road.

Brett left the horses tethered in the grooming stall inside the stable and strode toward the house. Normally, caring for the horses was his top priority, no matter what. But he needed to see for himself that Hannah was safe and sound, and figure out why she hadn't answered the phone.

When he passed by the darkened office, a movement caught his eye. The door was ajar and fluttering open and closed with the wind. He climbed the steps and pulled the door open. Then he gasped.

Even in the darkness, he could tell that the place was a disaster. Something was written on the side wall, though he couldn't tell what, given the angle. What he could make out was the sign of the cross done in dripping spray paint on the back wall. Eyes on that, he reached in and flipped on the light.

A curse escaped his lips. The office had been trashed. Every file drawer was open and papers were scattered all over the desk and floor. The computer had fallen over, its screen smashed. He took another step into the room and slid on something slippery. He windmilled his hands, catching his balance.

"Hannah?" he called.

A book sat open on the desk. From it protruded the hilt of a knife. He walked the rest of the way into the room, straight to the desk. His first glance was under the desk, in case Hannah was there, but all he found were more scattered papers. The book on the desk was a Bible.

With one hand on the desecrated text, he lifted his focus and scanned the rest of the room. The words painted on the side of the room that he'd noticed before entering sent a fresh wave of sickening fear skittering over his skin.

God's watching you and so am I.

"Hannah!" he tried to shout, though the word caught in his throat.

What if she'd been here when this had happened? What if she'd been taken? Kidnapped? She'd tried to call him nearly twenty times and now she wouldn't pick up her phone. He'd never been so scared in his life. For all he knew, she was being held for ransom somewhere by whatever twisted scumbag had stolen money from their family. Unless…

What if his mother's attacker had returned for another victim?

A strangled noise bubbled up from his throat that sounded foreign to his ears, and he took off running.

CHAPTER SIXTEEN

BRETT FLEW THROUGH the house and up to Hannah's suite, calling her name the whole way. The door was locked.

He pounded on it. "Hannah? You in there?"

He'd never been so sick with worry in his life. After knocking again, he gave her two more seconds before shouldering it open. The trim around the door frame splintered as he ripped it from the hinges off. He heard a yelp from inside. As the broken door clattered to the ground, Hannah appeared in the bathroom, clutching a towel and shaking from head to toe.

"You scared the snot out of me!" she cried. "I thought you were Abra's attacker coming back."

Infinitely relieved to find her unharmed, Brett bridged the distance between them and grasped her shoulders. "Are you okay?"

"Other than almost having a heart attack out of fear, yes. Why in heavens did you break the door down?"

He pulled her into a giant hug. "Thank God you're all right. You almost gave me a heart attack, too."

She pushed against his chest until he backed up enough for her to look him in the eye. "Is this because I called you so many times? Why didn't you answer?"

"With the storm, I didn't hear it ringing in my jacket pocket. Are you okay?"

"Yes. The power went out, but Edith got it back on

without much hassle. I called because your mom's not doing well. She took a turn for the worse, but I've since heard from your dad that she's stabilized again."

"I know. Ryan and I talked to him, too."

She clutched the towel around her more snugly. "Then why are you so freaked out? About your mom?"

"I'm sick about her, too, but someone wrecked the office. I thought something might have happened to you."

She brushed past him and strode to her bedroom. "What do you mean 'someone wrecked the office'? I was just there a couple hours ago, and I locked up when I left."

She grabbed a pair of black pants from the bed and pulled them on.

"The computer was smashed and there's graffiti on the wall, papers everywhere. Someone left a Bible on the desk with a knife stabbed into it."

She pulled a green sweater over her head. "A Bible? Oh, heck, no."

Just like that, she took off out of the room. With Brett in tow, she jogged down the stairs and out the front door, paying no mind to the rain.

"Hannah, there's nothing you need to see."

"Like hell there is."

She threw the office door open and gasped.

"It's got to be the person who's skimming money, doesn't it?" Brett said. "He's sending you a message that he's onto you."

"Not a he, a she," Hannah said. She walked into the room and touched one of the dripping red crosses on the wall, her finger coming away with the wet paint. She whirled to face Brett and shoved her trembling hands in her pockets, but not before Brett noticed that they were shaking. Angry tears flooded her eyes. "I know who did it. It was Mavis Turnbolt."

"You think Mavis the laundry maid has something to do with it?"

Hannah shook her head. "She's not the laundress anymore. She quit after I confronted her about her leaving a Bible in my room with passages circled about the devil and sin and murder."

All Brett could do was blink, he was so ticked off at her for not being forthright about her problems around the ranch. "She planted a marked-up Bible in your room? I told you to let me know if she gave you trouble. Between her and Rafe and the possible embezzlement, you've been keeping a lot of secrets from me. Is there anything else you haven't told me?"

"No, and I'm sorry. I didn't want to add to your burden."

"Hannah, you've got a target on your back. How can I keep you safe if you don't tell me what's going on?"

"I hadn't thought about it like that, but I think you might be right." She fingered the edge of the Bible on the desk, then, after another shiver, wrapped her arms around herself in a hug. "Maybe it'd be safer for me and the baby if I left the ranch for a while. Until the danger's passed. Someone's out there who has it in for this place and the people in it, not just me. The hunting-blind fire, the damaged fences, Abra's jewelry showing up at the hospital. And now this. I love it here, but I can't be selfish right now. I've got to think of the baby first."

She was right and it pissed Brett off something fierce that some unknown perpetrator was threatening his woman and unborn baby so much that they had to seriously consider fleeing from the home he was trying to provide them.

Not wanting to take his frustration out on Hannah any more than he already had, he stalked out of the office, so spitting mad that he couldn't see straight.

He got Ryan on the phone. "Turn around. I need you at the ranch."

"Whoa, there, bro. What's going on?"

He got Ryan up to speed on the office break-in.

"I'm turning around. I'm about fifteen minutes away, though."

Brett climbed the steps to the Big House and stood on the porch, looking out over his domain, his family's legacy that was being destroyed before his eyes. Enough was enough. "It's time for a reckoning, Ryan. I'm sick and tired of standing around watching my family get hurt. Mom's dying, Tracy was the target of a hit man last month and now somebody's threatening Hannah. And I have a pretty good idea of who it is."

"You have a new lead?"

"Two possible leads. It's either Mavis Turnbolt, who's a member of Hannah's parents' cult, which is Hannah's theory given the religious symbols on the office walls, or it's whoever has been embezzling money out of the ranch's accounts. It's time to start knocking heads around until we get the answers we're looking for."

"What? Slow down and tell me what you're talking about. Embezzlement?"

Brett took a breath, trying to think past his fury so he could speak coherently. "Hannah just told me about the embezzlement this afternoon. She says she's been documenting it since she started working here and she was getting ready to lay it all out for us because she has proof that someone's been skimming from our accounts to the tune of twenty-three thousand dollars over the past year."

"Well, hell," Ryan said. "Could the embezzlement and vandalism perp be one and the same?"

"That's one theory. And another question is, could it be the same person who robbed Mom and beat her within an inch of her life?"

"That thought crossed my mind, as well," Ryan said. "Sounds like we need to figure out who had access to the ranch's ledgers and accounts. That'll narrow the list down."

"You don't sound angry enough for my taste," Brett snapped.

"One of us has to keep a cool head, and it sure as hell ain't you right now."

"I'm trying to make things right with the mother of my child. Do you understand me? I'm trying to show her that it's safe here for her and the baby, or else she's going to walk away. And then what? What the hell would I do without her?"

He flattened against the side wall of the house and squeezed his eyes closed while he got a grip on his spiraling fear. Until he'd voiced it, he hadn't processed how desperately he needed Hannah and their baby in his life. And not just on the periphery of his life, with occasional visits until the danger on the ranch passed—that was, if the police were ever able to catch the assailant. Beyond the Colton code of honor, beyond duty, he needed Hannah by his side. Forever.

"We're going to get this guy, Brett. Whoever did this, we're going to make him pay. I promise you that."

"We keep throwing that line around, about how we're

going to get this guy, but this is the second month in a row that our women and our ranch are in imminent danger as we stand by and watch, helpless."

Ryan let out a heavy sigh that seeped to well up from the depths of his bones. "Hang in there and don't do anything stupid. I'm on my way."

Brett ended the call, cursing. He swabbed a hand over his face and girded himself to face Hannah again, even though he had no answers for her, nor any real hope to offer. He'd promised to take care of her, to be a man deserving of her, but he couldn't even do something as basic as provide her with a safe home for their baby. He gritted his teeth, riding out a wave of anguish. He had let her down; he'd failed her and their baby in a fundamental way.

Forcing himself to go numb, he walked back to the office, dialing his dad's cell number again as he moved.

When his dad answered, Brett said, "I'm sorry to bother you again, but I have to ask you something, and I know this is the worst possible time, but you're going to have to forgive me."

"Are you on your way?"

He couldn't decide if his father's dementia was kicking in or if he was purposefully ignoring Brett's words. "Not yet."

"Her situation isn't so dire anymore. She's still fighting and the doctors were able to stabilize her. They're trying a new medication."

"Thank God." A rush of relief battled with his frustration. He fought for numbness again.

"What do you need to ask me?"

"I need to know if, over the last year, you've given anybody access to the ranch's finances and accounts other than Jack and me." Brett's voice was tight with harnessed emotions.

"Huh? It's the middle of the night and I'm at the hospital with my wife who's in a coma."

Brett stood at the base of the office stairs and closed his eyes. "I know, Dad. And I'm sorry. But someone broke into the office tonight and vandalized it. We're trying to fit all the puzzle pieces together to figure out what happened and if we're in any immediate danger here. Have you let anyone else have access to the accounts? Maybe someone to make bank deposits for you?"

Dad huffed. "Only Rafe, and he wouldn't break in and mess with the office. Why would he? He loves the ranch like it's his own."

"Rafe?" As in the man who'd been getting too friendly with Hannah since she arrived at the ranch. A storm of fury started to build in Brett as the pieces clicked together in his mind. The religious symbols didn't make sense if Rafe was the vandal, but there were too many coincidences for Brett to overlook.

Dad sighed. "Yes, Rafe. I didn't want to admit it to you kids, but I just wasn't cut out for the job anymore. My eyes got tired, and Rafe was a big help. I asked him not to say anything to anybody. And then Hannah came, and Rafe and I were both off the hook. But I'm telling you, Brett, he'd never vandalize the office."

Brett bit his tongue, refusing to disagree with his father or chide him while he was in such a vulnerable state of mind. He did his best to modulate his voice and asked, "Was Rafe the only other person you gave access to the ledgers and account information?"

"Yes, besides you and Jack."

"Brett?" It was Hannah, standing in the office doorway, as pale as a ghost. "I found something you're going to want to see."

Phone still to his ear, he followed Hannah into the office.

She pulled a small black camera from the bookshelf against the office's back wall, from behind one of the plants she'd decorated the room with. It had been aimed at the desk.

"That's not what I think it is, is it?" Brett said. He couldn't take any more new discoveries tonight.

"Looks like it's digital and wireless and…" She trailed a finger over the top of it, leaving a clear path through the dust. "It also looks like it's been here a while. Someone was filming me." Her gaze roved to the desk before locking with Brett's once more. "Filming us."

Brett's stomach turned. *God is watching you and so am I.*

He could feel his palm start to sweat and had to grip the phone hard to hang on to it. "Dad, did you have security cameras put in the office?"

"Huh? No. We've never needed to take precautions like that. If we didn't trust someone then we wouldn't hire them. I don't think I'd know how to operate one of those new whiz-bang contraptions, anyhow."

Hannah touched Brett's arm, her gaze imploring.

He shook his head. "It wasn't Dad's doing," he said under his breath.

A firestorm started inside Brett, tensing his muscles, making his breathing shallow. Some psychopathic pervert had been secretly taping Hannah, which meant that, somewhere, there existed a recording of Brett pleasuring her that afternoon—violating their privacy, violating Hannah. Whoever had done this to her, they were going to pay.

"I've got to go, Dad." He didn't wait for a reply. The rage inside him was too all-consuming for pleasantries.

He pocketed the phone.

Hannah's hand flew over her mouth, her eyes going wide all over again. "The jam," she whispered. "That's how he knew I eat jam straight from the jar in my bedroom suite." Her body shivered. She stumbled back against the wall, dropping the camera.

"What? Who?"

"Rafe," she said. "He made a comment last week about me eating jam from the jar and I wondered how he knew because the only place I've done that is when I'm alone in my suite. I figured that he'd seen me on the balcony or something, but what if…"

Only two coherent thoughts broke through the rage pounding through Brett. One, that his .22 was still fully loaded from his patrol that night and, two, that Rafe Sinclair had better be praying that the police caught up with him before Brett did.

CHAPTER SEVENTEEN

BRETT'S MIND SCREAMED louder than the keening of a tornado siren. If there was a camera, then there was a set of recordings somewhere either in Rafe's bunk or in his phone. Whatever Brett found first—the recordings or Rafe—he had only one plan: destroy.

He barreled out of the office and flew down the steps, over the road to the stable.

He supposed it was raining still, but he couldn't even feel it. He didn't realize Hannah had followed him until he was inside the stable, lifting his .22 from Outlaw's saddle.

"Let the police handle this. Brett, please." She stood in the stable doorway, and he bet she meant to block him from passing, but he wasn't letting anything or anyone stand in his way.

The police would probably want to save the footage as evidence, but the thought of explicit recordings of Hannah being passed around a police precinct or presented in court made Brett's stomach turn.

"Like hell I will."

Rather than try to get past her, he pivoted on his boot heel and strode along the center of the stable to the door on the opposite end. He was nearly there when Hannah grabbed his sleeve.

"Damn it, Brett. This is not the way. I don't want you to get hurt."

He yanked his arm out of her grasp. "Go in the house and wait for the police. This ends now."

She took hold of his shirt again, pulling hard until he stopped walking. Moving around the side of his body, she clamped a hand on his jaw and forced him to look at her. "I'm not going to let you do this. Ryan's on his way and for all we know, Rafe is armed."

"I don't care if he's armed. I'm going to find him and I'm going to destroy those recordings if I have to burn the whole bunkhouse down." He didn't recognize his own voice, it was so even and quiet with restraint. "Do as I said and get in the house. Or better yet, take my truck and go to town. I won't have you in danger any longer."

"No. I'm not leaving. You need to stay with me and keep me safe."

Nice try. "Fine, then stay here. But swear to me that you're not going to put our baby in danger by following me any farther than this barn."

She looked furious with him, but she held her tongue. Clearly, she knew he was right. "Don't do this," she repeated from behind clenched teeth. "I love you. I need you to be safe."

Her words just brought it home to him what he had to do. She loved him, and he loved her, too. And he wouldn't stand by and let her be violated by some greedy psychopathic scumbag.

"We're wasting time. Let go of my shirt and get out of my way. It's time for justice to be served."

HANNAH STOOD IN the barn, alone. In shock.

Brett was going to get himself killed. Or he was going

to kill a man and get sent to prison. Either way, the life of the most magnificent man she'd ever met was about to change forever and she couldn't simply stand by and watch it happen. But he'd been right about her not putting the baby in danger. She was a strong, brave woman who'd risk almost anything to save her man, but her hands were tied. Tonight, being strong meant sacrificing what she wanted to do for the safety of her baby. There was nothing left except prayer for the police and Ryan to arrive in time. Or maybe, if God saw fit, for Rafe to be long gone from the ranch.

She walked to Outlaw and stroked a hand over his mane. "He'll stay safe, right? He knows how much I need him, doesn't he?"

Outlaw's ear twitched. He pushed his nose into her chest.

She nodded and stroked the top of his nose. "I'm going to take that as a yes."

The odor of smoke hit her nostrils. Wood burning. She lifted her nose, confirming her suspicion, which was how she spotted the first tendrils of dark smoke crowding the ceiling of the barn.

She didn't think; she didn't have time to be afraid. She untethered Outlaw and the still-saddled horse next to him and pulled them out the door. They ambled, not getting the direness of the situation. They stood just outside the stable, looking around and not paying any mind to the danger.

She swatted Outlaw's rear, trying to get him to run away, and it was at that moment that she spotted movement out of the corner of her eye. She did a double take and saw a flash of white clothing worn by someone small in stature, the size of a woman, headed west. She shook her head and blinked. Was she hallucinating again or was that the ghost? More likely, it was whoever had started the fire—and they were headed straight toward the bunkhouse. *Brett.*

Every fiber of her being wanted to go after him, but running headfirst into this new danger was yet another risk she couldn't take. Besides that, there was a fire nearby, with smoke pouring into the stable.

She didn't see flames from where she stood, so she backed up and, shielding her face from rain with a hand on her forehead, took a close look at the building. The rain made the smoke hard to see, but it seemed to be coming from the east side. If the stable was on fire, then so many lives were at stake. There were at least ten other horses in the stable that she knew of. She turned a spigot on and, grabbing the water hose that was attached to it, ran around the building.

What she saw when she rounded the corner was the most horrific sight she'd ever witnessed. Worse than the ransacked office.

The fire licked up from the grassy earth in a straight line, as though someone had poured gasoline along a crease. The treated wood of the stable was burning, too, but slowly. Above the flames, pinned to the outside wall of the stable, were dozens of photographs. In each one, every person in the picture had their eyes gouged out, much like the engagement photo Greta had shown her a couple weeks earlier. Above the photographs, carved into the wood siding, were the words *ALL LIES.*

Hannah shook away her horror. There would be time to figure out who'd left such a message, but right now, all she needed to worry about was keeping the horses and other livestock safe. She angled the hose at the flames and sprayed, keeping her mind on the task at hand instead of the dark thoughts threatening to buckle her knees in fear.

She didn't hear the car approaching until it was right up on her. Ryan leaped out and ran her way, his clothes still damp from patrol and a pistol in his hand. "What's going on? Where's Brett? Who set the fire?"

"I don't know. I saw a woman dressed in white, running toward the bunkhouse, but I don't know if she did this," she said.

"Give me that hose. You shouldn't be breathing these fumes."

He tried to take it from her, but she wouldn't relinquish it. "The fire's almost out. I've got this. You've got to stop Brett. He has a gun and he went after Rafe."

Ryan's mouth fell open. His face whipped sideways to regard her. "Rafe, as in the Lucky C employee? Brett thinks he's the one who vandalized the office? I thought we were worried about your parents' church or whoever is embezzling money."

"Brett called your dad. He said he was having Rafe help him with the ranch's finances this past year."

Ryan's shoulders fell. He shook his head. "That doesn't explain why Brett went after the guy with a gun in the middle of the night."

"There's more. We found a secret video camera in the office. Someone's been recording me. Recording me and Brett this afternoon and recording me in my bedroom suite. And it's Rafe. I know it is, given some private things he knew about me."

Ryan cursed. He pressed a switch on his pistol and the magazine dropped out. He gave it a good look, then slid it back into place and cocked it.

Hannah aimed the hose at the last remaining flames. "You've got to go stop Brett before he does something he can't take back or gets himself killed."

"Where are they now?"

Hannah nodded toward the west. "The bunkhouse. And hurry."

Ryan got on his phone. "I need backup at my family's ranch. A fire engine, too. We've got at least one suspect on the loose, possibly armed and dangerous, and a minor structure fire."

"You're not going to wait for backup to get here, are you?" Hannah asked.

"Hell, no. Come with me." He turned off the hose and tugged Hannah's arm. "Let's get you in the house first."

"I've got to get this fire out. You go stop them and bring Brett back to me safely."

"Hannah, I've got to make sure you're safe first."

Hannah threw the hose down and set her hands on her hips. "There's only one violent criminal on this ranch and right now the father of my baby is trying to single-handedly take him on. I'm safe enough. Just go. Now!"

He rotated his jaw, a battle waging in his eyes. Then, with a terse nod, he took off running.

BRETT STOOD OVER the sniveling, pathetic excuse for a man that was Rafe Sinclair while the other ranch hands stood watch at the door. As soon as Brett had clued them in about Rafe's crimes, they'd let him pass and blocked the hall against Rafe's escape.

"Tell me," Brett roared, backhanding him across the cheek with a fistful of his mother's jewelry that he'd found hidden in the bastard's mattress. "Have the guts to admit that you attacked my mother."

"I didn't. I swear. She was already unconscious when I found her."

"Like hell she was."

"I'm telling you the truth. I'd never hurt nobody. I swear on my father's grave. I just needed the money is all. With that party y'all were throwing, I saw it as my chance to slip a little jewelry out of her room. That's it. You were all distracted and so I made my move. And I found her on the floor, lying in a puddle of blood."

Brett hit him again. "And you did nothing?"

"I thought she was already dead, so I figured there was nothing I could do for her."

Brett was nothing but fury. Rage. "She wasn't dead, you son of a bitch."

"I know that now."

"So what did you do?" Brett said. "You walked around her and riffled through her dresser for things to steal?"

He licked at the blood on his split lower lip. "That's it. That's exactly right. I stuffed my pockets full of gold and diamonds and other pretty stones from the jewelry case, which was already open, I might add, and I got the heck out of there before you all came running in to find her."

"What about the photo albums?" came another voice at the door.

Brett paused, his fist in the air, ready to lay more pain on Rafe, and looked to the door. Ryan stood in the doorway, his entrance blocked by a ranch hand holding a shotgun. "Get out of here, Ryan. I'm not ready to turn this scum over to the police yet. Not until I get the answers I need."

"Don't you think that's what I want, too?"

Brett ground his molars together. "Your hands are tied by the law."

"Not tonight, they're not." He shoved past the ranch hand barring his entrance and stumbled into the room.

Rafe turned his sniveling expression to Ryan, trying to crawl toward him, but Brett kicked him in the ribs and knocked him to the ground.

"Answer Ryan's question," Brett barked. "Why did you take the family albums?"

"I didn't. I have no idea what you're talking about. I just wanted some jewelry to sell."

This time, Ryan grabbed Rafe's hair and wrenched his pathetic face up. "You didn't take the albums?"

"I swear. I'm broke. Gambling debts. The forged checks, the jewelry, it's because they're going to kill me if I don't pay back the money I borrowed. But I didn't want no trouble."

"Then why did you set fire to the hunting blind?" Ryan said.

"I didn't! I was as surprised as you were when that happened."

Brett caught him around the throat and raised him up. "How do we know you're not lying to us?"

He pulled at Brett's wrist, trying to free himself. "I don't know. I can give you the name of the guy I owe money to."

"And the jewelry you dropped outside the hospital? The locket?"

"I didn't take no lockets. Not enough street value."

Brett gave Ryan a sidelong look. Brett's gut was telling him that Rafe was speaking the truth. Which meant that whoever had attacked their mother and set fire to the hunting blind was still on the loose, and was taunting them with a trail of mutilated family photos.

Time to move on to the most pressing matter, now that he had Rafe all primed and scared.

He got both hands gripping Rafe's shirt and shook him hard until he heard Rafe's teeth rattle. "Where is the video footage of Hannah?"

Rafe raised a weak hand and pointed to his desk. "In my laptop. But I didn't mean no harm with it."

"You gonna stand here and tell me you didn't watch us making love? You didn't watch her in any compromising states?"

Despite his bloody, raw face, one corner of his lips kicked up in a smile. "Of course, but only because I had to make sure she didn't tell you about the money skimming."

With nothing in his mind except red-hot rage, Brett slammed Rafe's head against the footboard of his bed, then grabbed him by the hair and wrenched his head back. "You violated her, you sick prick, and believe me, if it was just you and me in a room with no witnesses, I'd find a way to erase your memory."

Then Ryan was behind Brett, pulling him away. "Easy, bro. I'll take it from here."

But Brett wasn't quite done. He shoved at Ryan until he released him. Leaving Rafe in a heap on the floor, Brett strode to the desk and yanked the cord from the laptop. He raised it over his head, ready to crush it on the ground under his boot.

Ryan grabbed his arm. "Stop. We need that. Evidence."

"Nobody else gets to violate Hannah like this bastard did. Not the police. Not a judge. I've got to destroy it."

Ryan's grip was an unrelenting vise. "Remember Susie? Susie Howard. I'm going to give this to her to process. She'll handle it with discretion. Nobody's going to violate Hannah again. You have my word, but we need this so we can make sure Rafe never sees the outside of a prison again."

Breathing hard, and so conflicted about the right move to make, he let Ryan take the laptop from him. If this meant Hannah's peace of mind by putting Rafe in prison for the rest of his life, then they could endure the existence of footage of them making love.

With his gaze locked with Brett's, Rafe stood and brushed his knees off. Brett's fists twitched with the urge to knock him back down, so he took a step away, then another, backing out of the room.

Rafe wiped his nose with a handkerchief, then found Brett in the doorway and sneered, as though his sniveling had been nothing but an act. "Pregnant women don't usually get my blood pumping, but that sweet little Hannah is a hot number."

Brett snapped again. He lunged for Rafe, but was stopped midair when Ryan shoved against his chest and grabbed his arm. Someone else grabbed hold of the other.

"Let me at him," Brett roared. For the first time in his life, he felt capable of murder.

Ryan and the ranch hand dragged Brett screaming and thrashing into the hallway. Try as he might, Brett couldn't wrench his arms out of their grip.

The sound of breaking glass cut through their shouts. They turned back toward the room to see Rafe's legs disappearing through the broken window.

Ryan lifted his gun up. "Oh, it's on now."

CHAPTER EIGHTEEN

THE FIRE WAS out in no time, as Hannah had predicted, though her mind remained fixed on Brett and Ryan and the battle they were waging. Her stomach twisted into knots in fear for them. Straining her ears listening for police sirens, though hearing none, she pushed all the doors and windows of the stable open, airing the interior out the best she could.

She couldn't find a switch for the vent fans inside the stable, but the moment she stepped outside in search of one, she was shoved off-balance.

She braced her arms out, cushioning her fall. But Rafe was above her, screaming obscenities. His face was a bloody mess, with both eyes swollen and a split lip. His nose looked broken. *Brett did that.*

Rafe's hands tightened around her throat. "You bitch. You ruined my life."

She kicked at him and swung her arms. She clamped down on his forearm and sank her teeth in. He howled and released her neck. She gasped for air, but there was no time to recover. This might be her one window of opportunity to escape safely. She got her knee up and kicked out, catching him somewhere in his midsection. He stumbled back, smiling.

"I do love fighting women, but it's time for me to scram."

Then he turned tail and ran toward the saddled horse that Ryan had used for patrol that night.

The horse was jittery, but Rafe had caught his lead rope before the beast could skitter out of reach. Rafe hooked a boot into the stirrup and swung on, then took off southwest into the prairie.

"Are you hurt?" Brett dropped to his knees next to her, his expression bald with fear. "Hannah, talk to me."

"I'm okay. Just a little roughed up. Rafe took off on Ryan's horse."

He cradled her face in his hand. "I don't care. I need to know you're okay."

She clamped a hand on his wrist. "I'm okay. And I'm so glad you are, too. I was out of my mind with worry."

Ryan dropped to her other side. "Is she all right?"

"I'm fine," Hannah said. "Rafe took off on your horse, headed southwest."

"The police will never catch him in that direction. He's long gone."

"I could catch him," Brett said.

Hannah grabbed a fistful of his shirt. "Don't. Please. Who cares what happens to him now?"

Brett's jaw rippled. "I do."

"I'll stay with Hannah. You go get him," Ryan said. He handed him a pair of handcuffs. "Just don't kill him. I'd get a lot of pleasure out of watching him rot in jail for the rest of his life."

Brett stood. He set his top teeth on his lower lip and whistled.

Hannah pushed herself up to her knees, then stood and took hold of Brett's hand. "Brett, I'm begging you. Just stay here with me. Safe. Our baby needs a father."

He shook his hand away and stroked her hair. "Hannah, I love you so much. I have to do this. I won't live the rest of our lives in fear of him coming back."

Outlaw appeared at Brett's side. Brett brushed a kiss across Hannah's lips, then mounted the horse. Brett nodded to Ryan, then took off, man and beast flying over the countryside. Hannah stepped in their direction, drinking in the sight of him until he disappeared from view in the darkness.

SPYING ON HANNAH was a personal violation of the worst order, but there was no greater sin on this earth, in Brett's mind, than a man laying hurtful hands on the woman that he loved. Outlaw knew this prairie from memory, every scrub bush, every tree, every rock. With only the occasional lightning strike to illuminate their path, they flew through the outback—straight in the direction of Vulture Ridge.

He and Outlaw caught up to Rafe and Tumbleweed long before they reached the ridge. Though Brett was the only man armed with a gun, he didn't dare chance a shot that might accidentally hit the horse.

"Freeze, Sinclair. This is it. You're going down." Rafe looked over his shoulder. "Go to hell."

"Not tonight. But my horse is faster than yours and more experienced in this backcountry than yours. You've got no hope of getting away tonight."

"Stop flapping your lips and shoot me if you're gonna. I ain't got nothin' to live for anyhow. And if you're not gonna shoot me, then just leave me be because the only way I'm going back to that ranch is dead."

They rode neck and neck through the night. Outlaw could've run faster if Brett had commanded him to, but pacing Tumbleweed would preserve his energy if necessary. All they needed to do now was trap Rafe against the ledge of Vulture Ridge, their best chance of cornering him.

When the ridge came into view, Tumbleweed slowed. Rafe dug his heels into the horse's flank, but Tumbleweed was undeterred.

Brett reached into his saddlebag for a lasso. When the ridge was no more than a football field away, he let the rope go. It fell over Tumbleweed's head. Rafe sprang into action, pushing the rope, trying to free the horse, but Brett clicked his tongue and gave a tug on the lasso. On cue, Tumbleweed ground to a stop.

But Rafe wasn't ready to surrender. He swung off the horse and took off running. Brett stayed on Outlaw, crowding Rafe against the ridge of the gully. Now that Brett was close to the edge, he could see that the gully was rapidly filling with water.

"Déjà vu, Outlaw. I don't like the way this is going."

The next time Brett looked at Rafe, he'd taken a running jump over the ledge.

Cursing, Brett pulled Outlaw to a stop and looked over the edge.

Rafe stood in the middle of the gully, looking dazed. His arm swung at a funny angle, one that made Brett wonder if he'd broken it in his fall.

Gun in hand, Brett slid down the mud wall into the gully. He took aim.

"Now will you freeze?"

Rafe limped toward Brett. "I hate to sound repetitive, but go to hell."

Brett put his finger on the trigger. "You have no idea how badly I want to kill you right now."

Rafe panted, his nose and lip bleeding again. He limped toward Brett, but Brett held his ground.

Rafe bumped his chest right into the rifle barrel. "So do it. I won't go to jail. I won't. And if I don't pay back the money I owe, I'm dead, anyway. Just kill me and get it over with."

There had been a time that Brett was as impetuous as to do exactly that. When he was a hot-blooded, hot-tempered young punk. But now he understood the value of mercy. He understood the value in watching Rafe get handed justice by the courts. He straightened his trigger finger and rested it along the side of the rifle.

"I'm not going to give you that kind of mercy, Rafe. I've heard that committing murder changes a man. And I'm not willing to go down that road for a pathetic excuse of a human being like you. It's over, Rafe. I'm taking you in."

A roar sounded behind them, a sound Brett remembered all too well. A wall of water in the gully bore down on them. They had to get out of the gully immediately if they wanted to live.

"I know that sound, Rafe, and it's all kind of bad. We need to get out of this gully." Dropping the gun to his side, he grabbed hold of Rafe's shirt, but Rafe shoved at him, then stumbled back, out of reach.

He limped away from Brett, toward the roar. "This is God's way," he said.

There was no more time to spare or else they were both going to lose their lives that night. Brett took one last look at Rafe, then started his climb up the cliff face, digging his boots into the earth and clawing at the muddy wall with his fingers, blinking out rainwater and bits of mud as he used every last ounce of his strength to save himself.

He had his torso on the top of the ridge when water hit his boots, sucking at his legs. He clawed at the ground, fighting for a grip as water pushed him with the force of thousands of tons of pressure. Growling with the effort, he pulled as hard as he could, but made no progress. His muscles burned with the effort to keep from succumbing to the raging flood.

Outlaw nudged Brett's forehead with his nose.

"Not now, buddy," he said through gritted teeth as he clung to the lip of the ridge.

Outlaw's rein smacked him in the cheek. In a moment of perfect clarity, Brett knew what Outlaw was up to. Keeping one hand on the ground in the meager grip he'd created, he said a quick prayer, then let go with one hand and grabbed hold of Outlaw's rein.

Outlaw stamped the ground and tossed his head, scooting backward. Brett slid up an inch, then another, until his boot cleared the water and he could swing it onto solid ground.

He rolled away from the edge of Vulture Ridge and stood, then threw both arms around Outlaw. Breathing hard, his legs turned to jelly, he rubbed his face against Outlaw's cheek. "Thank you, buddy. Thank you."

With one arm still hugging Outlaw, he turned and looked at the raging flood.

"What a waste, Outlaw. But it's over now. Hannah's going to be safe."

When Brett got back to the homestead, he'd tell the police to start a search for Rafe and clue them in to the direction that the Lucky C's new mama cow's body was recovered a month earlier, but he had no doubt that all they'd find was the broken body of a broken man once the floodwaters receded after the storm had passed.

CHAPTER NINETEEN

"I THINK THIS shade of green is your color. Brings out the different shades of black in your hair." From his seat next to the examination chair Hannah sat in, Brett fingered the edge of the paper hospital cover-up she wore.

"My hair doesn't have different shades. Black is black."

He winked at her. "Just testing to see if you're paying attention."

She took his hand. "I can't wait to find out which color hair the baby inherits, yours or mine."

"We've got a few more months before we learn that, unless it's bald and then we have even longer. Either way, as long as it has your features, it's going to be one beautiful kid."

Though Hannah's original ultrasound appointment was scheduled for the following day, Brett had insisted that she have a full medical workup the morning after her attack at the ranch to make sure she and the baby were healthy and hale.

Hannah knew in her heart that the baby was fine. If anything, it was even more active inside her belly, having shifted from playing soccer to learning acrobatics. But Hannah didn't mind Brett's concern or having her appointment moved up. She was eager to find out if she was going to be a mother to Faith Elizabeth Colton or

John William Colton. And she couldn't wait to share the news with the rest of Brett's family—her family now, too—beginning with Abra.

Brett had talked to Eric that morning, who'd assured him that their mother had stabilized since last night's scare. The cardiologist thought her code blue had been the result of a bad reaction to a new medication. Now that they'd switched her meds up, she was back to a quiet, stable state and her doctors gave her 70 percent odds of pulling through and waking up. Thank the Lord.

"You look a million miles away. What are you thinking about?" Brett asked.

She took his hand. "Just how twisty a road we traveled to get here. But I wouldn't trade it for anything. Not one moment of it."

He tightened his grip on her hand and brought it to his lips for a kiss. "I love you, Hannah. You know that, right?"

She did know that. Even more, she felt it in her heart. Having Brett by her side, with motherhood only a few short months away, her life was close to being perfect.

Before she could answer, the ultrasound technician strode into the room, her head bent over Hannah's chart. "Hey, Mom and Dad. Are you ready to meet your little one for the first time?"

Hannah's eyes crowded with tears. Oh, how she loved the sound of that. "We're ready. More than ready."

The technician prepped Hannah's stomach with a thick drizzle of cold gel that made Hannah jump, then squished the ultrasound wand right into the goop, pressing hard on her belly.

"You hear that, Mom and Dad? That's your baby's

heartbeat. You can see it, too. There it is, right there on the screen. That flutter."

Hannah didn't think she'd ever seen a more amazing sight as the scratchy black-and-white image on the screen. "Hi, baby," she breathed.

In her periphery, she saw Brett dab at his eye.

"And that's our baby's face," he said, his voice thick with emotion.

"And two perfect arms, and two perfect legs," the technician said, pointing to various parts on the screen. "I have to take some measurements, and while I'm busy with that, how about you two count fingers and toes."

Hannah and Brett were riveted by the sight. Neither spoke, neither moved, unlike the baby waving its arms and bucking for them. For the first time, Hannah was able to put a visual with the movements she'd been feeling for weeks and weeks.

"Active little jelly bean, isn't it?" the technician said with a smile. "And perfectly healthy, by all accounts."

A tear jarred loose and traveled over Hannah's cheek. "Our little star."

Brett dropped his head to Hannah's shoulder. "We've had so much bad news lately. This, right here, is more than a star. It's our little miracle."

"Are you two ready to find out if you're having a girl or a boy?"

Brett took a deep breath. "Ready. I can't wait."

The technician slid the ultrasound wand over Hannah's belly. Grays, whites and blacks undulated on the screen, then refocused. "There it is," she said.

Hannah narrowed her eyes in concentration. If only she'd brought her reading glasses. "What?"

"You see that little thing between the legs?" the technician said.

Hannah's mouth dropped open. She was filled with a joy and love so powerful, she'd never experienced anything quite like it. "I see it."

Brett stood up, his eyes glued to the sight of his son. "Well, hello, John William Colton. I can't wait to meet you." His swabbed the back of his hand over his wet eyes. "But I'm glad you're here to watch me do this."

Confused, Hannah wrenched her gaze from the screen to study Brett. From his pocket, he pulled a little black velvet box.

This wasn't the life she'd been meticulously plotting and planning; this, with Brett and their son, was beyond her wildest dreams, and here he'd gone and made the moment even more perfect.

"We agreed when I found out you were pregnant that we wouldn't marry for the wrong reasons. We both agreed that love was the only reason for two people to spend the rest of their lives together."

"We did say that, didn't we?"

"Hannah Elizabeth Grayson, I'm in love with you. With everything about you. I can't imagine my life without you by my side, and I need to know if you love me, too."

"I do, Brett. I love you so much. It was impossible odds, wasn't it? Me falling for the man I met in a club one night. Impossible, but just like this little baby, the impossible can happen. We've proved that."

Nodding like crazy, tears on his cheeks, he opened the box, revealing a gorgeous solitaire diamond ring set in platinum.

Hannah sniffled at the sight. "When did you have

time to buy that, with everything that's been happening?"

"The day after we first made love and I told you that I was going to fight for you, for us. I knew that morning when we were lying in bed that I'd fallen hard for you. There's nothing I want more than to be a family with you and our children."

"Children?"

He gave her a watery grin. "We have to give John some siblings, right?"

"Yes, we do."

"So I guess there's only one question left to ask. Will you marry me?"

There was nothing in Hannah's heart or mind except love for the most amazing man she'd ever known. "Yes, Brett. It would be my honor."

He slid the ring on her finger, then wrapped his arms around her and kissed her. She poured her heart into the kiss, all the while feeling little John kicking and celebrating inside her. Had there ever been a woman as lucky as she?

"Let's finish this appointment, then go tell my mom," Brett said. "She's going to want to hear all about her new grandson. And after that, what do you say we take the long way back home and find ourselves some twisty roads to explore?"

Over the past five months, she'd discovered the joy of the long and windy road, not so unlike the path to forever that she and Brett had forged. She took the hand of the man she loved, the father of her baby—her hero. "As long as I'm with you, that sounds just exactly perfect."

* * * * *

YOU HAVE JUST READ A HARLEQUIN® INTRIGUE® BOOK

If you were **captivated** by the **gripping, page-turning romantic suspense,** be sure to look for all six Harlequin® Intrigue® books every month.

The moment Fiona found the letter in the bottom of Chase's
sock drawer, she knew it was bad news. Fear squeezed the
breath from her as her heart beat so hard against her rib
cage that she thought she would pass out. Grabbing the
bureau for support, she told herself it might not be what she
thought it was.

But the envelope was a pale lavender, and the handwriting
was distinctly female. Worse, Chase had kept the letter a
secret. Why else would it be hidden under his socks? He
hadn't wanted her to see it because it was from that other
woman.

Now she wished she hadn't been snooping around. She'd
let herself into his house with the extra key she'd had made.
She'd felt him pulling away from her the past few weeks.
Having been here so many times before, she was determined
that this one wasn't going to break her heart. Nor was she
going to let another woman take him from her. That's why
she had to find out why he hadn't called, why he wasn't
returning her messages, why he was avoiding her.

They'd had fun the night they were together. She'd felt as if they had something special, although she knew the next morning that he was feeling guilty. He'd said he didn't want to lead her on. He'd told her that there was some woman back home he was still in love with. He'd said their night together was a mistake. But he was wrong, and she was determined to convince him of it.

What made it so hard was that Chase was a genuinely nice guy. You didn't let a man like that get away. The other woman had. Fiona wasn't going to make that mistake, even though he'd been trying to push her away since that night. But he had no idea how determined she could be, determined enough for both of them that this wasn't over by a long shot.

It wasn't the first time she'd let herself into his apartment when he was at work. The other time, he'd caught her and she'd had to make up some story about the building manager letting her in so she could look for her lost earring.

She'd snooped around his house the first night they'd met—the same night she'd found his extra apartment key and had taken it to have her own key made in case she ever needed to come back when Chase wasn't home.

The letter hadn't been in his sock drawer that time.

That meant he'd received it since then. Hadn't she known he was hiding something from her? Why else would he put this letter in a drawer instead of leaving it out along with the bills he'd casually dropped on the table by the front door?

Because the letter was important to him, which meant that she had no choice but to read it.

Don't miss
Steel Resolve *by B.J. Daniels,*
available July 2019 wherever
Harlequin® Intrigue books and ebooks are sold.

www.Harlequin.com

HIEXP0619

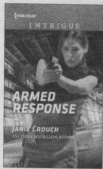  

Rebel asked more seriously, "How should a woman be treated, then?"

Avi smiled broadly. Now they were getting somewhere. "It would be my pleasure to show you."

She leaned back, staring openly at him. He was tempted to dare her to take him up on it. After all, no Special Forces operator he'd ever known could turn down a dare. But he was probably better served by backing off and letting her make the next move. Not to mention she deserved the decency on his part.

Waiting out her response was harder than he'd expected it to be. He wanted her to take him up on the offer more than he'd realized.

"What would showing me entail?" she finally asked.

He shrugged. "It would entail whatever you're comfortable with. Decent men don't force women to do anything they don't want to do or are uncomfortable with."

"Hmm."

Suppressing a smile at her hedging, he said quietly, "They do, however, insist on yes or no answers to questions of whether they should proceed. Consent must always be clearly given."

He waited her out while the SUV carrying Piper and Zane pulled up at the gate to the Olympic Village.

Gunnar delivered them to the back door of the building, and Avi watched the pair ride an elevator to their floor, walk down the hall and enter their room.

"Here comes Major Torsten now. He's going to spell me watching the cameras tonight."

"Excellent," Avi purred.

Alarm blossomed in Rebel's oh-so-expressive eyes. He liked making her a little nervous. If he didn't miss his guess, boredom would kill her interest in a man faster than just about anything else.

Avi moved his chair back to its position under the window. The hall door opened and he turned quickly. "Hey, Gun."

"Avi." A nod. "How's it going, Rebel?"

"All quiet on the western front."

"Great. You go get some sleep."

"Yes, sir," she said crisply.

"I'll walk you out," Avi said casually.

He followed Rebel into the hallway and closed the door behind her. They walked to the elevator in silence. Rebel was obviously as vividly aware as he was of the cameras Gunnar would be using to watch them.

"Walk with me?" he breathed without moving his lips as they reached the lobby. Gunnar no doubt read lips.

"Sure," Rebel uttered back, playing ventriloquist herself, and without so much as glancing in his direction.

It was a crisp Australian winter night under bright stars. The temperature was cool and bracing, perfect for a brisk walk. He matched his stride to Rebel's, relieved he didn't have to hold it back too much.

"So what's your answer, Rebel? Shall I show you how real men treat women? Yes or no?"

Don't miss
Special Forces: The Operator *by Cindy Dees,*
available July 2019 wherever
Harlequin® Romantic Suspense books
and ebooks are sold.

www.Harlequin.com